THE LOGO

Are we pawns
Controlled by masters of the game?

THE

LOGO

By *ALEXIS*

Pp
PROSEPRESS

Cover Art
O'BRIEN DESIGN

Comments: prosencons@live.com

ISBN: 978-1-950768-94-3

All characters in this book are fictional
Any resemblance to actual persons,
living or dead, is entirely coincidental.
Historical references are listed in the Bibliography.

Information relating to BayerAG's
past and current activities
can be found at
CBGnetwork.org

Published by ProsePress
Pawleys Island, South Carolina

PROLOGUE

The Logo is a mix of fact and fiction. It's meant to be a fun read based on a few historical facts.

FACT: According to folklore, Hans Schneider, a Bayer scientist, doodling while in a discussion with a fellow worker, wrote the word "BAYER" horizontally and then again vertically using the Y as a common letter. He added a circle to complete what has become known as the Bayer Cross.

As the story goes, Hans tore the page from his notepad, excused himself and took his sketch to the management, where it was greatly admired.

Today, the logo is embossed on every Bayer aspirin tablet throughout the world.

The Bayer cross logo is so important to the AG Bayer that a 236 foot version has been lighting up the skyline over Leverkusen Germany, Bayer headquarters, since 1958. The 100 plus year old symbol is truly one of the world's best-known trademarks.

Circular logos like Target, Starbucks, Volkswagen, Coca-Cola and GE have always been considered the strongest, most memorable images. The Bayer Cross is one of the best.

FACT: In 1882, New York Senator William Leanard Marcy said, "To the Victor Go the Spoils." This was an unfortunate truth for Bayer because even though the company was private, they provided munitions and poison gas and were considered part of the German war machine. As part of Germany's WWI war reparations, under the Treaty of Versailles, Bayer was forced to give away its registered trademark logo, as well as its right to do business in the USA and its WWI allied countries.

FICTION: After WWI, Painter Inc. was created by a small group of powerful men with industrial, financial, pharmaceutical, and chemical interests in Bayer. Its primary goal was to reestablish Bayer business and the precious logo back in the USA. The group has always been cunning, ruthless, and above all . . . successful.

CHAPTER 1
THE STRANGER

The man was a peculiar sort. An over-starched collar pinched his neck, making it appear even longer than it already was. Every blondish-gray hair was Brylcreemed in place, his pencil-line moustache was meticulously trimmed, and . . . those penetrating pale-gray eyes.

Despite of being focused on his chess matches, Joseph Westerfield caught an occasional glimpse of the hovering stranger. *Is he following my progress*? he wondered. The man stood motionless with his head tilted back. He peered through gold wire-rimmed glasses down a long narrow nose judging every move.

After being defeated in the semifinals, Joseph grabbed a sandwich, rehashed a few matches with other "also-rans," then joined his friends to watch the championship match. As the battle began, he saw the strange man in the group standing directly across from him.

Mr. Arrogant looks out of place, Joseph thought with an instinctive dislike. *Who wears a tailored suit to a chess match? And why has he been following my matches*? With one eye on the match and the other on the stranger

Joseph realized the curious man was watching him rather than the contest. *Do I know this guy?*

The five-match finale ended in four, with two draws and two impressive wins. The new Midwest Royal Chess Club champion, a lady from Fond du Lac, Wisconsin, demonstrated her superiority by trouncing last year's champion.

Joseph smiled to himself. *The game of kings has become the game of queens.* After a few good-byes, congratulations, and see-you-next-years, the room began to clear. When Joseph turned to leave, the stranger blocked his path.

"Excuse me, Mr. Westerfield," the man said. "My name is Hermann vonLeer. May I have a few minutes of your time?"

"Do I know you, sir? You've been my shadow all day."

"No. I don't believe we've ever met," vonLeer said with a squinty smile. "I hope my interest didn't alarm you."

"It didn't," Joseph replied but, at the suggestion, caution flags flashed in his mind. *This character bears watching, he's too patient for my liking, too confident. I'll bet he's accustomed to controlling every situation. Not this one.*

"What can I do for you, Mr. vonLeer?" Joseph asked, rushing his words.

The room had emptied quickly.

"Can we sit?" vonLeer asked, motioning toward the chess table.

"All right," Joseph said, sliding a backward chair between his legs. "What's on your mind?"

"I'll get right to the point, Mr. Westerfield," vonLeer said. "I represent a group of investors interested in purchasing Wesfield Laboratory."

This guy's a front for the same people I've turned down before, Joseph thought. He took a deep breath, staring into vonLeer's eyes. Speaking slowly he asked, "Precisely who are the investors that sent you here?" Are you a front man for people trying to get the Bayer Company a foothold in my country.

"I'm sorry," vonLeer said, sneering with opened palms. "I'm not at liberty to divulge that information at this time."

"Really," Joseph shook his head in disbelief.

"Let me assure you, Mr. Westerfield, the group is prepared to make you the offer of a lifetime."

"Is that so?" Joseph said. His eyes hadn't left vonLeer's.

"My client is a group made up of the most powerful men in the business and banking world. They are willing to pay you three times the value of your company, perhaps even more," vonLeer said, all the while holding Joseph's gaze.

"Why in God's name would they do that?"

"Their motives are not relevant," vonLeer said.

"Let me get this straight," Joseph said. "You want me to put

Wesfield Lab in the hands of strangers without knowing who I'd be selling to, or why whoever it is . . . wants it."

"Mr. Westerfield, our clients are highly respected world leaders. Many of them are vested in prestigious companies right here in the United States. I'm sorry I'm unable to provide more information at this time." vonLeer's tolerance was beginning to dwindle. "Let me assure you, this is a very sincere and generous offer."

"The answer is NO."

"That's not an acceptable answer, Mr. Westerfield," vonLeer bristled.

"NO . . . NO . . . NO," Joseph Westerfield was emphatic but totally composed.

With scarlet cheeks, vonLeer's eyes darted from side to side. "If that's your position, you're making powerful enemies–here and abroad."

"This conversation is over," Joseph pushed away from the table and snapped to his feet.

"I resent your attitude, Westerfield."

"Mr. vonLeer, your client has tried to acquire Wesfield Laboratory twice before. I know the people that make up your holding company. I know their history, and I know their motivation."

vonLeer's face seemed to pinch around his mouth as he spit out each word in his response, "You may think you know, Westerfield, but I doubt it."

"I will be damned before I sell to those you represent," Joseph said. "I will fight them with all my strength, down to my last dime. Wesfield Laboratory will never become part of your organization. Your people have too much blood on their hands."

"I'm sorry you feel that way, Westerfield. You and your family may not live long enough to regret it."

"Are you threatening me, vonLeer?"

"Let's just say . . . it's out of my control."

CHAPTER 2
SAILING

Sundays in springtime were Jeff's favorite days. The routine was often the same: six o'clock alarm, wolf down a doughnut, hook up the boat, head for his favorite Lake Michigan public landing, hit the water before eight, and, after a morning sail, spend a couple of hours with his best friend and mentor, his grandpa, Joseph Westerfield.

The wooden 17-foot Day Sailor was at least 25 years old, but Jeff couldn't have loved her more if she were brand new. He bought the boat 13 years ago with the first money he ever earned; it was quite an achievement because he was only fifteen at the time. On the day he bought her, as he was taping the end of the mast rope, he christened her the "Nipper," the name given to very young British sailors responsible for nipping off and retying frayed rope ends in the days when wind powered all ships. The name apparently appeals to the British, too; they often refer to their children as "little nippers."

A light westerly breeze enabled Jeff to clear the dock area and get up to speed in moments. His efficient tacking routine allowed him to go directly west, into the wind, by veering back and forth, slightly north then slightly south. After the shoreline dropped from sight, where the wind was constant, he maneuvered the Nipper in all directions. Jeff always enjoyed putting her through her paces because she responded so smoothly to every adjustment; just like she knew exactly what he wanted to do.

After a good morning sail, he turned toward his grandfather's place. Jeff easily guided the Nipper into the little inlet formed by the creek bordering the southern boundary of the Westerfield property. Only a small boat with shallow draft could get in that inlet; it was perfect for Jeff.

The "cottage," as it was called, was a 4,000 square foot, rustic New England-style home that sat squarely in the center of 43 heavily wooded acres. It was located far enough back from the water to avoid erosion problems often caused by westerly winds, but close enough to have a magnificent panoramic view of the lake. Growing up, Jeff spent every summer and most weekends at the lake. It would always be home. There was nowhere Jeff would rather be, and no one he'd rather spend time with than the man who raised him. Joseph Westerfield was his grandpa, parent, and trusted friend.

They were so much alike. Both loved nature, sailing, sports, fishing and hard work. Each knew the other was honest, moral and loyal. The old man never once told him what to do, yet Jeff learned everything he valued from him. As a boy, Jeff thought his grandpa was about the smartest person alive. He still did.

Lunch topics varied: sports, politics, fishing, and Wesfield Laboratory. They spent hours critiquing problems and solutions for each subject. Seldom did either change the other's mind, but that was okay; each respected the other's opinion. Fortunately, their values were so similar, they only disagreed on minor issues.

After securing the Nipper, Jeff charged up the wood steps he'd built into the steep bluff. Joseph Westerfield was pruning wild roses along the ridge.

"Hi, Jeff."

"Hey, Grandpa, how's it goin'?"

"How's the sail?"

"Great, wanna go out? She's ready to go."

"No, I was just about to put on a little lunch before the game."

"Cubs?"

"Of course, who else?"

"How can you stick with that bunch?"

"It's habit forming," Joseph joked.

"Lippy Leo Durocher has taken the Cubs from bottom feeders to contenders every year for the last six years," Jeff said. "His reward– they dumped him."

"I have to admit, it wasn't too bright," Joseph agreed. "If they don't start winning a few, Whitey Lockman better start looking for work. You're stickin' around for the game, aren't you?"

"Depends. What's for lunch?"

"Ballpark food, of course," Joseph said.

"Let me guess; hotdogs, chips and beer. Right?"

"Right."

"Sounds good to me," Jeff said. Then he went to a small square table set under a lakeside window. Picking chessmen from the drawer and placing each on its designated square, he ask, "Ready for a match?"

"Think today's your day?"

"Could be?" Jeff responded with a grin.

"How's the ExRelief Cold Medicine rollout coming along?" Joseph asked unwrapping a package of hotdogs.

"Not bad; the bureaucrats are starting to get to me. I need no less than eight approval signatures before anything can get done. Other than signing their names, I can't for the life of me figure out what most of those guys do. From where I'm sitting, Product Manager is a misnomer. We don't manage squat."

"It wasn't like that in the old days. Guess I got out at the right time."

"You did," Jeff said. "The group approach would drive you nuts."

"When are you going to bring that agency gal out so I can get to know her?"

"You're always pushin'," Jeff said, shaking his head, but still smiling. "Who are the Cubbies playing today?"

"Braves. Rick Reuschel is pitching for us."

"That's a plus."

When the game came to an end and the cursing was over, the Cubs had managed to pull out a 7 to 6 win.

Jeff asked, "Would you like to go out on the lake now?"

"No," Joseph said. "Watching the bums is enough excitement for me. You go. I'll clean up."

"I'll head back to the landing then," Jeff said. "I'll give you a call later this week; maybe we can have dinner."

"Sounds good," Joseph said, giving him a brief hug before Jeff headed out the door.

Jeff liked to close the weekend with an hour-long sail into the sun. The wind had done a 180-degree shift since morning. Now offshore, it was blocked by the high bluff, forcing him to paddle straight out from the inlet. He went about 50 yards before the mainsail billowed as it caught the wind. He let the Nipper run with it. Sailing was a time when he felt close to God, alone with the wind, the water, and the boat, all working together in harmony.

He eased into a right turn. With his feet firmly tucked under a centered floor belt, he leaned back; cold water slapped his back as he hung over the side, creating ballast to counterbalance the wind. Achieving maximum speed, he flew north, enjoying the gentle wind for almost four miles. When the Nipper came parallel to the lighthouse, a favorite landmark, he brought her about, sailing southeast back toward the landing.

Jeff's plan was to create enough speed to glide through the windless space along the bluff. He brought down the jib to simplify the maneuver and grabbed the mainsail rope, releasing it from its cleat. He loved the control he gained when he could judge the wind by the tension on the rope in his hand. It let him get the maximum out of his Nipper.

Suddenly, with a quarter of a mile to go, something violently slammed the side of his head. The force threw him from the boat, pulling the mainsail rope from his hand. The sail flapped freely in the wind. Partially dazed and confused with water erupting from his mouth, Jeff found himself in Lake Michigan ten yards away from his boat. His temple shrieked with pain, as something pierced the water inches from his ear. Seeing the line of bubbles where it hit, he realized someone was shooting at him. His only hope was to dive. In spite of his life jacket's extra buoyancy, he managed to swim underwater, coming up alongside the Nipper. He surfaced, exhausted, struggling to catch his breath. Fear overtook fatigue and pain as he realized he was in a fight for his life.

Thud, thud, thud, more bullets hit the boat. Then nothing except the sound of the wind and small waves lapping the boat. Shielded by the Nipper, Jeff couldn't see the shore; therefore, he figured, anyone up there couldn't see him either.

Numbed by the frigid water, too frightened to move, he waited, listening for a hint of his assailant's whereabouts. Oh no, the wind was taking him and his beloved Nipper back out on the lake. Darkness was falling fast. He realized Lake Michigan would take its toll if he stayed out there. Unless he took a chance, he would surely die. Unable to get back into the boat, with little strength left, he started to dog paddle toward shore. He was very, very cold . . . then everything went black.

CHAPTER 3
GUNTHER

A man of many faces, Gunther ironically chose one of the last bastions of genuine civility and genteel charm as the place where he fit in: Charleston, South Carolina. He was an appealing man, just over six feet with steel-gray eyes under thick dark brows and a disarming smile. Trusting Charlestonians treated him with the respect due a successful businessman and quickly welcomed him into their inner circle. Gunther saw himself rightfully belonging with society's upper crust and enjoyed rubbing elbows at cultural events: ballets, plays, gallery shows, and concerts. He was, after all, the very best in his chosen profession. His Charleston face was that of an Import-Export dealer, allowing him to routinely travel without arousing suspicion. His real face, beneath the congenial mask, was that of a ruthless murderer . . . a cold-blooded assassin. He favored "Special Services Operative" as his title and "performer of unpleasant tasks," his job description.

He became an operative quite unintentionally. In the summer of 1958, after he achieved the Army's prestigious number two sharpshooter status, the CIA plucked him from the service and put him into "Special Operations Training." Gunther saw humor in the language. "Special Operations" actually meant to eliminate, terminate or replace human beings perceived to threaten U.S. interests. He was amazed at the number of varying techniques he was taught to accomplish that mission. An enthusiastic student, he easily mastered martial arts, explosives, poisons, disguises, accidental events, and many other sinister ways to annihilate an adversary. Discipline, research, caution, and creativity – all CIA basics – became building blocks to Gunther's success story.

Upon completion of a year-long, very successful South American mission, Gunther was ready for some stateside R&R. His first stop, as always, was at Langley for the ritual debriefing. It was conducted by

Fred Dobbins, the lean, soft-spoken, Special Ops agent who initiated the project. Gunther gave a crisp account of the mission, from the night he was dropped out of a cargo plane, to the day General Sandiaga and his three main hatchet men met their Maker. Dobbins was pleased to discover the reconnaissance was accurate; the drop-off, pickup, and undetected surveillance came off without a hitch.

At the conclusion of the report, and after receiving accolades for a job well done, Gunther was handed a slip of paper that read, "Mr. Smylee, Manhattan's Park Lake Hotel, suite 701, 8:00 p.m. Today."

"What's this?" Gunther asked.

"It came from on high. I think it may have originated with a congressman. I'm out of the loop, so I can't tell you for sure. Can you make it?"

"If I have to."

"There's a plane at the strip," Dobbins said. "You'll have to book your own hotel."

Arriving at the hotel with little time to spare, Gunther hurried through the lobby and took the elevator to the seventh floor. Hand extended, a small man peering through round-rimmed glasses rose from a highly polished long black walnut table. "Thank you for coming, Mr. Gunther," he said. "I'm Mr. Smylee."

Like I had a choice, you limp-wristed little twit. "Nice to meet you, sir."

"How was your stay in South America?"

"That's classified, sir."

"Of course it is." The eerie little man's smirk barely changed throughout the introduction. After a series of personal questions, Gunther was asked if he would be interested in performing his services for industry, rather than government. He answered with a smile. "That would depend on the value you place on my particular expertise." In September, 1963, on a cool day in New York City, Gunther decided to go into business for himself.

The financial proposal was breathtaking: $1,000,000 annual retainer, plus $500,000 per assignment. Initial funding began with a $400,000 money transfer from Manhattan Bank & Trust to a Charleston Federal Bank savings account in Gunther's name. He also was given a briefcase containing $600,000 in stocks and bonds registered to Victor Vargas and Verner Delmar. Papers establishing the two identities were included, along with instructions that read, "Create a sole owner company in the Grand Caymans or Switzerland with off-shore banking." All future deposits would be made to that account with one exception: A $150,000 annual expense account would be funneled through a front company called *Gunther's Quality Imports.*

The new company would have a showroom on Adger's Wharf, a quaint little street at the south end of Charleston's downtown. Smylee suggested a small inventory of high end imports that he would initially provide. Gunther agreed to create business cards and stationery and open a business checking account at Charleston Federal. It was to be his company – profit or loss would be of no concern to Smylee's people.

The peculiar man talked, almost in a whisper, as he explained he had many clients who would be using his services, but Gunther would never meet the party requiring a project, nor would he be told why his services were needed. This was fine with Gunther; the more distance between the client or target and himself, the less likely the probability of detection. He definitely favored carrying out his assignments without personal judgment or sentimentality, either of which could cloud his thinking.

As it turned out, the closest he got to personal contact was a three-word recording. The system was simple but effective. The message, "Call your secretary," along with a number that changed with each assignment, was left with Gunther's answering service. Since he didn't actually have a secretary, it was the perfect message. He would use a public telephone to return the call. Smylee insisted on the extra callback to ensure Gunther received the correct communication without third-party involvement. All communication was initiated by Mr. Smylee. The only way Gunther could contact Smylee was to leave a message using a special emergency number he had been given when he was hired. He was told, "Emergency means emergency." Gunther never needed to use the number.

Over the years, Gunther's reputation as a ruthless but proficient agent had grown in the eyes of the few who were aware of his exploits.

In March of '74, responding to a "Call your secretary" message, Gunther listened as the answering machine transmitted a name, "T. Staniak, Niles, Michigan." He neatly packed the tools of his trade into his van, then drove 20 hours straight through to a motel along the Indiana Expressway, a few miles south of his pick-up.

After an eternity standing in line at the Niles Post Office, he asked, "Do you have a package being held for T. Staniak?" The clerk never said a word, just disappeared into the back. Another five minutes passed before he returned and handed Gunther a standard mailing envelope with no return address. "Thanks," Gunther said. The clerk nodded.

The information was brief. "Joseph Westerfield, 76, retired. South Station, Michigan. Jeffery Westerfield, 28, Wesfield Laboratory, South Station, Michigan. Weekend sailors on Lake Michigan. ASAP." A picture of each was enclosed.

In addition to Smylee's "No direct client contact rule," Gunther created a few simple ground rules of his own. They included: choose remote locations whenever possible; dress like the locals with some disguise, hair and eye glasses, mustache, etc.; use common weapons which increase the number of potential suspects. In addition, do not stay at local hotels or motels within two days of the event; have multiple exit strategies; know your subject's daily and weekly routines; formulate a secondary plan. And the most important rule: never, never gamble – abandon rather than risk.

Whenever two subjects are involved in a single assignment, it's logical to eliminate both at once, establishing a single crime scene and thus half the risk. He doubted that scenario would present itself in this case because the old and young seldom had common interests. During his 23-day surveillance, however, he was surprised and pleased to learn he couldn't have been more wrong. Young Westerfield had been at his granddad's lake house three Sundays in a row. They spent a couple of hours inside, or barbecuing on the deck. When dishes were done, they routinely went sailing together.

Gunther saw two obvious possibilities. Walk up to the house, introduce himself, and eliminate them with a silenced hand gun. This approach could incur resistance and the possibility of leaving evidence at the crime scene.

The other choice, which he favored, meant waiting until their afternoon sail was coming to an end. Then, as the boat slowed to drop off the senior Westerfield, the perfect opportunity for easy targets would present itself. A modified 30-06, one of the rifles preferred by local hunters, should do the trick. He viewed the "in house" plan as a little more risky and less civil, than the purer "sniper" approach. Fortunately for the Westerfields, he saw himself as a very civilized professional who didn't really like close contact with his target. Gunther made the wrong choice.

Just north of the inlet, the bipod-mounted rifle peeped out of the underbrush. Two o'clock passed. Three o'clock, then four. Apparently, the Westerfields were not following their usual routine. Following his most important rule, Gunther knew it was time to abandon the effort or, at least, change tactics to the "walk up to the house" approach.

Normally he would pack up his toys, go back to the hotel, and develop optional plans, but the Charleston Spring Symphony was being performed next Tuesday night and he wanted to be part of the festivities. In order to get there by Tuesday, he needed to wind this up today. Violating one of his own rules, he let his personal life get in the way of business. His second bad choice.

As he began breaking down and packing the 30-06, he saw Westerfield's sailboat gracefully moving out onto the lake. He would have to wait until they were finished sailing before he could do anything. It was okay; the plan was back on, and being patient was being professional.

Gunther reset the rifle support as he watched the Nipper go straight east, then north. She sailed over a mile before coming about to head back. She was closing fast when he realized something was wrong; only the young one was in the boat. Although it was reasonably close to shore, the boat wasn't close enough to be coming back to the inlet. "Damn, he's taking her in." His snap decision was to carry out both plans, taking them out separately. Gunther's third bad choice.

After quickly reassembling the 30-06, he took careful aim. The scope's cross-hairs were centered on Jeff's chest. Only his finger moved as he squeezed the trigger. Jeff flew out of the boat at impact. Gunther didn't see the bullet hit but was confident it did, because he always hit his target. He took several additional silencer-muffled insurance shots making sure his target was dead. He waited. No activity. Satisfied, he thought to himself, *I believe that should be the last swim you'll ever take.*

Time to head for the house and finish the job. He cautiously walked through the brush and up the road to the house, only to discover Joseph Westerfield was gone. Not a good day.

CHAPTER 4
ROSEY'S DINER

Highway AA, a desolate two-lane blacktop, ran east and west along the north rim of the Central Railroad freight yard. Across from the yard's main gate, a single building turned its lights on at 5:00 AM, seven days a week. Rosey's Over Easy Diner served breakfast and lunch to the late night and early bird railroad workers. In Rosey's mind, the place had a rustic western look, but to most of her customers, it was just a ramshackle dump. To say the food was average would be complimentary; what lured you in was the false promise of the coffee-bacon aroma that met you at the door.

In spite of its imperfections, Russ Atkinson had breakfast there a couple days a week. It was the only place that served Donald Duck orange juice, his favorite. Although he didn't realize it, starting his day with the unpretentious railroaders helped fill the emptiness that had crept into his life after his wife, Sylvia, decided one of his closest friends was the love of her life.

Russ had no idea how lucky he was. He was just not exciting, or shallow, enough to fill Sylvia's superficial needs. At 33, he and his 11-year-old daughter, Sarah, nicknamed Sassy, found themselves living alone in a comfortable house he built on three wooded acres along the river. It had been six years since Sylvia ran off. Sassy became his entire world.

At six foot three, Russ was in excellent condition. After playing basketball in high school and college, he tried to hold on to a bit of his youth by playing in a noon hour pickup game on days he could get away. Unfortunately, running the airport didn't leave many free hours. He only took that job after the management position he held with a northern Indiana musical instrument manufacturer disappeared when the company moved its operation to the Far East.

With his severance pay, he had enough money to purchase four rental properties. He hoped they would help supplement his income, but they turned out to be more work than profit. His time for basketball was becoming harder and harder to find.

Single women throughout southeastern Michigan knew this soft-spoken, attractive, and congenial gentleman was an available target, but none could penetrate his defenses. Then Kristi came along.

She walked in with a graceful glide. A hush came over the room as she drew attention from the weary bib-overalled customers. The athletic five-foot eight-inch beauty usually got that reaction, but Kristi tried to ignore it. Along with wide-set green eyes, flawless light complexion, and shoulder-length red hair that bounced ever so slightly as she walked, she had a friendly open smile that could make your day, if you were lucky enough to be on the receiving end.

As soon as Russ saw her, his heart began to race. He stood up and waved her to the table. "Morning, Kristi. Glad to see you could make it."

Rosey came over with coffee. "Hi, Kristi. Ya havin' yer usual?" she asked in a raspy voice.

"Good morning, Rosey. Eggs up, bacon, rye, skip the Donald Duck orange juice."

"How about you, Russ?"

"Same, but I want the juice."

"You know, Russ, except for Rosey and her daughters, I don't think I've ever seen another woman in here."

"At least nobody here calls you 'Chief,'" Russ said.

"Thank God." Kristi was the new South Station police chief. They met when she investigated an apparent break-in at the airport office.

"What's going on at the airport these days?" she asked.

"Not much. Well, at least not much I can understand."

"What do you mean?"

"I mean things are happening that don't make any sense."

"Russ, are you going to tell me about it or just talk in circles?"

"Remember, I told you about the weird stuff going on out there?"

"Vaguely. Would you mind going over it again?"

"I'll give you the short version. It started about 18 months ago.

One morning, when I arrived at the airport just before dawn, I noticed fluorescent red spots, spaced about ten feet apart all along the border of the airport property."

"You didn't know what they were for?" Kristi ask.

"Not at first. Then I saw a workman at the far end of the property peering through a transit and motioning to his crew to as they worked over each spot. They were using a hydraulic auger that looked like a giant katydid to dig post holes. It could sink a hole in a heartbeat."

"I'll bet you were shocked to see all that going on before dawn," Kristi said.

"Wouldn't you be?"

"I'm sure I would. What happened then?" Kristi asked.

"I asked what was goin' on. According to the Project Manager, the guy on the transit, a twelve-foot industrial grade, galvanized chain link fence was being erected with a five-strand barbed wire topper. He didn't know who was paying for it, but he said it had to be expensive."

"I've driven along it many times. It is impressive," Kristi said.

"What really annoyed me was that a fence was being built around the airport I'm supposed to be in charge of, and I didn't know a damn thing about it."

"So, what did you do?"

"I called Clarence Loecher. He's a natural born 'pompous ass,' but he's the only airport board member that takes any responsibility."

"Did he know what was going on?" Kristi asked.

"After a fashion. Clarence explained to me that an attorney named Smylee showed up at his office a couple of weeks ago representing an anonymous client who wanted to donate the fence. Smylee had specifications, a schematic drawing of the airport, permits, and everything needed to do the job."

Squinting with a questioning smile, Kristi pointed out, "Maybe in the break-in where nothing was missing, something was taken after all . . . airport information."

"Do you think . . .?"

"It's a possibility," Kristi said. "Did Clarence ever find out who the anonymous client was?"

"Nope. He told me the attorney was very guarded on that point.

Smylee called the client 'they,' but Clarence couldn't tell if he represented a business, a group, or a person. The contractor was hired without even asking my opinion."

"I can see why you're miffed," Kristi said.

"I told Clarence, it would have been nice if someone from the board had given me a heads-up about this before they started digging. He just hemmed-and-hawed, said it just happened so damn fast, blah, blah, blah."

"Did he say anything else about this lawyer, Smylee?" she questioned.

"He must have made quite an impression because he described him to me in detail. He told me Smylee grins with a kind of smirk when he talks, but there isn't any humor in what he says. The guy wears round wire-rimmed glasses, over round little eyes that pop out of a round little head. Clarence said Smylee was topped off with 'Hitler style' slicked down black hair, all combed to the left."

"He doesn't sound very appealing," Kristi smiled.

"No, he doesn't," Russ smiled back; he couldn't help it. "Smylee came back to see Clarence a month later with all the paper work needed to expand the runway."

"Did they expand it?"

"Started the next day – took less than three months. I have to admit they did a real nice job. I would just like to know who paid the bill and why did they do it?"

"Why don't you go back to the board member, Clarence, and get more details?"

"I've questioned him so often I doubt he'd take my call. Besides, I think I know everything he knows." Russ was showing a bad case of frustration.

"From a cop's point of view, I think I would concentrate on Smylee for the answers."

"Apparently, the devious little twit walked all over Clarence. I can't help wondering why Smylee was so closemouthed about who paid for our airport improvements. We're not a charity, so they can't write it off. The whole thing really bugs me."

"Want me to find out who paid the bill?" Kristi smiled.

19

"You could do that?"

"Not officially, of course, but I have friends who owe me a couple of favors. I'll need a little more information."

"Like what?"

"Like the names of the companies who did the work, and where their headquarters are."

"Well, let me think. Seems to me the fence people were called J. Ward Cyclone Fence and Gate. I don't know where their offices are, but they had Michigan plates."

"How about the runway?"

"That was done by a contractor. I think the name was something like 'Petaway.' I'm really not sure about the name, but I do know they were out of Indianapolis."

"Can you think of anything else?"

"Not really. The fence company's head honcho mentioned they were going to put up a couple mechanical gates over at Wesfield Labs. You know, the kind that takes a special card to operate."

"Was that the foreman?"

"Foreman, project manager, I don't know what his title was, but he called the shots."

"Sounds to me like you looked them over pretty closely," Kristi said with a snicker.

"I am supposed to be responsible for the airport, you know."

Suddenly a squawk from Kristi's two-way radio filled the room. "Chief, are you there?"

"Sorry," Kristy said to the rest of the patrons, starting to blush. "You've got me, Jake. What's up?"

"I've got a call I think you need to take . . . I'm patching it through."

"Okay."

"Hi, Pat McHugh here. Is this Chief Christopher from South Station?"

"What can I do for you, Mr. McHugh?"

"I'm at Pat's Boat Service & Storage, north of Highway 12 on Red Arrow. One of our clients towed in a sailboat. I think you better take a look at it."

"I don't believe my territory includes the beaches."

"I understand that, ma'am, but this boat is registered to a Jeffrey Edward Westerfield of South Station. And, I'm not absolutely sure, but it looks to me like it has four bullet holes in the hull, just below the deck."

"Thank you, Mr. McHugh. I'll get there as soon as I can."

"I understand, ma'am. Even I recognize the Westerfield name. Just ask for Pat."

Kristy finished wolfing down her food, excused herself, and headed out the door.

CHAPTER 5
PAT'S BOAT SERVICE

Lights flashing, Kristi raced down U.S. 12 finding little traffic to slow her. She got back on the police band radio to let Jake, her second in command, know where she was going. *Thank God for Jake*, she thought, *it's nice to have competent backup people.*

After several attempts, she located Gus Arven, the Berrien County Sheriff, to report the suspected foul play and asked if he wanted to meet her at the boat service.

"I'll be there in about 20 minutes," Arven said matter-of-factly.

"It will take me a little longer, about half an hour," Kristi replied.

She turned north at Red Arrow Highway, keeping her eyes to the left, searching for Pat's Boat Service sign. After fifteen minutes of wishing she had better directions, she relented and swung into a gas station, only to learn she was practically there. "It's half a block farther north. Turn left, follow da sign," a jewelry-covered teenage attendant told her. Walking out, she wondered, *was that a boy or girl?*

She parked in front of the boat yard. "Where can I find Pat?" she asked a white haired woman seated at a beat-up gray metal desk.

"He's out back," she said, glancing up from her books, "with the sheriff. Through that door."

As Kristi went into the yard, she just had to shake her head. Boats, boats everywhere, most were in pieces; an expensive junkyard without room to turn around. A man wearing tennis shoes, jeans, and tank top was talking to a "county brownie" standing beside a small boat on a trailer.

"Are you Pat? And you must be Sheriff Arven?"

"Chief Christopher?" Pat questioned.

"Yes. Thank you for calling me," she replied. "This must be the Westerfield boat? Looks small for Lake Michigan."

Pat was quick to answer, "It is the boat, and it's not too small. A good sailor could take this baby anywhere."

"Nipper" was painted across the stern in gold-leaf with a dark maroon outline. It had a glossy royal blue and white hull with teakwood trim and decking. The Nipper's smooth flowing nautical design reminded Kristi of a well-kept piece of art. The Nipper was the picture of tender loving care.

"Take a look at this, Chief." McHugh was pointing out four quarter-inch holes about three inches apart.

Biting her lip and shaking her head, Kristi said, "Sure as hell looks like bullet holes. What do you think, Sheriff?"

"I'd say a 30-30 or 30-06, could be smaller, but if those are bullet holes, where did they come out? They had to hit something, or they would have come out the other side of the hull."

"There's probably a spinnaker, an extra set of sails, and God only knows how many life jackets under that deck. Could that stuff stop a bullet?" Pat asked. "The boat wasn't flipped so everything is probably still aboard."

Kristi climbed aboard, using the trailer wheel and a boost from Sheriff Arven. Bending down, she stuck her head below the forward deck. "You were right, Mr. McHugh. The floor is filled with sailing paraphernalia in there."

"You see anything else?" the Sheriff asked.

Four small beams of light came through the holes about four inches above a duffel bag. She strained to get her head in a little farther. A matching set of holes in a bright yellow life jacket vest came into view. "They're bullet holes all right, no doubt about it," she said, crawling out of the boat. "Somebody better call the Coast Guard Search and Rescue boys, let 'em know where the boat was found and the possibility of a missing sailor, or perhaps sailors."

"I'll take care of that, Chief Christopher," Sheriff Arven volunteered.

"Thank you, Sheriff," Kristi said congenially. "The shooter must have been well above the target for the bullets to hit the life jacket. I'd say the trajectory would be at least 20 degrees."

"So, what does that mean?" Pat asked.

"It means the boat was shot from the bluff while it was close to the shore. Right, Chief?" Arven said with a grin.

"Very astute, Sheriff. I think that's logical, and very probable. How do you want to handle this? Whatever happened, although it didn't take place in South Station, evidently one of our citizens was involved."

"Let's just play it together for awhile, at least till we figure out who did the shootin' and why."

"I'd like that," Kristi said, brushing back a wisp of auburn hair.

"Hell, this might be the Coast Guard's case," Arven said. "Speaking of the Coast Guard, I better call now; we don't want to tic them off. Do we know where the boat was found?"

"The fishermen who brought her in said it was about four miles out, directly northeast of here," McHugh reported.

Kristi turned to him. "Have you got any ideas where Westerfield's boat might have been moored?"

"When a boat is that small, chances are it's kept on a trailer and could be launched anywhere. There is a Westerfield estate a few miles north of here but, as I hear it, an old guy only uses it off and on, summertime mostly. It would be difficult to get a boat in there; bluff's too high."

"Did you get the name of the fishermen who towed her in?"

"The Miller brothers, Roger and Gene," McHugh said with a smile. "They keep their boat with us."

"Did they tell you anything else, anything unusual?"

"Actually, they did. Roger told me one of the mast cables was broken. That doesn't make much sense. It would take hurricane force winds to break a cable. They just don't break."

"Show me," Kristi said, raising her eyebrows.

The mast was taken down and securely rigged horizontally on top of the boat. McHugh agilely hoisted himself aboard and began to loosen and unwind the three cables. As he worked, he explained that their function was to keep the mast from bending in a strong wind. He held up the broken end in triumph, "It's busted, alright." Then looking at the location where it should have attached, he said, "I'll be darned, here's the rest of it still fastened to the boat."

The Coast Guard was none too happy about the timing of his call, Arven reported, but in spite of the delay, they would get a boat out there to look around. They also said an unconscious man, found on the beach just north of here, had been taken to Memorial Hospital.

"Any ID?"

"No, but they said he was young, late twenties, early thirties."

"Sheriff, do you have a good ballistics man? Unfortunately, South Station is not well equipped with specialists."

"Neither are we, but I do have a guy who's not bad. He's good at evaluating trajectories, and he knows his guns. Why don't I have him come out here to check out the boat?"

"If you'll do that, I'll check in at the hospital, and see if I can track down the guy who found our John Doe."

"Okay by me," Arven smiled. "I'll keep you posted. You do the same."

Kristi was amazed at his willingness to co-operate, as well as his congenial, competent manner. *We're a long way from New York City, Toto*

CHAPTER 6
NEW PRODUCT MEETING

Wesfield Laboratory was a short distance north of the Indiana border in Michigan's beautiful fruit orchard and grape country. Having spent most of her adult life in New York City, Lori was always impressed when she entered the Wesfield complex. Majestic oaks formed a canopy over the half-mile driveway leading up to the main office. Flanked by acres of plush lawn, the road passed a three-acre lake before reaching the visitor's parking area.

After eight years of grunt work, Lori Smith finally became an account executive at Hutchins, Keller & McDonnell Inc., one of Manhattan's more creative advertising agencies.

She had to overcome two barriers on her path to becoming an account executive. The first was the age-old problem of being a woman playing in a man's sandbox. Second, she looked young for her age with light flawless skin and rosy cheeks. Her large, pale blue eyes often suggested she had more questions than answers, which didn't help her credibility.

Fortunately, after several years of providing a multitude of creative solutions, her intellect eventually prevailed. Once she got her chance, people whose accounts she managed had nothing but praise for her abilities.

She was told to be at Wesfield Laboratory, her main account, for a ten o'clock Monday morning meeting.

Getting there was no easy feat, since there wasn't a commercial airfield nearby. Lori had to fly into O'Hare and drive 100 plus miles, but the hassle was worth the effort. She liked the unique Middle America company and its friendly people.

Like a teenager on her first date, Lori bounced up the steps of the traditional red brick building and through the heavy glass doors. Passing the receptionist, she said, "Hi Kathy, I'll be in the ten o'clock meeting."

Kathy put up her hand. "Hold it Lori. You have to sign in, get a visitor's badge, and I have to call back to get you an escort."

"What's going on, Kathy? I've never had to have my hand held before. Why now?"

"It's not personal Lori, just a new policy. I've been told, in no uncertain terms, 'No Exceptions.'"

After a couple of minutes, one of the Marketing Department secretaries stuck her head in the door and loudly announced, "Miss Smith." In lockstep, they headed up to the third floor.

When they arrived, she found bureaucratic movers and shakers of the Consumer Products Division management team already packed in the meeting room. Sales, Marketing, Legal, Purchasing, QC, Manufacturing and Inventory Control were heavily represented. Lori immediately felt the tension. The usual pre-meeting chatter was nonexistent. Folks were worried, and they should be. It wasn't often Gordon Wieldey, Marketing Department vice-president, called a meeting, especially an "emergency meeting."

"Ladies and gentlemen, before we start the meeting," Wieldey said, "I have some really bad news. Early this morning Jeff Westerfield was found unconscious, washed up along the Lake Michigan dunes. Luckily, he was wearing a life jacket, but he had a nasty gash on his temple. He was taken to Memorial about six o'clock this morning. That's all I know except, as of 15 minutes ago, he was still unconscious."

Tears welled up in Lori's eyes. She couldn't breathe. She and Jeff were much closer than most Account Executive/Product Manager relationships. They had not been intimate, but they had spent a lot of time enjoying each other's company. Lori was the first girl Jeff had shown any interest in since his divorce two years ago. She was so emotionally concerned about Jeff, the new product marketing program she and Jeff put together seemed to lose all importance.

"When did it happen? Was he missing, or what?" someone asked.

"I am not sure, probably Sunday night," Gordon replied. "I realize you're all concerned; when I find out more details, I'll get the word out. Unless there are more questions, I'd like to get this meeting started.

"Our company has not had a successful new product launch since our nutritional line was introduced, almost 50 years ago. Life cycles of our brands have been on the decline, in spite of pumping a ton of advertising money in an effort to find new consumers. We have updated existing products and launched a few line extensions, but nothing truly innovative or profitable. If we are ever going to become a leader in the 'over-the-counter' market, 'ExRelief' Cold Medicine will be the first step. The success or failure of this launch will shape our future.

"Since Jeff is the Product Manager for this project, and he can't be here, you may have to bring me up to speed on a few details.

"It has been brought to my attention that the illustration on the national rollout package is a far cry from this gorgeous test market package." Wieldey held up both boxes. "I can't imagine how we could use a different package for the rollout than the one we tested and, I might add, based our projections on. Who approved this piece of crap?"

Panic swept the room. Heads were going to roll. There was no place to hide. A very authoritative voice spoke up, "I okayed it." The rest of the room started breathing again. Apparently, Margaret O'Brien was too new with the company to realize the consequences of volunteering.

"Would you please explain how you came to that decision?" Wieldey said, even more authoritatively and with one eyebrow raised.

Fortunately, Margaret's knowledge of printing was extensive. She simply stated, "The job was quoted to run on a rotogravure printing press like most of our products. The test market package, because of the small quantity, was printed on an offset press. On box board, because of varying box board thickness, you cannot achieve the same quality with rotogravure that you can printing on an offset press."

"Are you telling me that this is the best we can get?" Wieldey asked, holding the inferior package forward.

"I'm saying that's the best you can get at the price we are willing to pay," Margaret answered, not giving an inch.

"Why wasn't this brought to our attention before we got to this stage?" Wieldey asked.

Margaret took a deep breath and apprehensively continued, "Sir. You were notified. Both Jeff Westerfield and I pointed out, in separate memos, that the package illustration would suffer unless the boxes were produced using the same printing process for the national rollout that was used in the test market."

"Who stood in the way?"

Thinking, *You did, you bureaucratic ass,* she answered, "Actually, Mr.Wieldey, your finance committee wouldn't authorize the cost increase that we requested. It chose to hold the line on manufacturing costs to original projections. Packaging estimates were based on our existing products which, as you know, don't have illustrations and therefore do not require a superior printing process. So, we did the best we could within the financial parameters the committee authorized."

Dismissing his own shortcomings, Wieldey moved on to a solution phase. "How much would it cost to get back to the test market quality?"

"I can't tell you off the top of my head, but I think a safe range would be between 1.5 cents and 3 cents for each carton. That could increase the printing cost by as much as $30,000 for every million boxes we use."

"Thank you, Margaret, I had no idea," Wieldey said. "Agency people, Marketing, Purchasing and Estimating, please stay. Everyone else can leave. Maybe you better stay too, Margaret."

As the room cleared, Margaret realized she not only came through unscathed, but possibly advanced her credibility. Gordon Wieldey seemed to like her "eye-to-eye" approach. He didn't see that type of confidence very often.

"Okay, folks," Wieldey said, pausing to give his 'I-mean-business' stare. "Rework the packages. Lori, rework the TV commercials using the test market package. How about selling sheets, 'point-of-purchase' material, public relations releases, coupons and newspaper inserts? Have any of our support materials been produced with graphics showing the wrong package?"

"Offhand, I don't remember seeing a package illustration on the in-store point-of-purchase stuff, but selling sheets, coupons and inserts are another matter," Darin Rauguth, a sales materials and packaging buyer, explained. "We may have to reprint a lot of it, but I don't think anything has been sent out yet."

"Get me costs and a new timetable," Wieldey responded. "We

need to get this done fast; our sales people are already selling it. As you know, it's crucial to be on the shelf for the coming cold season. ExRelief Cold Medicine has to be launched without any more hiccups. It's just too important, and . . . we *will* do this to the best of our ability."

"Margaret," Lori said, loud enough to get her attention. "If I'm going to be able to get the commercials changed, I will need at least a dozen test market packages. Can you get them for me?"

"No problem," Margaret said, suspecting the reason for Lori's urgency. "I'll call my department now; they'll be at the receptionist desk before you get there."

"Thanks."

The meeting ended abruptly. Lori raced to the reception desk, put the boxes in her briefcase, and ran to her car. Memorial Hospital was a 20-minute drive. Jeff was still unconscious when she arrived.

CHAPTER 7
HOSPITAL

Earlier in the day, as the morning crew was being briefed, the "incoming" phone went off.

"Memorial Hospital, Emergency, this is Ila May."

"Hi, Ila May. Bobby, Paramedic with Berrien Ambulance."

"What do you have, Bobby?"

"Some joggers running on the Lake Michigan beach found an unconscious guy half in, half out of the water. My partners just brought him up the bluff. His temp is, let's see, 86 degrees, breathing slow and shallow. He's wearing a life jacket and all-weather gear, so he might have fallen out of a boat. There is a laceration on the side of his head. We'll keep you posted on his vitals, start an IV, and try to warm him. Should be there in about 30 minutes."

"Sounds good, Bobby. We'll be ready for him."

"Okay, Ila May, see you in thirty."

"That's Jeff Westerfield," one of the candy striper volunteers exclaimed, as the patient's gurney was wheeled into a curtain-walled cubicle. Dr. Turek's efficient medical team went into action. Oxygen and heated blankets were immediately put to use as machines measured Jeff's vital signs.

After careful inspection of the patient he, turned to his head nurse. "Fran, I need to get this guy's history; see if you can track down a relative."

Without answering, Fran's long strides quickly took her down the hall. After calling Wesfield's Personnel Department, she eventually located Carol Ackerman, Jeff's secretary, who gave her Joseph Westerfield's private phone number. Joseph Westerfield listened without interruption as Fran gave him a brief rundown. Although he was obviously shaken, he methodically answered all Fran's questions: no drug allergies, no metal pins or plates, no high blood pressure, no heart problems, no nervous disorders, and he was not on any medications. He started to list childhood illnesses, when Fran interrupted, "I have enough for now, thank you very much. You were extremely helpful." Fran thought to herself, *Grandpa knows more than most parents.*

"I'll be there shortly," a breathy-voiced Westerfield said.

Upon arriving, he checked in with the Emergency Room receptionist and was asked to have a seat. Fran, the nurse he had talked with, came out. She instinctively gave him a hug which told him she understood how important Jeff was in his life. His eyes filled with tears as Fran reported Jeff had suffered some hypothermia and seemed to be in shock; on the positive side, he was stable and holding his own.

One hour passed, then two. They seemed like days to Joseph, sitting alone in the dreary waiting room. An attractive girl rushed in, interrupting the silence. After a brief discussion at the reception window, she approached Joseph with a teary smile. "Hi, I'm Lori Smith, I work with Jeff on his . . ."

Westerfield cut her off mid-sentence, "I know who you are, young lady. I have been looking forward to meeting you, but under different circumstances, of course."

"Have you heard anything?" she questioned, as she reached up and locked her arms around Westerfield's neck.

He was no longer alone, instantly adopting Lori in his mind. They just stood there, comforting each other, for several minutes. Finally, Lori snuffed back her runny nose. "I'm sorry," she sobbed, then snuffed again. "Oh, my."

"It's too soon for grief. Now is the time for worry and prayer. Jeff is a strong lad. I believe with God's help, he'll recover," Joseph said, forcing a sober smile.

Lori dried her tears; his strength was contagious. Another hour passed.

A South Station police car pulled into the parking lot directly opposite the glass doors. Chief Kristi headed straight for the receptionist. After introducing herself, she said, "I was told a man was brought here this morning who apparently had a boating accident."

"Jeff Westerfield?"

"I believe so, but I don't have a name."

"One of our people recognized him. He is Jeff Westerfield, all right. What can we do for you?"

"It's important I talk to the attending physician as soon as possible."

"I'm sorry, Chief Christopher," the receptionist said, "He's with the patient now. I don't think the wait will be too long, but I can't say for sure. He knows people are out here."

When she walked over to the waiting area, Joseph Westerfield and Lori introduced themselves as Jeff's grandfather and friend. "Can you shed any light on Jeff's accident, Chief Christopher?" Westerfield asked.

"The boat was towed in by a couple of fishermen, and I'm afraid there were signs of foul play. I don't know anything about his condition. Hopefully, the doctor will be here soon."

Before Joseph could press Kristi for more details, a tall self-confident looking man in scrubs walked up to him saying, "I'm Dr. Turek."

"Hello Doctor, I'm Joseph Westerfield, Jeff's grandfather. This is Lori Smith and Chief Christopher. What can you tell us?"

"He's showing signs that he's starting to regain consciousness. It could take awhile."

"Do you have any idea what happened, doctor?" Joseph asked.

"Not really. He must have been in the water quite awhile because his body temperature was extremely low, but how long or how he got there, I have no idea."

Kristi interrupted, "Doctor?"

"Are you here as a friend, or on official business?" Turek questioned.

She didn't answer his question. "I don't have a delicate way to ask this," she paused, "but I need to know about his injuries. In particular, are there gunshot wounds?"

Lori and Joseph were stunned by the question, but Dr. Turek just said, "That would explain the wound on the side of his head. I couldn't see how the boom or any part of the boat could make a groove like that."

"Are you telling us someone tried to kill my grandson?"

"Unfortunately, it is more than just a strong possibility," Kristi replied. "There's other evidence that points in that direction."

The nurse came out and whispered something in Dr Turek's ear. "Fran informs me Jeff is starting to come around. Let me examine him and I'll be back when I know more. It will take the better part of an hour, so if there is anything you need to do, this would be a good time to do it."

Lori called back to Hutchins, Keller & McDonnell, instructing the creative people to rework the commercials with test market packages she was sending special delivery.

Kristi contacted Jake back at the station. "Would you believe we have an attempted murder on our hands? Jeff Westerfield was the target."

"Whoa, Westerfield. Nothing like starting at the top. What do you need me to do?"

"Call Berrien Ambulance; Bobby was the paramedic who handled the communications. Find out exactly where Jeff was found and by whom. I understand some early morning joggers called for help. Get statements if you can track them down. Keep me posted."

Joseph took most of the hour making several phone calls. He was extremely quiet when he returned. After a short time, he leaned toward Kristi. "We need to talk."

"He's awake," Dr Turek announced as he entered the room, "but not particularly coherent."

"Can we see him?" Lori asked.

"Yes, but please keep it low key. Why don't we give Mr. Westerfield a few minute alone with him."

"If you don't mind, I would prefer Miss Smith go in with me. Jeff might like that, too."

"That's okay with me, but he needs a little time before he'll be ready to answer questions."

Jeff smiled, as Westerfield and Lori came in together. "I see you've met."

Lori surrounded Jeff with a smothering hug, Joseph grasped his hand. "Glad to see you, boy," he said, teary- eyed. "How are you doing?"

"I'm a little groggy. Not bad though, considering I spent the night on the beach in my life jacket. How are you two getting along?"

Lori smiled, "I think we have some common interests."

"She's a keeper." Joseph's sincerity was written all over his face.

Jeff started a sentence, but drifted off before he could get his thought across. He woke a few minutes later. "Are you up to answering a few questions?" Joseph asked. "Let me get Miss Christopher, the police chief, before you get too tired." A minute later he ushered her into the room.

"Hi Jeff, I am Marilynn Christopher, the Chief of Police in South Station. Do you feel up to telling us what happened?"

"Nice to meet you, ma'am. I'll tell you what I can remember, but it's kind of fuzzy."

"That's all I can ask. If you get too weary, just let me know; we'll do it later."

"Let's give it a try."

"Okay."

"I was heading south, back to the landing where I put in that morning. Because the wind was out of east, I had to stay out from the shore to catch it. I had dropped the jib because I wanted total control and, as I remember it, I held the mainsail rope in my right hand. I often do that in swirling inconsistent wind." Jeff laid his head back tight to the pillow with his eyes shut.

"Are you okay?" Kristi asked. "We can do this later."

"I'm alright, just trying to remember. The next thing I know, I'm in the water and I'm freezing. I must have been knocked out for a second. My head was hurting and I think it was bleeding." He paused again. "Then, I remember, what had to be bullets, piercing the water inches from my face. I realized I was being shot at. I managed to get behind the Nipper. Several more shots hit the boat. You know, the Nipper saved my life. Thank God her sail wasn't cleated; if it was tied down, she would have been blown away from me. Anyway, when things quieted down, I tried to swim to Grandpa's shore. It was straight in from where I was. I can't remember reaching it; I guess I must have."

"Did you see an assailant?"

"No, but I'm positive he was on shore."

"How can you be so sure?"

"The bullets hit the shore side of the boat and I was the only one still on the lake."

"Thank you, Jeff," Kristi said, "Are you holding up well enough to continue or would you like to rest awhile?"

"I'm holdin' up better now that I'm waking up."

"Good. Your Nipper may have saved you more than once," Kristi paused. "I'm not positive, but it's very likely the bullet that hit the side of your head first glanced off one of the mast cables. One was severed. It's not a stretch to think it changed the trajectory enough to avoid a direct hit."

"Where is my Nipper?"

"A couple of brothers, the Millers, brought her to Pat's Boat Service."

"I know Pat's. We need to thank the Millers," Jeff said, looking toward his grandpa, "Maybe get them a gift or something."

Trying to keep him on track, Kristi said, "If you don't mind, Jeff, I need to know a few more facts. Are you up to it?"

"Yeah, I'm okay."

Kristi went on to establish the basics: Jeff's divorce was painful but civil, he wasn't aware of any enemies, no jealous husbands, and he couldn't see how this could be work-related. No one, it seemed, would benefit from his death. Then she said emphatically, "I don't want you speaking to the press under any circumstances. There are way too many unanswered questions for us to provide information to your attacker. Okay?"

"Okay. I doubt they even know I'm here. Why would I want to talk to them, anyway?"

"You don't. Given half a chance, they could do a lot of damage to our investigation."

"Enough said. I get it," Jeff said, with hands raised as if to surrender.

Kristi turned to Joseph, "Mr. Westerfield, are you up to filling in a few blanks for my record?"

"Of course. Let's grab some coffee in the cafeteria. Lori, keep an eye on him, will you?"

"Thank God, Jeff came around," Joseph sighed as they sat down.

"I can see you're very close."

"We're a great deal more than close. He's my world."

"What time did Jeff arrive at your lake house Sunday?"

"Jeff showed up late in the morning, maybe just before 11:00. We shot the breeze for a while, had hotdogs and beer, and watched a ball game. Normally, we would have gone for an afternoon sail together, but I was a little tired, so I cleaned up and headed back to town. Jeff left before me, some time after 5:00. All in all, I'd say it was a typical Sunday. We usually spend the day together."

"Did he seem anxious or upset about anything?"

"Quite the contrary. Other than a little frustration with Wesfield Laboratory's bureaucracy, he was in great spirits."

"You seem extraordinarily close for an adult grandchild-grandfather relationship."

"We've been through some trying times together. My wife Patricia and I raised him since he was six."

"What became of his parents? Are they still alive?" Kristi wished she could retract the question the instant it came out of her mouth.

"His dad, our son Frederic, lost his life trench fighting along the 38th parallel at the end of the Korean War. It happened in May, 1953. We received word on the third of June. He was a remarkably loving husband and father; I was very proud of the man he turned out to be. Freddy was a lieutenant in the National Guard when he was called up. He accepted it as his duty, in spite of the fact that he knew it was a poorly managed UN bureaucratic nightmare."

"He must have been quite a man."

"He was a loyal patriot who believed in doing his share." A long silence revealed the grief in Joseph's reflections.

Kristi sensed Joseph Westerfield was a master at controlling his emotions. "Can I get you anything?" she asked.

"No, I'm okay. I haven't thought about Frederic lately. These are trying times."

"You're doing fine."

After a few moments he went on, "His young wife Sophia was unstable before it happened. They had lost Jeff's three-year-old sister,

Sally, to polio the previous year. Sally was named after my younger sister, and she was cute as a button. Sophia was just beginning to recover from that tragedy when two Army officers appeared at the door. Even before they spoke, Sophia knew in her world, all was lost. She didn't cry, she didn't talk, she didn't eat, she didn't seem to sleep. She stared endlessly out the window as if she expected her beloved Freddy to walk up the sidewalk at any moment." Kristi could feel his sorrow as he said, "I believe Sophia's frail spirit was shattered."

He went on to tell her how, in addition to deeply grieving themselves, he and his wife Patricia were extremely concerned with their son's wife's despondency. "We thought maybe having Sophia's parents here might snap her out of her depression. We arranged their transportation from Italy and met Ida and Alfonso Antisdale at O'Hare. On the ride from the airport to the lake house, we tried to prepare them the best we could, warning them not to expect much."

"Did it help at all?" Kristi asked.

"Sophia's response to them was not what we were praying for; she expressed little recognition. Having Ida here to look after Sophia was a big help to us. We didn't know what to do and needed her help. Ida's always been a patient, capable woman. Having her here made a lot of difference.

"Being all mother, Ida soon realized Jeff was feeling the effect of his mother's condition. Fearing psychological damage, she came to us with a plan to save Jeff from an ongoing incomprehensible situation that few adults, let alone children, could ever understand."

"That's when they took Sophia back to Italy?" Kristi asked, giving Joseph a chance to pause.

"They left Jeff with Pat and me, hoping they could return when their daughter improved."

"That had to be hard," Kristi said with a wrinkled brow.

"Yes, it was. Jeff was pretty somber at first, but my wife's loving attention was just what he needed. We didn't realize, at the time, what a blessing it would be for us. In many ways, it felt like raising Freddy all over again.

"It was a terrible time for all of us." Silent for a few seconds,

Joseph swallowed a gulp of air to regain his control. "Especially the day Ida and Alfonso took their little girl back to Bardolino, where she was born.

"They were optimistic a rest in the Alps could help in her recovery," Joseph continued. "I think they were probably a little homesick, too; I would have been. Unfortunately, nothing ever changed. Such a shame. Sophia was nineteen when she and Freddy were married–a gentle, sensitive budding flower."

"What became of her?" Kristi cautiously asked.

"She's still there, still childlike, still in her own world." Although his face didn't reveal a hint of sorrow as he spoke, pain filled the room as it seeped from the depths of his soul.

Kristi's eyes started to mist ever so slightly, and Joseph, who never seemed to miss anything, picked up on it immediately. "There, there, young lady, you're an objective police officer. Cops don't cry."

"Chiefs could if they wanted to, but I'm not crying," Kristi said, backing off with an embarrassed smile.

"It's okay. I feel like that myself more often than I'd ever admit. There was an upside; I enjoyed watching Jeff grow into a remarkable young man. Let's go see how he's doing."

Lori reported that Dr. Turek expected him to sleep for several hours and that he could be released in the morning, barring any unexpected complications.

Kristi and Joseph left, but Lori wanted to stay.

When they reached the main entrance, three local reporters had set up their ambush. "Chief Christopher, can we have a statement? Laura Garnes, South Bend Tribune."

"Certainly. On what issue would you like me to comment?"

"The unconscious man that was brought in this morning from Lake Michigan."

"I heard he was doing alright," Kristi said, "But that's just hearsay. For an accurate medical report, I'd ask the doctor."

"Who was found?"

"I can't tell you that. I haven't been authorized by the party involved."

"You're not going to tell us his name?"

"Miss Garnes. Is there some crime here that I am not aware of?"

"No, I guess not," the reporter murmured.

"Well, in that case, I don't believe it's up to me to repeat anyone's personal stories as though the public has some right to know."

"You sure have a way with the press," Joseph smiled.

"It's a gift."

CHAPTER 8
BEVERLY'S PHONE CALL

Joseph Westerfield was pondering the "who and why" of the assault on his grandson. Annoyingly, the phone rang, interrupting his contemplation. "Hello."

"Hello, Mr. Westerfield, this is Beverly Neubauer."

"Beverly Neubauer? From South Station? My God, it must be thirty years."

"Thirty-five. How are you, Joseph?"

"You've just brightened my day. I am so happy you called. Where are you? What have you been up to?"

"I've been in New York since I left South Station, and it's Beverly Collins now."

"Well, congratulations, he's a lucky guy. I'll never forgive you for running out on me. I thought we worked really well together. You know, you were the only secretary I ever totally trusted."

"Thank you, Joseph. I always considered you a friend first and a boss second."

Joseph was never aware Beverly was in love with him, even though he was twenty years her senior. An unsolvable dilemma for her, because he adored his wife, and with a man like Joseph, unfaithfulness wasn't even a consideration. Loyalty was one of his most appealing attributes. Realizing it was hopeless, she decided to move on, but somewhere, down deep in her heart, she would always love Joseph Westerfield.

"Are you in town?" Joseph said. "Can you come to lunch?"

"No, I'm still in Manhattan."

"What have you been doing all this time? Any kids?"

"Oh yes; we have two grown girls and three granddaughters."

"That's nice." Joseph's sincerity was evident.

"After I left Wesfield, I bounced back and forth between secretarial jobs in the Big Apple, but they didn't hold my interest. During that time

41

I was a secretary by day and student by night, eventually graduating with a paralegal degree."

"That's great, Beverly; I'm proud of you. So now you do all the work, while some lawyer makes all the money."

"Not too far from the truth, but I like it, and I'm good at it."

"What does your husband do?"

"He's a retired commercial pilot, American Airlines. You'd like him."

"I'm sure I would, if you say so. I always thought you could read my mind."

"More often than you ever knew. As pleasant as this conversation is, I called for another reason."

"Is there some way I can help you, Beverly?"

"No. No. I ran across a letter that had your name in it, and, of course, it piqued my interest. At first I didn't think much about it, but the more I thought about it, the more alarmed I became."

"Are you sure you should be telling me this, Beverly?"

"From a legal ethics perspective, absolutely not. Morally, I would feel remiss not alerting you. You are a special friend I believe to be in danger. Besides 'legal ethics' is a contradiction in terms."

"You sound a bit apprehensive, Beverly. I wouldn't want you to put yourself in jeopardy."

"I have to admit, I've been fretting about this call most of the day, but if something bad happened and I hadn't warned you – I couldn't live with that."

"Since you already have your mind made up," Joseph said, "Tell me, why are you so worried about me?"

"Let me give you a little background. Richardson, Deckmann & Smylee is not your average law office. We represent only the wealthiest companies on the planet. They are so secretive that in 25 years with the company, I still don't know who most of our clients are.

"I work for the Deckmann head of the hydra. We represent large auto companies in the U.S., as well as abroad. My role consists of union negotiations, plant building approvals, and franchising agreements.

"I don't have a good handle on the company's big picture, but I can tell you things just don't add up here. First of all, ninety-nine percent of our lawsuits are settled out of court. We either pay, without much of a fight, or the litigation just seems to conveniently disappear. There have been too many ugly rumors surrounding some of the disappearing suits.

"Unfortunately, I suspect there is more truth than fiction in the rumors. We seem to avoid publicity for our clients at all costs. I'm afraid we take a ruthless approach if the partners deem it necessary. I don't know how far they would go, but I think the worst is probable.

"Another thing that puzzles me is our largest client. Manhattan Bank & Trust, Inc. pays us a $50,000,000 annual retainer. That's great, especially when you consider, to the best of my knowledge, we haven't litigated a single issue involving them. I believe they must be getting something for their money, but I can't fathom what it could be.

"Joseph, do you know anyone named vonLeer or a group called Painter Inc.?"

"vonLeer, yes. Painter, Inc.? Not that I can think of."

"Well, Mr. vonLeer, in a letter to Mr. Smylee, one of our partners, said the Painter people were having trouble with a very important acquisition. There seemed to be an urgency in his concern.

"The letter singled you out, Joseph, as the most influential force blocking their initiative. The line that scared me the most was, 'he will have to be dealt with.' I don't know what they have in mind but, with my company, that kind of talk frightens me."

Joseph was silent for a long moment. When he finally spoke it was barely above a whisper. "It frightens me, too, Beverly. Thank you for the warning; your concern truly touches me. Tell me, have you ever had occasion to use Wesfield as a reference, or have you ever told anyone at Richardson, Deckmann & Smylee where you're from?"

"You think I may be in danger?"

"It's possible. Please think about the question. Are you calling from home?"

"Yes, I am calling from home. I can't recall who I talked to about Michigan. I'm sure I have many times, but with whom and when, I have no idea."

"Let me make a few inquiries and I'll get back to you. I'll need your phone number and address. Thanks again, Beverly, I hope you haven't stuck your neck out too far."

Having a positive first impression of Chief Christopher, Westerfield decided to get her advice. He called the South Station Police Department and was instantly patched through.

"Hello, Mr. Westerfield. What can I do for you."

"I need help, Chief Christopher, and I hope you can point me in the right direction."

"I'll do what I can," she said, sensing the concern in his voice.

"I need to locate someone who can detect surveillance devices in my lake house, my home in South Station, and in a home on Long Island. It's very important that the Long Island house is done quickly. Money is no object. I was hoping you might know someone, or know someone who knows someone, who does that type of thing."

"Mr. Westerfield, we need to talk. We need to talk now."

"I'm staying at the lake. It will take me a while to get to the station."

"It's a little late to do that," Kristi said. "Why don't we meet in the morning? Jake and I have an 11:00 AM meeting with Sheriff Arven and the girls who discovered Jeff on the shore where he was found. We could talk at your lake house before that meeting, if you can arrange to be out there."

"That would be great," Joseph responded. "Right now, though, I'd like to talk about finding someone who can detect a wiretap."

When they had finished their conversation, Joseph was surprised how many people Chief Christopher knew in the surveillance business. He called Beverly back to alert her that someone would be coming to check her phone. She felt he was overreacting, but Joseph was not a man to take chances when a friend's safety was involved. He wanted to know if she had put herself in danger.

Three hours later a crusty old guy rang the doorbell to Beverly Collins' sixth floor apartment.

"Hello. Who is it?"

"Joseph Westerfield told me to tell you, 'shutters can go in the bathroom.'" Beverly smiled as she buzzed him up, remembering the many times they laughed about the order she placed for inside shutters to go adjacent to his office bathroom glass block window. She had hit the " i " key on the typewriter instead of the "u."

When he knocked gently, she opened the door with a smile, "Hello. Come on in."

"Hi, I'm Charley," he said, handing her a card. It read, "Charley

Tanner, Clean Sweeper At Large. We Hate Bugs."

"Nice to meet you, Charley. Joseph told me you'd be stopping by to check out my phone for eavesdroppers."

"That's about it, ma'am." After disassembling the phone, he pulled some kind of electric wand from his bag and began checking in drawers, behind pictures and mirrors, lamps and baseboards, inside and outside. Three hours later, he said with a cute little grin, "You have a very clean house; sure makes my work more enjoyable. The good news is – no bugs."

"Thank you. I didn't think there would be."

"I was told to come back every week until further notice. At your convenience, of course."

"Are you sure that's necessary?"

"I don't know, ma'am. I think this Joseph guy just wants to be sure you and your hubby are safe. That would be my guess."

"I think you're right." They worked out a convenient time for both. *She liked Charley.*

CHAPTER 9
FORCES AT WORK

Jeff walked through his office door to find his friend Skyler, one of the two Wesfield pilots, planted in his desk chair, doodling cartoon airplanes. "Morning, Skyler. How's the little one?"

"She's demanding and nocturnal," he happily replied.

"Why aren't you flying some of our hotshots off to make Wesfield's fortune?"

"I've got an 11:00 takeoff," Skyler said, masking a genuine concern. "Thought I better check on you; make sure you've still got all your parts."

"I'm doing just fine now. I have to admit it was scary as hell out on the lake with someone shooting at me."

"I'll bet. Got any idea who it was?"

"I don't, but Grandpa has a few suspicions," Jeff responded.

With his broad smile, Skyler said, "Joseph always seems to know more than the rest of us. Why is that?"

"It's a mystery to me, Sky. But you're right, he's perceptive."

"Ruby Sue wanted me to ask you to dinner Saturday night. Six, six-thirty."

"Sounds good. But I may want to bring someone along," Jeff said. "Think that would be okay?"

"Like a girlfriend?"

"Like a friend who happens to be a girl," Jeff said. "And thanks for checking on me. I'm doing okay."

"The phoney tightass you call a boss is headed this way. I better get out of your chair."

"Gordon's not so bad," Jeff commented, seeing his friend to the door. "Be sure to tell Ruby Sue I'll be there."

"Don't turn your back on that guy," Skyler whispered. "See you Saturday."

Skyler left as Gordon Wieldey approached. Jeff couldn't help but wonder, *why does Skyler have such a bad feeling about my boss? He didn't think much about the girl I married and he sure as hell was right about her.* "Come on in, Gordon; it's good to see you."

"Jeff, welcome back," Wieldey said, shaking Gordon's hand. "We didn't think you'd recover so quickly. Great having you at the helm again."

"Thanks, it's good to be back," he said, shaking his hand. Getting right down to business, Jeff said, "I hear we're going to use the test market package design for the national rollout."

Gordon was quick to answer. "I hope you don't mind. I wasn't trying to go around you. You weren't here. I thought we . . . "

Jeff held up a hand to cut off his babble. "Not a problem. I fought hard to stay with that package right from the beginning. The money boys on the committee, especially Purchasing, forced me to stay within the cost estimate. They cut me off at the knees for a couple pennies; you got the job done. I couldn't be happier."

"In hindsight," Wieldey said, "I should have gotten involved when the issue first came up. I didn't understand how drastic the difference would be."

Jeff thought to himself, *how can you look me in the eye and pretend I didn't show you the proof sheet specifically pointing out the differences?* "What now? Do you want me to pick up the ball, or where else can I help?"

"Are you kidding?" Gordon asked, distancing himself from the whole mess. "I just stepped in because you couldn't be here. This has been your baby from the start, but I will share the credit when it succeeds." Gordon grinned, handing him a progress report. "Here, this ought to keep you out of trouble."

"There is something else," Jeff said, "I'd like your opinion on something that has me concerned."

"My opinion? You want it, you got it. What's bothering you?"

"You've been around Wesfield long enough to get a feel for how long it takes to get things done. And you've worked with different product managers on several brands. My question is, have you noticed an inordinate number of roadblocks put in the way of this project?"

"Roadblocks?"

"Yes. Roadblocks. Take this approval sheet, for instance. Some of these guys took several months to sign off. Many of those who took the longest don't play a roll in production or distribution. I don't get it. Why would Quality Control, Inventory or Purchasing take months to ponder this? What's to approve?"

"I'm glad to hear you ask that question; I thought it was just me," Gordon said. "I could have gotten this product through both houses of congress with less opposition. It doesn't make any sense to me either, Jeff. You'd think these people would be doing everything in their power to get ExRelief off the ground."

"Speaking of things that don't make sense: are you aware of any revolutionary products in the development stage?"

"No. I can't say that I am," Wieldey said. "Nothing's new in the lab, just the same old crap they've been working on for years."

"If we don't have some new wonder product to protect, why do you think we're beefing up security?"

"What's got you so riled up, Jeff?"

"When I got here this morning I couldn't get to my parking place. The problem was, I didn't have a coded ID card. I ended up parking in the visitors' lot and going through the lobby. As it turned out, Kathy, the receptionist, had my name badge complete with picture, and what is apparently my personal Universal Person Code number."

"I know; we all got one," Wieldey said.

"Gordon, are you okay with being scanned just like our products? Every time we come in, Security will know we're here. Do you imagine they actually need that information?"

"No, but I don't have a problem with it."

"What troubles me the most," Jeff said, "is not knowing who's behind the security push and why anyone would think it's necessary."

"Beats me. You know the old Wesfield saying, 'If the competition stole our latest formulas, they could end up twenty years behind.'"

"That would be funny, if it weren't so damned true."

Wieldey left with Jeff wondering if he was overreacting. When Darin Rauguth appeared at his door, he came back to reality. "Come on in, Darin. Nice to see you." Of all the self- important incompetents in Purchasing, Darin was the one exception who could actually get things done. Jeff liked working with him, and Darin liked working with Jeff.

"How are you doing, my friend? Let me be the first to ask: is it true that somebody tried to shoot you?"

"Afraid it is, Darin. I imagine the rumors are running rampant."

"You'd be right, and I'm not the bearer of good tidings, either."

"I suspected as much. Let's have it; what's our problem?"

"I'll start with the most urgent. The supplier we used for the national rollout can no longer produce the total quantity using offset equipment. They would have been okay with the change, but someone vandalized two of their largest offset presses. I guess they were damn near totaled. I don't know what's going on there, unless it's a union problem or disgruntled employees."

"So, how far behind are we? What are our alternatives?"

"I already split up the order with two additional suppliers. We've lost at least a week, maybe a little more."

"What's the problem? Sounds like you already solved it."

"Money."

"Money?"

"Yup, authorized money. Money for three sets of plates, three sets of cutting dies, and most of all, three individual orders. Smaller quantities mean higher costs."

"How much higher?"

"As of today, 3.4 cents a package."

"I'll approve it, especially since you've already stuck your neck out. What's the rest of the story?"

"All the 'point of purchase' material still works. On the selling sheet the package illustration isn't very big; it might be acceptable. What do you think?"

Eyeballing the sheet, Jeff asked, "How much are we talking?"

"We've spent $10,200 so far. It would cost about the same to rerun it."

"I think you're right, Darin. That picture isn't going to influence a single order one way or the other. We'll stay with what we've got."

"All right." Darin's animated response revealed his enthusiasm for the decision. "You know you're leaving yourself wide open to the second guessers."

"I'm not going to lose any sleep over them."

Using the "Will it influence a single order" criterion, Jeff approved everything that had already been printed. New color separations would be created wherever possible, but only if they didn't jeopardize the timing. Fortunately, Sunday newspaper magazines and free-standing inserts, the two largest printed consumer promotions, would go to press with the correct pictures. Darin left Jeff's office with a bounce in his step.

Carol Ackerman, Jeff's secretary, buzzed his phone. "Lori Smith is on line one."

"Hi, sweetheart."

"Is that how you answer a business call?"

"I was hoping this wasn't business."

"Oh, you were, were you? Well it is. I thought you'd like to know the reworked commercials will be ready to view in a couple of days. Maybe I'd better bring them to South Station?"

"I like your business-type thinking. Convenient. Since I can't get to the Big Apple any time soon, it's only logical for you to review the changes with me at Wesfield."

"A Monday or Friday would be best for me."

"Works for me, too. Sounds great. Thanks again for staying with me at the hospital. It meant a lot to me. I still don't have a clue why anyone would want to kill me. The more I think about it, the more confusing the whole thing becomes. I'll be looking over my shoulder for a long, long time."

"I know what you mean. When I got to my apartment, I had a peculiar feeling that someone had been there. This might sound strange, but it didn't smell right."

"What do you mean, 'smell right'?"

"Like a heavy smoker had been there. I'm sure it was all in my mind. I'm doing just fine now."

Mrs. Ackerman stuck her head in the door to tell Jeff Joseph Westerfield was on line two.

"My Grandpa is on the other line, do you want to hold?"

"No; say hi to him for me."

"Okay. See you in a couple of days, sweetheart," Jeff said, then hit the push button to switch lines.

"Hi, Grandpa."

After the standard "how you doing" chitchat, and regards from Lori, Jeff told him about her apartment paranoia. An alarm went off in Joseph's mind. "Jeff, I need Lori's work and home phone numbers. Where do you think I could reach her?"

"I think she called from her office. Why? What's going on?"

"Maybe nothing at all. But, I believe there's a possibility the sniper who shot you could have been just part of a much bigger plot. I think there may be a major effort being launched to take over Wesfield Laboratory, and it could involve anyone close to us. Even Lori. If you're free tonight, we could get a pizza or something, and I can share my suspicions."

"See you at Nicky's Italian Restaurant about seven." *My second offer for a free meal this hour – everyone wants to feed me.*

Lori was surprised, yet relieved, to hear Joseph's concern for her welfare. It felt like having an extra grandpa watching over her. "A man named Tanner will check out your place," he told her, "and please do whatever he tells you. It's important."

An hour and a half later she walked out to the lobby to meet Charley Tanner. Handing her a card, he said, "Joseph Westerfield thought I might come in handy."

It was mid-afternoon when Joseph received the call he had been anticipating. "This is Charley Tanner. Is Mr. Westerfield there?"

"Hi, Mr. Tanner. How are we doing?"

"Not good, this place is totally infested. I found bugs in several places."

"Did you remove them? Where are you now?"

"Out in front of her apartment sitting in my van, and no, I didn't touch a thing."

"Can you take some of her clothes without attracting attention?"

"Not a problem."

"Good. I'll have her meet you across from the Park Lake Hotel by the Central Park entrance. Check into the Plaza. Register as man and wife."

"Don't I wish. No one would believe that gorgeous kid could be my wife."

"Alright, father and daughter then."

"That'll work. For how long?"

"Make it indefinite, guarantee a week if you need to. I doubt she is being followed, but I'd like you to make sure."

"Yes sir, I'll make sure." Charley sure liked the old man's style.

CHAPTER 10
THE LAKE HOUSE

On a cool crisp Michigan morning, Kristi found herself, once again heading north on Red Arrow Highway, this time trying to find the Westerfield property. Arriving at 152, the road address, she expected a walled estate and gated entry; she found faded numbers on an old galvanized rural mailbox sticking out of a sea of dusty weeds. Turning down the dirt road, she asked herself, is this really a rich guy's estate? No neatly trimmed shrubbery, no manicured lawn, only last fall's leaves covering the ground beneath partially thinned oak and hickory woods.

Although the legend of Joseph Westerfield III was common knowledge, no one, it seemed, knew much about him or what made him tick. One message, however, was consistent in every account: he was highly respected as a man as well as a business leader. His delicate balance between aggressive marketing and patience made him the force that steered Wesfield Laboratory through its mid-century success. Some people thought he was quite reserved, others considered him downright antisocial. In truth, those he loved, he loved deeply; the others didn't matter.

According to most accounts, 20 years ago on a windy wintery day, Joseph Westerfield left the office at 11:30 to have lunch with his wife. He always found time for Patricia; he treated her as if she were his most cherished treasure.

No one knows exactly what changed that noon hour, but something must have. He called his secretary with instructions to cancel all existing appointments and not to schedule anything in the future. He didn't go back that afternoon, or any other day after that. Around the office he was nicknamed "Kingston," after the Kingston Trio's hit, "The Man That Never Returned." Patricia died 18 months later.

After he lost her, most people thought he would return to run the company. He never did, but he remained on the board of directors, nudging the company along a positive path. Joseph Westerfield was still considered the most powerful man in the company.

Kristi pulled into the lake house driveway about 10:30. She felt a little apprehensive as she approached the door. Kristi peeked through the side window to see a barking Sheltie enthusiastically wagging its tail. Before she could ring the bell she heard, "Tootsie, sit!" As Westerfield opened the door, Tootsie paid little attention.

"That's okay, Mr. Westerfield, I'm a dog person. I especially like Shetlands."

"She's everyone's best friend. Come on in, Chief Christopher."

"Please, my friends call me Kristi."

"All right, Kristi it is."

Passing through the foyer, she could feel the presence of the woman Westerfield treasured long ago. Unpretentious elegance was created by comfortable furniture surrounded with tasteful accents, an environment you wanted to be part of.

"First of all, Kristi, thank you for your help securing people to check out my surveillance suspicions. I'd be at my wit's end to get that accomplished. You did it the same day; I am truly impressed and very grateful."

"Independent agents can be very responsive when you say the magic words, 'Cost is no object.' It's only when you're forced to go through a government funded service that time becomes a problem."

"You knew where to go and what buttons to push."

"I'm glad I could help," Kristi said. "Today perhaps you can help me."

Joseph responded eagerly, "If I can."

"As you know, Gus Arven, the Berrein County Sheriff, Jake Jacobson, my right-hand man, and the joggers who found Jeff are meeting me where they found him in about half an hour. Since you know sailing and the winds here, I'd like you to come along."

Immediately sensing the invitation was mostly a courtesy, Joseph said, "I appreciate your consideration, Kristi. No one wants to find out what's going on more than I do. My grandson is the most important person in my life."

"That's obvious, Mr. Westerfield."

"I doubt that I can help," Joseph said, "but I promise to stay out of your way. Most of my friends call me Wes or Joseph. If we are not already, I hope we're going to be friends. Good friends."

For an old guy, he doesn't miss a thing and he's one smooth talker, Kristi thought. *I wonder if he would consider adopting me.*

Joseph interrupted her playful speculation. "Since we have a little time, how about a cup of coffee?"

"Black. Only if it's already brewed."

Joseph returned carrying a tray containing two filled cups, cream and sugar, and a plate of assorted sweet rolls. Kristi was studying an old sepia-colored copperplate photo she'd taken off the fireplace mantle. The picture showed three rugged looking middle-aged gentlemen wearing vests and white shirts with rolled up sleeves. They were standing in front of a huge locomotive, each with a foot resting on a railroad tie.

"Those pioneers are my heroes, Wesfield's founding fathers," Joseph said with pride. He went to stand next to her and pointed at the smallest man in the picture. "That's Dr. Frederic Eugene Champeau. He was the country doctor who created the products the company was built around.

"The one on the left is Ethan Baylor. He was sales – the front man, so to speak. As I understand it, he could charm the virtue from a preacher's wife. Rumor has it he tried a time or two."

"Sounds like a rascal."

"I'm sure he was. The pudgy fellow was my grandfather, Joseph Westerfield. He was my namesake. Actually I'm the third Joseph Westerfield because my dad was Joseph Junior. When the company was founded, Jo Jo, that was grandpa's nickname, was considered an investor of some regard. His partners found out later that little of the money he put into the company was actually his."

"When did they create the company?" Kristi asked.

"In the spring of 1876 their first medicine show hit the road with WESTERFIELD MEDICINE COMPANY painted on the side of the wagon. By the end of 1879 they had 73 tent and wagon shows, all servicing the bustling towns that were springing up along the transcontinental railroad lines."

"That's why the locomotive is part of the photo?" Kristi said.

"That beautiful old engine is called a 'Consolidation.' Railroads were key to the company's success. Along with providing customers, the rails offered an efficient distribution system." As he talked, Joseph realized Chief Christopher was showing more interest in Wesfield's history than many of their employees.

"How long was the company called the Westerfield Medicine Company?"

"In 1929, it made sense to lose the 'Snake Oil' image. So we modernized with the name we have today: Westerfield was shortened to Wesfield, and the Medicine Company was replaced with Laboratory."

"'Snake Oil?' What kind of products were sold in the old medicine shows?" Kristi asked as her green eyes widened.

"Typical remedies," Joseph said, "tonics, liniments, elixirs, patches, tablets and pills. They were successful because Dr. Champeau's pharmacopeia was laced with some very effective ingredients: alcohol, quinine, alkaloids, opiates and bitters."

"You'd have a hard time getting that lineup approved today," Kristi said.

Joseph smiled, "They were state of the art medicines back then. We had loyal, possibly addicted, but very loyal customers."

"I'm sure you did," Kristi said. "When you talk about Wesfield Lab, it sounds like you care a great deal about the company's fate."

With a distant look in his eyes, Joseph replied, "More than anyone will ever know."

Choosing to change the subject, Kristi pointed at a brass plaque featuring a raised chess pawn lying on its side. Etched in a formal type style, "The Toppled Pawn - 1961 Grandmaster" appeared above the pawn. The name, "Joseph Westerfield," also etched and written in script, was prominently displayed at the bottom.

"Are you a grandmaster, Joseph?"

"Hardly," Joseph said. "'The Toppled Pawn' award simply means I managed to win our local chess club's annual tournament."

Kristi, with a flash of intuition, suspected the award meant more to Joseph than his casual response revealed. "I like the plaque," she said, leaning in to get a closer look.

"We had some very tactical thinkers in our group that year; I was lucky to defeat them." Joseph moved next to Kristi, and touched the pawn with his forefinger. "I can still remember every move in the championship match. Winning 'The Toppled Pawn' was the highlight of my chess career."

"Do you still belong?"

"The group still meets, but I'm not as active now."

She crossed the room to a well-worn 4' x 4' table with an in-progress chess match centered on the top.

"I love this little table, Joseph. It's the perfect chess-table."

"It's one of my most valued possessions," Joseph said with a hint of pride. "Jeff built it for me in a high school woodworking class."

"Very nice," Kristi said.

"The table's oak. Jeff inlaid birch and black walnut squares to create the board and turned the chessmen on a lathe. They're made from the same two woods."

"How did he make the knights?" Kristi asked. "I love their simplicity."

"He whittled the horses with an old army-knife that once belonged to his dad."

Gently, Kristi brushed the table top with her finger tips. "I see why you treasure it," she said feeling the smooth satin finish. "By the look of the board, I'd say you've got a very close match going."

"You know the game," Joseph said raising one eyebrow.

"I've played a few times," she said mischievously.

"Jeff and I started that match the afternoon he was shot; we never got around to finishing it. I guess it's time to reset the board."

"Were you black or white?" Kristi asked.

"I'm always black when Jeff's my opponent."

"Why? By the look of the board, he doesn't need any special favors."

"It's a holdover from his adolescence," he said. "As a boy, he liked to move first, so . . ."

"He was always white," she finished his sentence. "I like Jeff's chances in this match." She looked over the board again. "And I prefer white. Want to play out the match?"

"Sure. If you think we have time." Joseph said.

"If we use a timer," Kristi said with wily smile.

Joseph recognized her penetrating stare as a signal. *This lady can't resist a challenge,* he thought. *And, I'll bet she's a tough little opponent.*

"I haven't played with a timer in quite some time," he said, pulling one from the table drawer.

"I was hoping that might be the case." she said. "Two minutes. Okay?"

"Okay," he agreed. "At 11:30 it's a draw. We'll have to head down to the beach."

"Whose move?" Kristi asked. "Better yet, do you remember the last move?"

"I do indeed," Joseph said. "It was my king-pawn, two spaces forward."

"Great." Almost mimicking Joseph's move, she slid her king-pawn one space forward and smacked the timer.

Kristi was disappointed when Joseph seemed to be plodding, showing little offense or defense. She, on the other hand, with a surge of confidence got off to a strong start. Then, one move before she could implement the conclusion of a well-concealed queen-double knight offensive, Joseph castled, neutering her strategy. After 40 minutes of rapid-fire combat, the match ended in a draw.

I almost had him, she thought. *But, if it wasn't luck, he saw the attack coming all along. Could he have been toying with me?*

"Thank you, Kristi," Joseph said, "I enjoyed your aggressive flair. An assertive temperament is a rare trait in a public official."

"I don't know how to take that, Joseph. I've always considered defense the strongest part of my game, but I am after all, a policeman, not a councilman."

"Take it as the compliment it was intended to be."

"Thank you, Joseph. I look forward to a re-match." She couldn't help thinking, *we can learn a lot about each other from a chess match.*

"We'd better get going," she said pushing her chair back. "I don't want to keep the others waiting. I would like to continue this conversation later, Joseph. I need to know who, or what, you're afraid of."

CHAPTER 11
THE BEACH

Holding tight to the rail, they carefully went down the steep steps along the inlet. Arriving at the beach, they could see the group about a quarter of a mile to the north. Joseph was surprised to see how close the location was to his property. He couldn't help thinking, *if Jeff hadn't passed out, he might have made it to the house.*

Jake had easily tracked down the joggers; they'd left their number with the emergency ambulance operator. Graduate students from St. Mary's College, Yvonne and Janice liked to start their day with a run on the beach. After introductions all around, they told their story, showing the group exactly where Jeff was lying face down, with legs partially in the water. They carefully dragged him out of the water, then Janice went to find a phone and Yvonne said she tried to warm him. No one pursued the obvious question, but Kristi saw Jake and Sheriff Arven flash each other a "I-wonder-how-she-did-that" glance. Kristi thanked them for their help, and they sashayed back down the beach.

Sheriff Arven's ballistics man reported finding four bullets in the boat. They were shot from a 30-06, a hunting rifle commonly used in the Midwest. Traces of copper were found on the stainless steel ends of the severed mast cable. As Kristi suspected, it had undoubtedly deflected the bullet. The ballistics man also substantiated their preliminary trajectory conclusions; the shots came from a minimum of ten degrees above the target. In all probability, the shooter was on the bluff.

Kristi thanked the Sheriff for handling the ballistics. Gus tipped his hat, "No problem, ma'am; glad we could be of service."

Unexpectedly, Kristi's next question was directed to Westerfield. "Jake checked with the weather people; there was a ten mile an hour easterly wind around sundown on Sunday. With your knowledge of sailing, where do you think the boat was when the shots were fired?"

He pursed his lips while he thought for a moment, "I believe Jeff was heading south, back to the landing. Knowing a little about how he sails, I think he would have been catching the wind at the edge of the calm, out maybe 50 yards, maybe a little farther. Based on where he ended up, I'd say he was straight out from here."

Looking toward Kristi, Sheriff Arven and Jake nodded their heads in agreement. She turned toward the bluff, "Somewhere up there our shooter found a hiding place that served his purpose. If it's alright with you, Sheriff, I suggest we spread out along the base of the bluff and try to find a place where he may have climbed up. Then we'll see what's on top."

"Sounds like a plan," Arven said.

"Do you want me involved?" Westerfield asked.

"On our budgets we use anybody and everybody; just look for disturbed sand. Foot and hand impressions would really be nice."

Spreading out, they started examining the area. With four people searching it didn't take long to canvass. Forty yards to the north, Jake found hand and knee impressions indicating someone had indeed climbed the bluff. Nowhere could they find signs of a corresponding descent. Sheriff Arven said, "Assuming the shooter went up here, he's either still up there, or he used a different exit route. One of us contaminating the scene would be better than all of us. What do you think? Chief Kristi?"

"I think you're doing fine, Gus," she smiled, using Sheriff Arven's nickname for the first time.

Accepting it as a friendly gesture, he returned the smile with one of his own. He liked her, too.

Turning to the youngest and fittest member of the group, Sheriff Arven said, "You're the man, Jake." Then he walked a few yards farther up the beach and pointed at the bluff. "Scamper up here. I don't expect you to find any footprint detail with such dry sand, but keep an eye open. We might get lucky. Hopefully some indication of the shooter's movements may still be evident."

Fooling no one, Jake tried to make the climb look easy. He quickly found disrupted sand at the top of the bluff, right where he expected. Carefully following an intermittent path paralleling the ridge, he came to the corner of Westerfield's property. At that point, his heart began to race; he could see the location where the sniper crawled under the brush. Jake was extremely careful not to disturb it. He shouted down to the others to meet him at Westerfield's house. The path continued south, until it vanished in the leaves. He looked up, discovering he was only thirty yards from the house.

Enthusiastically, Jake recounted his findings and suggested they go back with a brush pruner. Leaving Joseph behind, Kristi and Sheriff Arven followed closely as Jake kept warning them not to mess up the sniper's path. He seem to be enjoying his newly acquired authority. Thanks to the pruner, a man's horizontal impression was uncovered with minimum effort. Using elbow, toe, and knee impressions as a guide, Kristi and Sheriff Arven concluded the shooter was a male about six feet tall, give or take an inch.

Jake pointed at two holes in the sand, slightly back from the crest of the ridge and close to twenty inches apart. "What do you make of these?"

"Looks like the rifleman used a Bipod to help steady his aim," Kristi said. "They're common in shooters' circles. Even with that he must have been one hell of a shot." The group scrutinized the area for details, but came up empty.

The enticing fragrance of grilled hamburgers increased as they approached the house. "It's past twelve," Joseph said congenially. "I thought you'd be ready for lunch by now." The spread included hamburgers, hot dogs, tomatoes, lettuce, chips, condiments, and drinks. Westerfield had it covered.

With a chorus of thanks, the group quickly moved to the food. Joseph graciously checked to see that everyone found drinks as well as food that suited them. He asked each of them personal questions, drawing them into friendly conversation. The old man's people skills were out-of-the-ordinary. The dichotomy between Westerfield of the legend and Westerfield their personable host was extreme.

As Kristi watched Joseph hover over the lunch, she pondered, *doesn't he know he's rich? He could have had a servant prepare lunch, had it catered, or taken us to get a Big Mac. Why did he do this?*

The reason, just a tad devious, was one that eluded her. Joseph simply wanted to be part of the conversation he knew would follow the meal. He not only achieved his objective, but established himself as a welcome member of the team.

"Here's what I think we've got," Kristi said, putting a recorder on the table. "A professional assassin."

"How do you figure?" Jake asked as the Sheriff nodded affirmatively.

"First, only a well-trained, exceptional, I could even say remarkable, marksman would have the confidence to choose that shot. Second, the shot was right on target, only an eighth-inch wide cable saved Jeff's life. Third, he researched the territory and the target. His choice was an isolated spot with plenty of cover, on a Sunday when Jeff and his grandfather routinely went for a sail.

"Although we were able to track his movements, we didn't find a single clue left on the ridge – no footprints, no cartridge casings. I doubt we'll find anything when we take a closer look. He was in excellent condition, or he wouldn't have climbed the bluff when he could have walked in from the road. Right, Jake?"

"I'll say."

"Joseph? After Jeff left that Sunday, what did you do?" Kristi asked.

"I went back to South Station. I only came out to the lake to spend the day with Jeff. Once he left I had no reason to stay."

"When we were following the shooter's tracks, it looked like he was heading straight to your house next. You could have been a target, too."

"I'm sure I was."

"What did you say?" Gus said, leaning forward.

"In fact, I believe I was the primary target. Also Kristi, with limited information, your conclusion about the shooter being a hired assassin was brilliant. I'm certain you are right."

Mouths and eyes opened wide. "Would you care to share with us what makes you think so?" Kristi asked.

"It's about ownership and control of Wesfield Laboratory. Ruthless people are making a move to take it over. Jeff and I, because we're the major stockholders, are in their way. They have a history of using violent means to overcome obstacles. I'm frightened, but I'm not easily intimidated.

"I must warn you all before you're too involved, being closely allied with me could be very dangerous. These people are not your average criminals. They have unlimited resources and they usually achieve victory at any cost, monetary or human."

Even though Kristi had an inkling, being aware of Joseph's security concerns, she, along with Jake and Sheriff Arven, was still in shock. Westerfield's perspective of the crime was much broader than anything they had previously encountered. At first it didn't sink in. "Are you telling us we're in the middle of some kind of diabolical international plot?" Arven's curiosity was piqued.

"I strongly suspect; I don't know for sure, but I believe my suspicions are warranted. There are international investors behind BayerAG, a powerful German pharmaceutical conglomerate, who want to see them regain the place in this country they lost at the end of the First World War. I might also point out Bayer was banned from the U.S. a second time after World War II because they were the most menacing member of IG FarbenindustriesAG, a company convicted of war crimes. If I am right, the people backing Bayer view Wesfield Laboratory as the first step to gaining entry back into our country. The most important step."

"Why is it so important?" Arven asked.

"Wesfield is a small company with old recognizable American products. They want the image our product lines communicate, and Wesfield is small enough to be considered an easy takeover target. They've been pursuing us for a long time."

"What do you mean by a long time?" Sheriff Arven asked.

"According to my father, Bayer first made overtures in the 1920s, but that's just hearsay. My first contact was in 1939, when a Swiss holding company called American IG made me a very generous offer. With a little investigation, I learned they were owned, lock, stock, and barrel, by IG Farben, now BayerAG, and the people that funded them."

"Do you think the people promoting a Bayer takeover at Wesfield are living in our country now?" Jake asked.

"Could be. I don't think they ever totally left. There is also the possibility that I have it backwards. Financial interests in this country may actually own, hence control, BayerAG."

"Do you mean to say Americans could be calling the shots?" Kristi asked.

"It's hard to tell who really holds the power. Wealth is international."

"Do you know who these financial interests are?" she continued.

"I can tell you this: prior to World War II, $30 million in American bonds were issued by National City Bank to help finance the IG Farben-Bayer expansion. And, I can tell you that Standard Oil of New Jersey, Alcoa, DuPont, Dow Chemical, and many other companies in our country worked closely with the IG Farben empire. Thanks at least partially to American funding, IG Farben became one of the most powerful and ruthless cartels the world has ever known. Can I tell you who these financial interests are? I wish I knew."

"Do you think you and Jeff are their only interests at Westfield?" Kristi asked.

"Heavens, no. As I see it, any of our stockholders could already have been contacted by the people pushing BayerAG. It's possible, let me stress, only possible, they could already be working on Bayer's behalf. I hope not, but God only knows what promises may have been made.

"This coming Wednesday I've invited some friends, who happen to own stock, to a lunch at the Chalet Restaurant. They represent the majority of Wesfield's ownership. It's not unusual for us to meet every couple of years. We all live in the Midwest and being part of Wesfield Laboratory is a common interest we've enjoyed together. I intend to present my reasons for not selling. There will be a lot of Bayer history some people are not aware of, or in some cases, may have lost sight of. You're all invited. It might be helpful to observe how people react to my comments."

"Why did you wait until now to tell us all this?" Kristi asked, with her green eyes burning into his.

Westerfield explained he received Beverly's "heads-up" phone call only yesterday. As he went over the details of the call, the name of the legal firm caught Kristi's attention. "Richardson, Deckman & Smylee." A man named Smylee handled the airport renovations. *Could it be*, she wondered.

Joseph Westerfield ended, saying, "I still don't really know what's going on, but I'd bet this is only the beginning."

CHAPTER 12
STOCKHOLDERS LUNCH

Joseph had played shortstop; Sally had been at second base. It always amazed him to see his gangly thirteen-year-old sister field and throw better than most of the boys. She was the only girl playing summer recreation baseball. With her short hair and wearing a uniform, Joseph didn't recognize her as a girl, just his pal, and together they were the best double-play combination in the league.

By the time she graduated from high school, a complete metamorphosis had occurred. She became a new person, slender and graceful, confident and composed, an elegant young lady. Joseph never tired of spending time with his second baseman.

Throughout Joseph's life, Sally had been not only his closest friend, but also his most trusted confidante.

It was only natural he would turn to her now for support and counsel. He was about to try to convince Wesfield stockholders to reject the recent barrage of attractive offers he suspected they were getting to buy their stock Having Sally aboard was important to him not only for moral support, but she could be a very convincing ally. If ever he needed strong allies, it was now.

"Hi Sal, this is your big brother, Joe."

"I was just thinking about you. How's Jeff?"

"Under the circumstances, pretty good," Joseph answered. "Do you think you might find time to drive over Tuesday to attend a stockholder lunch on Wednesday?"

"I should be able to handle that."

"It could be dangerous to spend time with me."

"Joseph. Why on earth would you say that?"

"I think the people who shot Jeff also intended to kill me at the same time. They're still out there."

"Really? Why? What's going on, Joe?"

"In a nutshell – some very ruthless people are trying to gain control of Wesfield Laboratory. One way or another, they will eliminate any resistance. Jeff and I, and any other stockholders who lobby against them, are potential targets. That would certainly include you, Sal."

"I can't imagine my piddling number of shares would make a difference," Sally said.

"Nor do I, but I thought you should be aware. It is a possibility."

"I'm just not that paranoid, Joe. I'll see you Tuesday."

"Great. I'll have dinner on." They went on to chit-chat for almost half an hour, which was surprising since Joseph was a "just the facts, ma'am" type of telephone conversationalist.

Sally LaPoint couldn't care less about the fate of Wesfield Laboratory, but she sensed the urgency in Joseph's voice. On Tuesday morning she skipped or pawned off her usual chores, quickly packed an overnight bag, jumped in her Caddy, and headed west from her Ohio farm.

South Station, a drive of more than 200 boring miles over some of the Midwest's flattest farmland, took the better part of the day. Although Sally was only a minor stockholder in the company, she was a major supporter of the brother she loved and admired. If he wanted her there, nothing could keep her away.

Tootsie, the official greeter, shot though the doggie door before Sally was halfway up the driveway. Somehow, with Sheltie instinct, she could distinguish between a vehicle containing a friend like Sally or one delivering a stranger to be challenged. "Okay, Toots, settle down – I love you, too." Tootsie always brought a smile to Sally's face

"Hey, Sally. Thanks for coming." Joseph gave her a hug, grabbed her bags, and they headed to the door. The aroma of simmering onions, carrots, potatoes and beef was the perfect welcome for the weary traveler. Joseph had slow-cooked a pot roast most of the day.

"Wow, that smells fantastic," Sally said, "I'm starved."

"I do my best." Joseph had the table set, ready to dish up whenever she arrived. Hunger kept conversation to a minimum while they ate. They cleared the table together as they had many times as children. With most of the dishes still in the sink, Joseph pointed at the porch door saying, "Go out there. I'll bring my special dessert."

With crickets fiddling in the background, a cool lake breeze brushed her face as she settled into a comfy over-pillowed wicker couch on the screened-in porch. Sally kicked off her shoes, still unwinding from the drive. Strawberry shortcake with whipped cream and chocolate sauce topped off a great meal. The man could cook.

Their late night chat seemed like old times. Growing up, she was uncomfortable talking with others, but didn't have a problem sharing the secrets of adolescence and early adulthood with Joseph. More than just a brother, he was always a wise and understanding friend. Now that they were adults, roles were reversed. Although her thinking was seldom the same as his, he trusted her ability to see things clearly, with a perspective different from his own. Joseph often used her as a sounding board when he was in the process of formulating or refining his thinking. Opposite opinions or variations in thinking never affected the closeness of their relationship.

They talked mostly about family. Sally had a list of "remarkable grandchildren" stories and   Joseph managed to hit the highlights of tomorrow's meeting. Around one o'clock, after another hug, Sally sauntered off to bed. Joseph looked over his notes.

*****

"Hi. Glad to see you, Mrs. Kelly; how's the new grand-baby doing? Garner, I'm so happy you could make it. Charlene, nice to see you, ma'am. . . ." Kristi watched in amazement, as the stockholders entered the room. Joseph greeted each as a personal friend. He knew everyone's name and, more often than not, made some comment about their personal lives. By noon, about 200 people were seated at circular tables and lunch quickly appeared.

Savory food, the result of a skilled chef and served by a friendly staff, was key to starting the meeting on a positive note. Friendly chatter brought everyone up-to-date on social events, children and grandchildren, successes, and even a few failures that occurred during the last 19 months. Dessert was the same gourmet quality as the main meal. Because he wanted their complete attention, Westerfield patiently waited until everyone finished before standing to speak.

Joseph Westerfield III looked considerably younger than a man in his seventies. Quick-witted, tall and straight with a full head of bright white hair, he was the picture of self-confidence. Although he hadn't been active in Wesfield's day-to-day operations for more than fifteen years, stockholders still looked to him for direction.

His formidable bass voice signaled authority. "People," the room went silent. "Thank you for coming on such short notice. It's surprising to see how far some of you will drive for a free lunch." As intended, the casual comment instantly put the group at ease. "I realize many of you had to rearrange your schedules and I appreciate your efforts.

"I asked you here because I believe the time has come for us to determine the future of Wesfield Laboratory. Although you won't read it in any newspaper, I've been told a group of people with an interest in BayerAG is in the early stages of a takeover assault on our company. Feel free to ignore this question but I have to ask it: Have you recently been contacted by anyone interested in purchasing your shares?"

Gagliano, Zacher, Harlin, Herlt, and Senchak, were quick to share their stories. Each had been contacted by an East Coast attorney representing an unnamed client. The interested parties had noble motives ranging between medical philanthropy to a better world through research. Offers starting from $75 a share to $95, were generous considering a share was valued at $40 tops.

"Why didn't you sell?" Joseph asked. "That's a big offer; I can't say I'd have blamed you."

Almost to the person, they said something didn't feel right. Too much mystery, unrealistic price, didn't like the lawyer, et cetera.

"I'm pleased you didn't," Westerfield smiled. "In the event that anyone should need to sell at this time, please give me a call. I may be able to help find a buyer. I truly believe the stock will rise considerably by this time next year, so please have patience. Although most of you are younger than I am, with few exceptions you have always shown a great deal of interest in Wesfield Laboratory's success. Much more, I might add, than the average stockholder who only cares about dividend checks. That's impressive thinking, my friends.

"Most of my life has been spent trying to build Wesfield Laboratory into a company families would want to build a community around. We tried to treat our employees special and hoped they would be happy working with us. The result has been a hard-working, loyal labor force. I love this company and I care deeply about the direction it is going to take. From the very beginning, we have always been an 'All-American' company with All-American ideals. We are – and I hope always will be – a company that cares about its people, its products, its community, and its country. I am proud of who we are. I am proud of the company we've become.

"Before the takeover progresses too far, I'd like to tell you a few things about BayerAG and its place within the IG Farben cartel. The story, I believe, may also answer the question, why they're offering an inflated price.

"When Westerfield, Baylor, and Champeau founded Westerfield Medicine Company, ownership was divided into three equal portions. Unfortunately, most of the Westerfield parcel was funded with European money. My great granddad, Joseph, they called him Jo Jo, actually only personally owned one-third of his allotment. The other two-thirds belonged to a small group of international businessmen, some of whom also had a stake in the partnership, called 'Farbenfabriken vorm Friedr. Bayer & Co.'

"In the beginning, the investors showed little interest in their American gamble. They were preoccupied with endeavors closer to home. Their major project, in terms of time and money, was building the Bayer Pharmaceutical facilities in Leverkusen, Germany.

"Just before the turn of the century, both Farbenfabriken vorm Friedr. Bayer & Co. and Westerfield Medicine Company, that was Wesfield's name back then, discovered they could utilize one another's sales and distribution networks. Bayer needed a means to promote their dyes and chemicals in the U.S., and the Westerfield Medicine Company would benefit from incremental sales that Europe offered. Both companies gained markets across the Atlantic.

"The First World War brought that little arrangement to an immediate halt. Two events severed any possibility of future interaction.

"The first is very personal." He paused to take a drink of water. "At age thirteen, my mother lost her mother to consumption. From that day on, because she was the only girl and the oldest, she became more mother than sister to her two younger brothers. Necessity forced her to be responsible for their rearing. When our country entered the war, the boys went off to fight together. They trained together, shipped out together, fought together, and unfortunately, were killed in action together. They died in a poison gas attack along with 300 other Yankee boys. My mother was never quite the same woman after that. She loved those boys as sons, as well as brothers.

"Chlorine, phosgene, and other byproducts of the dye industry were turned into chemical weapons by the Friedr. Bayer Company. They introduced the hideous weapons in battle at Ypres when Chlorgas was used on 15,000 allies – a third of those exposed, died. To ensure success of the new product line, Bayer provided a school in Leverkusen with the sole purpose of teaching how to safely use poison gas as a weapon. Selling what used to be a nasty byproduct as a very profitable weapon was Bayer's first joint venture with the devil.

"My mother's brothers didn't deserve the horrible death most likely caused as a result of Bayer's greed.

"Undoubtedly, many of you are unaware that my mom was Dr. Frederic Champeau's great granddaughter, Ramona. I find it ironic that my mom ended up with all the Champeau family shares as the result of her brothers being killed with poison gas. To this day, I regret it was my family that introduced people who sponsored Friedr Bayer Company to the Westerfield Medicine Company business.

"The other event severing ties between Bayer and Wesfield was initiated when World War I ended. Because they had produced a large portion of the explosive and chemical weapons, Bayer was at the top of the list of companies to be punished. The Treaty of Versailles ordered the confiscation of Bayer assets in allied countries and also denied them the right to conduct future business in those countries. Bayer products, patents, logos, and buildings, were auctioned off to local companies.

"In the United States and Canada, Sterling Drug's bid of $5.3 million was accepted for the right to sell aspirin using the Bayer name and logo.

"The people vested in Bayer will pay any price to get their assets back and regain a place in the U.S. market. In particular, they want the products, symbols, and logos that reflect positive elements of their past corporate image."

"Excuse me," interrupted a young woman accompanying her parents. "After over 50 years, do you really think they still care?"

"Germany is an old country with old values and a long timetable; the United States is a young country with a short timetable, still searching for its values. Perceptions of value can vary."

"Still, that was a long time ago and, if Sterling has the assets they want, why are they interested in Wesfield?"

Uncharacteristically, Westerfield's patience began to wane. "Madam, I am just trying to let you know to whom you would be selling. If Bayer made a direct play for Sterling, the authorities would stop them in their tracks. No. They're taking a more subtle approach just as they did in the past."

"How would they do that?" someone asked.

"I don't know for sure," Joseph replied, "But this is what I suspect they are trying. A holding company controlled by Bayer interests will attempt to buy a small pharmaceutical company with established products and potential – Wesfield Laboratory fits those criteria and happens to be a familiar target. If they succeed, it would be the stepping stone they need to get back into our market. The holding company will use Wesfield's name to ensure an American image, while gradually taking over management with their own people. After a few years, when the company is totally in their hands, it will offer to buy or merge with Sterling Drug.

"Simultaneously, I suspect Sterling will accept an offer from another international company with a cleaner image, before it's passed on to Bayer. That maneuver will be the smoke screen that creates an international transaction rather than one which could be closely scrutinized by our government. The final move will enable them to operate Wesfield and Sterling as divisions under the Bayer umbrella.

"I'm sorry. I got off the track. Let me continue with the reasons I don't want Wesfield to become part of BayerAG.

"Those early years represented the most positive aspects of Bayer's legacy. In 1925, in an effort to compete in the world market, Carl Bosch of BASF, and Carl Duisberg, Bayer's chief executive, formed alliances with five other struggling German chemical companies to form IG FarbenindustriesAG. We call it by the short name, IG Farben.

"By the late 1930's, with a large amount of Wall Street funding, the Farben cartel became the world's largest chemical company. Prior to World War II, IG Farbenindustries provided a large amount of the funding necessary to advance the Hitlerian or Nazi philosophy. Senator Homer T. Bone told the Senate Committee on Military Affairs in June, 1943, 'IG Farben was Hitler and Hitler was IG Farben.' I believe he was right.

"The Bayer Division of Farben distributed the prussic acid tablets (Zyklon-B) which was, my friends, the horrible little tablet that released gaseous hydrogen cyanide to human beings at Auschwitz-Birkenau, Dachau, and the other death camps.

"Being one with the Third Reich, IG Farben was asked to build and run industrial facilities at Auschwitz to produce synthetic fuel and rubber, which is called buna. The advantage in choosing Auschwitz was an unending supply of slave labor. The SS was paid a small fee to provide the labor force. The final product, of course, was then sold back to the Third Reich at a substantial profit. Cozy little arrangement.

"At the direction of IG Farben/Bayer out of Leverkusen, tens of thousands of prisoners were infected using pills, food, injections and enemas contaminated with typhus, tuberculosis, and many other illnesses. More than 90 percent of these human experiments died a horrifying painful death. The gas chamber would have been a humane blessing by comparison.

"Remember, the SS didn't have any scientific interest. These appalling experiments were conducted at the initiative of IG Farben/Bayer exclusively for their own benefit. These are the same people trying to buy Wesfield Laboratory.

"One of the Nuremberg trials was called the 'IG Farben Trial' because it focused exclusively on IG Farben management. Thirteen of the twenty-four directors on trial were sentenced to between 1-1/2 and 8 years. One of those, Fritz ter Meer, found guilty in 1948 of plundering and enslavement, was sentenced to seven years' detention. I personally feel that was only a slap on the wrist considering the thousands who died in Auschwitz IG, the slave labor camp he managed. Fritz ter Meer also arranged for and was in charge of Monowitz, a concentration camp privately owned and operated by IG Farben. That's right, Farben, using Bayer Division leaders, had their own concentration camp where their enslaved workers were housed.

"Fritz ter Meer was released in 1952, three years short of his seven-year sentence. Three years later, in 1955, he became a member of the supervisory board of BayerAG and was quickly promoted to chairman of that board, serving from1956 to1964. Only ten years ago, Fritz ter Meer, the convicted Nazi war criminal, was a leader in the Bayer organization." Joseph shook his head as his voice dropped.

"BayerAG was banished from our country for war crimes, and here they are again, trying to come in through the back door. Wesfield is the door. We can keep it shut or, if we become apathetic, they will walk right in.

"Are any of you familiar with Elie Wiesel?" A few people raised their hands.

"Wiesel is one of my heroes," Westerfield went on. "He was sixteen years old when he survived Auschwitz, Buchenwald and Gleiwitz. He went on to become a Nobel Peace Prize winner and Holocaust scholar. Let me read a short passage that reveals a little of what he went through and how he sees our role in the future:

> 'Let us remember, let us remember
> the heroes of Warsaw,
> the martyrs of Treblinka,
> the children of Auschwitz.
> They fought alone,
> they suffered alone,
> they lived alone,
> but they did not die alone, for something in all of us died

with them.'"

Westerfield continued, "I'm paraphrasing here, 'our moral obligation is to remember the wishes of the victims and protect the future of humanity from such evil recurring.' Wiesel believes, '...to remain silent and indifferent is the greatest sin of all...' If we allow this takeover, are we protecting humanity, or is our indifference allowing the company that underwrote Nazism a foothold in the USA?

"I realize we are becoming a global society, but I ask you, do we want to become a part of the historically untrustworthy Bayer heritage or remain the righteous company we are?

"Thank you for your attention. Are there any questions?"

There were none, but before they left, several of his friends let Joseph know they were standing with him. He had a hard time holding back the tears.

CHAPTER 13
PARK LAKE HOTEL

Seated at the head of the sixteen-foot hand-crafted black walnut French Provincial table, Hermann vonLeer's eyes slowly surveyed the room without moving his head. He had no title, but as he quietly waited with tented fingers, everyone knew he was in charge.

The dining room, with a marble fireplace, satin drapes, gold chandeliers, candelabra, and nine-foot ornate antique mirror, made an opulent meeting room. The Painter Management Company held the lease on the 2000 square foot executive suite located on the 60th floor of the Park Lake Hotel in midtown Manhattan. It was just down from the Plaza on Central Park South. The elegant suite had views of the park as well as the New York skyline, a luxury few can afford. The ten-year contract-lease was paid annually with a money transfer drawn on Manhattan Bank & Trust Inc.

"I would like to thank Mr. Smylee of Richardson, Deckmann & Smylee for negotiating our current arrangement with the Park Lake," vonLeer said, acknowledging Smylee sitting to his right. "We will meet here monthly. Would every second Wednesday be acceptable to everyone?" The seven other men and one woman each nodded agreement as Hermann vonLeer glanced around the table.

The people in the group, except for vonLeer, were all Americans. None was employed by BayerAG, but Bayer's success was apparently very important to each one. They were the same nameless people that financed IG Farben's worldwide cartel in the 1930s. They represented some of Wall Street's strongest companies: big oil, big auto, big chemical, big pharmaceutical, and big financial. One of the men was a board member on the U.S. Federal Reserve. They wore hand-tailored understated clothes with very little jewelry. Everyone was relaxed, obviously accustomed to lavish surroundings. Attendees were pleasant but showed little genuine interest in each other. Unlike most business meetings, writing materials were nowhere to be found; minutes were not being taken.

"Lady and gentlemen," Hermann vonLeer leaned forward signaling he was getting to the substance of the meeting. "As you know, since the end of World War I, BayerAG, one of our most profitable companies, has been banned from doing business in the United States." Then, almost whispering, but with extreme conviction, he said, "We have waited long enough. The time is now for us to re-emerge in the U.S. market.

"Over the last 50 years you have invested heavily in our endeavor. It was your support, when we became part of IG FarbenindustrieAG, that allowed us to flourish, perhaps even saving us from extinction. Thank you for that. When Germany was defeated in WWII, you stood strong again. Your faith in the organization is about to be rewarded." A murmur of approval came from his audience.

Hermann vonLeer paused until the room fell silent. "The first step, acquiring an American company, is already underway. Research has narrowed our choices down to a single takeover target...Wesfield Laboratory. It's a small enough operation for us to overpower, and Wesfield has trusted products with the solid American reputation we were looking for.

"The stage has been set," he continued. "Congress, of course, has been the highest hurdle. For several years, our people have been supplementing incomes and investigating lifestyles of senators and representatives on both sides of the aisle. At this point in time, believe me, we have the leverage to force Congress to do whatever we want, whenever we want." Hermann vonLeer's audience knowingly smiled, nodding their heads to indicate they completely understood controlling Congress was perfectly plausible.

"Up until now, Wesfield's successes have been limited. Their leading brand provided the funding for line extensions and the creation of their nutritional line, but that was a long time ago." After stopping for a drink of water, vonLeer continued. "The takeover needs to occur quickly because Wesfield is about to introduce a new cold remedy that, we believe, will be superior to all the other products in the category. If we allow this to happen before our plans are executed, stockholders will perceive future increase in value and be evermore reluctant to sell.

"We will strike quickly, taking over Wesfield Laboratory before they realize what's happening. They're our ticket into the U.S. market and we must accomplish that before we can even think about acquiring the Sterling Drug Company and retrieve the products, patents and logos that are rightfully ours. As a bonus, we'll use Wesfield's sales and distribution systems as a pipeline for many of our worldwide products." His audience reacted favorably, but without comment.

"You may be able to help," vonLeer said, looking at each person individually. "A list of Wesfield stockholders will be sent to each of you. Any personal knowledge you have about these people may help in our investigation and negotiations with them." With a slight smile, he explained, "Uncovered secrets can provide the leverage to convert stockholders into stock sellers.

"Acquiring Wesfield Laboratories is key to our success. Are there any questions?" Contrary to most business meetings, no one felt the need to be personally acknowledged by raising questions on minor issues. "Thank you for taking the time to be here. We look forward to rejoining the U.S. business community." The group quietly adjourned.

How very civil, Smylee thought to himself. *It is amazing to watch these people in action. They say so little and control so much.*

Once the room cleared, vonLeer approached Mr. Smylee. "How do you really think the project is proceeding?"

No one intimidated Smylee as totally as Hermann vonLeer. His heart was pounding and moisture appeared on the palms of his hands as he began his report. "Security measures are moving along nicely. South Station airport has been physically changed to comply to your specifications, but as you know, plans to employ security people are far in the future."

"How did the airport people react to our offer?" vonLeer snarled.

"They were more than happy to let us bring them into the twentieth century."

"What about the laboratory's security and the product launch?" The way vonLeer asked questions made Smylee feel any answer would be inadequate.

"Plant security is a little harder to achieve, but we're in good shape. We recruited three of their executives willing to work with us, at a very inflated price I might add. They were also guaranteed attractive positions at the top after the takeover, but of course, nothing is in writing."

"I see. Are these 'inside Wesfield' people in a position to initiate the security changes required?"

"Everything on our target list is already in motion."

"Very good, Mr. Smylee. What about our efforts to acquire a majority of the stock?"

"They're not going anywhere near as well as we originally anticipated."

"What is the holdup? Is there something we can do to help?"

"The old man, Joseph Westerfield, is the biggest problem. We knew he was not favorable toward Bayer; we could deal with that. His disdain is more than just unfavorable; he hates Bayer/Farben with a passion."

"I met him a while back," Hermann vonLeer reflected. "He was strong-headed then, too."

"Apparently he has been told, or has sensed, that we are moving in on Wesfield Laboratory. Although he's seldom heard from, when he does say something, his opinion is highly regarded. Joseph Westerfield has the influence to sway borderline stockholders not to sell, and he's assertively trying to block us. In addition to that, he and his grandson personally own 34 percent of the stock, and probably control another ten percent. He's tough, no skeletons in his closet, and he can't be financially influenced or intimidated. On the plus side, our efforts to neutralize him have just begun."

"I am sure you will handle it, Mr. Smylee. You always do."

"Thank you, Sir. I assure you, we'll do whatever it takes."

PART TWO

CHAPTER 14
POLICE STATION

Sides were being chosen. Eight-year-old tomboy, Marilynn Christopher, nicknamed, Kristi, assigned Joey, Bobby, Karen, Sharon and Freddy to be the bank robbers. The rest would be the posse: Prince, Clemmy, Susie, Hank, and little Sara Jane. "I'm the sheriff," stated Kristi.

"Why do you always get to be the sheriff?" Clemmy said, frowning.

"Because I am," Kristi said, pouting, with laser green eyes declaring her authority.

The game was on. Riding imaginary horses, slapping thighs, the posse galloped after those dirty-rotten bank robbers most of the afternoon. In the end, the robbers were first to tire. Kristi and her posse caught the bad guys. That's just the way the game was played.

Sixteen years later, Kristi's parents, Judith and Melberg Christopher, two of Manhattan's finest prosecuting attorneys, were agonizing over her career choice. They always expected her to follow in their footsteps. She flourished in the halls of academia. After graduating in the top ten percent of her class at Harvard Law, however, she was one of the first women accepted into "NAT" by joining the FBI's New Agent Training Unit in Quantico, Virginia. She still wanted to be the sheriff. Judith and Melberg never totally forgave her for that choice, but more or less came to accept it.

Kristi spent three years and a month with the Bureau. Her title was Specialist rather than Agent because, although the FBI wanted women on their team, they weren't quite ready to allow females to become Agents. She was an agent in every way except title.

Her sponsor and friend, Field Supervisor agent Marti Towne, made sure she was given challenging investigative and protection assignments, providing her the opportunity to develop analytical thinking and problem-solving skills. For a rookie, she achieved outstanding results and soon came to be recognized as one of the FBI's "up and comers." Several opportunities became available to her within the organization, but in spite of her successes, the petty, nit-picky group-thinking and the self-important pomposity smothering the Agency drove her out. She said later, "If I could've answered the phone 'Agent Christopher,' I'd probably still be there." Towne gave her an outstanding recommendation.

Manhattan's Midtown South Precinct was her next stop before she became South Station's first female Chief of Police. Midtown South Precinct, in the heart of the city, handled a wide variety of crimes committed between 34th to 40th Streets and from Madison to 9th Avenue. The area included Grand Central and Penn Stations, Manhattan Mall Plaza, the garment and fur districts, theaters, residential neighborhoods, jewelry manufacturing and Times Square. The diverse precinct, composed of many ethnic and religious groups, offered a broad training ground.

Six years spent defending and protecting the residents and tourists in the Big Apple gave Kristi a chance to combat crime "up close and personal." As an investigating detective on the streets of New York, she expanded and fine-tuned many of the skills she would need later in her career.

She lived with the same frustrations as her prosecutor parents, putting criminals behind bars only to watch the liberal courts and the crowded penal system give them a 'Get Out of Jail FREE Card.' Murderers, sex-offenders, armed robbers and other brutal criminals were too often plea-bargained down to shorten the jail time served. Manhattan's 'revolving door' approach to criminal punishment sent the guilty back to the streets over and over again.

When the South Station job became a possibility, she viewed it as a more civilized, and possibly more effective, place to do police work. She thought it would be a total contrast from the Manhattan "rat-race." She would learn it wasn't so different.

After 19 years, Chief Ginnegan was planning to retire in a few months. When he was suddenly sidelined by a stroke, South Station's town council was forced to quickly name a replacement. Kristi's name was at the top of a potential replacements list the chief fortunately had just prepared. She got the call on a Tuesday afternoon and was early for the interview at 9:00 Wednesday morning.

Marion Cooper, a distinguished retired school teacher, headed up the six-member town council. "I realize how hard it must have been to get here so quickly," Cooper said. "Thank you for coming."

"No problem," she replied.

The council members liked the spirited, young, yet mature woman who quickly answered questions with a friendly confident smile. She liked them, too.

A three bedroom, bath-and-a-half "cape-cod" built in the early 1950's served as the Police Station. The homey colors and wallpaper had to go; Kristi preferred comfortable, but not cozy. It was, however, an improvement over the offensive shades of mustard, the Midtown South's color scheme.

The budget provided for six part-time officers. The council, with a "parking meter" mentality, reasoned part-timers without benefits were a good dollar value. Kristi's instant analysis was 'quantity did not equal quality.' After talking with each of her new crew, Sue Ann Broadway, whose only qualification was being a pleasant good-looking woman, was the first to go. The move allowed her to offer Peter (Jake) Jacobson a full-time job as her second in command. Kristi found out later Jake was crushed when the council brushed him aside as a candidate for the new chief position. His ego quickly recovered when Kristi, with her stellar credentials, recognized him for his past dedication and qualifications. His undivided loyalty to Kristi began the first day on his new job.

The part-timers were: Dick Hastings, a local basketball star; Randy Robertson, a very successful high school coach; Fritz Massey, owner of a "mom-and-pop" restaurant; and Carolyn Spice, who was a housewife and a very quick thinker. Kristi thought with four part-timers, assigning work hours would be a problem, but scheduling was not especially difficult because the close-knit group made every effort to consider their co-workers' outside commitments. Jake's promotion also had a positive effect on the staff, and the daily routine was restored with little change.

Compared to her previous law enforcement career, the first ten months of her South Station tenure was a breeze. Although there was an abundance of drug and organized crime trafficking taking place to the south along the Indiana Toll Road, parking tickets, traffic violations, fender benders, domestic squabbles, a few break-ins, and a lot of underage drinking dominated the department agenda.

The city council's thinking, on the other hand, was clouded with visions of parking meters stuffed with nickels, dimes and quarters. Kristi's focus was law enforcement, not funding. She was as bored as a palace guard. Then someone started shooting at the grandson of South Station's first family and it all changed.

*****

Sheriff Gus Arven walked into the station at 11:00 AM sharp. "Hey, Kristi, how you doing?"

"Hi, Sheriff," she said cordially, "Let me get Jake. How about coffee?"

"I'd love some."

The three sat around one end of the rectangular glass top table. Taking the center seat, Kristi unconsciously assumed control of the meeting. Looking Sheriff Arven in the eye, she said, "I think we're playing with some very big boys here. What do you think?"

"Scares me. We spent over twenty man-hours going over the bluff. I personally interviewed all the local residents, gas stations, hotels, and bars in and out of the area. Nothing. Not a single clue. All we know for sure is the rifle was a 30-06."

"I hate to admit this, but I think our efforts might be better spent protecting the Westerfields," Kristi said. "For that matter, all the stockholders could be in danger, and in all likelihood, they don't even know it."

Sheriff Arven and Jake agreed.

"Problem is, we don't have the resources to even come close to doing what may be needed."

"Us either. You think we should call in the Feds?"

"They won't come in," Kristi said. "No Federal laws have been broken. No interstate probability. 'RICO' might work, but we can't guarantee the shooter was a pro, let alone belonged to organized crime. I think we're on our own."

"Yeah, you're right," Gus Arven said. "I hear they aren't easy to work with, anyway."

"It's against my better judgment to get civilians involved in police procedure, but I think it's only fair to let Joseph and Jeff Westerfield know where we stand," Kristi said.

"I have to agree," Gus said. "I guess we better call Joseph?"

"The way I see it, he seems to know more than we do most of the time," Jake cautiously chimed in.

"You've got a point," the sheriff said with an understanding smile.

Jake was pleased Kristi had included him in the meeting, and now Sheriff Arven was acknowledging his observations in a friendly manner. He thought, *it couldn't get better than this.*

Joseph picked up on the second ring, and she briefly relayed the pertinent information. With her hand over the mouthpiece, Kristi asked, "Sheriff, can you hang around long enough to meet Joseph for lunch at the Shoreline Fish House?"

He flashed her a "thumbs up." Driving to the restaurant they quickly reviewed the protocol, making sure they were in sync before talking to Joseph. The Sheriff would stay with the forensic and crime scene details, and Kristi would concentrate on the "who's and why's." Both realized their assignments overlapped and that luck would play a big part in any solutions.

Joseph was already seated when they arrived. The best of the four South Station restaurants, Shoreline's Friday special was Lake Michigan perch, fries and coleslaw. The red and white checkered oilcloth tablecloth had been the decor for longer than anyone could remember. The place was "wall-to-wall" with the usual patrons. A cross-section of local workers, railroaders, and a few salesmen who arranged their schedules around Shoreline's perch.

Joseph had commandeered the table in the back room usually used for small parties or families with rambunctious youngsters. It was private yet relaxing, perfect for a working lunch. Westerfield announced lunch was on him. "Eat hearty," he said enthusiastically. To his delight, no one gave him an argument. Everyone there could feel genuine friendships forming. Joseph recognized it as what he called the "common goal effect."

Conversation was casual as they waited for their food. "Joseph, do you realize you're somewhat of a living legend here in South Station?" Kristi was teasing and Joseph knew it.

"To quote George Burns, 'Being a living legend is better than being a dead legend,'" Joseph said grinning.

"Some philosopher," Kristi came back.

"I can understand him, anyway," Joseph said. "He's only a few years older than I am."

Jake smiled at the casualness of the banter. Joseph was the biggest of all the "big shots" he had ever known. He couldn't believe what an easygoing guy he seemed to be. To think Kristi had the wherewithal to jerk his chain and he joined right in, enjoying the give-and-take.

After devouring the beer-battered fish, fries, and coleslaw, washed down with a couple of whatever was on tap, Kristi spelled out the situation. There was no mistaking her point. She was warning him that neither she nor Sheriff Arven had the resources to protect him and Jeff. "I'm sorry to have to tell you so bluntly, Joseph, but we thought you needed to know what we're up against."

"I appreciate your candor and your concern."

"We had to tell you as soon as we could, Joseph," Sheriff Arven repeated.

"When I was in business and found myself without the necessary resources to accomplish my goals, I would explore outsourcing as a possible solution."

"What are you suggesting?" Kristi asked.

Looking directly at her, he asked, "Do you think there are people, or groups of people, we could hire to provide the security that would be required?"

"Not locally, but yes, for a price it could be done."

"Let's assume the cost could be handled. Could we achieve effective results?"

"Sheriff Arven, correct me if I'm wrong," Kristi said. "I don't think either of us wants a bunch of armed guards lurking around. It could be dangerous and would alarm the locals."

"That's not what I'm after," Joseph said. "I would like you, all three of you, to consider employing the people you would need to do the job. They would report to you, not me. You would have an unlimited budget, my support, and my total cooperation."

"Those kind of people don't grow on trees. Where do you think we'd get them?" Sheriff Arven asked.

"With Kristi's background in the FBI and NYPD, I believe they could be found," Joseph said with a slight smile.

Kristi's green eyes fixed on his as she replied, "And just how do you happen to know so much about my credentials?"

The smile broadened, then, disappeared, "I like to know who I'm dealing with. Do you think I would trust this type of responsibility to just anyone?"

"Damn. You checked us out?" Gus Arven said, showing a little dismay.

"Using your words Gus, damn right I did. And you also checked out very well."

"This is far from standard operating procedure," Kristi said. "Let us talk it over, make a few calls, and we'll get back to you, Joseph."

Kristi was back in charge.

CHAPTER 15
OFFENSE & DEFENSE

Even with the long summer days, Joseph was up with the sun. As always Tootsie was waiting at the side of his bed. He quickly went through his morning routine. He let the dog out, filled her bowls, poured juice, put bread in the toaster, turned on the news, brought in the paper, let Tootsie back in, ate breakfast, cleaned up, and started the project of the day. Today's task was a letter to the stockholders.

It was an invitation to join with him in the fight to protect Wesfield Laboratory from the takeover attempt by the people interested in reinstating Bayer in the US market. The letter included a synopsis of the Bayer-Farben history and an offer to help find a buyer for anyone who found themselves in a position where they had to sell their stock. Although he tried, he failed to keep it short, but it would accomplish his objective, reinforcing loyalty to the cause. He ended with a simple "thank you."

After lunch with Kristi and her crew, Joseph stopped at Wesfield Laboratory to check on Jeff and pick up a copy of the Registered Stock Owner's Listing. Giving him a hug at his office door, Jeff said in his ear, "Know anything about Lori's new digs?"

With a positive nod, Joseph said, "How's the coffee in the cafeteria these days?"

"You can get it down. Let's get some."

After choosing cold drinks, they settled at a secluded corner table. Joseph and Jeff were the only suits amidst the lab coats and hairnets decorating the break-room filled with packaging line plant workers. After reviewing Tanner's findings, Joseph explained the precautionary action that sent Lori to one of the truly great hotels in the world.

"Thanks, Grandpa. Nothing like going first class."

"I thought the Plaza would be a comfortable place to avoid trouble. I doubt 'they' will catch up to her there."

"You never cease to amaze me, Grandpa. I'd like to know who 'they' are, and I can't imagine why on earth 'they' would bother wiretapping Lori."

Although they had previously discussed the power struggle for Wesfield Laboratory, Joseph spent the next half-hour detailing how badly the powerful people with an interest in promoting BayerAG wanted the two of them out of the way. He also explained that the unknown "they" could very easily reside right here in the USA. "Bayer may be located in Germany," Joseph stressed, "but it's owned by 'big money' people all over the world."

Jeff patiently listened, thinking *it's time to move on.* "Did you know Lori will be here Friday night?"

"No, but in that case, I would like to invite you both to spend the weekend with me at the lake."

"I'll ask her, only if you promise not to promote me as a potential husband."

"Jeff. How can you say that?"

"Promise?"

"Okay. I promise."

*****

The lake breeze had fallen off and a swarm of lake-flies fluttered around Joseph as he hurried from his car. He hastily inserted his key and quickly opened and shut the door, trying to avoid as many bugs as possible. Standing in the dark room, the message machine's little yellow light looked like a firefly flickering at the edge of a deep woods, signaling mysteries within.

Tootsie's tail was a windshield wiper of happiness as she slobbered enthusiastically over Joseph's extended hands, a scene only dog owners would appreciate. He let her out, glanced at the mail he'd picked up at the mailbox and crossed the room to listen to his messages.

"Joseph, please call me about possible security solutions, Kristi"

"Hi, it's Beverly. I need to talk to you. It's 10:30 AM Wednesday."

"It's Beverly again, you better wait until tonight to call. I'll be at home. I sent you a little note. Keep an eye open for it."

He decided to try Kristi first. The phone rang several times before she picked up, "South Station Police, this is Chief Christopher."

"Hello, Chief Christopher. This is Joseph Westerfield. Sorry I took so long to get back to you."

"No problem," she said cheerfully. "When can we get together?"

"How about in the morning?"

"That works for me, but I'll be stuck at the station for awhile."

"Is Tootsie welcome?"

"I'll be waiting for you both. There might be a leftover hamburger in the fridge for Toots."

"See you about 10:30."

"Okay."

Joseph called Beverly at 8:30 and 9:00 with no answer. He was beginning to worry when at 9:30 a man answered, "Collins' residence."

"This is Joseph Westerfield. Is Beverly there?"

"Hello, Mr. Westerfield, this is her husband Frank. She's not home yet, but I know she's eager to talk to you."

"Does she usually get home so late?"

"It happens. Not often, but more than she'd like."

"Thank you, Frank. Please ask her to call no matter how late it is."

*****

Joseph's alarm went off at 6:00 AM, but he'd been awake for an hour wondering why Beverly never called. Tootsie was whimpering at the door. He let her out, dropped a piece of bread in the toaster, and poured himself a generous glass of orange juice. He tried Beverly again at 8:00. No answer. A walk around his property with Tootsie and a little paper work, dotting the "I's" and crossing the "T's" on the stockholder letter, filled the hour before he headed to the police station.

Kristi had been looking forward to this "one-on-one" with Joseph. His suspicions were profoundly believable, and he had an indescribable charisma that drew her in.

He arrived at 10:30 sharp. After a couple of doggy licks, Kristi brought Joseph up to speed.

Sheriff Arven's commissioner wouldn't go along with guarding or protecting anyone outside their jurisdiction. "I guess it was the smart political decision," Kristi said, "but Arven was just sick about it. He hoped to stay in the loop by pledging his people would be available as backup. I told him we would keep him involved anyway, as a friend and as a courtesy."

"If we keep him posted," Joseph pointed out, "He may end up more involved than his commissioner would like. I wouldn't want him to get in trouble over this."

"Don't worry about Gus Arven; he can handle himself. Now about security," Kristi said, "I think I may know some people who could do the job."

"I'd like to hear about them."

She told Joseph how she became friends with Lieutenant George H. Brown. When she was with Midtown South, he was 'the man' at Manhattan's 19th Precinct who, as the story goes, knew more about guarding and protecting dignitaries than Betty Crocker knew about baking. His responsibility was protecting the "International Dignitaries" who had diplomatic immunity. The group, mostly affiliated with the United Nations, was a mix of bureaucrats, prima donnas, and high rollers who happened to reside in the 19th Precinct. The precinct was home to 32 foreign missions, 12 consulates and more than 68 ambassador and counsel general residences. Brown worked with 90% of the private security agencies employed to keep them safe. He knew them well and counted the ones he trusted as friends.

Philandering ambassador's assistant Carlos de la Zaldro was one of Brown's perpetual headaches. The smooth-talking Latin seduced a never-ending string of socialites anxious to be included on his "favorites" list. The lieutenant had been picking up after Carlos for too many years. One damp New York night Brown was called to a grimy 4th floor single room residential on 34th street. He found Kristi's team of four had inherited a situation where a jealous husband had a 12 gauge firmly planted under Carlos' chin. Kristi methodically talked her way into the potential shooter's head, became his ally, and slowly nudged him to change direction. Any time no blood is spilled, the NYPD called that "success." So did Brown.

The lieutenant praised Kristi for a nice piece of work, but also kidded that he wouldn't have lost any sleep had the jealous husband put an end to Carlo's escapades. She trusted George Brown to provide them with a list of several qualified professionals.

"If you think your friend Brown will help us, let's make the call,"

Joseph said eagerly.

On the first ring, he snapped up the phone. "This is George Brown."

"This is Chief Marilynn Christopher of South Station, Michigan."

"Well, Kristi, how are you, girl?" he said thinking, *if only I was born 25 years later*. "What can I do for you, sweetheart?"

Kristi explained who Joseph was and that he would be listening on an extension. She went on to describe her dilemma, "I need security support people working independently of my department, but who would be willing to take some direction and coordination from me."

"Sounds a little unorthodox," Brown said.

"It is," she admitted, glancing at Joseph. At the end of an hour-long conversation detailing the aggressive assault on the Westerfields and her suspicions of future efforts, Brown had only one question, which he asked as if Joseph was no longer on the line. "Do your friends realize how much it would cost to do this right?"

"I don't know Joseph Westerfield well, but from what I've observed, results, not money, will drive his thinking." Kristi continued the conversation, ignoring Joseph's ear to the phone.

"Even if we are talking tens of millions?"

"George, he's not the type to do things half-assed. We want the very best people available."

"I am sorry to leave you out of the conversation, Mr. Westerfield, but it was Kristi's opinion I was looking for."

"I understand, sir," Joseph said. "I appreciate your help. Thank you." Westerfield couldn't remember ever being ignored before. The irony amused him.

Brown's recommendations were all based on personal experience: Tanner Security Systems, Protection Force & Associates, Sandora Guard and Protect Consultants, and Worldwide Executive Protection Ltd. The four diverse companies were composed of well over 500 specialists. Contact numbers and names would be sent overnight by Federal Express. Representatives from each group would be available tomorrow evening in South Station if it were deemed necessary.

"Where do we go from here, Chief?"

"That's up to you, Joseph. It's your friends and family that need protecting and we're spending your money. You can have these people report directly to you, or they could get their direction through my department. Either way will work, but the idea of having hired guns out there on their own makes my neck hairs bristle."

"I can understand your concern. How do you see it playing out?"

"I think Lori may need only protective surveillance. She could be aware of it but it wouldn't interfere with her lifestyle. You and Jeff, on the other hand, need, in my opinion, close protection. That means..."

"I know what that means. Bodyguards in the form of chauffeurs, gardeners, companions and the like."

"That's just a start. We will also need new security systems and monitors on all residences, cars, and frequently used areas. Several investigators and surveillance programs. That's just off the top of my head."

"Pretty big order for a small-town cop," Joseph replied factually, "And that's only half of it."

"What do you mean, half?" He caught her by surprise.

"That only covers our defense," Joseph said leaning forward. "I would like to create a corresponding offensive campaign with even more muscle. I'm not talking a hired gun approach. What I mean is finding out exactly who these guys are, foiling their plots, and bringing them to justice. I hope that's not too covert for you."

Kristi smiled in amazement; *this guy brings hardball to a new level.* "I like it, but I'm afraid the energy that drives you may get in the way. If we choose to pursue this through the department, only one of us can be in charge, and it's not going to be you. Since you're paying the bills, we could have a major authority conflict."

"Kristi, you are totally wrong. You've heard that I was a strong executive, right?"

"The force that drove the company is how I heard it."

"Do you know what a strong executive does, Kristi?"

"Within reason."

"A strong executive finds talented people, puts them in charge, provides ample funding, and gets out of the way. After success is achieved, he shares in the credit. This is no different."

"It's a lot more personal."

"Which is all the more reason to stay out of your way. You're my talented cop; I'm only here to give support. This is not going to stop unless we stop them first. I need you, Kristi. I think we'd be a tough team. *Your* team, Kristi," he concluded. "Are you getting hungry?"

"Famished," Kristi said. "You want to order in or walk down a block to get the Colonel's Kentucky Fried Chicken?"

"Both. Let's call so it will be ready when we get there."

They called down, ordering an extra dark meat for Jake, who should be showing up any time now. Kristi left him a note: "Tootsie is inside. She won't give you any trouble. Getting you a chicken."

Their order was ready and waiting. They picked a secluded table in the corner and dug right in. Between pieces of spicy chicken, Joseph announced an account had been opened at the local bank in the name ProTect & Associates. It was funded in the amount of $25 million, with a $50 million line of credit. Signatories included himself, Jeff and, to her surprise, Marilynn Christopher.

"I don't want to be in that position. I'm police chief here; I can't have a part-time job."

"Slow down, Kristi. You would only need to sign checks if Jeff and I were dead or unable to do it. You wouldn't want our support team to go unpaid, would you?"

"Of course not."

"If they manage to eliminate Jeff and me, I would expect you to carry on with every ounce of energy you could muster."

"I can see how you would."

"Are you going to accept my offer?" He asked with concern in his voice.

"You knew I would." *What am I getting myself into*? "Won't the bank people be aware of the new company and start gossiping?"

"Absolutely not. The new accounts manager takes a no-questions-asked approach with my business. And," he said with a smile, "I hold close to 40% of the stock in that bank. Are you going to tell the city council you'll be enlisting outside help? If they find out after the fact, they won't be happy campers."

"That may be true, but it could possibly jeopardize our efforts. I think I'd prefer to include one or two of them by simply asking them what they thought was the best way to utilize the outside contractors. Get their input, so to speak."

"Why, for heaven's sake? What could they possibly contribute?" Joseph responded quickly.

"Support, latitude, and possibly cover my ass if this thing gets out of hand. Ask a man his opinion and he'll be an ally forever. We need all the allies we can find."

"That's downright manipulative," he said with a smile.

"I may be the Chief of Police, but my tactics can be very feminine at times."

"You would have made a wonderful business woman."

"I just want to be a good cop. Are you done? Jake's dinner is getting cold."

When they got back to the station, Jake was happy to get a free dinner, hot or cold.

Joseph asked to use the phone. He had been trying to reach Beverly all day. On the third ring a rough male voice said, "Collins residence, who is calling please?"

"This is Joseph Westerfield. Is Beverly there?"

"What's your business with Mrs. Collins?"

"Is this Mr. Collins?"

"No, this is Detective Gartzke. May I ask why you're calling?"

"I'm returning her call. May I ask what you're doing there?"

"Where are you calling from and what is your business with Mrs. Collins?"

"I'm calling from South Station, Michigan. Beverly Collins is a friend of mine, and my business with her is none of your business."

"I'm afraid anything concerning Mrs. Collins is my business. I am sorry to have to tell you she was shot to death this afternoon, right in front of her apartment."

Without a show of emotion, Joseph handed the phone to Kristi. "Please."

"Hello. This is Marilynn Christopher, Chief of Police, South Station, Michigan."

"Detective Gartzke here."

CHAPTER 16
SURVEILLANCE

Sick to his stomach, anxious, with cold sweats, Gunther, unfamiliar with failure, was handling it poorly. His directions, "return to the same Edwardsburg Post Office Box," told him that Smylee's people were aware he'd totally botched the project. After a day, deciding to skip the concert, Gunther returned to South Station to begin surveillance all over again.

No one paid attention to the hunched-over old-timer shuffling down the sidewalk, enjoying the pleasant summer day. He stopped for a few minutes to watch work crews scurrying around Joseph Westerfield's South Station residence. Two men were digging a narrow trench a foot or so inside the property line. Gunther immediately recognized the wiring was for pressure, sound, and motion sensors being installed in random patterns. Doors and windows were also being worked over, and spotlights were positioned to eliminate every shadow. *I wonder what special little surprises they have prepared for me inside the house?*

Gunther repeated the sham outside Jeff's apartment. Although no one was working the grounds, he found a similar scene with workers carrying wire and equipment in and out of the building. There wasn't much he could accomplish there. Once satisfied he understood all he could learn about the systems being installed, the old man hobbled around the corner and slowly got into a two-year-old Chevrolet.

Gunther, always careful to respect the traffic laws, headed for Red Arrow Highway. Driving back and forth as often as he dared, he could see a good deal of activity, more than one would expect on standard security installations.

Tighter than a tick, Gunther thought to himself. *Very sophisticated. Only pros could pull this off, virtually overnight, and it sure as hell isn't local people doing it.* Gunther realized the Westerfields would no longer be easy targets. He still needed to check the shoreline for possible vulnerabilities, but it was obvious it would be difficult, if not impossible, to approach the buildings on the ground.

Decked out in typical fishing garb, with plenty of deep water paraphernalia in plain view, Gunther walked into "Nautica Marine." The store had a little bit of everything: food, bait, equipment, guides, charters and most important, rentals. He used a credit card to purchase an out-of-state fishing license and rent what the clerk called a "worthy craft."

Gunther, who captained his own boat out of Charleston, South Carolina, easily navigated the twenty-foot Boston Whaler. Once adjacent to Westerfield's, he set a course north for a mile, then south paralleling the initial line, a pattern consistent with down-rigger trolling for Coho salmon. Through a pair of 7 x 35 wide angle binoculars, he watched three carpenters constructing an outbuilding alongside the Westerfield main building. What appeared to be a gardener was working along the edge of the bluff. *If he's a gardener, I'm the Easter bunny.* The longer he observed the area, the more convinced he became that a successful attack from the lake was not an option either.

From the inlet where young Westerfield used to dock his boat, Gunther saw a mast moving behind the small dune. Suddenly the entire boat was visible with sails hoist. It was Westerfield's boat heading in his direction and closing fast. About twenty yards away, as the boat turned to the north, someone cheerfully shouted, "How they biting?" Gunther displayed a thumbs-down sign and waved with a smile. They were so close he could see pleasure on all three faces. *My God, I could take them out with a pea-shooter and here I sit in rubber cloth, grinning like a half-wit with a fishing pole in my hand....Opportunity wasted.*

While eating dinner at the Holiday Inn restaurant, Gunther reviewed Westerfield's new precautions over and over in his mind, as he pondered his options. Although he loved a challenge, the security surrounding his targets was going to be a very difficult problem. Appearing out of nowhere, Mr. Smylee was standing at his left elbow. *How in the hell did he know where to find me?* Before Gunther could utter a word, Smylee cut him off with a finger to his lips.

"No names, please," he said quietly. Smylee wasn't smiling.

"I understand. Please have a seat. Would you care to order?"

"No. Please give me an update starting with what went wrong on your first attempt."

I wonder how much he already knows. This, it's so degrading. Gunther proceeded to go over every detail, starting with surveillance and ending with the ride back to Charleston. He tried to add a positive spin wherever possible.

"If you thought you had succeeded with the boy, why didn't you stay to finish the job with the old man?"

God, I hate this. "I immediately went to the lake house to do just that, but he had already left. I didn't know where he went, nor did I have a plan developed for the in-town location. I felt I needed a day to regroup. I was already back here when I got your call."

"I know." There was the familiar Smylee smirk. "Tell me about your observations over the last couple of days."

"They're installing a wide range of first class security devices," Gunther explained. "The system includes total perimeter underground touch and motion sensors, well-concealed, well-placed electric eyes, located right where you don't expect them. At the lake they're building what I believe is a command center up close to the house. The town house, too, is covered from stem to stern."

"How about the subjects' daily routines?" Smylee asked.

"Nothing definite, even the grandson has adjusted his schedule to avoid repetition. They've both acquired some pretty savvy looking chauffeurs, gardeners, and new companions."

"What are your suggestions? Frankly," Smylee sneered, "I don't think you will be able to pull this off alone."

"Maybe, maybe not," Gunther said.

"Do you have any ideas, any type of plan yet?"

"Yes. Prearranged travel and destination."

"I'm not sure I understand."

"You will."

"Time is our enemy." Smylee said grimly. "You know failure is not an option."

"I know only too well," Gunther answered. *Only too well, you arrogant little twit.*

CHAPTER 17
LORI AT THE LAKE

When Tyler Zelinski got his pilot license, his young wife Ruby Sue, using her most southern of southern drawls, playfully started calling him, "Tyler the Skyler." Originally, it was an affectionate nickname used between the two of them. Over time, the nickname was shortened to just Skyler. When their friends overheard her calling him Skyler, they assumed it was what he wanted to be called. The mild-mannered pilot never bothered to correct anyone–he thought his new name was fine. If Ruby Sue liked it, he liked it.

Skyler was holding the Wesfield plane motionless in the loading area. The hour that had gone by seemed like forever to the four sales executives eating chips and drinking beer in the back. Skyler knew they were becoming more irritated with each passing minute. He was ready when, finally, one of them, stuck his head in the cockpit, "Skyler. What the hell is the holdup?"

"We're waiting for an account exec from Hutchins, Keller & McDonnell," he replied. "Mr. Westerfield asked us to wait."

"Jeff Westerfield. He's just a product manager. I could call your boss; I doubt that he'd want us to wait any longer."

"You could, Sir, but Joseph, not Jeff, Westerfield, had the plane held." Skyler smiled to himself, as he thought, *These peons really think they're hot stuff.*

"Oh. Well, I hope he gets here pretty soon," the salesman mumbled, heading back to his seat.

Lori Smith arrived on a shuttle that ran between the passenger terminals at O'Hare and Butler Air Field. They stopped fretting over the delay when they saw the appealing passenger running to the plane. Entering with a burst of energy and a youthful smile, she said, "I'm Lori Smith. Sorry my plane held you up. I didn't think they were ever going to let us land."

"Don't worry about it, Miss Smith," someone said, as they transformed themselves from middle-aged salesmen into teenage bantam roosters trying to gain the favor of this single chick. The other man on board, Lori's new friend Charley Tanner, simply smiled with an all-knowing nod.

After twenty-five bumpy minutes in the air, they bounced down at the South Station airport. The suits became middle-aged businessmen again. Tanner helped with Lori's luggage, and they all scurried to exit the airport. Lori smiled to herself as she noticed four wives patiently awaiting their loyal husbands. Tanner had an Avis rental car waiting, and Jeff was there to pick her up. Lori had the best ride of the lot.

More questions than answers dominated their dinner conversation, but there wasn't any doubt; just being together was all Jeff and Lori really cared about. She ordered fish. He wanted beef. Like many old married couples, they ate off each other's plate throughout the meal. Lori was thinking, *sharing anything could be the first step to sharing everything.*

Neither of them paid a lick of attention to the burly guy in the corner. His head was in a novel as he waited for dinner to arrive. Although no one would ever know it, he was aware of everyone and everything in and out of the restaurant. When Jeff and Lori left, he was quick to follow.

About 9:30 every Friday night, Red Arrow Highway darkened with deep black shadows as beaches closed, shoppers and early diners went home, leaving only a few barflies buzzing along between their favorite watering holes. When Jeff pulled into the lake house entrance road, he thought he got a glimpse of someone about ten feet off the north side of the road. *I must be getting jumpy,* he thought.

A gracious Joseph greeted them at the door with an extended hug for both.

"So this is your cottage, eh, Joseph? It's not up to my usual accommodations at the Plaza, but I'll make do." Lori's eyes danced with merriment.

Jeff winced at her directness, but Joseph knew behind the kidding she was seeking the explanation she deserved.

"I hear your concern. I popped some corn. Let's grab a drink and I will, to the best of my ability, try to explain why I thought a few days away from your apartment was merited."

Joseph became deadly serious as he explained his belief that ruthless unknown financiers promoting BayerAG were trying to eliminate any and all resistance to an upcoming takeover attempt at Wesfield. He and Jeff, along with a few select stockholders, were the biggest barriers to their success. "I believe they bugged your phone to gain information about Jeff – his intentions and routine. I don't believe you were ever in any real danger. But I wasn't sure, and I'm not a person to gamble with people I care about."

"Why the Plaza?"

"Well, I just thought you might enjoy staying there and I didn't think anyone could track you down there. Especially after checking in as Tanner's daughter."

"Tanner's daughter? I didn't register as his daughter."

"You didn't? Who did you register as?"

"Mr. Tanner provided me with a husband. A very rich and attractive one, I might add. My new name is Mrs. Willis McQuillan."

Making a mental note, Joseph thought, *Charley Tanner is not afraid to take charge.*

Jeff, not one bit enthusiastic about this turn of events, didn't say a word – Smart guy.

They spent a couple of hours reviewing details, possibilities, and building camaraderie. Joseph avoided telling them about his friend Beverly at this time. No point in spoiling their weekend. Before retiring, Joseph turned to Lori and asked, "Have you ever been sailing?"

"No, I can't really say I have. But it looks like fun."

Then turning to Jeff, he said, "How about sailing up to Benton Harbor for brunch in the morning?"

"In the Nipper?" Jeff's heart started to pound.

"She's moored down in the creek. The people at Pat's Boat Service did a great job."

"Thank you. You must have bribed them handsomely to get on their schedule. I can't thank you enough, Grandpa."

"Tomorrow, we'll see if you forgot everything I taught you about sailing. As for me, I'm going to bed. Good night."

Morning couldn't come soon enough for Jeff. Up at six, he bounded out of the house for a look at the Nipper and an early morning run. Much to his surprise, a work crew was already trenching in several places throughout the property. Another worker was high on a ladder buried in the tall Blue Spruce. As a youngster, Jeff remembered planting it with his grandpa after first using it as a live potted Christmas tree.

Seeing his boat was like rediscovering a lost love. He started his run filled with the energy pure happiness can deliver, but his joy turned to apprehension as he passed the spot where he'd come ashore. He couldn't block out the memory of the cold, cold water, the fear, wondering why someone tried to kill him, and how he managed to reach the sand. *Thank you God,* he said to himself over and over, as he ran for the next thirty minutes.

Coffee, juice, and the other two sailors awaited him at the kitchen table. Silence consumed the room as he walked in. Guilt was written all over their faces. Clearly, he was the subject of the conversation. What propaganda was his grandpa spewing?

"What's going on here?"

"Nothing you need to concern your little self about," Lori smirked.

"So that's how it is, huh?"

Lori responded, "It's on a 'need to know basis' and you, my dear, don't need to know."

*****

A beautiful lady deserves attention and a chance to strut her stuff. McHugh Boat Service people had given the Nipper plenty of loving attention and, now it was time to let her kick up her heels. A southwest wind filled her sails the moment she cleared the inlet. She effortlessly cut through the choppy waves as Jeff, holding tight to the mast-rope, realized he was, once again, one with his cherished old friend, the Nipper.

Shortly after clearing the shore, a fisherman in a Boston Whaler waved as they passed. Jeff and Lori gave it little notice, but Joseph waved and shouted, "Any luck?" thinking to himself, *I don't recall anyone fishing quite that close to shore before, and it's not often I see a boat with a lone fisherman.* He made a mental note of the Whaler's registration number. A half-mile farther out on the lake another boat, a 20 footer, seemed to be just bouncing around in the summer sun enjoying the solitude. The skipper of that boat also thought the Boston Whaler was just a tad too close to the shore for down-rigger fishing. He kept him in sight at all times, ready to respond to any movement indicating the craft was heading toward shore. It moved on after fishing for a couple of fruitless hours.

Jeff sailed the Nipper all the way to Benton Harbor, but after brunch he decided to share the joy of sailing the boat with the others. After extensive coaxing, Lori grabbed the rudder like she was born at sea. When Jeff told her to tighten the mainsail, she was amazed at the wind's force as she tried to pull the mast a little closer to the boat. He showed her how to bring the Nipper about when she was sailing into the wind and finished with a short course on tacking. Seeing Jeff and Lori sharing the fun, Joseph declined his turn as captain.

*****

Charley Tanner shook his head in disbelief as Kristi summarized the details of Beverly Collins' murder. The police report stated the doorman was the only witness. He saw her get out of the cab. A six-foot-tall man with long dark hair, wearing a gray sweatshirt and jeans, was walking south along the curb of the sidewalk. As he passed four to six feet away from the Collins woman, he shot her in the head. The doorman didn't hear the shot over the traffic, so the killer evidently used a silencer. The exit wound was extensive. The shooter continued to walk without increasing his pace. The doorman didn't see a gun or the killer's face. There were no other willing witnesses. The husband was up in their apartment at the time of the shooting.

Kristi explained to her new team of independents that Beverly had warned Joseph of danger from her company and/or one of their clients. "Gentlemen, Beverly Collins was only a pawn and they killed her anyway. This was not just a random incident; it was premeditated murder. These are ruthless people, let's remember that. Be careful, execute your assignments accordingly."

Tanner added, "Our people checked out their apartment after the shooting and it was still not wired."

"What are you getting at, Charley?" Kristi asked.

"Only that whatever the reason for the killing was, it wasn't the result of overhearing a call from her apartment. Maybe someone found out she was snooping around the legal group she worked for, Richardson, Deckmann & Smylee. That would be my guess."

"Mine too, Charley," Kristi said. "Any other thoughts?"

"Whoever's trying to force Westerfield to sell could just be sending him a not too subtle message. If so, they're willing to do whatever it takes," said Sandy (Donald) Sandora. He owned Sandora Guard and Protect Consultants. His people had the toughest assignments, personal security for Joseph and his town and lake houses. His "Close Protection Security Specialists" were trained to handle potential assassinations, kidnapping, industrial crimes–including espionage– and public events.

"You could very easily be right, Sandy," Joan Voss observed. She was from Protection Force & Associates. "Or possibly, Richardson, Deckmann & Smylee needed to send a 'whistle blower' warning to some of their own. Either way, we seem to be dealing with some very bad boys here."

Joan's group was assigned to be the invisible guards, providing surveillance by using mobile operatives and technology. They were picked because they had a strong New York team, where Lori spent most of her time. Kristi decided to keep Willis McQuillan in the picture as Lori's husband under either name. Joan thought it was a good precaution.

Worldwide Executive Protection Ltd., with a presence already in Italy, was assigned to watch over Sophia and Ida, her mother. Sophia's father, Alfonso, had died a year ago leaving the two women to live alone in the house where Sophia was born. It was located just far enough from Bardolino to be considered rural. This was a tough assignment; Joseph didn't want them to be aware they were being protected. Sophia's mom just didn't need more worry. He had previously told Kristi he had a feeling they could very easily be targeted because they were so isolated. Kristi, trusting Joseph's instincts, was glad Worldwide Pro had branches in Europe.

Kristi learned, in a conversation with Jeff, that Joseph regularly took him to visit his mother throughout his adolescent years. She also discovered he had provided for their welfare since Sophia's returned to Bardolino. Knowing Joseph, it didn't surprise her. "If they are in danger," Jeff told her, "It would put a great deal of pressure on both of us. They're family."

Worldwide Executive had a phenomenal track record, which influenced Kristi's decision to pick them for this sensitive duty. She stressed the danger and managed to get their top people.

Charley Tanner and his Systems people were needed to monitor the large variety of alarms and sensors that had been installed. They would be constantly reallocating and adjusting as situations changed.

As Kristi evaluated her talented team, she realized Joseph trusted her enough to put the lives of his loved ones in her hands. Standing alone, a long way from the FBI or NYPD, she realized how frightening being in charge could be. *Be not afraid. Fear is only a warning not to abandon your instincts or your training. You are not alone; your teachers are always with you.*

CHAPTER 18
MOVING IN

"Hi stranger, how're you doin'?"

"Hi, Russ. The Westerfields have me jumping," Kristi said.

"I know. Not many secrets in South Station. I didn't tell anybody you'd be here. Maybe we can have a quiet dinner," Russ said with a captivating smile.

"I hope you're right, I could use a little R & R. Jake can always reach me, but he's proving to be very capable and seldom needs my help."

Being a single dad had forced Russ to learn more about cooking than he ever wanted to know. His speciality was charcoal grilled filets. Unless he overcooked them, they were always a safe and tasty treat.

Entering the backyard, Kristi was hit with the aroma of water-saturated, husk-on corn and baked potatoes smoldering on the grill; the promise of a typical Midwest barbeque. Wine, beer and soda, rolls, tossed salad, baked beans, cold watermelon and devils food cake were the other offerings. Kristi thought, *boy's food, but a gallant effort . . . I hope I don't get corn kernels stuck between my front teeth.* It had been a long time since a man cooked her a meal. She liked it.

Sassy and her best friend Kerry giggled their way through the meal and quickly departed the world of adults into one where Russ, it seemed, was never allowed. Detecting his distress, Kristi said, "It's okay, Russ, you're not supposed to know everything – you're just a parent – they need a little space."

"That's good. I sure as hell don't have a clue what's in her head half the time," he said with a befuddled look.

"They are just little girls acting like little girls," Kristi said. "That meal was topnotch. I'm impressed with your culinary talents. How about a little more wine?"

Russ was pleased. Although he was with people all day, he seldom shared his concerns and values with anyone. He saw Kristi as an accomplished lady, with the accent on lady. She was the first woman to interest him in a long time.

When the small talk was over, as it always happens, the conversation took a turn to the serious side. "You wanted to know who paid for the fence and runway extension?" Kristi asked.

"Are you telling me you found out?"

With her sly little smile she said, "I can't give you the names of the people, but I can tell you both companies were paid by wire-transfer through the Manhattan Bank & Trust Inc. The money was drawn on an account belonging to the Painter America Reestablishment Fund."

"I've never heard of a Painter America," Russ said.

"We did a little digging on their behalf," Kristi said. "I managed to find out Painter America has been around for over fifteen years. They're a holding company that owns, among other things, several small real-estate companies. Their business, as much as we could determine, is owning upscale homes they rent to Europeans with big bucks."

Russ said, "I might know who the people with the big bucks are, or at least where they came from."

"Really?"

"Don't sound so surprised. I pay attention to what's goin' on, too." Russ enjoyed the moment.

Kristi said, "You've got my attention."

"You know the runway extension was finished about five weeks ago?"

"I didn't know, but so what?"

"So, the first plane to land at our airport that needed the bigger runway was a modified 727 out of Leverkusen, Germany. According to the co-pilot, they went through customs at Kennedy, picked up two more passengers and came straight here."

"Do you know who owned it?"

"It was a charter. Their home base is Berlin; however, the co-pilot made it sound like Leverkusen was a regular departure point."

"Did you happen to see any of those aboard?" Kristi asked.

"I told you I pay attention. Two men in suits, medium height and build, were picked up at the plane by a man I couldn't see well enough to recognize."

"The car?"

"Big black Caddie, four or five years old. The other four people, three men and a woman, piled into a van with a Judy Realty sign on the door."

"I'd say you certainly did pay attention," Kristi grinned. "How about some of that chocolate cake now?"

"You got it."

The pleasant evening ended early, but then Kristi lingered at the door, reached up, grabbed Russ by the neck, and planted a meaningful kiss on his lips. "Thanks for dinner," she said slyly.

Russ thought, as she walked to her car, *it's a start.*

Kristi thought, as she walked to her car, *the people trying to take over Wesfield Laboratory needed an airport with longer runways and better security. Even more important, they had the wherewithal to get the changes made. Impressive.*

The smell of Russ's cologne followed Kristi home. Even after a quick shower it still lingered. *Why did I have to put so much emotion in that kiss? What was I thinking? Thinking didn't have much to do with it. There is nothing quite so appealing as an attractive guy not pushing too hard. He simply enjoys my company . . . right.* She slept restlessly.

*****

The next morning Kristi was greeted by Judy McKibbin's generous smile. It signaled her confidence and ability, qualities needed to run a successful real estate company. "What can I do for you, Chief Christopher?"

"I prefer Kristi."

Judy extended her hand. "Kristi."

Nice grip, Kristi thought as she said. "I need a little information you may be able to help with."

Judy was the complete business woman, with a quick mind that sensed she was about to be interrogated. Real estate contracts are public information for those willing to do a little digging, so she suspected Kristi's inquiries would be of a personal nature. Her intellect said, "On guard."

Prior to any questions Kristi said, "Let me assure you, I am not interested in any privileged or confidential information."

She read my mind, Judy thought. *I better keep on my toes.*

Kristi went on to say she was interested in the people Judy picked up at the airport last month. She asked how her company, Judy Realty, acquired them as clients. Kristi also asked her to briefly trace her steps from the time she picked up the passengers in the morning until they got back to the plane that afternoon.

Judy had no problem with that. "A secretary from Manhattan Bank called to make the airport appointment for 10 o'clock Thursday. She told me a Mr. Tuchscherer was interested in purchasing a small farm, about 100 acres. He would prefer someplace close to South Station. I made it clear to the secretary very little land was available. She showed little interest in my opinion."

"I wonder why?" Kristi mused. "You'd think she would want to know how many possibilities there were."

"She didn't." Judy picked up the story when the 727 landed. "They came in right on time. Four of the passengers came to the terminal where I was to meet them. Three men and a woman, all middle-aged. Mr. Tuchscherer, the buyer, didn't say much. Mrs. Isabel Quinn did the talking for the group. Other than grunt hello, I'm not sure the others could speak.

"They wanted to get oriented first, so we drove downtown. Then, Mrs. Quinn asked if we could take a swing past Wesfield Laboratory. From there we drove five miles north to the Mac Orchard. It was 75 acres larger than they requested, 175 acres, but I knew Mac's owners, the Loebes, were having a tough time the last couple of years and might be receptive to an offer."

"Were they?"

"We only did a drive-by at that time," Judy said. "They wanted to see the entire area first. We drove around for a couple of useless hours looking at farmland."

"Did they see anything else they liked?"

"Not really. Like I said, there was nothing for sale. Not where they wanted to buy. I tried to make conversation by explaining how the hills in this area were created by glaciers during the ice age, but they couldn't have cared less. In the end, we went back to Mac Orchard for a closer look."

"I guess you knew you'd end up there all along."

"I did. But, I wasn't sure my assessment of Loebe's financial situation was accurate."

"Was it?"

"It must have been," Judy said. "I went to the door by myself to present the unsolicited offer. I got all I could have hoped for – a neutral reception, which meant in my mind it's negotiable."

"I'll bet he was surprised, when you showed up out of the blue," Kristi commented.

"He was. But he did everything in his power to help."

"How?"

"He took his time escorting us around the grounds. Mr. Loebe pridefully pointed out the quality of the fruit trees, soil and drainage advantages, the outbuildings and the fruit market's potential."

"How did they like it?" Kristi asked.

"Orchards, by their very nature, are charming places. This one, with a crystal clear little stream weaving through it, was particularly appealing. When the tour ended, Mr. Tuchscherer looked toward his silent associates and without a word spoken, they gave him an affirmative nod with a hint of a smile."

"Sounds like it was your day," Kristi said.

"It was," Judy smiled. "The stream made it an easy sell."

"How about the price?" Kristi asked.

"With orchard farm land selling at $4,000 an acre, Mr Tuchscherer's offer of $45,00 an acre plus $30,000 for the farm house, was more than Loebe had ever imagined.

"I could have gotten a better price for the farm, but I seemed to be sidelined once the group had decided to buy it. I wrote up the offer to purchase for $789,530 sitting at the kitchen table. The 10%, $80,000, down payment was written with a check belonging to Painter America Holding Company. They actually purchased the property."

"Nice day's work," Kristi said.

"Better than nice. Their legal people cleared the title, wired the money into escrow, and closed in four days. According to Mr. Loebe, in a separate deal, they agreed to pay his family $3,000 to be out in three days. He said it was hectic, but being debt free with pockets full of money more than made up for it."

"Where did they go?" Kristi asked.

"They bought Jack Johnson's empty two-story on the boulevard. I heard Mr. Loebe was hired to keep up the orchard for the Painter people. He's probably making more than when he owned it."

"I'll bet I know who had the Johnson listing," Kristi said with a smile.

"It was a good week. But just between us, I didn't charge the full 6% commission. I use a fixed fee under 4%. Still, like I said, it was a good week."

"That was nice of you, Judy. And I appreciate your cooperation. If you have time, I'll buy your lunch."

"You're on, but only if we're finished with the questions."

"Fair enough." They enjoyed one another's company over an all-salad lunch.

*****

Up down, up down, pot-hole patches dominated the blacktop road dividing fields of endless rows of fruit-filled trees. The Mac Orchard sign, torn down and lying in the weeds, was being replaced with wide brick columns on both sides of the entry road. Kristi thought, *the gate can't be far behind.* Well into the orchard, a culvert bridge passed over a crystal clear stream meandering over a sandy bottom. Downstream, ripples danced over a patch of pebbles hinting a strong current flowing beneath. A little over fifty feet back from the stream, a hole had been dug and foundation construction was well underway.

At lunch, Judy McKibbin mentioned Bailey Construction, a local firm she recommended, had been chosen to build three additional houses.

A balding, round-faced man, pointing at blueprints on a makeshift easel, was instructing a hard-hat who kept nodding with understanding after each statement. When they were finished, he turned to Kristi with a smile, "What can I do for you, Ma'am?"

"Hi, I'm Marilynn Christopher, South Station's police chief."

"I'm Ron Bailey," he said, extending his hand. "I heard you were our new chief. How do you like it?"

"Fine, thank you. I'd like to ask you a few questions about the houses you're building out here."

"Why would the police have an interest in my work?"

"It's not your work that interests us, Mr. Bailey, it's the company that hired you."

"Not to be disrespectful, Chief Christopher, but my deal with them is between them and me. I don't see how it's any of your business."

"Let me ask a couple of questions. If you think they are too personal, you can say so. Okay?"

"I guess that will be okay."

Patiently, Kristi asked, "How many houses are you building?"

"We're starting with three, but they indicated more would be built later."

Good, he's volunteering information. He's a pussycat once you get past the bravado.

"Your customer is Painter America Inc., right?"

"That's right, Ma'am."

"They called you out of the blue?"

"I think Judy McKibbin of Judy Realty may have recommended me."

"She told me she did. I might suggest you send her some wine or something." Kristi flashed a conspiratorial smile.

"That's a good idea." Bailey smiled back.

"Did Painter ask for a quote, or are they paying on a cost plus basis?" Kristi waited for Bailey to balk at that question.

He surprised her. "Not that it's any of your business, Chief Christopher, cost plus with a high-low range quote. I draw from an escrow account at the local bank. So far they seem like very generous people."

"I'm sure they are. How big are these houses?"

"Big. Bigger than I'm used to building. All three houses are well over 4500 square feet."

"Are you doing all the work?"

"That seems like a strange question, Chief. Yes, I am, everything except the security system. Apparently, they have their own people for that, but they do show some special wiring on the blueprints."

"Thank you, Mr. Bailey. I trust I haven't kept you from your work."

"It was nice to meet you, Chief Christopher. I hope I was helpful."

"It was nice to meet you, too, Mr. Bailey. You were very helpful." As she walked to her car she couldn't help thinking, *The people promoting a Bayer takeover haven't managed to get Wesfield to sell, yet they're already moving in . . . they must be a very confident group.*

Kristi stopped at the station on her way home, hoping to find an uneventful routine day winding down. She was not disappointed – with one exception. Joseph left a message; he would stop in the office in the morning to talk about a note he'd just received from Beverly. If that was inconvenient she was to get back to him. *Thoughts of poor Beverly followed her home.*

CHAPTER 19
OFFENSE

Although she hadn't been consistent lately, Kristi tried to start her day with the exercise routine she learned at Quantico. It didn't take too much time or equipment, and it could be done in her apartment. After the workout and a quick shower, she headed for the station.

Joseph and Jake were embedded in Cub's talk when she walked into her office. She said, "Joseph, you're up early; had breakfast yet?"

"I put sweet rolls on the counter," he replied. After giving her time to pour coffee and grab a pastry, he continued, "The reason I'm here is to show you this." He handed her an envelope. "Unfortunately, it's taken a few days to catch up to me because it was sent to my attention at Wesfield Laboratory instead of my home. I guess Beverly either needed to send it quickly, or didn't have my home address handy."

Uncharacteristically, her note appeared hastily scribbled. It read, "Joseph, I saw part of another memo from Hermann vonLeer, I think that's how it was spelled, to our Mr. Smylee. It said monies had been provided to expand efforts to include the people in Italy. There was more to the memo that I didn't catch because Mr. Smylee walked in as I was reading it, but I did manage to see, 'execute the plan immediately – we must get Westerfield under control –NOW.'"

"I don't know what it all means, but it doesn't sound good to me. I hope this finds you safe and well. I'm worried. It seems someone associated with our company is trying to harm you. If you get a chance, call me at home. I'd like to know you're alright. As always, Beverly."

"Do you want me to get additional protection for Sophia and Ida?"

"What do you think, Kristi?"

"I don't believe anyone suspects our people are even there, and I have a great deal of respect for the people at Worldwide Executive Protection Ltd. I guess I'd just give them a 'heads up'."

"Very well, call them – see what they think."

"There's something else we need to go over, Joseph."

"And that is . . . ."

Kristi reiterated Judy McKibbin's story from beginning to end.

"I can't believe it. You mean to tell me the South Station Bank was involved in the sale of Mac Orchard to the same people trying to buy Wesfield?"

"It's only holding escrow monies, Joseph," Kristi answered. "Besides, I believe it can work to our advantage."

"What kind of advantage?"

"Your bank may be key to answer the 'who paid for it' question."

"My bank? I don't own the bank, you know."

"I know, but I'm betting they treat you like you do. Before we get to that, I'd like to share some of my observations."

"Okay. What are they?"

"I think 'the money people' behind Bayer have a multifaceted plan already in motion," Kristi said.

"I'm listening," Joseph acknowledged.

"The crucial component, of course, is to free up stock so Wesfield can be purchased. You, Jeff, and that tribe of stockholders that follow your lead are their biggest problem."

"Their tactics may be ruthless, but I don't intend to sell them a single share. I'm glad you're helping us, Kristi; God knows we need your help."

"You and Jeff have both suggested that stumbling blocks have been placed at every turn on the road to ExRelief's introduction."

"That's been pretty obvious." Joseph said.

"I see diverting the new product rollout as a secondary goal." Kristi said, as she paused in a moment of contemplation. "It will keep profits and stock prices down so stockholders may be inclined to consider any solid offer."

"I see your point," Joseph said. "You think it's just a ploy aimed at enticing stockholders to sell."

"Right. Remember they're already offering an inflated price. I think the power brokers behind Bayer feel they will succeed even if ExRelief gets launched on schedule. But, if ExRelief gets out for the cold season on time, and it's as successful as you told me the test market shows, stock prices will go through the roof." With a penetrating gaze, she said, "People will be very reluctant to sell a rising stock, and I think our enemies know it."

"You're analytical, Kristi. I have to agree with the probability of your conclusions."

"Which brings me to my next point," she said. "The people behind Bayer are so accustomed to success, the idea of failing isn't a consideration. They are, I believe, already taking steps to provide security for their executives."

"Really?" Joseph said.

"Three programs are in motion: building a housing complex, security changes and improvements at the airport, and the new 'beefed-up' security at Wesfield. I could be wrong, but I believe these are all integral parts of the same scheme."

"What's the airport got to do with Wesfield?" Joseph asked.

She told him about her friend Russ and his concerns with the "donated" airport fence and "donated" runway extension. She was hesitant, but continued, explaining that a friend who owed her a favor traced the contractor's payments to a wire transfer from Manhattan Bank & Trust Inc., the same bank involved in the property transactions.

"I can see your point. You're undoubtedly onto something, but what I really want to know is how you know people with the expertise to hack into bank records."

"If I told you, Joseph, I wouldn't be much of a friend," Kristi said with a hint of a smile peeking from the corners of her squinting eyes.

Kristi went over the details of the land purchase and Bailey's arrangement to build the houses. When she finished, becoming deadly serious, she said, "Here is where we start our offense if your bank will help us."

"I can guarantee it," Joseph quickly responded. "What do you want done?"

"First, using a 'trace route program,' find out where the money came from that went into Bailey's escrow account. Second, review any wire transfers to South Station Federal customers that originated at Manhattan Bank & Trust. We need to know if any locals are in their pocket."

"What's a trace route program?" Joseph asked.

"It's a common computer program developed to trace bad checks, wire transfers and the like. Your bank people should know about it, but if they don't, I know people who do."

"Do you think we should be spying on bank customers? The bank is going to fight me on that."

"Joseph, this is not a time to play nice," Kristi said, flushing. "We are looking for people who are trying to kill you. Wouldn't you like to head them off before they succeed?"

"Okay, Kristi, okay. I get it."

"I thought you might."

"Do you think we could get into some legal privacy trouble?"

"Contrary to public opinion, bank records are not protected information." A convincing and persistent Kristi said, "You want to take the offense. Let's take it. Identifying the enemy is the first step."

I wonder if the good people of South Station will ever know, or appreciate, how protective this foxy lady can be. Thank God she's on my side.

Kristi accompanied Joseph to the bank to give their request a legitimacy it may not have had without the badge. Mr. Wienbergen, the bank president, wearing an unwrinkled suit coat and with perfect posture, marched into the lobby to greet them. He showed a bit too much cordiality to suit Kristi, as he directed them into a nearby conference room.

Putting on his bank director face, Joseph became the picture of authority, a man impossible to deny. Kristi was a silent partner, watching as Joseph spelled out the details of their requests to the pompous banker. S*o that is what real authority looks like,* Kristi thought, as Wienbergen, metamorphosed into a wimpy 'yes-man.' He nodded agreement and understanding with each request, never questioning Joseph on a single issue.

On the way back to the car, Joseph said, "That went better than I expected, Kristi. Thanks for your help."

"No need to thank me. You didn't seem to need any help," Kristi said, with a twinkle in her smiling green eyes. "Besides, we're in this together. This was just the first step. Finding where Painter America gets funding is the hard part. Once we know account numbers we will probably need to use a hacker to get much further. Know any good hackers?" Kristi said, needling him as a friend and co-conspirator.

"Young lady, you are corrupt – insightful, but corrupt."

"What a thing to say to the chief of police."

CHAPTER 20
WESFIELD SECURITY

Still asleep, Jeff tried to ignore the unwelcome ringing of his telephone. *I'm not up yet – my alarm hasn't gone off.* "Hello."

"Good morning. This is Marilynn Christopher. I hope I didn't wake you."

"Morning, Chief, I need to get going anyway. What can I do for you?"

"Can you meet me at the Coffee Shop? I would like you to do some snooping around and I don't want talk about it at Wesfield."

"Sure, say, 45 minutes."

After working their way through more doughnuts than either needed, Kristi explained what she wanted and why. She stressed that she didn't want Jeff trying to catch anybody, only identifying people who were in a position to influence the Wesfield security effort. She would then take those names to the bank, so to speak, and check their deposit history.

"Would it be okay if I included my secretary in this subterfuge?"

"How much do you trust her?"

"I trust her."

"With your life?"

"I think so."

"Okay."

She was Jeff's ally in their quest to overcome bureaucratic forces that often stifle success in corporate efforts. Carol Ackerman always said, "No one works *for* Jeff Westerfield, only *with* him." She had the best secretarial job in marketing. Jeff, her boss, had a realistic open approach; her opinion was often asked for and always considered valuable. He was easy to work for, fun to be around. She trusted him; he trusted her.

"This is strictly on the QT, Carol," Jeff said, looking her in the eye with concern written all over his face.

"So, what's new?" she replied flippantly.

"What's new is that I would like you to do some spy work."

"Ooo. I shall be known as Madam Carol, Private Eye."

"I can see the humor from your point of view, but let me explain what I need to find out and why."

"You know I'd be happy to do whatever you want, so let's have it." Sensing Jeff's seriousness wasn't going to be tempered, Carol's look became every bit as intense as his.

"This is just between you and me," he said, "and it could even be dangerous."

"Dangerous. You mean *real* danger?" Carol said, her eyes widening.

"It's possible. Let me tell you why." He explained a takeover attempt was underway and that he believed the "money people" behind it were ruthless. "They were the ones who tried to kill me," he said, "and they came very close to succeeding."

"Why are they after you, Jeff?" He had her full attention now.

"Because my grandfather and I own a good deal of stock – almost enough to block their efforts. In addition to that, my grandfather's stockholder friends have always followed his recommendation. We're in their way and we're not budging."

"I had no idea," she said.

"You're not alone; only a few employees have a clue what's going on." Jeff went on to tell her Chief Christopher and Joseph believed that whoever started the increased security programs at Wesfield was being paid by the same people trying to buy the company. He needed to find out who they were.

"Why? What does security have to do with anything?" she asked.

"The people trying to take over are fearful of retaliation for Nazi war crimes."

"Like Nazi gas chamber, concentration camp war crimes?"

"Exactly," Jeff answered.

"You're telling me a company involved in war crimes is trying to buy Wesfield?"

"Someone, or some group, is working to get BayerAG back in this country," Jeff said. "During World War II, Bayer was part of a company called IG Farben. Thirteen IG Farben executives were convicted of war crimes and we know the Bayer division was heavily involved in the worst atrocities."

"The Bayer Aspirin company?" she asked in disbelief.

"Yes, and no." Jeff said with a smile. "After World War I, Friedr. Bayer & Co., which today we call BayerAG, lost the Bayer Aspirin brand when the Treaty of Versailles forbade them from doing business in this country as part of their punishment for war crimes."

"I still see Bayer Aspirin in all the stores," Carol noted.

"When Friedr. Bayer was forced to sell, Sterling Lab bought them for $5.3 million. They have owned and distributed Bayer Aspirin here in the States ever since. Over the years, I'm sure they made a bundle on it. It's the people trying to get BayerAG back into our country that we fear, not the Sterling Drug Company."

"How do you know all that ancient history?"

"My granddad. Joseph knows a good deal about BayerAG's past. He wants no part of that company."

"Okay. That is scary and I get it," Carol said. "So, how are we going to discover who initiated beefing up security?"

"Follow the paper trail. Start with a copy of the minutes from the Executive Committee meeting authorizing funding, and work backward."

"I'll see what I can dig up," she said.

"Great. Just ask for copies of memos, without letting on why you want them."

"And if they ask?"

"Use me – you don't know why I want them."

"You want me to lie?" Carol asked with a smile.

"No, just don't volunteer any more than you need to."

"You're a devious boss, Jeffrey Westerfield."

"I know."

Carol's telephone calls got the ball rolling. The lack of resistance from her secretarial peers was alarming. Not a single 'why' or 'for whom,' came forth when she asked for copies of meeting summaries or minutes.

Their bosses' lives were an open book – all you had to do was ask.

When she talked to meeting participants, however, resistance was inherent. Her technique was simple, but effective. She told her targets everything she knew, then asked if they had anything to add. Being self-proclaimed authorities, almost everyone put their own spin on the conclusions that led to improving security.

*****

The fruits of Carol's efforts were staggering in their intricacy. "I would like you to know I had to promise things that will guarantee my place in hell to get this information."

"That bad, eh, Carol?" Jeff replied.

"Worse."

"I'll make it up to you. I promise."

"Do you want the information in the order I got it or chronologically?" Carol asked.

"Either way, whichever works for you," Jeff said.

"I think chronological is easiest to follow. Okay?"

"Shoot."

"Our esteemed group leader sent the earliest security memo I could find," Carol reported.

"Gordon Wieldey?"

"Eighteen months ago, our very own Gordo sent an inter-office memo to Plant Security questioning our degree of protection. He was particularly interested in security for the new products under development."

"What new products under development? He must have been smokin' something if he thought we had some new secret formulas to protect. ExRelief is the only product within years of becoming a reality."

"That may be true. I'm just telling you it was the first memo I could find questioning our security readiness."

"I'm sorry," Jeff said. "It makes no sense."

"Moving right along – that inquiry spawned a meeting called by Security that was intended to calm Gordon's fears. Gordon, three

Security people, and apparently Manufacturing and Finance people were in attendance. I couldn't find out exactly who they were. I guess Gordon's fears weren't calmed because it didn't end there. As you can see from this copy of the minutes from that meeting, funding would be provided to conduct an independent analysis of current security effectiveness." She handed a copy of the minutes to Jeff. "Guess who knew a great consultant group that might consider taking on the project?"

"Gordon?"

"Bingo. Give that man a cigar."

"I don't see Gordon's recommendation in the minutes," Jeff objected.

"I told you I sold my soul. Rowland Thomas, the head honcho in Security, remembers the meeting only too well. He resented anyone poking their nose in his department, especially, as he put it, 'by some uppity marketing butt-wipe.'"

"I can see how he might become a bit defensive."

"A bit defensive? Gordon will be his enemy for life."

"Did we use Gordon's consultants for the study?" Jeff asked.

As she turned over a copy of the quote and study, she said, "Those hard-to-get-consultants were at the door the next morning. They had a quote in our hands by the end of the week."

"Where did the trail go from there?" Jeff asked.

"I don't know how they got involved, but Purchasing called the next meeting."

Jeff explained, "A purchase order probably needed to be cut; they were undoubtedly just flexing their muscles. It's standard bureaucratic positioning – who's responsible for what."

"I think there's a possibility someone in the Purchasing group may also be in Bayer's pocket."

"Really?" Jeff said.

"They put a lot of pressure on accelerating the recommendations. And, who do you think seconded their approach?"

"Gordon?"

"You are batting a thousand," Carol smiled.

"Who was pushing from Purchasing?" Jeff asked.

"He may have spoken on behalf of one of his bosses, but Darin Rauguth was the pitchman. The conclusions from that meeting went to the Executive Board for approval, but that was just a formality."

Rolling the report into a tube, then slapping the tube on his other hand, Jeff asked, "How long did these so-called outside experts take to produce this study?"

"The report was mailed to us in five weeks, which seems odd to me – how are you going to question, or even discuss the conclusions? According to Thomas, 'they did a 'half-ass job – weren't here long enough to do anything else.' When I asked him to explain, he told me three young punks tied up his people for three days, asking the stupidest questions he'd ever heard. He said they didn't know squat about security or the over-the-counter pharmaceutical business."

"I'm sure he was right." Jeff sounded disgusted.

The next morning, Jeff sat in his car for 35 minutes waiting for Wieldey to arrive. Gordon slowly swung into his basement parking spot. When he shut off his engine, Jeff got out of his car, holding up for a few seconds, making sure he and Gordon would walk in together.

"Good morning, Jeff." Gordon's teeth sparkled unnaturally in his permanently fixed smile.

"Hi, Gordon, how's it going?"

Gordon replied with some superficial blather Jeff wasn't hearing.

When they got to the door and inserted their ID cards, Jeff said, "I wonder what all this increased security is all about. It sure is a pain in the butt."

"It sure is," Gordon agreed.

"Do you know why it was put in or who asked for it?" Jeff asked.

"I don't have a clue," Gordon replied.

"I thought you always knew what was going on around here, Gordon."

"Not this time."

Jeff smiled to himself. *Why would you lie, Gordo? Why would you lie?*

CHAPTER 21
PARK LAKE MEETING

SUBJECT: Wesfield Laboratories, Progress Inquiry
TO: Richardson, Deckmann, & Smylee
FROM: Hermann vonLeer
ATTN: Mr. Smylee

We are falling behind with our efforts to change the
balance of Wesfield stockholder ownership.

We must become the controlling partner.
Stock purchases are almost zero.
Joseph Westerfield is matching all offers.
He has convinced his followers to holdout for ExRelief's
 potential profits.

The Westerfield problem must be neutralized – NOW.

ExRelief – Package manufacturing hasn't been slowed
sufficiently to delay the introduction.
Additional in-plant action must be taken.

Update security and housing projects

NOTE: The Reestablishment Committee, including the
Painter Group, is concerned with the progress in the Wesfield
Laboratory acquisition.

Be prepared to address these issues at the next
Park Lake meeting.

*****

Mr. Smylee resented being forced to report to the committee. The people that made up the committee, and in particular Hermann vonLeer, always sneered when they asked their stupid questions. They all expected programs to be carried out without complications, and when things didn't work according to plan, it was always his fault. In Smylee's mind, the committee members didn't have a clue what it took to actually do the dirty work they created. But, they'd pay handsomely to get his services. He entered the Park Lake Hotel filled with anxiety masterfully disguised behind a businesslike image.

After a general welcome to the members of the Reestablishment Committee, Hermann vonLeer quickly handed the meeting to Smylee for his update.

"Let me assure all of you I totally understand our dilemma," Smylee said, pausing to catch an inner breath. "At this very moment, we have two separate programs in motion designed to eliminate Westerfield's hold over the stockholders."

Feeling the need for clarity, vonLeer interrupted. "An additional effort has been authorized and funded." Speaking just above a whisper, his serpentine demeanor flooded the room. "With our time constraints, a second program was called for as an assurance to achieve a satisfactory outcome."

"We have been solving problems together since the turn of the century," Smylee said. "This, too, will come to a satisfactory conclusion, and it will happen shortly."

Uncharacteristically, one of the committee members entered the conversation. "Mr. Smylee, I fail to share your optimism; time is running out. Westerfield's influence is increasing. Stock is not changing hands. ExRelief is back on schedule. We only see positive results in the areas of security and housing. Without acquiring Wesfield Laboratory, we will need neither security nor housing."

Smylee, not accustomed to being challenged by a committee member, was rattled, but no one would ever know it – his face, a mask, hid all emotion. "It should not take long for us to realize our goals, three weeks, maybe less. As I said, we have dual strategies in motion to deal with the Westerfields. The second initiative is simply backup insurance. Either project will produce success, but after the first attempt failed, we felt it was necessary."

"Are you using the same agent that got us into this untimely dilemma?" vonLeer asked, already aware of the answer.

"With this one exception, this operative is the most successful agent we have ever used. He was chosen because of his abilities and long history of success under pressure."

VonLeer continued to manipulate the conversation to provide answers he wanted the others to hear. "Is there any connection between the two programs?" He asked.

"None whatsoever," Smylee replied. "The parties involved are not aware a second program is being carried out."

"Tell us how the new product launch is being diverted," vonLeer continued.

"I can say with absolute certainty that all the ExRelief Cold Medicine produced in the initial run will not be commercially acceptable. The Quality Control Department will find the tablets contain too much moisture to hold their shape in the pressing function."

"Thank you, Mr. Smylee. Do you have anything you would like to add?"

"Only that I would like to apologize for the poor start and promise a quick recovery. Thank you for your patience," he said thinking, *wouldn't it be nice if these pompous asses actually had any patience.*

CHAPTER 22
SALLY

Labor 50 years dawn till dusk, often later than dusk, and if you're not blind-sided by frost, flood, drought, hail or poor crop demand, your farm might, just might, have an adequate year.

In the late 1920s, a young Claude LaPoint inherited his parents' failing farm. Being young and an optimist, Claude paid little attention to the fact the farm's value was less than the mortgage. His enthusiasm didn't fool Sally. Just like her brother Joseph, she was a Westerfield realist, willing to stand beside Claude with full knowledge of the task ahead.

Their uninsulated two-bedroom home needed new roof shingles to stop the leaks and wiring that didn't blow fuses with morning toast. Beginning with that house, Claude and Sally personally built and rebuilt their farm buildings during a lifetime of sweat, tears, and an abundance of love. Although built separately, the sheds, silos and barns fit together as though some master architect's only objective was to create harmony. The farm acquired the personality of the owners: strong, functional, and well cared for.

Amidst the daily drudgery of a farm routine, the LaPoints managed to find the time to raise four boys and a girl. With Claude and Sally as role models, the kids grew up understanding what a good work ethic was all about. The family grew into a smooth running, well-coordinated work force, but they also managed to find time to support one another's individual goals and ambitions.

Sally was content with the life she'd chosen, but after her babies flew the nest, she often found herself alone with what she called, the tedious "Cs": chickens, cooking, and cleaning. Farming by its nature is a very isolated lifestyle, but within the routine, positive elements create a unique peacefulness seldom found in city life.

One of the positives came on weekdays at two o'clock sharp when the mail was delivered. Sally looked forward to a break, and her walk to the mail box to see if the world knew she was still there gave her a few precious moments. Thistle and goldenrod with a sprinkling of daisies bordered the quarter-mile dirt road that meandered from the LaPoint's farm complex to the county highway. A warm summer breeze rustled poplar leaves and carried the sweet scent of fresh cut hay, lifting her spirits as Sally strolled down the familiar lane to the mailbox.

A package leaned against the base of the post. The old galvanized box was stuffed with junk mail and a few letters of interest. As always, she stood before the mailbox leafing through the envelopes hoping to see if, by chance, one of the kids had sent her a letter.

It was sudden – it was loud. The devil's howl filled the air as the engine's roar pierced her ears. Glancing up from the mail in her hand, terror consumed her. With evil at the wheel, a black sedan was barreling down the edge of the road directly toward her. *"Oh, God, help me. He's trying to run me down."* She leaped toward the fence, willing herself to jump farther than she could possibly expect.

*****

Having spent three days studying the farm routine, Gunther already knew Sally's habits. She would be an easy target standing at the road scanning her mail. He patiently waited with the motor running, so he could keep cool with the air on. Sure enough at 2:10, right on time, she was a pretty picture sauntering down the road without a care in the world, taking her own sweet time. His breathing quickened and heart began racing as the adrenalin surged into his blood stream.

Wait . . . wait. Timing is everything. She will look at the box on the ground first. Be patient, another thirty seconds. She did pick up the box, then put it back down. She pulled the door of the mailbox down, bent over and peered in, looking hopefully for actual letters.

Your time's up, lady. The rush was magnificent as he tromped the accelerator, eyes fixed on his target. Wheels half-on half-off the shoulder, the car threw gravel all the way. Just before impact, she jumped to his right. He responded quickly, jerking the car to compensate for her sudden attempt at evasion. *No way will I let you get away*. Taking out the mailbox with the left headlight caused the car to overcompensate and veer farther right than he anticipated. The fatal outcome was predestined, but he didn't intend to hit the scrub elms or the fence made from field boulders, along the way. Now both lights were out, and blood was clearly visible down the center of the car. *Sally was in the hands of God.*

Luckily, nothing was rubbing against the tires or dragging on the ground. Keeping to country roads, Gunther headed north and west. At a particularly desolate stretch he got out to evaluate the damage. Wiping blood from the bumper and grille, Gunther smiled to himself as he thought, *It took demolishing both headlights, both fenders and a grille to eliminate one little old lady. Is anything going to go smoothly on this project?*

*****

Two days later, the car was found at Cleveland's Hopkins Airport when an alert guard, seeing the Avis logo sticker on the window, thought it didn't make sense to park a rental all day long in short-term parking.

Only the most obvious blood had been wiped off, and no fingerprints were found inside or out. The contract was no longer in the car, but it only took a few minutes to uncover the name, Victor Vargas, on the Visa receipt and rental contract in the Avis computer. The transaction originated at Indianapolis International Airport. After spotting blood left from the half-hearted effort to wipe it off, the car was identified as a candidate linked to a rural hit and run downstate. It proved to be the deadly vehicle.

*****

"I missed you guys; how're you doin'?" Sheriff Arven asked.

"We've missed you, too, Gus. It's nice to hear your voice," Kristi said visualizing his friendly smile. "Did you get the copies of my notes?"

"I did, thank you. You're a lady of your word. I'll bet you're swamped," Gus replied.

"You'd win that bet."

"How are you and your contractors getting along?"

"Great. I wouldn't have an ice cube's chance in hell without their help. They know their stuff. You'd like them."

"I am sure I would, but I'll bet you didn't call me to just chit-chat."

"You know me too well, Gus. I could use your help locating a boat. I hope it was rented on the southeast corner of the lake."

"I'd be glad to poke around a little. What can you tell me about the boat?"

Kristi had to think a second, "She was a small Boston Whaler called 'Love of My Life.' Mr. Westerfield got a look at the number on the bow, but he said his old eyes couldn't be positive. He thought part of it was IN24???0SL."

"It's nice to be working with you folks again, Kristi."

"Well, I don't want to get you in any trouble, but nobody knows the shore as well as you do."

"It won't be a problem. Do you have a particular time or day in mind?"

"Oh, of course. The boat was sighted last Sunday morning, but I have no idea when it was rented."

"I'll get right on it. You should know, one way or the other, by the end of the week."

"Thanks, Gus." Kristi hung up the phone. *Gus Arven has got to be the most cooperative cop I've ever worked with. I need to do something special for him one of these days.*

The phone rang for the umpteenth time. To hell with it – it was getting late. Kristi listened as the answering machine went to work. Joseph sounded devastated. "Kristi, this is Joseph. Please call as soon as . . ."

She grabbed the phone before he could finish. "Joseph, what's happened?"

He could barely speak. "My sister Sally was run down at her mail box."

"Where are you? I'll be right there."

"I'm at home, here in town."

In minutes, Kristi was hugging Joseph for all she was worth. It seemed like an eternity before he let her go.

Eventually, with a long deep sigh, he leaned back, "Thanks for coming, Kristi. I think the losses are becoming more important to me than the cause. These people have no soul. Killing is just another business tool to them."

"Are you sure it was Wesfield related and not just an accident?"

"The Seneca County Sheriff said it was intentional – no doubt about it."

"What can I do, my friend? How can I help you?" Kristi knew there was nothing she could do. She only wanted him to know he was not alone, that someone cared.

"Why would they kill Sally?" Joseph questioned. "She only has a couple hundred shares and I'm entrusted to vote them. I'm confused, I'm frightened, and I'm angry.

"She was my closest friend for as long as I can remember. When we were little kids we slept in the same bed. Even though she was two years younger, she tutored me all through grade school; Sally always read better than I could. I just can't understand how anyone could harm that dear, good-hearted lady. I feel like they stole her from me."

"They did. Have you called Jeff?"

"He's on his way over."

"Good. Is there anyone else you want me to locate?"

"No. Thanks for asking, Kristi, but we don't have any local relatives. I'm sure Claude has already called his kids, and farm neighbors are quick to spread the word among themselves."

Jeff came in long-faced and red-eyed. Visibly shaken, he and Joseph embraced without a word. Kristi quickly said her goodbye, leaving them alone in their sorrow. She kept asking herself, *Why is this happening to such wonderful men?*

CHAPTER 23
TIBBYVILLE

After leaving Joseph and Jeff to their sorrow, Kristi quickly assembled the leaders of her team: Jake, Sheriff Gus Arven, Sandy Sandora, Joan Voss and Charley Tanner. By eight o'clock they were crammed around what was once a dining room table in the police station's only large room. "Thanks for coming on the spur of the moment. You're here because we learned this afternoon Joseph's sister, Sally, was viciously run down right in front of her house." Kristi said. "As I understand it, she was out at the road picking up her mail."

"Did we have her under protection?" Joan asked.

"I wish we had." Kristi said quietly.

After the standard "how horrible" comments by the group, Gus Arven asked, "Do we know the details?"

"I talked to Sheriff Surratt over in Seneca County," she told him. "That's in northern Ohio where their farm is located. The Sheriff said the tire tracks told the story. They indicated a car was parked on the shoulder about 40 yards from the mail box. The driver gunned the car down the side of the road taking out Sally, the mail box and part of the fence. She flew 35 feet, so the car had to be really moving at impact. The Sheriff said there wasn't any sign of an attempt to try to brake. His only possible conclusion – a deliberate murder."

"It's too bad we didn't know she was a target," Joan said.

"That's just it. There wasn't any reason to think she was a target. Joseph told me he voted her few shares right along with his. Annihilating her doesn't make sense unless . . . ." Kristi paused. "Let my friend, Gus, give you a report on a project he did for us first, then I'll tell you why I think she was killed."

"Just in case you don't know who I am or where I fit, I'm Gus Arven, Sheriff of Berrien County. Originally Kristi and I worked this case together, but my superiors felt I was being stretched too thin so they reined me in. This case snagged my interest and thanks to Kristi, I've kept up with your progress. I'm impressed.

"A week ago Sunday, Joseph Westerfield became suspicious of a boat fishing close to his shoreline. Being the savvy old guy he is, he remembered the boat's name and a partial ID.

"Kristi asked me to check with local boat rentals to find out if, by chance, the boat belonged to one of them. I know most of the boat people around here, so it made sense to use me to make a few calls. We got lucky. Turns out it was rented at Nautica Marine from Joddy Willard who is a friend of mine. The guy that rented it was named Victor Vargas, out of South Carolina. A red flag went up when I contacted the folks in Carolina. They never heard of a Victor Vargas. He rented the boat for a week at $250, but he returned it less than four hours later. No one I know pays 250 bucks for three hours of fishing – no matter how bad they're biting."

"Did Joddy remember what he looked like?" Jake asked.

"He said he looked like a typical middle-aged fisherman, but he did better than that." Holding up a few pieces of paper, "Here are copies of his South Carolina driver's license. It's only black and white, but there is a picture on it. Poor quality, but a picture. Proof of identity is required to get a fishing license, in or out of state. Copying the driver's license is standard procedure at Nautica. The guy probably didn't even know it was copied."

"That's great," Joan Voss said.

"That's not all. Here are copies of his receipt. The Visa card was issued by Manhattan Bank & Trust Inc. in New York City. It's paid automatically from an out of state bank. I couldn't get that information yet – but I will."

"Nice work, Gus. Thank you," Kristi said. "I would like the rest of you to know it only took Gus two days to uncover our mysterious fisherman. Thanks again, especially since you're not working with us anymore."

Gus smiled and said, "I'm not done yet. When I traced Vargas's credit card history, I discovered he checked into two different motels about 25 miles from here during the last nine days. I'd say this guy has been here awhile."

Kristi, with a big smile, looked him in the eye and shook her head. *He's something else – I like him – too bad he doesn't work with us. Hell, he'd be in charge.*

A pizza man walked in with three boxes, "I got the beer and soda in the car."

The pizza quickly disappeared from paper plates. Kristi continued the conversation as the crew finished the snack. "I believe this man, this Victor Vargas, is the assassin who shot Jeff. He's back to finish the job."

"Do you think he's alone or possibly part of a team?" Jake asked.

"It's hard to say for sure," Kristi said, "but my guess would be, alone. This guy is a pro. He wouldn't want, or need, anyone else to worry about. Also, I don't think the people who hired him would involve any more people than necessary. I believe he is here for one reason, to plan and carry out another attempt."

Although a little hesitant, the rest of the group seemed to agree.

Kristi continued, "Thanks to Gus, we know he's been here long enough to realize our defense programs are extensive."

"You can bet on it," Gus said. "He probably watched us install the electronics."

Charley Tanner spoke up, "We didn't think much about it at the time, but there was an old guy who watched us trenching the perimeter at Westerfield's town house. He didn't stay long."

"I think our shooter is knowledgeable enough to evaluate our defenses, and I'll bet he doesn't like what he sees," Kristi pointed out. "The question is, under those circumstances, what would you do in his place?"

Joan Voss replied, "Try to force the targets out of the protected area, into one where he has the advantage."

"Exactly."

"You think the sister was killed just to force Joseph and Jeff to leave the area?" Jake asked.

"Not just leave the area. Our killer has to know where they will be and when they'll be there. That way, he can create a plan he feels comfortable with."

"I think Kristi could be right," Sandora said. "What do the rest of you think?"

After a few minutes of "back-and-forth," the group agreed that murdering Joseph's sister probably was only a means to an end.

"That's the reason I thought we needed to meet tonight," Kristi said. "The Westerfields will undoubtedly be at the funeral, playing right into the killer's hands."

"Due to the size of the family and the distances some relatives need to travel, the funeral won't take place for four days. In that time, let's create some diversionary tactics of our own."

"What do you have in mind, Chief?" Charley asked.

"If we use all our around-the-clock teams, we must have at least 20 people guarding Joseph and Jeff at the three locations. Simply moving them to Tibbyville, especially around the funeral home, church, and cemetery, would alert the killer we're onto him."

"Can we avoid that somehow, Kristi?" Sandy questioned. "I get the feeling you have some 'diversionary tactics' in mind."

"I do. Try this on. We create a second funeral around an imaginary corpse. Our dead man, we'll call him Monty I. Cranston after Lamont Cranston, The Shadow. He will be buried a day before Sally, and we will make sure the same rituals occur both days. As mourners, we can evaluate the areas of opportunity our killer might try to capitalize on. If we know where he is likely to hit, hopefully we should be able to stop him.

"Tomorrow, a woman and a couple of men from our group, posing as family members, will arrange for services at the funeral home. Together with the funeral director, they will look over the church as well as the grave site. We'll plan and pay for a regular funeral, except we just won't be able to see Monty in the casket. The funeral itself will be attended by all of us equipped with concealed cameras used to record potential hiding places. With a walk-through like that, we should be able to discover and rectify most weaknesses."

"Kristi, that's one of the craziest schemes I've ever heard," Charley Tanner said.

"Do you think it could work?" she asked.

"Absolutely. It's crazy, but I love it."

"What about the rest of you?" Kristi asked. "I think this could be our best chance to apprehend or eliminate this monster."

"I have to agree with you," Joan replied. "We have a chance to go after him because he thinks he's outsmarted us. We're on the offense, girl. Let's call this, 'the Shadow Project.'"

That brought a smile to Kristi's face. "I like your optimism, Joan. Thank you. Are you all comfortable with it, or do you have any suggestions? I need all the thinking I can get."

"I suggest we guard the Westerfields with our regular force. If they drive, use a standard guard motorcade, front and back cars with a chauffeured car in the middle. Any reduction in protection might tip our hand. We sure as hell don't want this guy to get suspicious because it looks too easy."

"Good point," Charley said, "That applies to the hotel, too."

Gus chipped in, "People visit grave sites all the time. I think elderly ladies mulling around the cemetery would appear perfectly normal. Little old ladies can be very covert."

Everyone contributed a variety of ideas that fine-tuned the concept. As they rallied around their leader, Kristi became the loving coach of a championship team. The relationship was more than friendship – it was trust.

"We'll need to keep a skeleton crew here to run the department as well as keep an eye on the Westerfield properties. Jake, I'm afraid I need you to mind the store."

"I understand," he replied. "Don't worry; I'll take care of things here. Go take this guy out."

"Thank you, Jake. It's good to have you to fall back on. Gus, maybe you could check on the lake house? What do you think?"

"I think you are hard to say no to."

"Before you all arrived tonight, I talked to Mr. Kestler, the funeral director, to be sure he would go along with the sham in the event you agreed to it."

"Sounds like you were quite sure of our reaction, aye, Kristi?" Joan said.

"I was hopeful. Mr. Kestler is trying to get an obituary in tomorrow's local paper. He just changed the name and updated one printed last year."

"I think your Mr. Kestler must be a very cooperative guy," Sandy observed.

"He was a friend of the victim – thought she was a great person."

"That'll help."

"Joan, I would like you, Charley, and one of your people to show up at the funeral home in the morning to put things in motion. It's a long drive, so you'll need an early start."

"Does Mr. Kestler expect us?"

"Yup, he's ready for you."

"Good."

"I still need to call the Seneca County Sheriff to let him know what's happening in his territory. I'm going to try to get him involved. Maybe he will help get a few more female mourners for Monty."

Sandy pointed out, "If roadblocks are needed, we can't get them set up without his help."

"Right, that's a good point. I hope the sheriff is as cooperative as Mr. Kestler. Pick up extra expense money before you leave, and remember, the killer is very good at what he does."

The group didn't budge – they were just not through exploring the plan. Kristi appreciated their enthusiasm for a half hour, then told them to go get some sleep. The conversation moved to the sidewalk.

*****

The morning call to Seneca's County Sheriff wasn't going well.

"Let me get this straight, ma'am. You're tellin' me there is a professional hit man lurking around here who is gonna strike some time within the next four days. Right?" Sheriff Surratt asked cynically.

"That's correct," Kristi replied.

"Your idea to stop him is to have a make-believe funeral on Friday. Right?"

"Right. Only as a means to introduce agents into the area without arousing suspicion."

"You say Kestler has no problem burying an empty casket with all the fanfare as though some poor slob was in it?"

"You got it."

"I'll be damned," the Sheriff said, sighing.

"I thought you would like to know what was going on, and I hoped we could get your people involved."

"Well, I'm glad you didn't carry out this scheme without cluing me in. Thank you for that."

"We intend to keep you up to the minute on everything as the plan unfolds," Kristi said.

"Before it unfolds," Surratt snapped.

"Of course. What we would really like is for you to join in our efforts."

"Exactly what did you have in mind, ma'am?"

Sensing the chief was still very skeptical, an exasperated Kristi went over the reasoning in the utmost detail. Just before Kristi was ready to throw in the towel, Sheriff Surratt asked, "What precisely would you like us to do?"

"First, we need more women, maybe a few children, at the services. I was hoping you could recruit them."

"How do I accomplish this in one day?"

"Money," Kristi responded. "Whatever you need. How about a hundred bucks a head?"

"For a hundred bucks my wife and kids will cry real tears."

"You have $1500 to spread around, but remember we're needing mostly women with a few kids, we have too many men already."

"Okay. There are some church ladies I think might be interested."

"I'll leave all that to you," Kristi knew he just came on board. "I will be there later today with the cash. If you need more, we'll do whatever it takes."

"That must be nice; Seneca County runs on a little smaller budget."

"It's a long story. I'll tell you about it over a beer."

"That sounds good. What else can we help you with, ma"am?"

"Please call me Kristi. There's one more thing we would appreciate."

"And that is?"

"Design, and be ready to implement, a roadblock system that seals off all escape routes from the funeral home, church and cemetery."

"I doubt I'd have the personnel to do it right."

"How about off-duties? We'll pick up the tab."

"It could happen. Let me do a little checking."

"Thank you. We really need your help. I'll see you later this afternoon with some money."

"I have to tell you, ma'am, this may be the most unorthodox, bizarre operation I've ever been part of."

"See you later, Sheriff, and thank you for keeping an open mind. We appreciate your cooperation."

"I'm looking forward to meeting you, ma'am." Sheriff Surratt hung up shaking his head with a grin on his face.

CHAPTER 24
CONTAMINATION

Marketing executives, from Product Managers to Division Presidents, loved nosing about in the New Product Laboratory. Checking on their precious brands was a legitimate chance to get out of their offices and out into the world of people who actually produced something tangible.

A little winded, Gordon Wieldey and his friend Dick McLane, the Purchasing Department's Materials Director, arrived at the top of the steps to the third floor. They were greeted by a sign, "DO NOT ENTER WITHOUT COMPLETE LABORATORY ATTIRE." A closet to the right of the door contained "one-size-fits-all" paper lab coats, hair and shoe coverings. Smiling at each other they climbed into their temporary duds. Funny how dressing in paper suits becomes a great equalizer – one can't tell the officers from the peons.

Wieldey and McLane "glad-handed" each member of the team tending five mixing machines resembling miniature cement mixers. The hoppers contained carefully measured amounts of the ingredients used in ExRelief Cold Medicine. They asked a few general questions as they poked their executive noses in areas they didn't begin to understand. The workers didn't mind, though, because Wieldey and McLane appeared very pleased with each person's efforts. Surprisingly, they spent most of the morning observing the progress.

Having previously tested the contents, a standard procedure, and working in a humidity controlled area, no one initially suspected foul play when the tablets failed during the pressing stage. After reconsidering the results, Diane Lackey, one of the more curious Quality Control technicians kept thinking, *how did water find its way into the original batch destined for the national roll-out?*

As it turned out, Diane Lackey and Carol Ackerman were neighbors who often took their break together. "I just don't see how any type of liquid could get into the product–we are so careful about humidity," Diane said with a puzzled look.

"What do you mean, exactly?" Carol asked.

"I mean it's my job to be sure the humidity doesn't fluctuate any more than three percent. And, I can tell you, it didn't change one iota all week."

"I see," Carol responded trying not to alarm her, "I wouldn't worry about it."

"It just doesn't make sense. If there really was moisture in the mixers, it didn't get there by wavering humidity."

"Forget it," Carol said trying to put her at ease; all the while suspecting this might be more important than she could imagine.

*****

"Jeff?" Carol said, walking into his office.

"You look like the Cheshire cat. What's on your mind?"

She relayed her friend Diane's suspicion. Jeff didn't respond immediately, but when he did, Carol could sense resolve building within him. "I think your friend Diane is a very smart girl. The questions are: Did an employee add liquid to the mixture? And, if so, why was it done? Even more important, how do we keep it from happening again?"

"Maybe your grandpa was right? Didn't he suspect people promoting Bayer were trying to delay the ExRelief roll-out?"

"Actually, we both thought it was a good possibility. Now I'd say it's a probability."

"Well, do you want me to get Security on the phone?"

"No. Let's stir the pot a little. I think a memo to Security asking the question, 'who introduced water into the mixers?' will get a lot more attention. We'll suggest they review tapes from the new surveillance cameras and compile a list of people who had access to the mixing area."

"You mean a list of possible suspects?"

"Exactly."

"That's going to turn a few heads, all right," Carol said with a broad grin. "You have a devious side, Jeff Westerfield, a very devious side."

"We're dealing with very devious people," he replied.

After dictating the memo, he instructed Carol to back-date it by one day, then hand carry the original to Security as well as copies to the Lab, Manufacturing, Purchasing and Quality Control. He was emphatic that Gordon get his copy well after the others. Finally, Jeff asked her to make sure her friend Diane kept her suspicions to herself. He didn't want her viewed as a whistle blower or troublemaker.

A surprised Diane appreciated the consideration, especially after Carol explained that her observations were likely to create quite a stir. The next morning, Diane found a box of chocolates at her desk with an unsigned note that read, "Good Work."

Dick McLane called Wieldey before the memo landed on his desk. Gordon, after a few minutes of panic searching, located it in his in-basket. "What do you think?" McLane asked.

"Just stay calm, Dick. We are not going to have a problem here–I guarantee it."

Gordon Wieldey always pondered his options before acting. After three hours of office seclusion, he decided it was time to get more information.

Poking her head in Jeff's door, without a change in expression, Carol announced, "Gordon Wieldey would like to see you in his office when you have a chance."

"Sooner than I expected. Thank you, Carol."

Jeff thought to himself, *I think I'll let him stew awhile*. He called Lori to use up a little time. It's amazing how long it takes to say nothing when you're talking to the right person.

An hour later Jeff arrived at Gordon's office; the secretary announced his arrival. Opening the door, a congenial Wieldey said, "Come on in, Jeff. Thanks for coming over so soon."

Thinking, *the man can play the game*, Jeff asked, "How are you, Gordon? What can I do for you?"

Ignoring the first question, Gordon said, "I just got your memo on the humidity problem."

"And?" Jeff said, without showing emotion.

"Don't you think it's a tad accusatory? It might be a good idea to call a meeting of the people you sent the memo to and make sure they know they aren't under suspicion. We don't need to create enemies if we're going to pull off this introduction."

"You're welcome to do that, Gordon, but I meant the memo to be an accusation. It's obvious to me that someone, or possibly a small group of our colleagues, is intentionally undermining our efforts to get ExRelief to market in time for this year's cold season."

"Do you really think so?"

Jeff knew Gordon's ego wouldn't allow him to play dumb for long. "How can you deny the obvious?"

"Obvious? What is so obvious?" Gordon stammered.

"Sabotage, Gordon – Industrial sabotage."

"That's a strong statement. Would you mind explaining it?"

"First of all, I happen to be the ExRelief Product Manager who someone tried to kill. I think that's a pretty strong clue. You may recall, we've discussed many of the 'roadblocks' over the past few months. Start by looking at approvals. They took more than twice as long as normal and they were held up by departments like QC with no pertinent reason to delay the project. Then, Purchasing's Cheap-Charley decision on the package changed the product image from quality to junk. Did you give them the authority to make graphic changes?"

"Of course not," Gordon snapped back.

"I didn't either, but don't you think, at the very least, they would have run it by us?"

"Yes, I have to agree." Gordon was making his turnaround.

"Timing was backed up for months by that little maneuver. Then, on the rerun, our suppliers experienced an epidemic of vandalism. Their presses were so badly damaged they were forced to crawl to their competitors for help. Do you think that was just coincidence, Gordon?"

"You've made your point. I'll call Security and get those tapes," Gordon said, knowing full well that if they still existed he'd be moved to the top of the list of suspects.

"Okay," Jeff said. "We should also get a copy of the humidity control record, just to make doubly sure we didn't just have some technical problem. I'll walk up there myself so they understand that I need the report now."

As Jeff left, Gordon said to himself, *I wish I'd thought of that damn humidity variation data.*

Simultaneously, Jeff thought to himself, *I'll bet good old Gordo didn't stop to think about the humidity record.*

Ironically, Gordon organized the meeting to take action on Jeff's memo. The head of Security, Rowland Thomas, apologetically explained that the tapes showing the mixers during the correct time period couldn't be located. He said the equipment was in perfect condition and there was ample film in the cameras, but unfortunately his people could not come up with the tape.

"How is that possible?" a manufacturing manager asked.

"I don't have a good answer, ma'am, but we're still looking."

"I would like to suggest an answer," Jeff broke in. "One of your people intentionally took, or recorded over, the tape."

Thomas was on his feet. "How dare you accuse my department of something so devious?"

"How dare you, sir, a person responsible to protect us, be oblivious to the sabotage taking place before your eyes?"

"Jeff Westerfield, I resent that. We do a damn good job. We always have."

"Rowland, drop your defenses for a moment and look at the facts."

"Okay," Thomas said, "I'm listening." He realized, in spite of currently being only a Product Manager, Jeff was destined to run the whole show someday, and he liked working at Wesfield.

Holding the humidity report in the air, Jeff softly stated, "There hasn't been a significant variation in humidity in the mixing area for months. The only way liquid could have gotten into the product mix was for someone to have put it there. Assuming I am right, destroying the evidence also seems logical. If anyone can imagine a different scenario, I would like to hear it."

A long silence consumed the room before Thomas finally broke the tension. "We will talk with each person from the manufacturing crew and, of course, make sure we have the surveillance tapes after every shift."

"Thank you, Rowland," Gordon said with a smile as he stood up to signal that the meeting was over.

Jeff asked Rowland to stay a few minutes after the meeting. When they were alone, he affirmed that he knew Rowland would never do anything to hurt Wesfield. Then, although it took some time, he elaborated on the reasons that led him to believe someone was methodically sabotaging the ExRelief launch. He said, "Rowland, I really need your help. We've got to discover who's working against us."

"You can depend on me, Jeff."

"I knew I could. There are a couple of things we might look into."

"And they are?" Rowland couldn't help liking Jeff, in spite of the fact that he knew he had just been recruited into his army.

"Let's find who was overseeing the surveillance cameras when the lapse occurred."

"And?" Rowland said with a smile.

"Could you check with the manufacturing folks and put together a list of the visitors they can remember? This would be on the QT."

"No problem. I'll get back to you as soon as I can."

"Thank you, Rowland."

CHAPTER 25
BANK RECORDS

Using the intercom, Carol Ackerman buzzed Jeff to tell him Mr. Thomas was on the line. She smiled to herself, *I know what you're calling about – being on the inside is such fun.*

"Rowland, how are you doing? I didn't expect to hear from you so soon."

"I think I've got everything we need."

"That's great. I'll be right up." It pleased him to hear "everything *we* need," rather than "everything *you* need."

"No, I've got to come down anyway. Are you free?"

"Come on down."

A couple of minutes later, Rowland was sitting in Jeff's office. The list was a lot longer than he expected; apparently a lot of people liked to stroll through the plant. The paper contained fourteen names, three of whom were women.

Rowland pointed out that his new Security Specialist, Nancy Woolf, was overseeing the new camera recorders for the duration of the initial run. He said, "We might want to take a real close look at her – she came to us from the company that installed the system."

"Really?"

"We hired her because she understood the system, its installation, and she knows the 'ins-and-outs' of the equipment."

"I don't know why," Jeff said, "but it never dawned on me to consider a woman as a possible industrial clandestine agent."

"Think about it, Jeff. I can tell you from personal experience women can be devious and conniving." Rowland left the office humming to himself with a smirk on his face.

Jeff asked Carol into his office. "Here's the list of plant wanderers that Rowland's people could remember."

"Do we need to combine it with the names from the original security investigation?" Carol asked.

"Right. Did you notice we have a couple of people on both lists?" Jeff asked.

"I sure noticed one in particular. Gordon Wieldey."

"Do a combined list with no title. Keep one copy in your bottom left desk drawer instead of the files. I'll get the original to Kristi in the morning. No other copies. Okay?"

"You got it, Mr. Westerfield." She seldom called him that in private, but it was her way of showing she liked his take-charge attitude.

"Carol."

"Yes."

"Thanks for your help. Nice job."

Jeff left a message asking Kristi to meet him in the morning, same time, same doughnut shop. She had already ordered for both of them when he arrived. Jeff beamed as he told the story of how the combined list was created. He went over every detail, crediting Carol for going beyond his expectations.

Kristi thought to herself, *What a capable, generous man. I can see a lot of Joseph in him.*

The phone was ringing when Carol got to her desk. She answered with a breathy "Hello, Carol Ackerman."

"Good morning, this is Marilynn Christopher. Do you know who I am?"

"I surely do, Chief Christopher. What can I do for you?"

"According to Jeff Westerfield, you've already done an admirable job on our behalf. I just wanted to thank you."

"Well, thank you so much," Carol said, pleasantly surprised. "It's nice of you to take the time to call. I do have one little concern."

"Shoot."

"I was supposed to put a dot by names that were on both lists. Did Jeff catch it by any chance?"

"He did."

"I should have known. Have a great day."

The list was still a work in progress. Kristi added the names of people whom she suspected received payment of one kind or another.

She throughly studied it one more time. *Time to do a little banking.*

I. J. Wienbergen, engraved in Old English letters on a gold plated door plaque, signified he was the main man at South Station Bank & Trust. Plush wall-to-wall carpet kept noise to a library level. After being escorted between a row of empty desks to his office, Kristi was greeted with a big smile and a handshake. "Good to see you again, Miss Kristi."

How would he know I'm a Miss. Maybe he's just southern. He wears a buttoned suit jacket, and it's hot as hell in here. Not a single hair out of place – must be a lot of grease on that noggin. "It's nice to see you too, Mr. Wienbergen."

"What can I do for you?"

"Do you remember our conversation about tracing the account activity of people who could be involved in industrial sabotage?"

"Of course." So far, the smile never left his face.

Handing him the paper, she said, "Well, here is the list we've assembled."

The smile turned up-side-down. "We're not going to hand you the record of this many patrons. Why, there must be over 20 names on this list."

"23, to be exact."

"That's way too many," he blustered.

"Look Mr. Wienbergen, you know as well as I do that there is nothing protected in financial records. If I need to, I'll come back with a subpoena."

"Maybe you better do that."

Kristi realized this self-righteous jerk was huffing and puffing just to show her how important he was. She wasn't falling for his theatrics. "Okay, I will. Before I do, however, you can be sure Joseph Westerfield, who probably represents your largest personal account, not to mention that he sits on your board of directors, will know you think his life and his grandson's life are not important enough for you to honor your agreement." She reached across his desk, grabbing the phone, "I'll gladly call him now if you like."

"Now, now, little lady, let's not jump to conclusions."

"I'm not a 'little lady.' I'm Chief Marilynn Christopher to you, the Chief of Police in your town, and I will not accept anything but total cooperation from you and every member of your bank. Do we understand each other."

"Yes, ma'am."

"Good. For each name on the list, I need a two-year transaction history for all monies that flowed in or out of their accounts at South Station Bank & Trust. That includes their personal and business accounts, wives' or husbands' accounts, children's accounts, IRAs, CDs, any college savings or Christmas clubs, and any other accounts I may have missed. I am particularly interested in large deposits or a series of deposits that add up to large amounts. They will probably be in the form of wire transfers, or direct deposits. Any problem?"

"When do you need this information?"

"If at all possible, I'd like to get it tomorrow."

"Tomorrow?" he repeated as though it were a monumental task.

"Look Mr. Wienbergen, lives are at stake here."

"I'll see what I can do."

He isn't a happy banker, but even with all his carrying on, every hair is still in place. "Thank you, Sir; we knew we could depend on you."

Wienbergen, being a macho chest pounder, was too proud to do anything that could cause him to look bad. Late the next afternoon, a folder containing the requested information was dropped off at the station. After adding copies of the credit card receipts from the boat rental and car rental involved in Sally's death, Kristi had the names and numbers she needed to start some major snooping.

*****

When he was a Special Agent in the Justice Department, John Snowden was known as "Mr. Money." He got that nickname because he was the most proficient man at "following-the-money" the department ever had. His partner, Jay Holmes, was a former FBI agent whose forte was racketeering surveillance. Holmes treated the RICO law (Racketeer Influenced and Corrupt Organizations Act) as his ticket to an eavesdropper's free-for-all. He tapped many big names in the criminal world, but his methods were often challenged in court.

When Snowden and Holmes broke from the establishment to form S & H Investigation, they were amazed to discover their former employers quickly became their largest clients.

Finally, they were being paid what they were worth –setting their own timetables – without anyone looking over their shoulders. Funny how valuable they became once they jumped ship.

Jay picked up the phone on the first ring. "Do you know a Marilynn Christopher?" he shouted with his hand over the phone speaker.

"Sure. She's the one who got me to do the freebie involving the construction people." Grabbing the phone, he cheerfully said, "Kristi. Good to hear from you."

"Hi John. First, I'd like to thank you again for helping me out."

"It's okay, it wasn't that complicated. How do you like running the big show in a small town?"

"It's not that different, except it can get very personal at times. I called because I have some good news."

"You've decided to go out with me?"

"Anytime your wife gives the okay. I have another job for you, and this time I have funding."

"Funding's good. When will I get the particulars?"

"I sent it special delivery so it should get there sometime today or tomorrow."

"Great. We're not too busy right now, so we'll jump right on it."

They went on to chat for awhile, Kristi inquiring about common friends and John checking to see if she was doing alright. Finally John said, "Thanks for the project, Kristi, I'll call you when I get the package."

A middle-aged postman strolled in with the package close to 4:00 that afternoon. John ripped it open and skimmed the note stapled to the packet of papers inside. According to Kristi, Gordon Wieldey, one of the names on the list, was a better than 90% possibility of being guilty of taking money for industrial espionage. She went on to say, "If your analysis of account activity confirms my suspicions, and I believe it will, you might consider a 'same-day-activities-analysis' with the other names on the list." She also mentioned Painter Inc., and Manhattan Bank & Trust, as a likely money source.

Kristi is one sharp cop, John thought, smiling to himself, as he dialed her number.

"South Station Police Department."

"Chief Christopher, please."

"This is Chief Christopher."

"Kristi, this is John. Let's talk time and money."

CHAPTER 26
GUNTHER'S EVALUATION

Gunther drove the battered rental into Hopkins' Airport at dusk. Carrying a briefcase and two heavy bags, he walked briskly from short-term parking to the bus and taxi loading area. An unkempt taxi driver took him to Cleveland's downtown Hilton. From there it was a little over an hour drive to Tibbyville. He registered and arranged to rent a Chevrolet Monte Carlo under the name Verner Delmar. He bought a paper and ordered dinner in his room.

Pleased with himself and the plan he had masterminded, his dreams were of success. *Right on cue, like puppets on a string, you foolish flies are about to land in my web.* Having the ability to manipulate a mark's movements gave him a sense of superiority that, he believed, separated him from others in his field.

Jolted by his alarm, Gunther woke with enthusiasm. "It's time to get to work," he said to himself. Grabbing a couple of doughnuts and a coffee to go, he located his rental and headed to Tibbyville. He arrived midmorning, drove around to get a feel for the town and found a newspaper at the drug store. It was an eight-pager called *The Tibbyville Truth* and came out in the morning, Monday through Friday. Gunther picked up the Tuesday edition and scanned the obituary section hoping to nail down the times scheduled for Sally's services. It was the second listing.

"Sally Ramona LaPoint, 70, died Monday as a result of a hit-and-run auto accident in front of her family farm home in Seneca County. The daughter of Joseph and Ramona Westerfield, she was born June 19, 1905 in LaPorte, Indiana. Surviving Sally are her loving husband Claude, daughter Sally, sons, Nolan, Joseph, Claude Jr., William, and brother, Joseph Westerfield."

The notice detailed an extensive list of Sally's personal achievements and interests, including volunteer work, schooling, social activities and religious affiliations. The last paragraph contained the information he was looking for: "The family will receive friends from 7:00 to 9:00 Friday evening at Kestler Funeral Home. Funeral services will be held at 11:00 AM Saturday, at St. John the Baptist Episcopal Church with the Reverend Alvin Livingston officiating. Burial will follow at Christ the King Cemetery."

After studying Sally's write-up, the words "Reverend Alvin Livingston" caught his eye in the obituary just above hers. As he read the details he realized some 90-year-old geezer named Cranston was being laid to rest with similar rituals. The timing wasn't quite the same as Sally's, but the funeral home, church and the cemetery were all identical. The one important difference: everything was taking place a day earlier, reception Thursday night and funeral Friday morning.

A pleased Gunther realized, *I'm getting a dress rehearsal, how lucky is that. It's time to see what Kestler's has to offer.*

*****

Kristi's enthusiastic team filtered into Tibbyville right on schedule. Being defensively structured, agents developed the ability to stay alert, survey and analyze, but their assignments were usually rather routine, often boring. This idea was bold and everyone approached it with extra passion. They still had to protect, but this time they were also trying to snare a ruthless killer.

Joan Voss and Charley Tanner walked into the funeral home just before noon. They didn't look like a typical married couple. Charley, partially bald and fifty-nine, was at least twenty years older than Joan, and a couple of inches shorter. Both walked with a confident motion and seemed to move in unison.

Kestler acknowledged them as he escorted an elderly gentleman to the door. "Thank you for considering us," he told him, as he closed the outer doors.

He turned to Joan and Charley with his most consoling look. "What can I do for you folks?"

So caring, so concerned, so understanding, so helpful –amazing how morticians were born with faces that so completely reflected those compassionate traits. Mr. Kestler, who identified himself as the funeral director, was no exception until he realized Charley and Joan were there to make arrangements for "The Shadow's" services.

A grin engulfed his face. "Yes, of course. Monty I. Cranston, poor soul. His obituary appeared in this morning's paper. It will be a closed casket affair. May I be so bold as to ask what does the 'I' stands for?"

Although she hadn't thought about it, with a straight face Joan answered, "Why, invisible, of course."

"Of course," Kestler said, still grinning. "I have to tell you a funeral home owner's life is dull to say the least. Being part of this project is the most fun I've ever had at the office, so to speak."

"Glad to make your day," Charley said, "But remember, we have to pull this off with all the sadness as if Monty were really in the box."

"I understand. What would you like to do first?"

"Follow your usual procedure. Show us the church and the burial site," Charley said.

"Does Rev. Livingston know the casket will be empty?"

"It's a 'need to know' situation. No need to share that information with him," Joan answered.

The grin re-emerged as they headed for the church. Kestler was enjoying the deception. "May I ask just why we are going through this charade?"

Joan answered, "You can ask, but all I can tell you is, we need to know exactly what will happen during the LaPoint funeral on Friday."

Charley and Joan took notes and a few pictures, as they observed possible vulnerable points at each location.

The funeral home entrance was protected by a huge blue spruce surrounded with low junipers that covered the center of the circular drive. The front door, where people would be dropped off, was completely obscured from sight. "Next, we can see St. John's church," Kestler announced.

Although the church was 40 years old, a master architect must have been given a free hand to display his forward thinking talents. Simplicity and continuity formed with powerful truss-beams lifted your eyes up to an enormous stained glass crucifixion scene, taking up most of the outer wall. Twenty feet in front of the wall, a freestanding altar appeared to be below the massive stained glass cross, thus becoming the focal point from every pew.

"I love this church," Joan said, as she spun around a full 360 degrees. "If I get married again this would be a definite possibility."

"Mr. Vargas, the fellow I took here earlier, liked it too."

"What did you call him?" Charley asked, recognizing the name.

"Vargas. Victor Vargas. He was just leaving when you came in."

"Was he making arrangements?" Joan inquired.

"No. His mother is terminally ill. She lives somewhere down south, but wants to be laid to rest here in Tibbyville."

"And you say he was the guy leaving your office when we came in?" Charley gazed straight ahead with his lips pursed.

"That's right."

"Did you notice anything unusual about him, Mr. Kestler?" Charley questioned.

"Now that you mention it, I thought his wig was a terrible fit."

"Anything else?" Charley didn't want to appear to be giving Kestler the third degree, but he wanted to be doubly sure of his suspicions.

"His hands didn't appear to be as old as his face."

"How's that?"

"His face looked old. In fact, he could have had a little accent color on the wrinkles, but his hands didn't show the same signs of aging. In my profession you notice stuff like that."

"I'm sure you do, and I appreciate your abilities," Charley said. "You've been more helpful than you could ever know."

"Okay, let's move along," Joan said. *It looks like Kristi was right, this is not just an elaborate waste of time. The killer is here and as Sherlock Homes would say, "The game is afoot."*

The front steps of St. John the Baptist Church were just the opposite of the funeral home's. "This entrance is wide open," Tanner noted. "We'll need careful positioning here."

"So are the fields across the highway," Joan replied. "A sniper could trench in for a shot, but his getaway would be dubious at best."

"Remember, he probably doesn't realize our people are on to him," responded Charley. "The cars will have to be watched closely while everyone's in church. I think this guy would use a car bomb as easily as a gun. Don't you?"

"Yes, I'd bet on it. Or, he might just crawl in a back seat and pop someone when they get in. Let's try to make sure all doors get locked."

"I see your point, but I doubt it. No escape," Charley said. "Let's take your standard route to the cemetery, okay, Mr. Kestler?"

"No problem."

The car pulled away from the curb and down two blocks before it was stopped by a train. It took over five minutes before the road was clear. "You allow an extra ten minutes for trains when you live in Tibbyville," Kestler said, as they turned left, paralleling the tracks heading west.

Charley looked for potential hiding places on the left side of the road – mostly tracks and ditches. Joan checked out the houses and farms on the right. It was only a preliminary appraisal, but their focus intensified with the knowledge that the hit-man was lurking in the area.

The Oak Garden cemetery housed generations of local forefathers from Tibbyville and the surrounding area. It was on a slight hill, a full city block back from the county highway. Turning left, the entrance road rose slightly as they crossed the tracks again. They had traveled only half a block when the blacktop split, forming two single lane roads. A ONE WAY sign pointed right, with DO NOT ENTER on the left.

The road eventually passed through an opening in the center of a sewer-brick fence about four feet high. A wrought-iron gate was wide open with weeds growing around it, indicating it hadn't been closed in years. The wall and entrance must have been built long ago, because today's cars barely managed to squeeze through. Once inside, the narrow road followed the perimeter of the very large "T" shaped cemetery, eventually coming out through another narrow opening 30 yards to the left of the entrance.

The Shadow's grave was being dug when they arrived. After standing close to the excavator for a few minutes, the group casually walked past the spot where Sally would be laid to rest. Since the entire group would be evaluating the area at The Shadow's service, they quickly did a general survey and returned to the car. No need to attract attention that might signal the assassin.

They checked into at the Tibbyville House Motel, dropped off their bags, and met in the bar to compare notes. Both felt Kestler Funeral Home was the least likely target location, the cemetery the most likely, and the church and funeral procession route somewhere in the middle.

They could hardly wait for Kristi to get there to tell her the assassin was moving about freely, without any apparent indication he suspected they were aware of his efforts.

PART THREE

CHAPTER 27
BARDOLINO

Ten thousand years ago God, using a dark ice mass, slowly gouged, heaped, dredged and forced the land up, down, back and forth until He created the Alpine mountain range. On the Eastern side of the range, His glacier penetrated over 11,000 feet deep into the ground. Then the earth-warmed water filled God's divot, forming what is now called Lake Garda. Tidy vineyards and olive groves decorate the foothills along the southeastern rim of the lake. Surrounding mountains stand guard, protecting a handful of Alpine-Mediterranean communities and the people who live there.

Bardolino, Italy, one of Lake Garda's special villages, is where Sophia spent her childhood. Her house, the Villa de Antisdale, with thick masonry-stone walls, heavy oak doors, and terra cotta tiled roof, was embedded in a flowered hillside.

The peaceful, safe environment should have been the perfect place to heal her emotional wounds. For over 20 years, Sophia's loving mom and dad, along with the best doctors in Europe, did everything in their power to bring her out of her private purgatory. Their efforts were only partially successful.

Having totally blocked out adulthood, Sophia found a form of serenity by reverting back to a happier time, her pre-teen years. She seemed to enjoy God's little creatures, squirrels, birds, butterflies and chameleons. Every morning she took it upon herself to provide a fresh bouquet of flowers to decorate the kitchen table. She always smiled when her mother told her, "How pretty, thank you, sweetheart." It was not unusual to hear her softly humming a children's song while strolling about the garden. Sophia had found a world where she could survive.

Half awake, half asleep, a muddled scene was recurring in Sophia's subconscious. *Walking dangerously close to the rocky edge of the mountain ridge, she could see the tall handsome man with a beautiful mysterious child on the hill across the valley. He lifted the little one high in the air; her long auburn hair and sheer light blue dress flowed freely in the wind, as she smiled her precious smile, beckoning Sophia to come to her.* The dream was always the same; no matter how hard she tried, it was impossible to cross the valley. They were waiting for her, hoping someday she'd get across. She knew they wanted to be with her as much as she longed for them. The dream made her feel happy and sad at the same time.

"Sophia! Rise and shine, sleepyhead," her mother called.

"I'm up," she responded, still lying under the covers. She rolled out, shuffled to the bathroom, sprinkled a trace of water on her face and moseyed into the kitchen. "Morning, Mama."

"Good morning, sweetheart. How did you sleep?"

"Pretty well."

"You want a buttered roll with milk and orange-juice? Raisins?"

"Yes, thank you."

"How about a banana?"

"That sounds good, too, Mama."

Ida, having been widowed for a year and a half, realized Sophia helped her survive her grief just by being there. She was someone to care for, and Italian mothers need someone to mother.

Frequent trips to Bardolino were not enough to satisfy Jeff's need to be part of his mother's life. Sophia, being almost a stranger to him, was confusing as a child and unacceptable now that he was a man. He and Joseph both often asked Ida and Sophia to come to America. Ida knew it would come soon enough, but for now she and Sophia were happy living in the house that was home. They were getting along fine; Joseph had seen to that.

Ida washed, Sophia wiped; the same routine every day. When the last dish was put away, Ida said, "You run along, sweetheart, and get us some pretty flowers for the kitchen."

There was only a whisper of wind, but it carried a multitude of garden fragrances and the sound of distant church bells echoing between the hills, as Sophia carefully descended the stone steps to her favorite place, Mama's garden.

How the garden came to be had always been one of Ida's most treasured memories. Alfonso Antisdale, having saved a small amount of hard-earned money, bought a small cottage on two acres of land shortly after marrying Ida. The first project on his "honey-do list" was a flower garden that he took great pains to build exactly as Ida wanted. To solve the problem of planting on a hill, he created the garden on three terraces, each three to four feet above the other, with steps on both sides following the new land contour. In front of each terrace, a wall was constructed using mortar and stone, which was plentiful all over the property. Using two wheelbarrows, he hauled cultivatable soil up to each plateau. Ida pitched right in; at the bottom of the hill, she filled alternate wheelbarrows. They always liked working together.

Ida planted clumps of taller flowers, like hollyhocks, against the walls with enough space between each clump to be able to lean over the wall to work with shorter plants. Like most flower gardens, the work was never done, but the rewards were ever changing as each season blended into the next. Without Alfonso around to do the heavy lifting, the garden seemed harder to maintain, but it was always a labor of love.

*****

Roberto Modica of Worldwide Protection Ltd. directed the surveillance program designed to protect Sophia and her mother. Modica was stocky with thinning hair, older than your average operative, but you knew by his handshake he was at the top of his game. He managed to rent an overpriced hillside pasture directly across from Ida's cottage. Modica and his two associates, Bella Salzarulo and Tony DiMarco, put sheep to graze in the field and trained Border Collies as a cover.

They quickly built a partially open lean-to shed to use as an observation blind. It was perfectly positioned to see over the low stone fence surrounding the lot, with a total view of the Antisdale garden, including the front of the house and down both sides. Although the house had been expanded many times, it was still built into the lower part of the hill allowing an observer to see the land above the roof.

Modica smiled to himself as he realized he couldn't remember ever being able to see the land on all four sides of a house at the same time. The shed would be manned 24 hours a day.

Always outside working with their animals, the team instantly became part of the neighborhood. At the first opportunity, they made friends with the ladies on the other side of the road. Bella, the youngest of the agents, and Sophia took to each other the moment they met. Ida appreciated the new relationship because her daughter had few friends. Worldwide Protection Ltd.'s people didn't miss a trick. They were every bit as good at clandestine work as their billing claimed.

"Is that an upside-down bathtub with wheels?" DiMarco asked, as the odd shaped orange and white vehicle headed up the hill.

"That, my boy, is a Westfalia Camper," Modica replied.

"Weird."

"Not really. Volkswagen has been making that critter for 20 years. They call it a Volkswagen Bus. It's becoming more popular every year. Did you notice the windows had curtains?"

"I can't say I did," DiMarco answered.

"Hard to know who or what's in there. We better keep an eye on it. Especially since I'm not aware of any campgrounds up the hill. The Westfalia Camper doesn't quite fit in this part of the country."

"You want me to take a ride up the road, see if I can find out where he went?"

"Can't hurt," Modica said.

Tony DiMarco took off without another word.

Modica watched the gentle Sophia glide around the garden. Her first stop was the little grotto built into the bottom wall. It surrounded a St. Francis statue holding a bird in each hand and one on his shoulder. With head bowed and hands folded, she spent several minutes at the grotto. Modica assumed that was where she said her morning prayers. Once she moved on to gather flowers, he noticed each selection was thoughtfully pondered. It was obvious to him only the prettiest bouquet would be good enough for Sophia. Her world was at peace, and if he had anything to do with it, that wasn't about to change.

Two hours later, DiMarco returned with a concerned look on his face. Modica was quick to ask, "How did you come out?"

"Not so good. I missed them on the way up," DeMarco replied, "But, on the way back, I spotted their bus parked about seventy-five meters down an overgrown lane."

"How far back?" Modica asked.

"It's about a half mile up the road. I didn't stop; thought maybe you'd want me to walk back along the hedgerows and olive groves."

Before Modica could answer, the Volkswagen Bus slowly cruised by on its way back down the hill. "Did you see that?" DiMarco pointed. "Two guys were in the front seat, I'm sure of it,"

"What I saw was, they were taking a very close look at the ladies' cottage. Fortunately for us, they didn't even look this way. I don't think they even know we're here," Modica said.

"That can't hurt," DiMarco replied.

"Follow 'em, Tony. Give them plenty of space, but let's find out where they're camped. Nose around a little; I'd like to know who they are and what they're up to."

Tony DiMarco was like a happy coyote, getting a second chance to stalk the prey. He was cautious, but thorough, an adept undercover agent.

It was after seven when the Border Collies started barking. Modica peeked out of the shed to see DeMarco's pickup pulling into the field. As he walked out to meet him, once again he asked, "How did you come out?"

"A lot better," DeMarco answered, still embarrassed about missing the bus on the way up the hill. He handed Modica a couple of sandwiches. "Thought you and Bella might be hungry."

"Good thinking. So what about the Volkswagen?"

"The boys, there are only two of them, are camping at Caesius Villa, an over-priced resort on the south side of town. It's first class, overlooks Lake Garda, with a restaurant, tennis courts, horses, the works. They looked totally out of place; they had 'thug' written all over them."

"Did you get names, descriptions . . ."

DiMarco cut him off. "I did better than that. Our office people are running a trace on the vehicle, as well as checking the name on the driver's license they used at check-in, as we speak. The license was Sicilian, belonging to Alto Camilo Cabellos. The concierge told me his buddy's name was something like Bonito or Benny. He said, 'They're quite a pair, but what are you gonna do – they paid cash.' If they both belong to the same 'camorra' organization, we'll probably find out who he is, too."

"Do you mind taking the night watch? I'm going back to the hotel to call the boss. I'll send Bella back around six."

"Nah, let her sleep. I'll be okay," DiMarco said.

*****

"Hello, this is Chief Christopher."

"Hello Chief. This is Roberto Modica with Worldwide."

"I know who you are Mr. Modica–I'm glad you called. Did you have any trouble running me down?"

"Jake, at your office, gave me this number. The reason I called is, I thought you'd want to know what I believe is going on at the ladies' cottage."

"Great. Give me your analysis."

"I am almost positive two men are going to try to kidnap one or both of the ladies."

"Go on," Kristi said, "you've got my attention."

"They've been casing the place, driving back and forth at different times during the day. If they wanted to take the women out, I think they would have tried by now. It wouldn't have been all that difficult. And, they're so intent on watching the cottage, I don't think they have a clue we're on to them."

"They sure sound like a threat," Kristi said.

"They drive a camper, but stay at a hotel. So why do they need a camper?"

"Good question. I agree with your conclusions, Mr. Modica. It sounds like they are going to attempt a kidnapping. It makes perfect sense," she noted, "hostages would create a great deal of leverage. Killing the ladies wouldn't accomplish a thing."

Modica continued his critique, "I also suspect they could be members of the Sicilian Mafia which has a history of 'snatch and

161

grab.' According to my partner, they've got the hoodlum, cocky-but-stupid look. They're scheduled to exit their hotel in the morning, so I would expect them to make their move tomorrow."

"Sounds to me like you've done your homework."

"We'll see, Chief Kristi . . . We'll see."

CHAPTER 28
THE TRIP

What now, Joseph thought, as the ringing phone interrupted his blank stare. Kristi, imagining his grief, didn't want to call, but thought he needed to know the conclusions of the meeting and the mock funeral plans. She tried to spin the group's deductions so they were not quite so directly related to him. He was too numb to react to the plan, but not numb enough to miss the significance of why Sally was killed. He knew her death was somehow related to the Wesfield takeover. Sadly, in spite of Kristi's attempt at softening the blow, he now understood that he was the "why." Guilt piled on grief can become an unbearable burden.

Silence became part of the conversation. Feeling his devastation, she patiently waited before asking, "Is there anything I can do, Joseph?"

"No. I'm having a hard time justifying things in my own mind."

"Do you want me to come over to talk about it?"

"No. Thank you. I'm not thinking straight right now, and Jeff and I and are about ready to leave for Tibbyville. I just can't seem to get myself out to the car."

"I understand. You can always get hold of me through the office number. Call me day or night, even if it's just because you don't want to be alone – okay? Okay?"

"Thank you, Kristi. You've become a valued friend."

The comment caught her by surprise; she felt the same way, and she knew Joseph was not casual about relationships. Tears welled up in her eyes, and they wouldn't stop. She was glad no one was there to see her. *I'm becoming too close to these people to be objective.*

Kristi used going out of town as an excuse to call Russ. In spite of her team's camaraderie, she'd been feeling very much alone. She hoped a few moments with her special friend would help.

"Hi, Kristi. How are you doing?"

He always sounds so happy when I call. "How about grabbing a cup of coffee?"

They met at Judd's, one of the few remaining drugstores old-fashioned enough to feature a food and soda fountain. Russ, sitting poised with his usual welcoming smile, was already into a pastry when Kristi straddled her stool. "Okay. What's up?" He knew he was about to become a sounding board.

"Thanks for meeting me," she said, flashing him her sweetest smile.

Kristi placed her order. After a bit of small talk, she finally got around to her concern. "I've been second guessing myself all night," she sighed.

"We all have second thoughts once in awhile." Russ was as patient as he could be.

Kristi explained her theory and detailed her plan, including the dual funerals.

Russ pondered the facts, eventually saying, "I don't see the problem."

"The problem is, it's a guess. How would I know why Joseph's sister was killed? I'm sending over 20 people to a farm town in Ohio and spending thousands of someone else's dollars on a hunch."

"You don't have a choice," Russ said. "The Westerfields would need to be protected no matter what was behind the sister's death."

"Of course, you're right. I guess it's just being in charge isn't quite what I expected."

"Did Joseph question your plan?"

"No. He's so broken up, I don't think he even heard what I told him."

"Well, let me tell you. Joseph chose you because he trusted your instincts. He's not concerned about the money and, as I see it, he gave you a free hand. Besides, I think you're right."

That brought a smile to Kristi's face. "Thanks. I needed that."

*****

Gentle hills decorated with rolls of summer hay, fields of corn or soybeans, and small lakes formed when the road was built went unnoticed as the three-Cadillac motorcade cruised east on the Indiana Toll Road. Kristi insisted the Westerfields use Sandora's cars because they were fortified with extra steel and bulletproof glass. Two guards were in the lead, as well as in the trailing cars. The middle car with Joseph and Jeff in the back seat, had only one guard, the driver.

Foremost in Jeff's memory, Aunt Sally always treated him as a special person, an important part of her life. He and his grandpa spent most holidays with her and her family. She loved to sing Christmas carols and play board games –winning most of the time. She had five kids that kept her hopping, but she always found time to talk to him. He imagined she was what his mother would be like if she hadn't had a mental breakdown. He would miss his Aunt Sally.

The ties between Sally and Joseph were a different matter. He had many female friends, but only three women were part of who he was: his mother Ramona, his wife Patricia, and Sally, who had been his lifelong sidekick. They grew up together as dependable allies, fighting their way through the challenges of adolescence. When she died, it left a hollow space in his soul that he knew would never be filled. Reminiscing together was no longer an option; the thread between childhood and adulthood had been broken. Joseph would accept the loss, disguising the depth of his grief to the best of his ability. He always did.

It seemed like forever before the Indiana Toll Road turned into the Ohio Turnpike. After an hour going east in Ohio, the motorcade turned southeast just below Toledo. The two-lane highway with its reduced speed limit dragged the trip out even longer. Eventually, a sign appeared: TIBBYVILLE CITY LIMITS.

Joseph chose to go directly to the farm. His approach was always to confront the most difficult issues head-on. Arriving at the farm, they found the yard randomly cluttered with cars and pickup trucks. Once they stopped, a guard climbed out of the rear car, and, using a three-foot pole with a mirror attached, quickly inspected each car's undercarriage.

Joseph asked his protectors to remain outside. He received a little resistance, but held firm. As usual, things were done his way.

The house was packed with relatives and neighbors. Sally's husband, Claude, met Joseph at the door. They immediately hugged each other, sharing grief, until their emotions were under control. "If it's possible, I would like to speak with you and your children privately," Joseph said quietly.

Only two of the boys and his daughter, Charlotte, had arrived. Claude motioned them into the kitchen. Joseph wasn't trying to be secretive, but he didn't want a crowd, either. The friends and neighbors gave them plenty of space.

Starting this conversation had to be one of the hardest things he'd ever had to do. "I'm so sorry I have to tell this, but I must. I believe our beloved Sally, your wife and mother, was killed because of me." Joseph broke down, breathless, as tears welled up in his eyes. He couldn't continue.

"Take your time, my friend," Claude said patiently.

After a minute, Joseph went on, "She was killed because of me. Because of my business connections and my ties to Wesfield Laboratory. I'm undoubtedly the most outspoken person among a group of people resisting a Wesfield Laboratories takeover. The people trying to get the company have an evil heritage, traceable all the way back to the Holocaust. They were barred from doing business in this country after both World Wars, and now they're trying to get back into the US by acquiring Wesfield.

"My opposition has triggered a series of diabolical acts, all designed to eliminate my resistance." He told them about the attempt on Jeff's life, and how close the shooter came to succeeding. He also mentioned that footprints leading to his cottage indicated he was also a target, and he included the story of how his friend Beverly tried to warn him and was quickly silenced.

"I believe Sally was killed to weaken my resolve."

"Sally has always believed in you, Joseph," Claude said, speaking slowly. "She would be the first to join in your fight."

Devastated, Joseph said, "I know I caused it, Claude."

"You weren't driving the car, Joseph – Evil was."

Joseph was relieved when Claude ended the conversation so abruptly. He was thankful for his perspective, but he didn't share it.

Joseph didn't go into the plot that could be unfolding around the funeral. It was just speculation, and these folks had enough to deal with. He and Jeff stayed for an agonizing hour sharing stories and heartache.

While friends and relatives consoled each other inside the house, on the outside, a three-year-old, dark green Chevy Monte Carlo slowly passed the LaPoint farmhouse. The driver saw about 30 cars and trucks parked haphazardly around the yard. *It looks like cars belonging to relatives and neighbors except for those three black Cadillacs parked in tight formation.* Gunther observed. *I'd say the Westerfields came with plenty of protection. Those rent-a-cops aren't gonna do you a damn bit of good, boys. They'll be able to lay both of you to rest right next to all your other relatives.* Gunther was pleased with the way his plan was coming together.

CHAPTER 29
THE PICKUP PLAN

In the mid-1800s, a *Mafioso*, a word which meant "manly," was considered an honorable man. Mafiosos were esteemed members of the Sicilian Mafia, formed when peasants joined together to defend themselves from their enemies. That changed in the 1920s, when a criminal element took over the leadership and turned the protective brotherhood into "La Cosa Nostra." By 1950, the Sicilian Mafia forcefully expanded into a major worldwide crime organization. With over 2,000 members in the United States, it's considered our most powerful organized crime group.

In the 1950s, Giovanno International, a food and wine import-export company, was created by the Sicilian Mafia as a front company used to launder money. With legal direction provided by Richardson, Deckmann & Smylee, Giovanno International opened branches in Los Angeles, Chicago, Kansas City, and Manhattan.

The company became so good at money-laundering, it managed to maintain a squeaky-clean image with a reputation for selling only the finest wines and cheeses. Stock in the profitable company has been privately held by many affluent business leaders throughout the US and around the world. In 1974, it remained one of Richardson, Deckmann & Smylee's strongest international accounts.

One phone call to Giovanno International was all it took to put the "Italian Plan" in motion. Anthony Roselli, the CEO of Giovanno International, assured Smylee he would take care of anything and everything, but he would like to get together to work out the details.

They met for lunch at Diamond's Steak House where Roselli promised to go to Sicily and personally oversee Sophia's abduction. Smylee felt reassured by Roselli's capable demeanor. They talked of kidnapping as though it were just any other day-to-day business venture; for the two of them, it probably was. By the time Smylee and Roselli left the restaurant, an agreement had been reached on all aspects of the project.

When Roselli arrived in Italy, things didn't go as planned. The Sicilians were under extreme scrutiny because of a recent political assassination. Trying to keep a low profile, they preferred not to get involved. Roselli had hoped to just broker the project, taking a percentage for providing the job without getting his hands dirty.

The best the Sicilians would do was to recommend one of the people they'd successfully worked with in the past. Roselli was told not to worry; Alto Camilo Cabellos was a man with considerable experience in the kidnapping-for-ransom business. He and his "grunt-man," Benito, had been successful on several occasions. Antonio Lombardo, the Sicilian Don, told Roselli he could depend on Alto for the strong-arm end of the project, but warned him to handle all the negotiating personally – it just wasn't Alto's forte. Roselli found himself without a choice.

Alerted by the sound of squealing brakes, Alto pulled the Volkswagen Bus Camper to the side of the road. He thought, *that guy must not know a thing about mountain roads*. When the teenaged driver in a dilapidated pickup passed, the smell of burning brakes confirmed his suspicions.

"I swear there's nothin' dumber than a kid with his first truck." Bonito said, shaking his head.

"You said it, Benny; he'll need brakes before he gets home for supper."

As Alto and Bonito rounded an unending hill, tiered roofs covering the hillside emerged from their sun-washed hiding place. They finally reached their destination, Bardolino. It was time to go to work.

Not only was this the biggest job they were ever involved in, it was by far the most profitable. They couldn't believe their good fortune.

Alto, being the more outgoing of the two, persuaded the client to pay $50,000 up front, before the kidnapping even took place. On top of that, the woman who was being nabbed would bring a huge ransom, $2,000,000, because she was provided for by a rich American. The client would only take 25% of the ransom. For that he would communicate the demands, establish a drop-off, and carry out the money pick-up. Alto and Benito didn't have an American connection, so it was a break to be working with someone who did.

Even though they were driving a camper, Alto and his sidekick chose to stay at the Caesius Villa, one of the fancy resort hotels that overlooked Lake Garda. After all, they could afford it.

A parking attendant grabbed their luggage and drove the camper around to a distant lot. Alto was left holding a ticket. He wasn't sure how the system worked, but was too proud to ask. After checking into the room, they turned on the TV and went out on the balcony. It was sunny, with a breath of wind under a flawless blue sky outlining the awesome Alps. Lake Garda, with its cerulean blue water, was the perfect setting for the sailing regatta underway. "Now this is living," Alto said, watching the yachts in full sail, as they maneuvered to gain wind advantage over one another. "Let's go take a 'look-see' at the Antisdale place. We need to put a plan together, and that's where we start."

"That's okay with me, Alto. The sooner we get started the sooner we get the ransom." Benito was raring to go.

Six months earlier, Alto purchased the Volkswagen Bus Camper, because it was well-suited for their line of work. With surrounding windows they could see the total landscape or, when necessary, close the curtains for complete privacy. The convenient side door provided easy access, in case two people needed to jam through simultaneously. And the floor was flat, perfect for transporting a wide range of cargo.

The attendant scampered off with the parking ticket. Alto breathed a sigh of relief when, a few minutes later, he saw the camper coming toward them. *No problem.*

Leaving the Caesius Villa, they drove down the narrow streets passing delightful shops and cafes with Lake Garda as a magnificent backdrop. Alto thought, *If everything goes without a hitch, this could be the last job we ever have to do. I may settle here when this job is over.*

A half mile north of town, they found the Antisdale property without a problem. The house was halfway up a slope with flowers blanketing the ground between it and the road. It was located in a quiet neighborhood with only the sheep across the street showing any signs of life.

A convenient location for achieving a very big payday.

CHAPTER 30
TRACING THE MONEY

"You were right, Kristi. Using Gordon Wieldey's bank account as a jumping-off place was pivotal in uncovering similarities with several of the people on your list of possibilities." John Snowden said. He always sounded so confident with his analyses.

"Glad to make your life easy, John."

"Your biggest contribution, however, turned out to be the freebie you talked us into last year. The Bailey Construction Co., 'draw from escrow,' information you provided simply confirmed our original findings. Manhattan Bank & Trust's client, Painter America Inc., was the group who paid the bills."

"I've never heard of Painter America. Who are they?" Kristi asked.

"We don't have any idea. I can tell you, though; they are a huge diverse organization, because along with the Painter America Inc. account, they have three additional accounts with varying focuses: Painter America Holdings Company, Painter America Reestablishment Fund, and Painter America Special Projects Ltd."

"Why would it be advantageous to have multi-accounts?"

"It's probably just a bookkeeping convenience. All four accounts contain many millions of dollars – I mean unlimited funding. These people have more ready cash than anyone we have ever been asked to investigate."

"Where does Painter's funding come from, or how do they make their money?"

"Good question, Kristi. I wish I had a good answer. What we've seen so far is a few protected trusts, holding companies, and associations, all with very nebulous memberships."

"Any indication BayerAG has contributed to Painter?"

"None whatsoever. In fact, all the funding seems to have originated right here in the USA, and the same groups have been putting money in Painter as far back as we could see."

"Now that surprises me, John," Kristi said quickly. "Since Bayer's headquarters is in Leverkusen, I expected the people behind the Wesfield takeover to be mostly European."

"You could very easily be right," Snowden said, "But, everything we've been able to dig up indicates the funding is coming from backers who live right here under our noses."

"That's hard to believe."

"Believe it. Real wealth is universal. Some individuals are worth more than some entire countries. Didn't you tell me Bayer was instrumental in creating the conglomerate called IG Farbenindustries?"

"Yes. Along with Carl Bosch, the director of BASF. That's what Joseph Westerfield told me," Kristi replied.

"And, that the Farben cartel had enough money to become the financial core of the Nazi movement?"

"So?"

"It may be coincidence but, unless my German falls me, Farben means 'painter.'"

"Really? How did you get so smart?"

"My mom was German. Getting back to our findings, you might be interested in knowing the legal group of attorneys that oversees the four Painter accounts is called Richardson, Deckmann & Smylee. They have been on board from the very beginning."

"Did you say Smylee?" Kristi snapped.

"Yes, I said Smylee. He and a guy named vonLeer are the only ones authorized to sign checks and move money."

"How many of the people on our list received money from these Painter people?"

"Quite a few. And I can tell you it was an extremely big payday for some of them."

"Like Gordon Wieldey?"

"He's at the top of the list. My findings will be in the mail as soon as I get them typed."

"How about the credit card charges for the boat and car rental? Were they paid by one of the Painter accounts?"

"No, that would be too easy. Victor Vargas and Verner Delmar's card charges were paid by check from an account belonging to Gunther's Quality Imports, an import-export company out of Charleston, South Carolina."

"Damn. I was hoping for a connection," an exasperated Kristi said.

"Not so fast. The connection's there, it's just buried a little deeper."

"Don't tease me, John."

"Well, everything we've managed to dig up tells us Gunther's import-export company is only window dressing as a means to provide funding to Mr. Gunther himself, with some money going to Vargas and Delmar. A woman named Hiening gets a monthly check. I'd guess she is probably Gunther's gal Friday."

"Anything else?"

"Oh, yes. He must be providing a hell of a valuable service, because he's been getting well over a million a year. And that's for at least the last nine years, which was as far back as we could go."

"Do we know who paid Gunther's bill?"

"In 1965, someone deposited $778,000 in his personal checking account. He used $650,000 to create his company, 'Gunther's Quality Imports. Since then, over 90% of the money in Gunther's company came out of a numbered account held with the International Bank of Commerce. We can only speculate, but we believe Gunther has an offshore company that uses that numbered account."

"I can't say any of that means a thing to me," Kristi said.

"Let's take a closer look at the bank," Snowden said.

"Okay, what about it?"

"At last count, the IBC – that's what the bank is called – was in 26 countries with main offices in Luxemburg and the Cayman Islands. Both countries have very secretive banking policies. Without a single central office, they don't come under the jurisdiction of an individual government. IBC has a lucrative business sheltering taxable incomes from countries all over the world."

"Are you telling me you can't penetrate their system?"

"Yes and no. They make things hard to track, but you can always use the back door."

"Like?"

"Like the yearly million dollar money transfer that takes place every January – Painter money is moved from Manhattan Bank and deposited in Gunther's IBC numbered account. There is an accessible record at the Manhattan Bank. And, we can get a peek at money transfer requests between IBC and the Gunther's Qualty Imports account at First Federal of Charleston. The transaction shows up on actual wire transfer, as well as in First Federal's monthly transaction information."

"So, there is a connection?"

"It's not quite as direct, but it's there all the same. One more thing that's even more conclusive, Manhattan Bank and Trust also transferred $150,000 from the Painter Reestablishment Fund directly into the Gunther's Quality Imports on several occasions. There was no apparent pattern, which probably means the money must have been in response to some purchase or service. I would love to see the paperwork that initiated those actions."

"Me, too," Kristi said.

CHAPTER 31
THE TRAP

Modica and Bella arrived with pastries and cappuccino just after seven. Sleepy-eyed, DiMarco stretched as he emerged from the shed. "Good morning, Tony. Did you get any sleep in the shed?" Bella asked.

"I did okay," DiMarco replied.

"Thanks for letting me sleep in. I appreciate the favor."

"No problem." DiMarco cracked a little smile, "I'm a nice guy."

They finished their coffee about 7:30, when the camper crawled past the Antisdale home. Seeing the Volkswagen so early heightened their awareness to full alert. Eyes wide with excitement, Bella's unease affirmed the obvious. "Mr. Modica, I think you called it. Today's the day."

"I think so," Modica replied.

The camper was still moving slowly when it returned a half hour later, and like clockwork, at 8:30 it was heading back up the hill again. Feeling confident, Modica felt the rush as he asked, "Are we ready for this?"

"We're never gonna be any readier," Tony responded.

"Sophia has been coming out around 9:00 so we better get set up. Bella, you're in the shed," Modica said, sounding like a drill sergeant. "Tony, let's go." The men headed for hiding places outside the stone fence that they'd checked out earlier. Modica took the south corner which had an abundance of underbrush, and DiMarco crouched 15 feet down from the north corner, well concealed in high grassy weeds.

The camper slowly rambled down the dirt road. After three days of surveillance, Alto figured the old lady shooed Sophia out after breakfast.

She sauntered out into the garden just before nine.

"There she is, Alto. She's out, just like you said she would be."

"Keep your eyes on the road, Benny. Don't stare."

"You want me to pull over?"

"No. Go up the road a little farther. This is good, let me out." Before exiting the camper, he told Benito to turn around and go back up to the lane, then come back and park at the side of the road near the north corner of the fence, a spot close to where Tony was hidden.

"Good luck," Benito said as he pulled away.

Sophia was well into her morning routine. She had already gone down the steps to the lowest terrace and said her morning prayers with St. Francis. After picking a few weeds, she began to select the best flowers for the bouquet. Humming an indistinguishable melody, she slowly moved along, appraising her options.

"Good morning, Sophia." Alto smiled leaning over the wall.

"Hello, how do you know that I am Sophia?"

"I am a friend of Ida, your mother. You've got a very nice garden. It's beautiful."

"Thank you. It's mama's, but I get to pick the flowers. I'm good at finding the pretty ones."

"Do you like these pink flowers, Sophia?" Alto held out three perfect Queen Elizabeth roses he had taken from of one of the hotel gardens. "You can have them for your bouquet if you like."

"Oh, how pretty they are," she said, as her face lit with delight.

As Sophia moved toward the stranger, Modica appeared at Alto's side like a silent phantom. Alto's body stiffened, his teeth clenched, his eyes widened. Panic gripped him, as he felt the unmistakable jolt of a revolver being thrust into the small of his back

"Do you train sheep dogs, too?" Sophia asked Alto. The question went unanswered.

"Good morning Sophia, it's nice to see you again," Modica said. "He doesn't train dogs, he's just a friend of mine."

"Hand the little lady the flowers." Modica whispered, jabbing the pistol several times to send an unmistakable signal to Alto – he meant business. "Tell her to get them in water right away." Alto did as he was told.

Sophia smiled, "Oh, thank you. They are so pretty – I'll go put them in water right now. Thank you, mister, thank you so much." She scurried up the steps and into the house. Holding the roses up she said,

"Mama, look what we have."

Concurrently, Bella walked brazenly up to the camper's driver's side door.

Who the hell is this? Benito thought. "What do you want, lady?" he glared. Bella's partner, DiMarco, was closing in from the other side.

She instantly stuck her revolver in his face. "Get out, pal, with your hands in the air." Bella snapped the command, keeping her eyes fixed on his.

Benito, panicking, started to raise the .38 from his lap. "Gun," DeMarco shouted, seeing the revolver start to move as he peered through the opposite front window. Before DiMarco could get off a shot, the blast halted his effort.

Bella and Benito shot simultaneously. Benito's shot went through the car door hitting Bella in the left leg. She realized she was hit, but held her ground. DiMarco came running around the car, put his arm around her shoulders, and opened the car door, prepared to shoot for any reason.

Benito rolled out with a small hole right between the eyes. The exit wound was an ugly ragged opening in the back of his head. Pinkish-gray matter and bone were splattered all over both seats and the opposite door. "Nice shootin'," DiMarco said, "But you could've used a little smaller caliber."

Modica, having already handcuffed Alto, was roughly dragging him toward the van. Seeing blood oozing through Bella's slacks, he waved his pistol, motioning her to the seat in the back of the camper. He followed, forcing Alto in through the side door and shoving him to the floor. "You okay, Bell?"

"I don't think it's too bad–it's kind of numb."

"Can you handle this bum for a minute?"

"No problem." With hands shaking badly, Bella pointed her revolver at his head. "Want to join your buddy? Make your move."

Alto didn't move.

Modica and DiMarco carried Benito around the bus and tossed him in the convenient side door. Then DiMarco got in and tied Alto's feet, as Modica used his belt to create a makeshift tourniquet above Bella's wound.

"Hey, why are you doin' this?" Alto's curiosity began to overcome his fear.

"Shut your face," DiMarco said contemptuously.

"All we did was give the lady some flowers."

"We know exactly what you were doing." DiMarco stood up and clubbed him, coming down hard across the side of his head with the handle of his Colt. "I don't think he'll be giving us any trouble for awhile."

They went straight to a friendly doctor so Bella's wound could be tended. Once their comrade was in good hands, Roberto used the doctor's phone to call the office to see if anyone had discovered anything about these boys.

"What did the doctor think about Bell?" Tony asked when he got back to the camper.

"He thought she'd be hurting for awhile, but couldn't tell much. He was shooting an x-ray as I was leaving. I got his phone number. We can call in a couple hours." Modica changed the subject back to business, "I also called the office."

"And?"

"They're both low-level Sicilian Mafia, but – get this, the Sicilians told our people they don't have a clue what they were up to."

"This wasn't a Mafia job?"

"You got it. Let's get rid of the stiff. I really don't know what to do with the other one."

"I've got an idea." Winking at his partner, DeMarco said loud enough to be sure Alto could hear, "We'll drop them both over a cliff."

DiMarco drove back to the field to pick up another car. Modica followed the Volkswagen camper closely, as they proceeded to drive higher into the mountains. When they finally stopped, the air was crisp and the wind brisk. They took the gag from Alto's mouth and untied his hands and feet. He hobbled out of the camper looking apprehensive. He asked, "What now?"

Talking in his softest voice, Modica explained his requirements. "That's totally up to you, Alto. Tell us who you are. Who hired you? And why? Then we'll let you live. If you can't convince me you're leveling with us – dead or alive, you're going over the cliff with your companion. You have one minute to tell us what you know."

"I am Alto Camilo Cabellos from Sicily. I don't know who hired us. We were contacted by phone. The call came to my house. I was told to 'think it over' and when I'd decided, call a special phone number I was given. It was an answering machine that told me to say either, 'accept or reject.'" He carefully pointed to his pocket and, using only two fingers, took out his checkbook. The number was noted on the first page. "They put money in my checking account, but I don't know how it got there."

"How much money?"

"Fifty thousand dollars. The ransom was supposed to be two million."

"Who was going to pay that kind of money for this woman and why?"

"Some rich American. I don't know who he is, or why the woman is so valuable to him."

"It's answers like that, Alto, will put you over the cliff." Modica was very convincing.

"I swear. The people who hired us were gonna do all the negotiating. I don't know who they were asking to pay the ransom. It's probably a relative. I just don't know."

"How were you going to contact them once you made the grab?"

"The telephone number I just gave you. We were supposed to leave a message on a machine and they would call back."

"How much do you have left in your checking account?"

"Why?"

"How much?"

"Probably about forty-five thousand in American dollars."

"Where were you going to stash the woman?"

"There's a shack in the mountains. It's not far from here."

DiMarco cautiously peered over the edge of the mountain. "It's a long, long way to the bottom, Roberto."

"That's the idea," Modica replied. "You want to drive the camper up to the edge?"

"Not really, but I can," DiMarco answered. Hating heights, he inched the camper forward, ever so slowly following Modica's fluttering finger signals. At last, Modica put both palms up and DiMarco let the air escape from his lungs. *Thank God that's over.*

"We'll let Alto here get his buddy into the driver's seat," Modica said.

"That works for me." Looking toward Alto, DiMarco said sternly, "You heard the man. Get to it!"

Although Alto was a strong man, he struggled to pick up the dead weight of an inert Benito. He dragged him to the front seat and hoisted him over, managing to prop him up against the steering wheel. Once in, he was told to put the Volkswagen in neutral, get out and give it a push. Alto did as he was told, happy just to be outside the camper. It didn't make much noise or burst into flames, just kicked up a little dust, vanishing as it entered the timberline.

"Get in the back seat, Alto. You're going to take us to the shack you'd planned on using to stash your victim. Sounds like the perfect place for you to spend a little alone-time."

He was right. It took less than a half hour to find the run-down cabin. They left him handcuffed to a metal column that supported the center beam. A small bowl of water was placed so he could lap it up but not reach with his hands. They pocketed the key and headed back to the doctor's office.

Bella was in good spirits considering she'd been shot. The doctor said she was lucky; the car door reduced the velocity or it could have been a lot worse. He wanted to keep her overnight, but Bella was quick to reject the idea.

When they got back in the car, Bella asked, "Well, where in the hell are they?"

Modica smiled as he said, "They won't be going anywhere for awhile." He went on to fill in the details, finally wrapping up by saying, "I'd say it's been a big day."

"We better call our new boss," Bella said. "She should know we're earning our keep."

Kristi listened carefully as Modica reported they shot a guy between the eyes and sent him and his camper over the edge of a mountain. Then if that wasn't enough, they abducted the other one and had him locked up in some Godforsaken hole-in-the-wall shack. It didn't go unnoticed to Kristi that no crime had actually been committed, except perhaps by her people.

Modica covered every detail of the very eventful day. Kristi was impressed with the team's ability, but concerned that Bella Salzarulo was shot. Even though she belonged to Worldwide, Kristi considered her and everyone else involved in this assignment to be part of her team. She asked to be kept up-to-date.

Modica told her his plan was to anonymously call the police reporting that he saw Alto shoot Benito, then push the camper down the mountain. He explained Alto's prints are all over it, so a call to the police would keep him out of mischief for quite awhile. Then, he really got her attention when he asked what she wanted him to do with the $45,000.

"What $45,000?" she asked.

"I had Alto sign a check in that amount – it's what's left of the 50 grand they had been paid to kidnap Sophia."

She thought about it for a moment, then said, "Let's use it to help pay your bill, and I want Bella to get something extra. We'll make it worthwhile."

"That's fine, except I don't want it written to our company – we don't need ties to this jerk."

"I see your point," Kristi said. "Are you sure it's in the account?"

"It's blood money. His blood now."

"You can write the check to ProTect & Associates, endorse it 'deposit only,' and send it to the South Station Bank & Trust in South Station, Michigan. I'll get the money back to you once it clears."

"It'll clear."

"Can anyone at Worldwide get a trace on the number Alto was going to call after the pick-up?"

"We're already on it," Modica responded.

"Great. Another thing that might help would be to find out where Alto's $50,000 came from."

"I'll try, but Alto's been kept in the dark . . . He doesn't know a damn thing. And, we don't have the expertise to trace money, so don't expect much."

"Do what you can. Even a copy of Alto's bank statement might be helpful."

"Okay. We'll give it our best effort. Alto also told us he was to leave the message, 'We picked up your sister for you' at a contact number he gave us. We're going to have him record it and play it into the telephone. Hopefully, they'll think Sophia is in Alto's control."

"I like the idea," Kristi said. "It sounds like you are doing a great job. Thank you; it's appreciated."

Their long day wasn't over. Modica unsuccessfully tried to get Bella to go home and rest, but she wouldn't even consider it. It took the better part of the hour to get back up to the shack where Alto was stashed.

He meekly recorded the "picked up your sister" message several times until all three were satisfied. Upon completing the chore, Alto couldn't believe his good fortune. They were letting him go.

Night was falling fast as they drove off, leaving Alto standing alone at the top of the mountain. His relief would quickly diminish, when he discovered the authorities had been told, by an anonymous caller, that someone saw him kill his partner and push their camper off the mountain. The police would be hunting him down before morning.

CHAPTER 32
THE SHADOW LAID TO REST

"He's here," Joan proclaimed as she jerked open the car door.

Kristi had just arrived at the Tibbyville Country Inn. "Hold on a minute, Joan." She popped the trunk, swung herself around, and got out of the car. "Now, you want to run that by me again?"

"He's here. We know the killer is here. And, it looks like he's planning to take action just like you figured."

A relieved Kristi asked, "How can you be so sure?"

"Victor Vargas checked out the funeral parlor, and according to Kestler, he also wanted to see the church."

"He used his Victor Vargas alias?"

"That's what Kestler called him."

"Now that's arrogance," Kristi said. "He apparently didn't think we'd be smart enough to recognize the motive behind Sally's murder. Victor Vargas, whoever he really is, thinks we're a bunch of hicks and that's going to work in our favor."

"He walked out of Kestler's as we arrived," Charley said. "If we had any idea he was our villain . . . well, we found out too late to take action."

Kristi called Sheriff Surratt and asked him to join them at the hotel for a 6:30 dinner. Sandy, arriving at 6:00, told them Joseph and Jeff were safe inside the farmhouse. His people stayed to guard the area. The meal was typical midwestern cooking, meat, potatoes and vegetables, served family style, and a choice of apple, cherry or pecan pie for dessert.

With bellies full, Charley and Joan reported their general observations. The fact that the killer was near heightened everyone's enthusiasm. In addition to funeral-related assignments, Joan bought 50 rolls of 35-millimeter slide film and extra cameras for agents who didn't bring their own.

183

They also hired Jim Neely, a local photographer, with instructions to set up a makeshift laboratory capable of instant turnaround. His operation was put in the room next to Kristi's because it had an interior joining door. Neely assembled developing and slide mounting paraphernalia in the bathroom, and by changing the lights to red, turned it into a darkroom. Folding chairs replaced the bed, and a projector with corresponding screen was quickly put together. The room was cramped, but everyone would fit.

The idea was simple enough. As the agents went through the motions of the mock funeral, each team member would discreetly snap pictures of locations well-suited to the assassin's needs. Access to the targets, concealment, and easy departure were key considerations. Slides would then be projected onto the large screen for evaluation by the entire group.

After listening to the intricate plan, Sheriff Surratt said he had never been involved in such a sweeping program. As a creditable, and hopefully, objective outsider, Surratt's flattering appraisal of their creative approach was very welcome. It helped reassure Kristi at a time when she uncharacteristically needed to be reassured.

The sheriff took out a county map showing where he would have roadblocks positioned. The group liked what he presented, and were happy to have him backing them up. The dinner meeting wound down at 9:00.

Before tucking herself in, Kristi called Russ to share the knowledge that Charley and Joan discovered the killer was lurking; the whole thing was not just a waste of time. Russ said, "Told ya." After a little small talk, they said good night.

Kristi needed a good night's sleep, but what she got was intermittent at best. Her burden was exhausting and exhilarating at the same time. A call from Joan's people in Italy got Kristi's day off to an anxious start. She was quickly reminded that the enemy was made up of ruthless, resourceful demons who would do anything to accomplish their goals.

Wednesday was a flurry of activity. As each member of the group arrived, they passed through Kristi's room where they were provided cameras, film, an earphone, and a clip-on microphone.

Before the agents left, Kristi reviewed the objectives and stressed the dangers with each one of them. It was totally unnecessary; everyone understood the danger and were on board – they had been all along. The review did, however, reassure her that she had the right people, in the right place, at the right time.

As Kristi prepared for action, she repeated a silent prayer throughout the day. *God help us defeat the evil, and keep us safe.*

At 6:30 sharp, people began to arrive at Kestler's. The mortician, with eyes glancing from side to side, looked like a cat sitting next to an empty goldfish bowl. Locals, who had no idea why they were there, got a smiling nod from Sheriff Surratt as they mournfully passed through the reception area. An old photo of an unknown, but handsome man, sat on top of a simple coffin. Kestler had volunteered to provide flowers, which encircled the viewing area. They were a droopier version of flowers used in a funeral that took place earlier in the week.

The locals were gone by 7:30, allowing Kristi to be alone with her team. She asked if anyone thought Kestler's was a good possibility for the attack. The group confirmed Charley's and Joan's analysis: "Very unlikely."

With that response, Kristi said, "Okay, folks, let's try to get a good night's sleep. I'll see you at St. John's; The Shadow's service starts at 8:30."

The group, along with Sheriff Surratt's hires, arrived at the church dressed in appropriately drab colors. After everyone was inside St. John's Church and the doors were closed, an old Monte Carlo slowly rolled past the church. The driver, a rough-looking old lady with curiously lifeless gray hair, took special interest in how the vehicles were lined up.

A police car would lead the procession, followed by what Gunther believed to be the pastor and the funeral director's cars. They were both dark Cadillacs with little flags reading 'FUNERAL' on the front fenders. Fourth in line was the hearse, followed by family vehicles, which all had a fixed place in the procession. General mourners would follow at random. When the entourage arrived at the cemetery, he would use field glasses to see where each car ended up parking in relation to the grave.

The Minister thought it odd that he was the only speaker. He also was painfully aware that the patrons seemed to be preoccupied while he rattled off his impassioned "rest-in-peace" sermon. Apparently, he wasn't especially moving, but after all, it's not like he really knew the Cranston family.

After a short program at the gravesite, the services came to an end a few minutes before 11:00.

Walking back to their cars, Kestler asked the Reverend, "What did you think of the funeral?"

"Funeral? You call that a funeral? In all my 20-some years of performing final services, this has to be the most disrespectful group of mourners I have ever seen."

Kestler could hardly hold a straight face, but managed to prod him on, "What do you mean?"

The Reverend stopped walking, turned and looked Kestler in the eye. "Don't you think at least one of the so-called friends of the deceased would say, at the very least, a few kind words about LaMont from the pulpit?"

With teeth clenched, Kestler just shook his head.

"They not only ignored my sermon, they were talking among themselves as I delivered it. And out here, they seemed to care more about every tree, bush and butterfly, than the poor guy they came to say goodbye to. The clincher was—one of the women took my picture while I was reciting the 23rd Psalm."

"Really?" Kestler smirked.

"Can you imagine, I'm walking them through the 'shadow of death' and this lady is snapping a picture like it's some kind of social event."

"She probably just liked your style." Kestler grinned to himself all the way back to the funeral home.

*****

When the team crammed into Kristi's room, they found there were sandwiches and an assortment of goodies laid out on a table. Some slides were available for analysis before they finished lunch.

As each slide was flashed onto the screen, one of the members of the group, usually the person who shot it, explained why he, or she, thought it met the criteria. The slides represented the most logical hiding places with visual access to the church, the procession route, and the cemetery. Each image was scrutinized, discussed and eventually rated for its potential. After the evaluation they were placed in one of three piles: likely, possible, or unlikely.

By 4:00 they finished evaluating the last slide. The "likely" pile contained only nine slides, four of which were locations in close proximity to the church. The other five involved the area surrounding the cemetery. There were only four "possible" slides, all pertaining to the cemetery. "Based on the numbers," Kristi concluded, "The cemetery is the most likely target area."

Joan pointed out, "There's a wealth of cover out there: bushes all over the cemetery, brush along the railroad, and huge, waist-high soybean fields. You could hide an army out there." Everyone murmured in agreement.

The agent who pointed out the dangers of a location was assigned to head a team of two or three agents to cover it. "We will work in waves," Kristi said. "First, we'll concentrate on the St. John's possibilities. If no attempt is made by the end of the service, and once all the mourners are in their cars, we'll move out ahead of them to secure the cemetery.

"Since we don't have to concentrate on the procession route, people assigned to the likely cemetery locations can get out there quickly; the rest will join in with the procession. Remember, try to draw minimum attention.

"Before we break up, I want to double check on tonight," said Kristi. "No one gets in Kestler's without one of us knowing who they are and why they're there."

"We won't have a problem, Kristi," Joan said. "Joe, the oldest son, is going to help identify everybody as they enter the building."

"How about the parking lot? Everyone knows their assignments?"

"Relax, Kristi, we've got it covered," Charley Tanner said. "Besides, you have us because we're good at our jobs. Stop worrying, we're as ready as anyone could be."

"Okay. Before you go, I want to remind everyone that our assassin is a very accomplished killer. Do not become one of his victims."

"We are pretty accomplished ourselves," one of Sandy's people said.

"Make no mistake, we're going to get him," Kristi responded, "but I don't want to lose any of you in the process. Think out your moves – stay alert – trust your instincts and cover each other's back.

"Oh. One more thing. Thank you."

As the last person sauntered down the hall, Kristi realized there wasn't anything more she could do.

At 6:30, as people file into Kestler's, events will occur which will be totally out of my control. God help us to recognize the signs – show us the way to defeat the evil, and keep us safe.

CHAPTER 33
SALLY'S FUNERAL

Only one of the double doors was open, forcing guests to enter single file. Joe, Sally's oldest son and Joseph's namesake, personally welcomed each person who entered. He recognized most of the family's friends and neighbors as they packed Kestler Funeral Home early Thursday evening to express condolences.

He simply asked the ones he didn't know who they were and how they knew his mother. Joan Voss was close by, ready to take any suspicious guest aside for further examination. There are no strangers in a close-knit rural community. Joan, the only inside security person, stood in the background, trying to look like she belonged.

The only guest that Joe or Joan didn't recognize was Lori Smith, who unexpectedly showed up to be with Jeff and his grandpa. Both welcomed her as though she were family.

As a result of the "shadow" run through, Kristi's team viewed Kestler's as the least likely place for the assassin to strike. She used a few well-concealed agents to police the parking area, but not enough to create a noticeable presence.

For the family, including Joseph and Jeff, there were too many people to have anything but brief conversations. The result was more hugs and tears than words. The entire night was an exhausting blur, where the most consoling comments seldom registered; words couldn't penetrate the pain.

By 9:00 everyone had gone.

*****

The clock in the courthouse bell tower bonged twelve times and, with few exceptions, Tibbyville's residents were sound asleep. Excellent visibility provided by a full August moon was reduced to zero, as heavy clouds rolled in from the west. The night had turned

189

into pitch-black darkness.

Along the north side of Oak Rest Cemetery, a man with a flashlight, using a long handled pruner, and a bow saw, was trimming bushes along the edge of the property. Although he was very selective, he didn't appear to have any criteria behind his hit-and-miss selections process.

When his midnight gardening was concluded, he picked up every branch, twig, and leaf, carefully depositing them on a pile at the back of the cemetery. He double-checked the area with his light, making sure he left no trace that any changes were made. *I'll have a clear view to your car, Westerfields. I'm ready for you. Morning can't come soon enough.*

*****

A drizzly rain slipped into Central Ohio in the middle of the night with every intention of staying for the day. Dawn was lost in charcoal-gray clouds concealing any hint of the sun.

The phone rang, then rang again. Having slept poorly in a hotel bed, Joseph rolled over to see 6:06 on the illuminated alarm clock. The phone rang again. Apparently it wasn't going to stop. He picked up and a familiar voice said, "Good morning."

"Hello, Kristi. What can I do for you?" He sounded half asleep.

"I'm sorry if I woke you, Joseph. I thought you told me you were an early riser."

"I usually am."

"Are you and Jeff up to meeting me in the downstairs restaurant? We'll have breakfast together if you feel like it. They have a pretty good smorgasbord."

"Anything special I need to be prepared for?"

"I'd say this is good news for a change, but I do need your input."

"Good news would be nice. Are you downstairs now?"

"I'm on my second cup of coffee."

"I'll call Jeff; he should be up by now. We'll be right down."

As Joseph and Jeff walked toward the table, Kristi could see by their somber faces that Sally's death was taking a heavy toll. She already had two extra coffees on the table. After a brief morning greeting, all three went through the food line. No one put much on his plate. After picking at his food, Joseph said, "So what's the scoop?"

"There has been a failed attempt to kidnap Jeff's mother and possibly Ida." Kristi was trying to treat this as good news.

In unison Joseph and Jeff said, "Are they okay?"

"Completely safe. Sophia doesn't even know there was a problem."

"Thank God they weren't hurt. They've had enough tragedy in their lives," Joseph said with his voice just above a whisper.

"You may still get a call demanding ransom."

Jeff was quick to respond. "I don't understand. If they're safe, why would anyone call?"

"It's possible the people behind the kidnapping are unaware that they have failed." Kristi went on to explain, "I don't have all the details, but I do know generally what happened." Taking her time, she gave full credit to the people from Worldwide Protection, describing how they carried out the actual interception with details of how one kidnapper ended up dead and the other was captured and willing to cooperate.

"Do we need someone to stay by my phone?" Joseph interrupted.

"We're taking care of it." Kristi told him. Then she continued, telling about Bella's leg wound, stressing it was not life-threatening and that the agent was being tended to. Concluding, she mentioned the attempt to trace the $45,000 check and the complicated telephone-recording communication structure.

"I'm sorry to hear about the girl who was shot," Joseph said. "It sounds like we have some capable people in Bardolino. Where do we go from here?"

Kristi paused, then said, "I would like to consider moving Ida and Sophia before anyone discovers they are still on the loose. Hopefully, it would spoil any follow-up plans that may be in the works."

"Do you think my lake house would work?"

Although Jeff seldom joined in strategic planning between the two of them, a concern for his mother prompted a comment. "With all the security systems that were installed there, it's the safest environment we have. But, do you think they'd be happy there, Grandpa?"

"That's a good question. I should call Ida, anyway. It's only fair to let her know what's happening, and I can see if she'd go along with the idea. What do you think, Kristi?"

"I'd definitely feel better with them at the lake where we can keep an eye on them."

"What time is it there?" Joseph asked.

"They're five or six hours ahead of us, so it must be early afternoon," Jeff replied.

"What about today, Kristi? Is there anything Jeff and I can do to make things easier?"

"There is one thing you should know. We are positive the killer is here."

Jeff asked, "How can you be so sure?"

"He used his Vargas alias, if it is an alias, when he checked out Kestler's."

"I thought you said the guy was smart. Sounds pretty dumb to me."

"He is smart, Jeff; he just underestimated us."

"Anything else?" Joseph questioned.

"I see Lori Smith came in from New York last night."

"Is that a problem?" Jeff asked.

"No. But we haven't planned for her security. I'd prefer that she sticks close to me today."

"I've already asked her to ride with us to the cemetery. I think she is planning on it," Jeff said.

"You and Joseph are the primary targets, Jeff. Do you really want her close to you?"

"She will ride with you, if that's okay. I'm sure you'll enjoy each other's company," Jeff said, smiling meekly.

"Good," Kristi said, thinking, these men are too distraught to resist anything.

"If there isn't anything else we need to go over, Kristi," Joseph said as he pushed his chair back, "I'll go make the call to Ida and Sophia."

"There is one more thing and it's important to you both." Kristi looked determined.

"And that is?" Joseph questioned.

"I would like you both to wear what is called a Kevlar vest with trauma plates."

"A bulletproof vest?" Jeff asked.

"I only wish it was totally bulletproof, but the vest, with the plates front and back, could possibly save your life."

Joseph realized he was out of his element – this was a time to listen. "Have whatever it is you want us to wear in our rooms before we leave for the services. We'll be glad to wear them. Thanks for your help."

*****

The Reverend unlocked the door and quietly entered the vestry. As he flipped on the light, he was startled by a woman peeping through the cracked door out into the church. "Who are you and what, may I ask, are you doing here?"

Kristi put a finger to her lips, made a shushing sound, held her badge high in her other hand and walked over to look the clergyman in the eye. "Will you please keep your voice down?"

"This is my church."

"I understand. I'm sorry to have startled you. We have a potential problem here . . . a possible murder attempt, and unfortunately it could happen in your church. Do you want blood all over the floor?"

"No, certainly not. What's this all about?"

"It's about protecting Sally's relatives. You are aware that she was murdered?"

"Of course," the preacher said with confusion showing on his wrinkled brow. "Do you really think they're in real danger?"

"I know they are; that's why I'm here."

"Are you working for Sheriff Surratt?"

"He's working with us."

"Oh. Do you think peeking out of the vestry door will help?"

"If that was all we were doing, it wouldn't. But we also have people in the pews, the vestibule, the choir, covering every door, watching the parking lot, and covering several locations across the street."

"I see. Didn't I see you here yesterday?"

"Probably."

"Who were you protecting then?"

"LaMont, of course."

"LaMont? He was already dead."

"Was he? Are you sure about that?"

"I assume he was."

"Look, Reverend, I'm sorry you're inconvenienced. But, it's time to cut the crap and get your show on the road."

"I guess I better. The place is already packed."

Concealing any sign of piety, the Reverend marched to the church podium like a five-star general ready to review the troops.

Mourners filled the church, the vestibule, and spilled out onto the steps. Umbrellas overlapped, but somehow the rain found its way to the ground without drenching anyone. They were dressed in the somber grays, black and dark blues that dominate most funerals – the last colors Sally would have wanted to be surrounded with.

She preferred pastels: delicate pinks, light blues, pale magenta and purple. She was a lot like her favorite colors, soft and gentle, creating an inviting atmosphere wherever she went.

At 8:45, once everyone was settled in the church, the green Monte Carlo again cruised past St. John's with its driver taking note of the vehicle lineup. Once past the church, the car picked up speed, making its way north to a small strip mall and gas station a mile south of the cemetery.

The service was filled with spiritual hymns, prayers, and friends and relatives telling of the wonderful experience it was to be part of Sally's life. After a short, but passionate speech by Sally's husband, Claude, he said, "Joseph, you are the only person who was part of her life starting with the day she was born. She loved you in a special way. Would you like to say a few words?"

"Thank you, Claude." Joseph, choosing not to use the pulpit, stood on the front of the elevated altar area. With his emotions under control, he talked about Sally's life with their parents. "Our father once complained to mother, every time one of us kids was being reprimanded the other would join, uninvited of course, in the discussion, always siding with the other sibling. He didn't like seeing Sally and me close ranks against authority, especially when mother was the authority.

"Mother smiled, telling him, 'siblings are allies by nature. They will always stand together because they have the same blood. Half yours, half mine. It's a natural instinct, don't take it personally.'"

He went on to tell the mourners that he didn't know if his mother's theory had any validity, but the result was hard to contest. "We always stood together; we will always stand together."

Constant rain was the final touch to a gray world, as the funeral procession slowly made its way through the town. It traveled down Tayco Street, turning left at Racine, crossed the railroad tracks and turned north on the county road paralleling the tracks on the left.

*****

Cocooned in a hedgerow 300 yards north of the cemetery, Gunther became an invisible part of the landscape. Annoying raindrops kept falling from the brim of his cap and under his rain gear. His pores spilled perspiration, creating enough moisture to render the waterproof poncho useless. *Where in the hell are they?* His patience was running thin.

Three cars arrived at the cemetery about 10:30. *The others can't be far behind.* Gunther was anxiously setting his bi-pod rifle mount when six dark umbrellas bobbed out of the cemetery.

Sandora took five agents to check out potential sniper hiding places along the railroad tracks and in the fields north of the cemetery. "Remember, this guy is trained to be invisible," Sandy said. "Check every possibility."

One of Joan's people, Scott Scruggins, nicknamed Scrugs, asked, "You think he's out here, Sandy?"

"I would bet a month's pay. And, I think his most logical points of attack are in the area we've been assigned to cover. So, shoot first, ask questions later."

"I know," Scrugs said, "The guy is a killing machine."

"Right, and we don't want to end up one of his victims."

Splitting up, one umbrella bounced along the entrance road to the slightly elevated railroad tracks. The rest spread out along the north border of the cemetery. Two men were positioned about five yards in from the borders, one went in up the middle, and the other two were in between. All of the umbrellas came down as the agents began their trek through the soybeans. Methodically, they moved in a line, scrutinizing the territory.

When the searchers appeared to be headed his way, Gunther began to wonder – could someone be on to me? He watched as they advanced, finally concluding they were Westerfield's bodyguards from the three-car motorcade he had spotted at the LaPoint farmhouse. Although they aroused his suspicions, he wasn't particularly concerned. *No rent-a-cops will ever stop me.* Even more important, by the time they discovered he was ever there, the Westerfields would be dead and he would be miles away.

Sandy's group was through the first field of soybeans. Climbing over the low hedgerow to get to the next field was as close as they would come to discovering him. Sandy himself, passed within 15 feet of the sniper. Gunther's Special Services training paid off again. Pleased with himself, he thought, *Who do you think you're dealing with, boys? The longer you search, the farther away you're going to get.*

From his hiding place, Gunther had visual access through the newly created clearing to the exact spot where he believed the hearse would stop. A second clearing would allow him to observe where the sixth, seventh, and eighth vehicles in the procession would end up parking. He believed Joseph and Jeff would occupy the seventh car.

As a backup plan, Gunther also had chopped out several clumps of brush assuring him a clear view of the grave site. It wasn't his first choice, because there was no way to determine where people would stand. *They should be here by now.*

Like continuous thunder, a freight train came rumbling down the track behind him. *Great. This is going to block the cars from turning into the cemetery.* To Gunther, the six minutes it took the train to pass seemed like an hour. He was soaked with sweat, and raindrops continued to fall from his hat at a steady pace.

As the train cleared the intersection the lead squad car turned, crossing the tracks and onto the cemetery entrance road. *It's about time – they move so damned slow.* At last, the hearse passed slowly through the narrow gate, finally coming to rest right on the spot where Gunther hoped it would. All the cars were in the same positions they had been in at the church.

His heart picked up to full throttle. The three black Cadillacs stopped in the six, seven and eight positions, just as Gunther anticipated. This was the moment – he was ready.

CHAPTER 34
THE CHASE

Outside, the warm drizzly rain made little noise as it hit the roof of the car. Inside, Jeff and Joseph stared out the back seat windows as the procession crept along. The mood was somber, but Joseph wasn't as quiet as Jeff expected. He spoke about already missing his sister. Then, looking inward, he said, "If I weren't so headstrong, Sally and Beverly would still be alive, Sophia would be safe in Italy, and you wouldn't have been shot."

"You didn't do it, Grandpa," Jeff said. "And you certainly didn't cause it."

Apparently it was too painful to dwell on, because Joseph changed the subject. "Sophia and Ida will be on their way to Michigan in the morning."

"That's good news. Ida doesn't have Alfonso to help anymore, and they will be a lot safer at the lake."

"I'm not so sure, Jeff. It sounds like Worldwide's people did a hell of a good job keeping them out of trouble."

"I'll like having them close – I'd like to know them better."

"Me, too," Joseph said. Then he changed the subject again. This time he talked about the enemy's unlimited resources and the fact that they could end up broke, dead, or both, trying to fight these evil people.

Jeff said, with a slight smile, "Is that why we're wearing the Kevlar underwear?"

"I guess I'm not telling you anything you don't already know."

"It's hard to miss," Jeff said. "Everything and everyone we care about is being attacked. I can't believe we're so important."

"We're not," Joseph said, "Wesfield Laboratory is what's important to them. You and I are just an annoyance they think can be eliminated or forced to relent."

"I'm glad we're not so manageable."

"I am, too, Jeff. I am, too."

Once the train passed, the motorcade made its way down the narrow road, coming to a stop inside the cemetery. The security guard-driver came around and opened Joseph's door holding an umbrella.

Joseph climbed out and waited as the younger Westerfield slid across the seat to get out the same door. The moment Jeff was standing, his Grandpa, with eyes and mouth wide open, let out a loud "ahh." His knees gave out and he crumpled to the ground. As Jeff reached for him, something that felt like a sledge hammer slammed into his sternum. With his chest tightening and breath gone, the world spun into darkness as he collapsed on top of his Grandpa. Although Jeff was no longer conscious, he was aware of people shouting, scurrying about, and rain hitting his face.

As they realized they were under attack, some mourners fell to the ground. Others scattered, hiding behind trees and large headstones. A few just stood there in shock, unable to comprehend what was happening. They too scurried off when their friends shouted, "Take cover. Get down."

Rushing words into his clip-on microphone, the agent-driver shouted, "Both subjects hit and down. Believe shots fired from north field."

"That's us, Scrugs," Sandy said. "He's out here somewhere." They were on the opposite side of the field from the hedgerow that concealed the sniper. As their eyes scoured the landscape, they could see small groups of agents emerging from the cemetery, moving into the fields and along the railroad tracks.

Scrugs saw the motion before he realized it was a man. Running along the hedgerow, Gunther resembled a four-legged animal, keeping extremely low to the ground and moving at remarkable speed.

Wishing he had a rifle, Scrugs sighted his Smith & Wesson .357 Magnum with patience and confidence. He deliberately took one carefully lined-up shot at a time. Although his shooting range pattern was within three inches at twenty yards, at this distance, Gunther made a very difficult target.

When Gunther reached the slight crest of the railroad tracks, many agents fired desperation shots, but it was Scrugs that took time to carefully line up his last possible shot. He squeezed the trigger and watched him fall. He rolled toward the cornfield on the other side of the tracks.

Scrugs, Sandy, and the agents coming from the cemetery ran toward the downed gunman. The closer they got, the slower they moved, increasing caution as they zeroed in on the potential danger.

When they realized he had escaped, a couple of the more brazen agents walked up to the spot, finding only a few drops of blood. Someone said, "Nice shootin,' Scrugs. Looks like you put at least one round in him with that pop pistol."

Quickly taking charge, Kristi shouted, "Fan out. We'll work our way through the corn. It looks like he went straight in."

Agents spread to about ten feet apart and began methodically plodding through the field. The pungent odor of mature corn was intensified by the warm drenching rain. The assassin's trail was clearly marked, but caution was necessary because, they all realized, they were in pursuit of an adversary as shrewd as he was lethal. He could barricade himself in somewhere up the way, or swing around to maneuver in behind them.

After 15 sweaty minutes shuffling between corn stalks, the searchers heard the unmistakable howl of a Harley as it exited the field and accelerated north along the fence.

Crashing helter-skelter through the corn, Kristi's team put every effort into clearing the corn to get another crack at the villain. His exhaust fumes and a speck on the horizon were all they got.

Kristi immediately went to the two-way radio, "Sheriff Surratt?"

"You got me, Chief."

"I hate to say this, Sheriff, but the ball's in your court."

"I hate to hear that. Is everyone alright?"

"Both Westerfields were hit, but, I don't know how bad it is."

"I'm sorry, Kristi. How did he get away?"

"He's on a motorcycle. Sounded like a Harley."

"You think he'll stay with it?"

"I doubt it," Kristi replied. "He's much too clever for that."

"Roadblocks are in place. What should we be looking for?"

"He will be a six-foot stranger – likes to use an 'old man' disguise, but he may have others. I believe he's wounded, probably in the leg."

"We'll do our best."

"I'm sorry to put you in this spot, Sheriff."

"Don't be; it goes with the territory."

"Please, remind your people, this guy has no qualms about killing. And, good luck."

The mourners hiding behind the larger headstones during the barrage of gunfire waited several minutes before emerging. Frightened, many scrambled to exit the cemetery.

*****

Fearing they might cause additional damage, no one disturbed either Joseph or Jeff. Joe, the oldest LaPoint brother, did manage to check their pulse and drape a raincoat over them. By using two-way radios, the ambulance arrived sooner than expected.

With great care, the paramedics maneuvered Jeff off Joseph and onto a flat board. They lifted him to a gurney, strapped down his head, body, and legs, and rolled him to the ambulance. The same procedure was followed with Joseph. The ambulance drove back down the one-way cemetery road, across the tracks, onto the county road, fired up the sirens, and headed to the hospital.

The grieving family chose to resume the ceremony in an effort to bring the dreadful day to an end. So stunned was the Reverend, he lost his authoritative demeanor, and fumbled his way through the rest of the ritual. Kestler became the humorless mouse he'd always been.

Sally's friends and family, too numb to do anything else, simply went through the motions as the cemetery service got underway. When the last tear was shed, the mourners slowly walked to their cars shaking their heads, and mumbling bewildered comments of confusion and tragedy between themselves.

CHAPTER 35
WOUNDED

Holding tight to the Harley's handlebars, Gunther negotiated every bump, boulder and rut like a professional dirt-biker. In spite of the burning hole in his thigh, he smiled to himself as the satisfying vision of both Westerfields falling to the ground recurred in his mind. At the end of the cornfield he passed onto a dirt road through an opening he had discovered earlier. A mile, two, then three – his confidence was building. No one was close enough to see where he was going. *I'm free and clear.*

At last, the woods were in sight. He slowed the motorcycle to a stop in front of a wide dilapidated gate. Pain shot through his leg when he hit the kickstand. He limped up to the gate and gave it a hard yank. It opened much harder than it had earlier when he stashed the Monte Carlo behind the brush a little way down the lane.

He laid the bike on its side and shed his wet camouflage suit, leaving it in a heap on the ground. Working efficiently, he toweled himself dry and carefully checked his thigh. There was only a single wound so the bullet was still in there. Even though there wasn't heavy bleeding, Gunther knew it would soon need a doctor's attention or he'd be in big trouble.

He slipped back into the house-dress. Using the rearview mirror, he put on and haphazardly adjusted the tattered gray wig, applied lipstick, and added a touch of blush to his cheeks. Although he changed into an older woman, his muscular hairy legs and men's boots were a dead giveaway – he was no lady. The disguise obviously wasn't intended for close inspection.

Skirting the cemetery, he brazenly pointed the Monte Carlo back toward downtown Tibbyville. He drove up to an outside telephone where he ripped the phonebook from its holder. Under Physicians & Surgeons – Family Practice, he found only two listings.

Doctor J. R. Rand's small fieldstone office had concrete steps with wrought-iron handrails. The building signaled "one-man show." Gunther impatiently waited across the street for cars to clear the front parking area. The last person to leave was a woman dressed in a nurse's uniform. *I'll bet you're the nurse-receptionist.*

When a CLOSED sign appeared in the window, Gunther turned into the doctor's driveway and pulled up alongside a station wagon. He hobbled to the front, went up to the steps and tried the doorknob. Locked. He pounded on the door.

Looking through the tiny door window, Dr. Rand thought to himself, *Is this a guy, or a very ugly old lady?* He unlocked the door, opened it a crack, and asked, "What can I do for you?"

Gunther thrust his body into the door sending the doctor across the room where he landed on his back. *What the heck is goin' on?* He saw the hairy legs, hunting boots and large masculine hand pointing a gun at his head. It was definitely not just an ugly lady.

"Are you here alone? And are you the doctor?"

"Yes, and yes."

"Good. Do as you're told, and I'll let you live."

The old doctor didn't intimidate easily. "What the hell are you supposed to be, anyway?"

"I'm supposed to be the guy that's gonna shoot one of your fingers off every five minutes until you either fix me up, or I need to find a doctor that can hold the scalpel."

Dr. J. R. Rand, being an excellent judge of character and nobody's fool, knew this guy was big trouble and not to be underestimated. "Come on, let's take a look at you," he said, turning around and marching into the back room with Gunther hobbling close behind. "Can you get on the examination table?"

"Yes, I think so," Gunther replied. Once he crawled up, he lifted his dress to show Dr. Rand the wound. "This is my problem."

"At least you don't have to drop your pants for me to see it."

"Enough humor already." Gunther was anxious to get this over.

"How did you get yourself shot?" the doctor asked as he cleaned the wound.

"That doesn't matter. Just dig the slug out and sew me up."

"It's going to hurt, unless I use an anaesthetic."

"You will not put me to sleep. If I start to blink, I'll put a bullet in your head. Got it?"

"Hold your water, Bucko; I will use a little numbing agent. It won't put you out."

"Lidocaine?" Gunther questioned.

"Something like that." Dr. Rand wasn't about to tell him he was right.

Forty years of patching farmers had honed the cantankerous old doctor's skills. He retrieved the bullet, sterilized the wound and did the stitching in less than half an hour. Fortunately, Gunther didn't blink. In fact, he didn't even wince in spite of the doctor deliberately using a lean dose of lidocaine.

"Give me a bottle of penicillin tablets," Gunther said, waving his gun. "Now."

First showing him the label, Dr. Rand poured over a dozen pills into a smaller container. "How's that?"

"Fine. Now we are going for a ride. You're driving." Gunther jabbed Dr. Rand with his gun, pushing him out to the driveway. "Get in the passenger side and slide over. Do it. Get moving."

"Keep your pants on, Ace." Dr. Rand said, as he backed out of the driveway.

"Keep to the speed limit and don't do anything stupid."

Dr. Rand quickly replied, "I'm not the stupid one in this car, Bucko."

"Just drive." They went north in silence until Gunther saw the police blockade about 50 yards ahead. "You're going to talk us through this, Doc."

"I am?"

"If you value your life, you will."

Surratt's men recognized Dr. Rand's car about the same time Gunther saw them. Seeing Dr. Rand was a daily occurrence and didn't arouse their suspicion. "Looks like Doc is having a long day again." someone said.

"Probably a house call. You know how he is," another commented.

"Yeah, too bad there ain't more like him."

As the doctor pulled to a stop, Fritz Vanderhide, a rugged looking policeman the doctor had delivered into this world 34 years before, walked up to the window. "Nice to see you, Doc. Where you goin' at this hour?"

"Up the road. Katy Keller's farm. I'm dropping off her aunt."

Katy Keller was Fritz Vanderhide's wife's maiden name. She didn't have any relatives she got along with. Katy and Fritz lived on the opposite side of town, and she would have run away rather than live on a farm.

The policeman yanked the door open with one hand, a .38 revolver in the other. Gunther, with lightning speed, using his good leg, kicked Dr. Rand into the policeman. Both men crashed to the ground. With the jolt, Vanderhide's gun discharged putting a bullet through the car roof. The sound of the shot sent the rest of the roadblock crew scurrying for cover.

In seconds, Gunther slid over, tromped the accelerator and barreled down the road blowing black exhaust in his wake. As the car cleared the roadblock, a barrage of bullets hit it with little, if any, effect.

After being banged on the top of his head by the door as the car pulled out, Dr. Rand asked "Can someone tell me what the heck is goin' on?"

"Not now," Vanderhide shouted, running to his car. A flurry of roadblock guards took off after Gunther, leaving the good doctor standing alone at the side of the road. *Damn.*

In the end, neither the intense pursuit, nor the "all-points" radio alert, succeeded in catching the elusive assassin.

Sheriff Surratt got Kristi on the radio. "Everybody can go home – he got past us."

Without a hint of disappointment Kristi asked, "Was anyone hurt?"

"Not so much anyone would notice. Dr. Rand took a pretty good bump on the head."

"Dr. Rand? Who's Dr. Rand?"

"He the guy that pulled a slug out of the shooter's thigh, then ended up being his hostage."

"Really. Can I talk to him?"

"I'm sure you can, but he's probably home in bed by now. Vargas, or whatever his name is, tried to use him as his ticket through the roadblock."

"What happened?"

"The brazen old geezer wasn't about to roll over. He signaled the officer at the roadblock with some very clever double-talk."

"Sounds like our assassin underestimated him," Kristi noted.

"He did. Old Doc was cagey enough to alert our guys. He probably saved his own life."

"I suspect you're right," Kristi said. "Go home. Get some shut-eye."

"I think we all could use some," Sheriff Surratt replied.

*****

You hicks are no match for me, Gunther thought, as he pulled into the farthest corner of a Toledo Ford dealer's used car area. He hot-wired a converted van and drove to the back side of the mall he'd passed a few blocks back. He parked alongside a couple of delivery trucks, shut down the van and stretched out across the back seat. He was asleep in thirty seconds.

CHAPTER 36
SAINT JAMES

Early afternoon rain evolved into sweltering heat as the sun failed to penetrate the humidity. Kristi's sweaty, plastered-down hair added to the defeated image she was trying to conceal. *What was I thinking, a woman floundering in a man's world. I couldn't protect the Westerfields with 20 of the finest security people and an unlimited budget. I don't seem to be able to catch the assassin either.*

Self-doubt and despair had replaced her confidence and optimism, but she was a professional, capable of tabling her emotions long enough to assign her people to constructive tasks. The majority were sent to help reinforce roadblock positions, others to question people who possibly saw the motorcycle, and four stayed with the Westerfields just in case the threat wasn't over.

The short drive to the hospital was a painful blur. Reality was devastating. Although she knew what was going to happen, she was unable to stop it – the worst of all possible outcomes. When she arrived at Saint James Hospital, Kristi noticed it was so small, it could easily have been called a clinic. As she got out of the car, she prayed, *Please God, let them be alive. Please.*

Her fear increased with every step as she pushed herself along the sidewalk from the front parking lot to the hospital's main entrance. One of her people, stationed at the entry, held the door for her without the slightest hint of acknowledgment. The lobby, which was also the waiting room, overflowed with Sally's family. *These poor people didn't have time to grieve, and here they are dealing with more violence.*

Lori Smith, recognizing someone she knew, came over to be with Kristi. "We've got to stop meeting at hospitals," she said.

"I know," Kristi replied, as she noticed everyone looked concerned, but tears were nowhere to be found. *Could it be that was a good sign?* "Any word?" she asked no one in particular.

Charlotte, the LaPoint daughter, said, "A nurse told us they were doing as well as could be expected, but that's all we were told, and I have no idea what it meant."

After a long moment of silence and a lung deflating sigh, Kristi whispered, "Thank God." In her mind she said, *Thank You, God, for keeping them alive. Thank You, thank You, thank You.*

Crowded together in the cramped lobby, they waited quietly. The family was apparently too exhausted and depressed to question the circumstance. For that, Kristi was truly appreciative.

An expressionless doctor moved briskly down the hall to the lobby. "I'm Dr. Hastings. I've been tending the Westerfields."

"What can you tell us?" someone asked.

"As you know, they've both been shot; Jeff was hit in the front, Joseph in the back."

"What are their chances?" Charlotte questioned. She apparently was the family spokesman.

"They'd be dead now, but for the extra protection they were wearing. As it is, both are still alive."

"Extra protection? What are you talking about?" Charlotte asked.

"Fortunately they were wearing bulletproof vests with metal chest and back plates."

"Bulletproof vest?" someone questioned.

"A vest made from a material called Kevlar, stopped the bullet that would have gone right through Jeff's heart, and probably saved Joseph from being mutilated beyond repair."

"What can you tell us so far?" Charlotte asked.

"Let's take Jeff first. Luckily, he just has contusions – that's bruising – and two cracked ribs. If there's any internal trauma, it hasn't shown up. He's going to be sore for a long time."

"And Joseph?" Charlotte continued. "Didn't you say he had one of those vests, too?"

"He did, but Joseph is in a lot more trouble."

A murmur of concern filled the room.

The doctor continued, "Even with a metal plate covering his back where the bullet hit, it wasn't slowed enough to keep it from entering his body."

"How bad is it?" Claude asked.

"Bad. Very bad. The x-ray shows the bullet lodged between the edge of the spinal canal and the spinal cord. We need to get him to a neurological surgeon and we need to get him there fast."

"What have you done so far?" Kristi asked, forgetting her despair.

"Jeff talked to a Dr. Turek, Joseph's doctor in South Station."

"I know Turek. He's good," Kristi said.

"He recommended Dr. Mikol," Dr. Hastings continued, "an associate he has a lot of faith in, out of Mount Sinai. We need to get him there soon, or I'll have to operate here."

"I take it you'd prefer getting him to Sinai?" Kristi asked.

"I would. I've dug my share of bullets out of soldiers in Korea, but this is a delicate operation. Joseph could end up paralyzed, in a wheelchair for the rest of his life."

"How are you planning to get him there?" Kristi questioned.

"That's a problem we haven't solved, yet."

"Do you have an airport?"

"Yes, it's only used by locals with small planes. We don't have a terminal, or air control or anything like that."

"How long is the runway?" Kristi asked.

"I'm not a flyer myself, but I think it's fairly long. At one time we had aspirations of getting a commuter airline like Air Wisconsin, but it didn't pan out."

Kristi got the name and number of a local pilot who, she was told, was an airport-knowledgeable person. After calling to make sure the pilot was home, she placed a second call to the South Station airport. "Russ, I need your help."

When she finished with the call, Kristi found Dr. Hastings in a small office behind the lobby. She interrupted his concentration to tell him he needed to contact Mount Sinai and arrange for Joseph's transport from Newark Airport to the hospital. The plane would take an hour to get to Tibbyville, and it would take a little over an hour to get from there to New York.

She went back and waited impatiently in the lobby. When Claude came out of the Westerfield room, he told her Jeff and Joseph would like to see to her before she left. Her despair returned as she walked to the room. *How can I face them? Get control....*

"Hi, there," she said, trying to look optimistic. "I'm glad to see you're still with us." Jeff was sitting upright in a chair, while Joseph was on the gurney lying on his stomach, still strapped to the body-board. His head, at least, was no longer secured. Kristi noticed he had a catheter tube hanging below. *The poor man.*

Ready to get it over with, Kristi said, "I'm so sorry we failed to keep you safe. You've given me all the tools I could possibly want, but the assassin was successful in spite of our efforts."

"Kristi," Joseph said, "In case you haven't noticed, we're both still here."

"Only by the grace of God."

"Nonsense. Without your precautions, we'd be history."

"We knew he was going to strike here. In spite of our elaborate precautions, the demon managed to elude us, get several shots off, and, worst of all, he's still on the loose. I don't call that success."

"The people we're up against are powerful, capable adversaries," Joseph said.

"I only wish I had tried to talk you out of coming here, instead of trying to capitalize on it."

"You couldn't have stopped us, Kristi, no matter what the risk," Jeff said firmly.

"I suspected that, but I feel terrible about the outcome."

"Being bold is one of your strongest traits, Kristi." Joseph said, talking deliberately – painkillers were slowing him down. "You secured our homes, saved Sophia, identified the plant sabotage, are tracking the money to find out who is behind this evil, and you recognized Sally's death was part of a bigger plot. Don't stand there and tell me how inadequate you are. It doesn't wash."

"Thank you, Joseph, I appreciate your confidence."

"The doctor said you also arranged for a plane to get me to Mount Sinai."

"Actually, Russ Atkinson, South Station's airport manager, worked it out. I think the plane should be taking off about now."

Looking toward Jeff, Joseph slowly said, "While I'm at Sinai, Jeff, you'll represent me. We have always thought alike on the important issues. I trust your judgment."

"Thanks for your confidence, Grandpa, but are you sure you want to do that?" Jeff's cracked ribs were forcing him to take short breaths. "I don't do things the same way you do."

"Our approach may vary and that's okay. Values, loyalty, passion, and tenacity are the traits we have in common, Jeff. How you get there isn't as important as knowing where you're headed."

Will I ever be smart enough to live up to his expectations? Jeff thought. *I hope I never let him down*

Kristi realized for the first time their bond was so total, each was an extension of the other. "We won't have a problem," she said.

"I know that," Joseph said slowly, obviously uncomfortable straining to keep his head up.

At 3:40, Kristi and a few of the LaPoints watched as Skyler, flying a Cessna 340, touched down on the weed-bordered runway. He turned the plane around and rolled back to a waiting ambulance. When it came to a stop, Russ came through the door with a seat halfway over his head. It was the first of four he had removed during the flight. He also took out two small walls that created a storage area. The sight of Kristi brought a smile to his face. "I think we've got space for him in there."

"I didn't realize you'd have to personally rebuild the plane." Kristi brushed back a lock of her hair as she walked up to give him a cheek kiss and a little hug.

As two hospital workers were moving Joseph to the plane, he elevated his head enough to smile at Russ, "Thanks, I owe you one."

"No big deal," Russ smiled back. "Good luck at Mount Sinai."

Turning the gurney, once it was partially inside the door, explained why Russ removed the walls. It was tight, but they managed to squeeze it through.

Russ suggested they take him off the cart and strap the board directly to the floor. When one of the men asked why, he said, "You can't fall off the floor." Two of Kristi's team used the other seats. They would be providing security for Joseph until further notice.

Twin turbocharged Continental TSIO-520-K engines easily powered the Cessna down the runway, quickly lifting it into the westerly wind. It gently banked to the northeast setting a course to Newark.

As the plane flew out of sight, Kristi and Jeff unknowingly shared the same thought, *Please God, watch over him.*

Jeff and Kristi lavished Russ with gratitude on the short ride back to Tibbyville. Ignoring the praise, he asked, "Where can I rent a car?"

"You're going back tonight?" Kristi asked, with a hint of disappointment.

"Afraid so. Sassy's with a neighbor. If I leave now I'll be home in time to tuck her in."

"I need to get back, too," Jeff said. "My mother and grandmother are coming over from Europe and, as much as I would like to stay with Joseph, we both thought I needed to be there when they arrive. How about keeping me company?"

"Sounds good," Russ replied. "How about you, Kristi? When are you coming back?"

Glancing at Jeff, she said, "We believe the shooter is still in the area. He hasn't shown up at any of our roadblocks and as long as he's here, I'm here."

"Kristi," Jeff paused, "Maybe we better talk about Grandpa's *'Jeff will represent me'* statement."

"It's not a problem for me, Jeff, unless there's something I'm not aware of?"

"Oh, no. Grandpa and I both think you have wonderful instincts, you know the most capable people, and you've become their respected leader. I just want to be sure you know you have my total support and I'll help any way I can. That includes keeping out of your way."

"I knew that; but it's nice to hear anyway."

After they parted, Kristi picked up her two-way radio.

"Sheriff Surratt here."

"This is Sheriff Kristi. Any sign of him?"

"Not a trace."

CHAPTER 37
COMING TO AMERICA

The community was sound asleep, traffic nonexistent. The possibility of being followed, or anyone realizing they were leaving was remote. The beginning of what would be a very long day started before sunrise, with a knock on the door. "Ready, ladies?" Roberto Modica asked, with a friendly smile.

"We're as ready as we can be with such short notice," Ida replied.

"Great. Got your passports?" DiMarco asked, as he picked up three of the overstuffed suitcases, dragging them to the car.

"Yes. We're ready. Aren't we, sweetheart?"

"I guess so, Mama." Sophia's response sounded extremely skeptical.

Modica grabbed the other three bags which he managed to jam into the trunk. As the Volvo began to move, Ida and Sophia strained to get one more look at their garden. The scent of jasmine lingered at the bottom of the driveway; they would miss it. The car turned south, staying on the coastal highway all the way to Lazise; then, as the sun peeked over the horizon, they turned east on their way to the airport.

Arriving at Aeroporto Valerio Catullo, just outside Verona, DiMarco loaded the bags on a luggage cart and pushed it into the terminal. Modica told the ladies he would be leaving them, but DiMarco was going to accompany them until they arrived safely in New York. At Kennedy Airport, Westerfield's people would take over.

Ida gave him a hug. "Thank you, Mr. Modica. Joseph told me how you were our guardian-angel yesterday – I can't begin to tell you how grateful I am."

"It's been my pleasure, Ma'am. And I thought you might like to know that I've been instructed to see to it someone keeps the weeds out of your garden while you're away."

"Joseph thinks of everything," she said. Modica, putting a

reassuring arm around her shoulder, gave her a little squeeze, then turned and disappeared through the revolving door.

Three tickets were waiting at the check-in counter. An hour later they were seated in a European Commuter Airline plane enjoying the majestic view of the mountain range. Heathrow, on the other hand, was an anthill of impatient travelers. DiMarco plowed a path for the ladies as they wove their way to the American Airlines boarding area. They only had time for bagels before the boarding call. Big seats, with more room in first class, gave the women space to relax, and eventually they both fell asleep. DiMarco hovered over them like a mother duck protecting her ducklings.

Thanks to a long nap, the ladies were well-rested as the 737 bumped onto the runway at JFK International. At US Customs, the line wove back and forth between metal rails. They handed the agent one Italian and one US passport.

Checking the last date on Sophia's renewed passport, the agent said, "Welcome home, Ma'am. You've been away for quite a spell."

"Thank you," she replied, flashing her friendly smile.

DiMarco moved them through the terminals, stopping to get hotdogs and French fries along the way. They arrived at a boarding area with time to spare. The sign behind the podium read, "O'Hare. Flight 347, Departing 6:05." It landed in Chicago at 8 o'clock.

Tony saw a sign saying "DiMarco" the moment he entered the terminal, and with the ladies, hurried to it. "Hi, I'm Tony DiMarco. This is Ida and Sophia."

"Jeff Westerfield," Jeff said, shaking DiMarco's hand. "I've known Ida and Sophia for a long time. Thank you for bringing them to us." He gathered one lady in each arm, hugging them enthusiastically. Although both women looked tired, Jeff could see they were excited and happy. He was, too.

DiMarco said his goodbyes to Ida and Sophia and went off to locate his return flight. Jeff introduced the ladies to his friend Sandy, who had been watching them from the other side of the room. "Nice to meet you," Sandy said, "I'm going to be your driver."

The luggage was gathered and Sandy cautiously drove out of O'Hare. Being past the rush-hour, he chose to go through town, down the Dan Ryan and over the Skyway. It worked out well: traffic wasn't all that bad.

Ida, with Sophia joining in, told him about the trip, stressing how helpful Modica and DiMarco had been and how fast everything was happening. "My goodness, we didn't have time to catch our breath," Ida told him, "But, we're here. That's the main thing."

You're so right, Jeff thought. *The last three days were dreadful: You were almost taken, Aunt Sally was buried, Grandpa was severely wounded, and you were uprooted from your home. It can't get worse. We will fight these people if it takes our last drop of blood.* Jeff realized, he had never been this angry before and that, indeed, it could take his last drop of blood.

Without revealing any more details than necessary, Jeff told Ida and Sophia that Joseph had been shot and was now in Mount Sinai Hospital. Rather than dwell on the devastating nature of the incident, he said, "It's lucky for us that you're here, because he will need you both to help him through this."

"He has taken care of us for so long; now it will be our turn to take care of him," Ida said, with a sad smile.

*****

Jeff was awakened early Sunday by the sound of a ringing phone. By the time he got to it, the answering machine had picked it up. Although Kristi told him this call was a possibility, he could hardly believe his ears. The recorded message was saying: *"Westerfields, if you want to get Sophia and her mother back alive, sell your stock this week. To make arrangements call 212-231-8399 before noon Monday."*

Unaware they were even in the room, Sophia and Ida stood behind him, listening. He jumped when Ida said, "Oh, my goodness," a habitual phrase she used whenever she needed to gather her thoughts.

"I didn't hear you get up," he said. "Did you hear the message? It doesn't make sense."

"We didn't mean to startle you, Jeff," Ida said. "It sounds like somebody thinks the kidnappers have us."

"I'll be damned," he responded. "That's exactly what somebody thinks."

The phone rang again. This time it was Joseph. "Hello, Grandpa. What are you doing up so early?"

"I'm not exactly up, but I can have phone calls. Did Sophia and Ida get there okay?"

"They are standing right next to me. I'll put them on."

Sophia talked first. Like a child, full of excitement and enthusiasm, she relayed details of the last three days. Ida's conversation was filled with concern, more questions than answers. She ended with a tearful "thank you" for always being there when she needed him most. She handed the phone back to Jeff.

He gave Joseph a brief summary of the threatening phone call, then played it on the answering machine. "What do you think about the kidnapper's demands, Grandpa?" Jeff asked.

"I think Kristi's people have won a major battle on the Italian front. Maybe we'll be able to capitalize on it. What are you all doing today?"

"Before I do anything else, I'm going to set a tape recorder next to the answering machine and make a couple of copies to take to the police station. Then, I think we could all use a nice quiet day."

"How are your ribs?" Joseph asked.

"Not bad at all. I've been taking aspirin, and the elastic bandage helps a lot. How about you?"

"The doctors either don't know much, or if they do, they're not telling me. Is Kristi back?"

"Jake told me he thought she'd be back sometime this afternoon."

"The kidnapper's message should boost her morale," Joseph said. "She's probably beating herself up right about now."

"I'm sure you're right," Jeff replied. "I won't let her wallow around long. I doubt if she would anyway. She doesn't roll over easily." *It felt so good to hear his Grandpa's voice.*

CHAPTER 38
WHAT NOW

7:00 AM. "Dr. Rand?" Kristi was standing at the door.

"Whatever you need, ma'am, my office opens at 10:00." He unsuccessfully tried to shut the door as Kristi pushed her way in. *What the hell? Not again.*

"I'm Marilynn Christopher, chief of police from South Station, Michigan. I need to talk to you and I don't have the luxury of hanging around till your office opens. Okay?"

"Okay." Grumbling, he led her into the kitchen. With a twinkle in his eye, he said, "I suppose you want coffee and toast, too?"

"Coffee would be nice."

He reviewed his ordeal in painful detail, getting plenty of sympathy from Kristi as he spoke. His description of the assailant was that of a man trained in seeing details. In addition to the standard "'all-points-bulletin info"; six foot one or two, 190 lbs., light brown hair under the wig, blue-gray eyes, he also noticed his attacker was very tan, well-groomed, in excellent condition, moved like an athlete, had an extremely high pain tolerance, and spoke with a slight southern accent.

Kristi apologized for the early intrusion and handed him a signed blank check.

"What's this for?"

"Doctor, it's time for you to get a car that's not full of holes."

"I can't accept this."

"Sure, you can. The Westerfields, that's who I represent, are just sorry you got dragged into this mess." With that, she turned and headed for the door.

As she got in her car, Dr. Rand said, "Thanks ma'am, I can use a new car."

"That's good, Doctor. We're all glad you're still alive to enjoy it." She had one more thing she needed to do.

"It's pretty quiet in here," she said as she walked into Sheriff Surratt's office.

"Hi Kristi, I thought you'd be on the road by now."

"I wanted to say thanks in person," Kristi said. "You and your people have been great."

"Well, I'm embarrassed, letting him get through our roadblock."

"Don't be. We knew right where he was going to hit and still missed him. He's good, very good."

"What's next with all this?" Surratt asked.

"Do you think we could keep the details out of the paper? There's no point in telling the shooter how much damage he did."

"That shouldn't be a problem; we don't have the *New York Times* here, you know. Besides, almost everyone that gets the paper was there when it happened."

"There's one other thing," Kristi said, with a sly little smile.

"And that is?"

"When we get this guy, and we will get him," Kristi said, "I would like to have him tried here in Ohio first."

"That sounds good to me, but why?" The sheriff asked.

"Evidence," Kristi replied. "It's where we have the most conclusive evidence."

She left the station knowing she had another strong ally in Sheriff Surratt. *Everything is done, it's time to go home.*

During the long ride back to South Station, Kristi's mind was traveling through unfamiliar territory; the world of second guessing and insecurity. *What have I done? What do I do now?* She drove back alone, choosing to put off the discussions and speculation she knew would come. Defeated, she tried to stay focused on the highway. Her brain was numb, except subliminal snippets of ideas about "bank transfers" and "follow the money" kept recurring. *Maybe I'm trying to tell myself something? I better pay attention.* It was a place to start.

Jake met her at the door with a hug. "Hey, I'm supposed to be your boss," Kristi said, after an extended stay in the hug.

"So. Start bossing."

"Hear any word on Joseph?"

"Jeff called me at home last night, and he stopped in this morning. As I understand it, thanks to you and Russ he hit the operating table about 6:30."

"And?"

"He told me Dr. Mikol sounded optimistic. The odds of retaining the use of his legs were favorable, but it sounded like he'll be stuck there for awhile."

"That's wonderful," Kristi sighed. "Anything else going on around here?"

"Jeff dropped off a tape of someone asking for ransom money for Sophia and her mother, and I gave him Charley Tanner's phone number in New York."

"The ladies are here? Aren't they?"

"Oh yes, safe and sound."

"That's the first good thing that's happened in a long time. Let's hear it."

After listening to the tape several times, Jake said, "I had Jeff call Tanner to have him recommend, or send, someone to hook up a monitor on the lake house phone. They'll probably call back. I hope that's alright."

"It's exactly what I would have done, Jake," Kristi said with a smile. "Good job. What else?"

"Not much. Marion Cooper, from the town council, came in to see you. Didn't say what he wanted."

"I've got a hunch," Kristi said. "He's probably wondering if I work here anymore."

"He didn't seem upset or anything," Jake said.

I'm just not ready to deal with Marion. She opted to call a safe harbor. The familiar voice answered. "South Station Airport."

"Hi, Russ. This is Kristi."

"Welcome back. I was hoping you'd get back today."

"How was your trip? How did you and Jeff get along?"

"Fine. He's good people, and I liked Lori Smith, too."

"I didn't realize she was going along."

"She's smitten with Jeff," Russ declared. "That's obvious."

"I don't know much about her," Kristi said, "But what I see, I like. He's a lucky guy."

The small talk went on for awhile before they decided to have dinner together. It was all Kristi really wanted.

I guess it's time to face the inevitable. She dialed Marion Cooper's number. "Hello, Marion, this is Chief Christopher. I heard you were looking for me."

"Thanks for getting back to me. I think we need to talk; when could we get together?"

"Now would work. Tomorrow is pretty well booked." The moment she hung up, she knew it wasn't a wise decision. Exhausted, depressed, with patience nowhere to be found – not a good frame of mind in which to be talking to your boss.

Cooper was a good guy, but Kristi recognized she was hired to run the day-to-day operation, and that job she'd delegated to Jake. She knew she was in trouble when he started the conversation with, "What've you been up to, Kristi?"

"It's a long story, but I'll give you the short version."

"Okay."

"Remember when Jeff Westerfield was shot while he was sailing?"

"Yes, but I didn't think that was our problem. After all, it didn't take place in South Station."

"True. But our goal is protecting our citizens, is it not?"

"Well, yes."

"Are the Westerfields not important South Station citizens?"

"Yes, of course they are, but . . ."

Kristi impatiently interrupted, "When we investigated Jeff's shooting, we discovered Joseph was also a probable target. The plot was to kill them both." Calling it a "plot," was a stretch, but she felt she needed to come from a strong position.

"I didn't know that."

"Few people do." She went on, "The first inkling of a plot came in 1972, when Joseph was threatened by a guy named Hermann vonLeer because he refused to accept an offer to buy his stock holdings in Wesfield Lab." It took an hour and a half for Kristi to provide him with a brief summary of where each piece of the puzzle fit. She touched on changes in airport and Wesfield security, Beverly's warnings and killing, Lori's phone tap, Orchard Farms building project, product sabotage, the banking investigation, Vargas's boat rental and suspected surveillance, Sally's murder, The Shadow caper, the bullet on Joseph's spine, and the company structure he created to pay the bills.

Cooper just sat there, shaking his head. After a long silence, he said, "All this has been going on, and you didn't think the council needed to be kept in the loop?"

"It kind of crept up on us," she replied.

"You hired 20 outsiders, Kristi. That's not a small thing."

"I know."

"Who do they report to?"

It was the question she feared the most. "Ultimately, Joseph Westerfield pays the bill, but their activities are run through me."

"Do you think we are set up to run an independent security force?"

"As long as Jake is better at running day-to-day operations than I am, I can't see where the department has suffered."

"He does a good job, I'll grant you that, but the town council should have been kept informed."

"Would you have approved?"

"I doubt it. We'll never know."

Silence filled the room as Kristi pondered her reply, "The handwriting seems to be on wall. I'm going to make it easy on you, Marion."

"I don't know wha, what you're talking about," Cooper stammered.

"Let's not play games, Marion. You couldn't justify my actions to the council and I'm not going to put you in a spot where you have to."

"But I . . ."

She cut him off again. "I have two conditions."

"And they . . ."

"Jake gets my job. He's proven himself to be more than capable."

"That would be up to the board, but I can almost guarantee it. He is, after all, the only one who knows what's goin' on."

"Your word is good with me, but I want to know you're going to back him."

"You have it. And your second condition?"

"I need a few days to deal with the conspiracy taking place at Wesfield Laboratory."

"Do you have enough evidence to arrest these people?"

"Some of them, but what I really want is information. An arrest would be up to Jake, or more probably, be brought as a federal case."

"Why federal?"

"It's only part of a bigger conspiracy, and it crosses state and national boundaries."

"Are you sure you want to do this?" Cooper asked.

"I've wanted to be a police officer since I was a little girl, but under the circumstances, it's time to give Jake the job he should have had all along."

"I'm sorry it's come to this, Kristi."

"I knew I was stepping over the line. I made the choice, Marion. I'd do it again."

"Are you so sure?"

"I wasn't until this very minute but, yes, I'm positive. Besides, not being a law officer has some benefits. It certainly will untie my hands."

Cooper smirked, "Seems like you've had a free rein all along."

"I can see how you would think that, but the safety of the people of South Station has always been my primary concern."

"Not just the Westerfields?"

"I would have done my best for any citizen. It just happens the Westerfields have resources that most of us would like to have."

*****

Greeted with smiles and hugs, Kristi walked into the world of Russ, the domestic. He'd prepared a backyard meal of grilled chicken laced with some sort of herb butter, tough late-season corn on the cob and vine-ripe tomatoes. It all tasted great. Relaxing at the picnic table gave her a chance to escape the dreadful feeling of failure long enough to share in Sassy's enthusiasm for the role she'd landed in the fifth grade play.

Kristi realized young girls, by nature, were protective of their single fathers, but fortunately, Sassy only encouraged the relationship. Kristi made a point of always taking the time to share in Sassy's world and, as a result, they truly enjoyed each other's company. When they finished eating, Sassy went inside do whatever fifth grade girls do.

"How are you holding up?" Russ asked, noticing her malaise.

"Poorly. I feel like I'm in a cattle stampede. Things are happening so fast it's overwhelming."

"Go back to basics."

"What do you mean?"

"When we were getting trounced in sports, the coach usually told us to go back to basics."

"This isn't sports."

"True, but if you concentrate on the positive aspects of your basic police work, it can keep you focused."

"There's not much positive when he's still out there."

"You've uncovered so many things that are tied together, certainly they can lead you to him."

Kristi's green eyes held his questioning gaze. "You're right. You're absolutely right. It's time to stop crying in my beer."

CHAPTER 39
PRESSURE

Marion Cooper opened his front door to find Kristi standing with papers in her hand. "Well, Kristi, come on in. Don't tell me you want your job back?" he said with a smile.

"I need a favor, Marion, but I'm not sure you can help."

"Why do I think it's going to be something devious?"

"Because you were going to fire me for being devious," Kristi returned his congeniality.

"You quit – remember?"

"Right. And for that, you owe me a favor."

"Okay. What are you looking for?"

She told the story of the how people from Leverkusen ended up with the Mac Orchard property. The new owner, Painter Holding Company, was tied in as part of the group fronting for people interested in bringing BayerAG back into this country. She included information about the three mysterious accounts at the Manhattan Bank & Trust, and stressed how and why Bayer came to be prohibited from doing business in the US. She closed by stating the assassin after the Westerfields was just a small part of the same movement.

"What do you want from me?" Cooper asked.

"I'd like you to put the screws to the building project."

"I assume you already have an idea how I might do that."

"The environment."

"What about it? Have they broken some environmental law?"

"Not that I'm aware of."

"But, you want me to 'put the screws to the project.'"

"Just put a few stumbling blocks in the way."

"Like what?" Cooper asked.

"The Berrien county chapter of Great Lakes Fishermen could have some questions about the septic system polluting the trout stream."

"Will it?"

"It's possible," Kristi answered, "But I doubt it. That doesn't mean they can't raise the issue."

"I see what you mean; cause them trouble. Right."

"Also, the stream on the property runs into Lake Michigan."

"And?"

"The Great Lakes Basin Ecosystem folks – they're part of the Environmental Protection Agency – may want to take a real close look at all that pollution before any more work is done."

Cooper said with a smile, "You get the Feds involved and it'll be years before they can move in."

"No, Mr. Cooper, it's you we need to get them involved. You have the credibility it will take to get their attention. I don't even work here anymore."

"I guess I could let them know there's a New York builder trying to sneak one over on them."

"I like your thinking, Marion."

*****

With a bounce in his step, an upbeat Jeff walked into South Station's cozy Cape Cod police station.

"Hi Jeff, how's Joseph doing?" Jake asked.

"Not that bad. He has some feeling in both legs, and they have him in a rehabilitation routine. We're encouraged."

"That's great; he's in our prayers."

"I'll tell him that, Jake; he'll appreciate it. I understand congratulations are in order."

"Thanks, but under the circumstances, I've got mixed emotions about it."

"You'll do a great job. Is Kristi here?"

"I'm in here," she said loudly from the side-room office. "Come on in." Kristi was throwing odds and ends in a cardboard box.

"Looking for work, ma'am?" he asked in his usual friendly manner.

"Got any ideas?"

"Sure do," Jeff said. "ProTect & Associates needs a full-time chief executive. Interested?"

"South Station's town council thinks I'm already full time with ProTect. That was the problem."

"Joseph and I are both sorry about that, Kristi."

"I'm not having as much of a problem with it as I thought I would. So, tell me Jeff, what's the pay like for a full-time executive?"

"How's three times whatever you've been making here?"

"That's not necessary, Jeff."

"I know that; but it's less than what you're worth."

"Are you so sure?" she asked, still haunted by the feeling she was somehow responsible for not preventing the shooting.

"I'm damn sure. And I know Joseph would say the same thing. Without you we'd be pushin' up daisies, and my mother and grandmother would be kidnapped or worse."

"I'll be happy to accept such a gracious offer." Kristi said, extending her hand to seal the deal. Shaking hands brought smiles, to both faces.

"Good. Where do we go from here?" Jeff questioned.

Kristi's green eyes held his tightly as she replied, "We are going after those people–no holds barred."

"What can I do to help?"

"You're going to have your hands full with Ida, your mother, and Joseph, when he gets home."

"It won't be a problem," Jeff said. "Taking care of Joseph will keep the ladies out of trouble."

"I want to be sure you're aware of, and whenever possible, involved in everything we have in motion."

Jeff interrupted, "That's not necessary. I'm no more of a second guesser than Jo . . ."

". . . in case something should happen to me," Kristi said with a smile.

"Of course. For some reason it didn't occur to me that you, too, could be in danger."

"You need to get with Jake. He wants your input on taking in and questioning the Wesfield employees."

"That's easy. Very discreetly."

Kristi reviewed the events involving Sophia's failed kidnapping and the possibility that the originators could be unaware of the outcome. She outlined her idea on slowing down the Mac Orchard building project, and told him her main focus would be the money trail.

"How do they follow the money?" Like his grandpa, Jeff wanted enough detail to understand what was going on.

"I don't know much more than you do, but according to John Snowden – he's my friend at S & H Investigation – checks, money transfers and direct deposits are just agreements between cooperating people and institutions. John claims, if you can gain access to the messages that carry those agreements, you will be able to verify who's paying whom. The 'for what,' however, is another matter.

"It helps to know what accounts you're looking into; that's why the list of suspects you worked on was so helpful."

CHAPTER 40
THE HACKERS

Forming a tent with his fingertips, John Snowden touched his nose as he pondered Kristi's request. "Let me get this straight. You want me to freeze a numbered account at the International Bank of Commerce, one of the Cayman Island's oldest and most secure institutions?"

"John, you're the one who told me they funded Gunther Quality Imports, the company that funneled money to the assassin," Kristi said.

"There is a difference between discovering banking patterns and changing them," Snowden said.

"Can you do it? Or better still, will you do it?"

"I've never tried anything like that. One thing for sure, I wouldn't take any money out of the bank."

"I'm not asking you to steal, John," Kristi said, "Just freeze the account."

"It would be illegal."

"That bothers you?"

"Not a lot," Snowden said with a grin. "I do have one idea that might work, but it would be a lot easier if we could discover the account holder's code number."

"I thought you discovered the account number?"

"I did. And with that number we can deposit money into that account without a problem. Taking money out, or changing the account, is a completely different ball game. For that you need to provide a code number in conjunction with your account number."

"I guess the code number is what makes it a numbered account?" Kristi said.

"You got it."

"Are you going to share your idea with me, anyway?"

"It's risky. How about this," he began. "We send a wire that says, 'Through no fault of yours, I believe my account information has been compromised. Would it be possible to change my account number. If it's convenient, I would like you to change the second group of numbers from G77 to G14. The other eight numbers can remain the same."

"That sounds good to me, John."

"The fact that we know the account number and are not trying to take money out may keep alarms from going off, but I think the chances of pulling it off are slim at best."

"I don't want you to end up in jail, John."

"That won't happen, but I would only do it as a last resort. If we knew the code number it would be a done deal."

"How would we know if they took the bait?" Kristi questioned.

"Get a Charleston P.O. box number. We'll ask them to send a confirmation there."

"They won't question that?"

"I doubt it. With a new account number, it makes sense to change the address."

"What would happen then?"

John was enjoying the speculative intrigue. Smiling , he said. "Fortunately, monies going into Gunther Quality Imports from IBC weren't drawn automatically. From everything we can tell, it has always been requested in the form of a money transfer. That's how we got the account number in the first place. Next time they send a request, Gunther Quality Imports should receive a message reading something like, 'INCORRECT ACCOUNT NUMBER, PLEASE RESUBMIT'."

"I'd like to try it, John, but I'm afraid we might just be sending up a red flag," Kristi said. She always liked John Snowden's willing style.

"Mind telling me just what you're trying to accomplish?"

"I'm trying to slow our assassin down and get him wondering, what's goin' on for a change. I also think, if money gets tight, he'll return to his home base."

"Where is his home base?" Kristi.

"I wish I knew for sure. Thanks to your efforts, John, we know Gunther Quality Imports in Charleston, South Carolina, covered at least some of the expenses for Victor Vargas and Verner Delmar. Both names are tied to the crimes we are looking at, which makes Charleston a very potential location."

"You have people there?"

"Just one, Charley Tanner, and he hasn't been there long."

"I know Charley. He's a great snoop and he knows his listening devices. How else can we help?" Snowden asked.

"Remember when you discovered Gunther Quality Imports paid the credit card bills for Vargas and Delmar?"

"Sure, of course I remember," Snowden replied.

"I need their credit cards canceled, overdrawn. I don't care what, just totally discredited and unusable."

"Now that I can do; no problem. Their cards will be invalid by the end of the day. And, I'll see to it they will not have clean enough credit to get new cards. What else?"

"I'd like to target the four Painter America accounts at Manhattan Bank & Trust, but I don't know what could be accomplished there."

"Can you get the Feds involved?" Snowden asked.

"There is a worldwide conspiracy here, and we'll need to pull them in when we get closer, but for now, they would probably just muck it up."

"Didn't you start your career with them?"

"Yes I did. My first job was a Specialist with the FBI – but they complicate everything they touch."

"Don't you have any friends there?"

"Why?"

"Because a call from the FBI requesting Painter records would have the place in a tizzy," John said confidently. "I think the Painter people would be very reluctant to forward any more money to someone funding a hit man, if they thought the FBI's snooping would tie them to a murder."

"I do have a few FBI friends that are still on my Christmas card list."

"Hey. What good are friends if you can't use them," Snowden joked.

"Thanks, John. I don't know what I'd do without you."

"You'll get a bill. Now get out of here before I end up in jail."

Kristi thought to herself, *As long as I'm out and about anyway, I could stop off to see my old friend Marti Towne. Maybe he could or would get unofficially involved. The feds would love to get their hands on this mess. Do I really want that?*

CHAPTER 41
THE GREEDY

Millions and millions of light yellow tablets marched along a vibrating stainless steel tray down to dividers grouping them into platoons of fifty. Once assembled, they were dumped into bottles, covered with cotton, and trapped with a childproof cap. Then labels were applied and the bottles were packed in corrugated boxes. The boxes were neatly stacked on pallets, secured with shrinkwrap film, and whisked into semitrailers.

Disrupting the hush of a dewy Michigan morning, the big trucks rolled before dawn. Thundering down the highway, up the hills, around the curves, they carried the future of Wesfield Laboratory to food and drug stores across the USA.

Hutchins, Keller & McDonnell, the advertising agency, created the "Stubborn Winter Colds" theme, using humorous sneezes and red noses to entertain as well as explain product benefits. TV and radio commercials were scheduled to hit the airways as merchants rearranged their shelves to accommodate the new item.

With perfect timing, print ads featuring testimonials that targeted winter cold and flu sufferers, were placed in magazines and national, as well as local, newspapers. Additionally, six million samples were bulk-mailed to upper and middle-income households. ExRelief Cold Medicine was about to become a reality.

News of the cold medicine's successful product introduction was vonLeer's first hint that he and the Reestablishment Committee could possibly fail. Early next year indications of consumer acceptance would begin to trickle in and, based on test market results, vonLeer knew it was going to be a smashing success. Once that happened, purchasing enough stock to gain control of Wesfield was going to become nearly impossible.

VonLeer's face revealed none of the panic and rage churning in the pit of his stomach, as he asked his secretary to arrange a meeting with Mr. Smylee. *What else could possibly go wrong? Don't these people know failure is unacceptable?* He hoped Smylee would have something positive to report. The meeting was not going to be one Mr. Smylee would soon forget.

*****

A 3:00 meeting at Wesfield Laboratory on a Friday afternoon; that was unusual. Most people were mentally too far into their weekend to be productive. Gordon Wieldey's secretary paid little notice as she passed along an interoffice communication titled "Security Violations." Rowland Thomas, head of Security, sent it to Wieldey, Dick McLane, Nancy Woolf, Jeff Westerfield, and a fellow from Manufacturing named Stodameyer. The memo briefly stated, "It has come to our attention that several people have infiltrated Wesfield Laboratory and are working counter to the goals and interests of the company." The last line asked people to "Attend in person – Do NOT send a substitute."

Jeff sat quietly on the sidelines, as Rowland, his ally in protecting the company, opened the meeting. "People, let me introduce our county sheriff, George Arven, and Chief Jacobson, the new police chief at South Station. Getting right to the business at hand, I would like to turn the meeting over to Chief Jacobson. Jake."

Jake was certain everyone could hear his heart pounding, as he rose from his chair. *Last year he was a part-time cop; now he was opening a conspiracy investigation. Well, here goes,* he thought.

"Thank you, Rowland," Jake paused to take a deep breath and look over the attendees. "Will each of you please give me your name and job title. We'll start with you, Jeff, and go clockwise around the table."

"Jeff Westerfield, Product Manager."

"Randy Robertson, South Station police officer."

"Marilynn Christopher, former chief of police – chief Jacobson's associate."

"Dick McLane, Purchasing."

"Nancy Wolf, Security"

"A stranger to all but Kristi, the stocky, middle-aged, smartly dressed gentleman looked at each person before saying softly, "Marti Towne, FBI agent." The room went silent.

Each person replied as instructed until it was Gordon's turn. "I'm Gordon Wieldey, Vice President of Marketing. What's going on here, Chief?" he asked, brushing back the hair above his ear.

Kristi proudly watched Jake take the offense. "Tell me, Mr. Wieldey, what is your connection to the Painter America Company?"

"What are you talking about?" Wieldey responded with a wild look flashing in his eyes.

"You received several large . . . I might say very large, sums of money from the Painter America Reestablishment Fund."

"Why do you think that?"

"I don't think anything, Mr. Wieldey. I know it."

"How's that?"

"You cashed personal checks written from their account at Manhattan Bank & Trust. The only question is, what did you do to earn all that money?"

"I ask you again," Wieldiey said, with his finger waving in Jake's direction. "What's this all about?"

"It's about trouble, Mr. Wieldey. You're in serious trouble. So are you, Mr. McLane, Mr. Stodameyer, and you, Miss Wolf. We have proof that you've been in the Painter organization's pocket for some time."

McLane's panic came to the surface. "Are you telling us we're under arrest?"

"Perhaps." Jake's matter-of-fact approach unnerved all four of the accused. "You are, after all, aware that you're part of a worldwide conspiracy?"

"Conspiracy?" McLane quickly stood, leaning forward in Jake's direction. "I don't have any idea what you're talking about."

"I don't, for a second, believe that, Mr. McLane. You received three payments of $30,000 each for your efforts."

"What efforts?" McLane said.

"You're caught up in a conspiracy, masterminded by ruthless, powerful people trying to take control of Wesfield Laboratory," Jake said, looking him in the eye. "Of course, you already know that."

"I do?"

"Yes. You do. You personally sabotaged the ExRelief product components with water."

"What?"

"When you visited the mixing room with Mr. Wieldey."

"Now wait a minute . . ." McLane said, without words to finish his protest.

"Sit down, mister. And stay down." Kristi saw a side of Jake she didn't know he had.

Jake continued, "So far the plot has involved two murders, three attempted murders, and an attempted kidnapping. More closely related to the product launch, Wesfield's main packaging supplier had their printing presses demolished in an attempt to cripple ExRelief's manufacturing timetable."

Gordon Wieldey shouted, "We had no part in that."

"Perhaps not," Jake said softly, "but you are part of a conspiracy that includes those crimes. It's not a team I would want to play on."

"What now?" Nancy Wolf cautiously asked. She was first to see the Chief and his associates knew too many details to deny.

"You all have the same choice. Tell us everything Painter had you do and we'll be as lenient as the law allows. Refuse, and you'll be in jail too long to watch your kids grow up."

"What do you expect from us?" Wieldey asked, beginning to realize the magnitude of the situation.

"Total cooperation," Jake replied.

"I'll tell you everything I know," Nancy Wolf blurted out, trembling with fear. McLane and Wieldey realized she alone could put them behind bars.

"Not now, Miss Wolf," Jake said. "You and Mr. McLane will go with Sheriff Arven to the county offices where you'll be individually questioned. Mr. Wieldey and Mr. Stodameyer will come back to the station with me."

"We can't go home first?" Wieldey asked, having lost all signs of composure.

"You'll get a chance to call your home, as well as an attorney if you feel the need, but remember, how well you work with us will be taken into consideration." Jake turned toward Kristi, "Do you have anything you'd like to add?"

"Thank you, Chief," Kristi said. "Although some of you managed to get the plant security altered according to Painter's instructions, you have failed miserably in stopping ExRelief from hitting the market in time for the cold season. You can bet the Painter executives are livid with your pitiful performance.

"You're only small fry in this pond," she continued. "It's the big fish we are after. Helping us catch them can only work in your favor. Or . . . the choice is yours to make."

On the way out, Kristi had to quickstep to catch up. "Jake. Hold up a second."

"Hey, Kristi," Jake said as he turned to wait.

"Jake. You did a great job in there."

"Thanks. I think I was as anxious as they were. I'm glad that part is over."

CHAPTER 42
CHARLESTON

Charley Tanner's wife, Bessie Mae, would never complain about it, but Charley knew she'd been lonely with him stuck in the Midwest for so long. He stopped off in New York, just long enough to pick her up. Charley had finagled a working vacation with her included. She didn't get to travel with him often, which made this trip to Charleston, South Carolina, a special assignment, indeed. The 6:07 AM flight on Piedmont Air took four hours because they changed planes in Charlotte, N.C. In Charleston, with a rented a car and the better part of the day ahead of them, they decided to check out the town.

Manhattan's frantic pace was replaced with the sound of clopping hooves from horse-drawn carriages taking tourists to share Charleston's charms. Charley and Bessie Mae had no problem making the transition. They enjoyed the narrow streets lined with two, three, and four-story buildings separated only by gentle pastel colors. The Battery, decorated with soldiers' monuments and cannons under a canopy of live oaks, was of particular interest. From there, out in the bay, they could see a hint of Fort Sumter where, they learned, on April 12, 1861, the first shots were fired beginning the War Between the States.

Bessie Mae shopped at a few boutiques and art galleries before they checked into The Lady Slipper Inn, a quaint little hotel on Pinckney Street, in the older part of town.

The next day, while Bess browsed the shops, parks and churches, Charley's first stop was the Charleston Metro Police Station. Calls from Sheriff Surratt and Chief Jacobson had paved the way for his visit. When Charley identified himself and presented a Michigan arrest warrant, he was received with smiles and friendly small talk about being a damn Yankee. The congenial Charleston police wanted to be kept in the loop, and they pledged their support wherever it was needed.

Charley worked to discover where Gunther lived, what his habits were, and when, if ever, he put in an appearance at his import company. When they met for dinner, Bessie Mae relayed the events of a fun-filled day. Charley did most of the listening.

Later that evening, while looking for things to keep her busy, Bess spotted an article in the *Charleston Observer* that piqued her interest. "Charley?"

"Yes, dear?"

"Didn't you say you're looking into a guy named Gunther?"

"Yes, dear."

"Does he own an imports company, by any chance?"

"Yes, dear, he does. Why?"

"I think I may know how to find him?"

"Yes, dear. I appreciate your interest."

"I'm serious, Charley. This piece in the paper says a Mr. Gunther and a couple other blue-bloods are being honored Saturday night for starting some financial fund. It sounds like the fund is designed to support the Charleston Ballet Company."

"Let me see that," Charley said, as he grabbed the paper and scanned the article. The words "Gunther Quality Imports," bounced off the page. "I'll be. Bessie May, you really have found him."

"Yes, dear. Haven't I, though?" she said with a grin.

Charley called the South Station Police station, only to learn Kristi didn't work there anymore. Jake gave him a number where he thought she might be reached, and told him he would be happy to pass along messages if he couldn't track her down. Charley looked twice when he saw the New York City area code.

"Hello, this is Kristi."

"Kristi. Are you still the boss?"

Recognizing his voice, she said, "Charley. Since when do you need a boss?"

"I just was told you're not a cop anymore."

"Well, to ease your mind, nothing has changed except I don't have to worry about the South Station Police Department."

"You okay with that?" he asked.

"Oh, sure. There really wasn't time for both, and to be honest, Charley, South Station doesn't need me. It never did."

"You're not movin' to the Big Apple, are you?"

"No, just trying to tie up a little banking. Now, why did you call?"

"This mysterious Gunther guy we're looking for."

"Yes."

"He's a regular celebrity down here."

"You've located him, then," Kristi said.

"My wife Bess did," Charley replied.

"What?"

"It's a long story. Next Friday night, at the Galliard municipal auditorium, the ballet company is honoring him, and a couple other local muck-a-mucks. I think they're givin' away a bunch of dough."

"You sure he's the right Gunther?" Kristi asked.

"He owns the import shop."

"Have you personally seen him yet?"

"I'm pretty sure I saw him this morning at the import store, but I need a confirmation before I can say for sure."

"Why do you think it was him?"

"Well, the store opens at noon, so he had to have a key to get in. This guy was pretty big, about six foot, well-built, I'd say in excellent condition. He left his Mercedes parked in front of the store, spent five minutes in there, then came out and took off. I'd bet a week's pay it was him."

"It sounds like he could be our man, all right," Kristi said. "Think you can get in there without attracting attention?"

"I've done things like that a time or two. What do you need?"

"Ties to Victor Vargas or Verner Delmar, bank records, itinerary, plane tickets; you know the routine."

"I'll see what I can do," he responded.

"Remember who we're dealing with, Charley. Bessie Mae doesn't need to go home a widow."

"Thanks again for letting me bring her. She loves this place; the people couldn't be any nicer."

"It's called civility, Charley. We don't see it much in the Northeast.

Where are you staying?"

"The Lady Slipper Inn."

"Sounds quaint. I'm glad you and Bessie Mae are having a good time. Good snooping, Charley, and stay safe."

*****

Adger's Wharf, one of Charleston's oldest streets, was originally used to load and unload merchant ships. In 1974, it had evolved into a bumpy cobblestoned shopping district with crepe myrtle trees and huge concrete pots of bright red geraniums along both sides. The exclusive shops were housed in pastel clapboard and old brick buildings with arched doors and windows. Walking down Adger's Wharf was like returning to the 1800s. Gunther Quality Imports was located at the end of the street, preceded by a gallery displaying expensive sculpture.

A Sunny Day touring bus squealed to a halt on East Bay Street. The doors swished open and a band of tourists spilled onto the sidewalk. Sticking together, they moved slowly, spending token time in each shop. When the shoppers turned east on Adger's Wharf, Charley managed to become one of the group by striking up a conversation with the lady he perceived to be the head know-it-all. She spent much of her time looking down her nose at price tags containing numbers that never satisfied. Her co-shoppers seemed pleased to see she'd found a new friend to keep her occupied.

Using the group as cover, Charley surveyed Gunther Quality Imports without drawing attention to himself. The first thing he noticed was how little inventory was exhibited. Although each piece or grouping was smartly merchandised, there wasn't much of it.

He casually took note of the two continuous loop video cameras, discreetly mounted to cover the shopping area, and the simple alarm systems installed at both doors. The narrow steps leading to an office above the back quarter of the floor space didn't appear to have an obvious alarm, but Charley thought there was one he'd have to find. Simple stuff, he thought, considering this guy is a pro. If I'm going to find anything here, it'll be up in the office. He would find out tonight.

It was close to midnight when Charley returned dressed in his dark, cat-burglar clothes. Without streetlights, the narrow alley behind Gunther's store was hidden in dark shadows. Heart pounding, he disabled the alarm, picked the back door lock, and began moving deliberately into the building. Rubbing his hand over his bald head, he took a long apprehensive breath on his way to the steps. *Here I am again, breaking and entering. I hate this.* He was right, the steps were wired, too. It only took a couple of minutes to disarm the system and he scampered up.

Across from the door, the floor safe was huge, taking up most of the opposite wall. Charley looked it over, wondering how they got it up the steps and why this little company would need this monster. As he suspected, it was too sophisticated for him to open. He decided to ignore the safe and concentrate on things he could handle – unlocking the desk and files. Without taking the time to read details, he methodically took pictures of anything that might contain pertinent information. His most important photos, as it turned out, were of a few hand-written numbers and letters scribbled on the inside cover of the checkbook. They didn't make sense to him, but somebody might know what they were.

When he ran out of papers to photograph, he turned his attention to his real expertise, implanting microphone-bugs in the soft tile ceiling over the office area. Charley was as meticulous and thorough in his departure as he was breaking in.

He got back to The Lady Slipper Inn around 3:30. Bessie Mae maintained a steady rhythm of mild snoring as he crawled under the covers. Relieved and exhausted, he instantly fell into the same rhythm.

They spent little time together the next few days, but Bessie Mae was happy not being left behind and Charley enjoyed having her along. Tonight was a first for both, dinner and the ballet. Dressed in their Sunday duds, they were escorted to their seats, seven rows from center stage. They couldn't figure out what the story was about, but the dancers were wonderful to watch. As the program progressed and intermission rolled around, they were surprised to discover they were totally enjoying the ballet.

*****

Gunther was a man haunted by childhood memories. In his

earliest memories, he was very poor, living with his widowed mother downstream from a spillway on the Crystal River. Their small rundown rented house was located in the lowland where the river widened to become Crystal Lake. His mother worked endlessly, cleaning, cooking and sewing for wealthy neighbors that lived in well-kept houses on the high end of the lake. Not only was Gunther financially poor, he felt inferior in his heart.

Each Saturday morning with earthworms and a cane pole, young Gunther walked the banks of Crystal Lake watching the weekly sailing regatta. He had never sailed, but he could feel the joy and freedom that sailing offered. He watched with green eyes as the wealthy gathered to enjoy parties and dances at the country club, and countless stage performances at the community college. He vowed someday he would be part of it all. Envy became his motivator.

In 1963, on the day Smylee's initial funding was safely in the bank, Gunther joined the Yacht Club and enrolled as a member of the group sponsoring the Charleston theater and ballet. Society welcomed him enthusiastically, more than happy to take his money.

Gunther was fidgeting in the wings, waiting to be officially accepted as one of society's true leaders. He was being recognized for his success and generosity. In his mind, he was finally where he always wanted to be.

The other three names were called first. At last, the loudspeaker bellowed, ". . . and Victor Gunther, would you all please come to center stage." The audience responded with generous applause. He tried so very hard not to limp, but injured nerves and muscles wouldn't respond to his will. Gunther burned with humiliation, but concealed it totally with a broad smile, as he hobbled into the stage lights. The others walked slowly so he could keep up.

Each recipient said a few words. Victor had his badge of total acceptance.

Charley Tanner could hardly stay in his seat as he watched Gunther limp out on stage. He leaned over and whispered in his wife's ear, "This guy not only paid the assassin, he *was* the assassin."

CHAPTER 43
THE NUMBER

Federal Express. A company you could depend on. They dropped off Charley's duplicate packages to Kristi at her South Station apartment, and John Snowden in Manhattan. They arrived at both destinations well before 10:00 AM. Kristi quickly paged though the material to discover Charley's camera had worked remarkably well, considering the lighting.

After closer inspection of the checking account records, Kristi concluded two things were certain: Gunther Quality Imports was generously funded, and Gunther, using the names Victor Vargas and Verner Delmar, had traveled all over the world.

She placed a call to her friend Snowden. "Hello, John. Did you get Charley's package?"

"Man . . . he struck gold with those pictures,"

"We sure have a lot of proof that Vargas, Delmar and Gunther are all the same man."

"Hell, Kristi, we knew that already," Snowden said. "I'm talking about the numbers written on the checkbook cover."

"What numbers?"

"Find the picture of the bluish checkbook; it's the inside cover."

"Okay, let me look . . . got it."

"Look at the bottom left corner. See the numbers?"

"Yes. I can just make them out, but I fail to see what they mean."

"Kristi, look above the number, a few inches up. Can you see any letters?"

"It looks like a C, and above that, I guess that's a B, then a one."

"It's not a one; it's an I," Snowden said. "IBC. The International Bank of Commerce."

"Do you think it's the code to the numbered account, John?"

"It's an IBC number, and it's not the account number. Everyone writes his code number down someplace, unless it's tied to something he can't forget."

"You mean like a birthday?"

"Exactly, but this number is too long for that. He probably didn't choose it." Snowden pointed out.

"I'm surprised how casually Mr. Gunther treated the code." Kristi said.

"I'm not. He's thinks like a predator. It wouldn't dawn on him that he could be a victim."

"Well, what do you think, John? Still too risky? Can we get away with it?"

"Hell, yes, we can get away with it. We won't be challenged now that we have the code."

"How soon can you get it done?"

"The money will disappear by the end of the day. And Kristi . . ."

"Yes?"

"Be sure to tell Charley, the bug man, he outdid himself this time."

"I'll do it. Let me know how you come out, okay, John?"

"Okay. Have a nice day."

Later that afternoon Kristi listened twice to a message left on her answering machine. The words brought a smile to her face. "Blood money. Now you see it – now you don't. John."

*****

Only a few people had the number to his private line; when that phone rang it was usually important. "This is Mr. Smylee, what can I do for you."

"Mr. Smylee, Jules MacFarlin, at Manhattan Bank & Trust." MacFarlin's most important responsibility was account executive assigned to oversee the Painter business.

"Jules, it's good to hear your voice. What's up?"

"An agent Towne from the FBI was in here interested in seeing transactions between Painter and several people in Michigan."

"Really, that..."

Jules interrupted, "That's not all. He was also interested in your business with Gunther Quality Imports. They're out of Charleston, South Carolina."

"I know the company." Talking very slowly, Smylee asked, "What did they want, exactly?"

"For the import company, copies of wire transfers you sent to them over a period of several years."

"How would they know if we sent Gunther Quality Imports any money or not?"

"I have no idea. But they had dates and information involving exact deposits; so they're not just on a fishing expedition."

"Do we have to provide the information?" Smylee was still talking deliberately, but the pitch of his voice seemed to be rising.

"We can slow up the process, but, when all is said and done, we don't have a choice."

"What about the people?"

"They gave me these names: McLane, Stodameyer, Wolf, and Wieldey."

"Did they want transfer information for them, too?"

"They did, but more importantly, they wanted copies of checks you wrote to them."

"That was on the up and up; they sent us invoices for consulting fees." Smylee was beginning to sound defensive.

"I'm sure it won't be a problem, Mr. Smylee, as long as you have the documentation."

"Where did you leave it, Jules – you didn't give them anything?"

"Of course not. I wouldn't do that, Mr. Smylee. Not without clearing it with you."

"Good. Just hold tight for now. I'll get back to you."

"No problem," Jules said.

How wrong you are, Smylee thought. *Things were not going well before, and this . . . vonLeer is not going to be easy to deal with.*

CHAPTER 44
CONFLICTING REPORTS

He listened to the phone message for a second time. "Park Lake, Sunday afternoon, 3:00." Smylee was anything but ready to meet with Hermann vonLeer. His information was more hearsay than reality, and the facts were so contradictory they only created more questions. No matter how distasteful, Mr. Smylee was a man who did what he had to do. He decided to walk the 16 blocks to the hotel. A little exercise always cleared his head, and whenever he met with vonLeer, he needed his wits about him.

It was 3:00 sharp when one of vonLeer's ever-present muscular assistants escorted him into the opulent conference room. Smelling a wisp of lemon oil on the black walnut table accentuated the woozy feeling Smylee had been trying to shake all day. He took a seat directly across from his interrogator. After a short businesslike greeting, vonLeer's first question caught Smylee totally off-guard. "How have we been funding the people we have working at Wesfield Lab?"

Smylee wondered, *could vonLeer already know the FBI was interested in Painter's payments to the people at Wesfield?* He answered, "They send us invoices for consultant services along with a separate report on their progress. Unless there is some issue with the report, we send them a check."

"Who signs the checks?"

"I do, of course. You and I are the only authorized signatures on the reestablishment fund account." The thought, *I'm standing out on this limb – alone*, flashed through Smylee's mind. "Is there some problem?"

VonLeer ignored the question. "What about the operative you have dealing with the Westerfields? How is Gunther funded?"

Smylee responded, "The bulk of his money is wire-transferred into his IBC account in the Caymans."

VonLeer's pencil moustache emphasized a contemptuous sneer

when he asked, "Where does the money that's not part of the bulk go?"

Unnerved, Smylee said, "It's only his expense money, and it's always been deposited directly into his export company account at Charleston Federal Bank in South Carolina."

"His expenses – what do they run a year?"

Smylee, fidgeting in his chair, answered, "Roughly, sixty to a hundred thousand."

"How easily can Mr. Gunther be tied to Painter America?"

"We have taken all the standard precautions. And, in his long history with us, he has never come under suspicion for any of his services."

"Mr. Smylee, that's all very interesting, but the question was, 'Can he be tied to Painter?'"

"Possibly." It was the last thing Smylee wanted to admit.

"What stage of this project are we in?" vonLeer pressed on.

Smylee's eyelids fluttered as he began the update. "Last week, Gunther sent me a report claiming he shot both Westerfields in an Ohio cemetery. He said he saw both men fall to the ground."

"If they're indeed out of the picture, our people will be very pleased." Hermann vonLeer said, his demeanor softening.

"Unfortunately, the Tibbyville newspaper only confirmed that there was a shooting without identifying the victims, or their condition."

"That doesn't sound like they're dead to me."

"I agree," Smylee said. "I checked the *South Bend Tribune* which covers South Station's local news; that's where the Westerfields live. There wasn't any mention of the incident."

"Is there anything else that ties into this?"

Smylee paused, wishing he could escape. "I also received word that someone claiming to be Jeff Westerfield has responded positively to our demands in Bardolino."

"What? The same Jeff Westerfield who was supposed to be shot dead in Ohio?"

"Yes. The same," Smylee said panicking inside without an explanation for the contradiction. "According to the information I have, he agreed to sell all Westerfield-held stock if Sophia and Ida's safe release could be guaranteed."

"If both Westerfields had been eliminated, who was responding to the kidnapping?" vonLeer said, with eyes penetrating into Smylee's soul.

"I am trying to find out." The pitch of Smylee's voice kept rising with each unacceptable answer.

"Mr. Smylee? Do you think Gunther has become a liability?"

"He has been an extremely effective agent, but maybe it's time to reevaluate."

Slamming his palm on the table, vonLeer shouted, "Reevaluate, my ass – Gunther has the feds all over him, and they're trying to link us to him."

"What do you suggest?" Smyblee feebly asked.

VonLeer leaned forward with his chin between his thumb and forefinger, "Hmm . . . it's time to limit our exposure."

"Where do you want to start?" Smylee said, having a premonition. *I know you'd like to start with me.*

"All funding will stop immediately," vonLeer said pointing at Smylee's nose. "That includes Gunther as well as our Wesfield people."

"I'll, I'll see to it immediately," Smylee stammered, backing his chair away from the table.

"Your office will also destroy all reports, correspondence, and copies of banking transactions, any trace of past dealings with those people."

"What about arrangements between our companies?" Smylee asked.

"Attorney-client privilege. It shouldn't be a problem."

"What do you want me to do about Gunther?" Smylee asked.

"Forget him," vonLeer replied. "He will no longer be your concern. I will deal with Mr. Gunther."

"Are you sure? I could have him leave the country, or possibly some . . ."

"In fact, Mr, Smylee," vonLeer interrupted. "I am considering scrapping the whole project. We'll just have to wait and see how the Italian program plays out. And, of course, find out if the Westerfields are still in the picture."

"I understand," Smylee said.

"I doubt that you truly understand. In spite of your efforts, we have already failed to derail ExRelief Cold Medicine from being launched in time for the cold season."

"Young Westerfield spotted what was happening, almost right

from the beginning. He had our people looking over their shoulders at every turn. They couldn't do what they promised," Smylee whined. "I couldn't control that."

"So. Do you think Painter America's people will care?"

"I guess not."

"Our clients are some of the world's most powerful people, and they're not accustomed to failure. They reward success, but failure? I have no idea how they'll react if we're forced to pull the plug. Even worse, God help us, if they are implicated in any way."

*****

Monday morning 10:00 AM, an hour later than usual, Smylee got out of his limo on Madison Avenue, made his way to the elevator and up to the offices of Richardson, Deckmann & Smylee. Eyebrows were raised in every cubicle; he had never been even a minute late before. No one realized how nauseous he felt inside; his face was all business, concealing the depression overtaking his spirit.

Settling into his plush leather desk chair helped settle his nerves. His intercom announced, "Mr. Tuchscherer and his assistant, Isabel Quinn, would like to see you."

"Set up an appointment for later this afternoon." *What the hell do they want,* he thought.

"They're here now, Sir; they said it was important."

"Okay. Send them in."

First, they apologized for showing up without notice, then Tuchscherer said, "We thought you needed to know the federal environmental people have forced us to shut down the Orchard Creek building project."

With his forehead vein popping out and his eyes going in and out of focus, Smylee whispered, "I thought you told me that project was all buttoned up?"

"I don't understand what's going on," Tuchscherer said.

"Well. Do you have any ideas?" Smylee seethed. "What are we paying you for?"

"I believe someone is deliberately attacking the project." He went on to explain someone had to have pointed out to the feds that the creek was a trout stream and that it ran into Lake Michigan. He left saying, "Let me know what you want to do."

"Please hold my calls," Smylee told his secretary over the intercom. He needed time to catch his breath, time to get a better understanding of why everything was going so badly.

Halfway through his in-basket, he found an envelope with Giovanno International's return address. An article from an Italian newspaper was attached to a short note from Anthony Roselli, the man who was going to take care of everything in Bardolino.

Roselli's note said he was alarmed by the attached information. The headline read, "Sospettato Arrestato Della Montagna Omicdio, *Suspect Arrested in Mountain Murder*." Alto Camilo Cabellos had been arrested for the murder of Benito Campanello. Benito had been shot in the head and dumped off a mountaintop in a small camper.

Roselli was concerned because these were the two men who carried out the Bardolino project. More importantly, he had received word from Alto that the first phase was complete after, according to the newspaper, he had been arrested. If he had already been jailed, how could he call in the "Mission successful" message? Things were not adding up.

Roselli reported he investigated the Ida and Sophia's home, but found only a gardener hired to fend off weeds from overtaking the flowers. He had no idea what had become of the ladies.

Smylee's confusion continued to grow. *If Alto didn't make the first call sending the message claiming that Sophia and Ida had been abducted, who did? And if, by some chance he did manage to get the message off, where the hell did he stash them? One thing is for sure,* Smylee thought, *I'm not calling vonLeer to tell him young Westerfield's agreement to sell is based on faulty assumptions.*

CHAPTER 45
TIGHTENING

"Mr. Gunther, this is Robert Raymond at Charleston Federal."

"What can I do for you, Mr. Raymond?"

"I'm having a problem with the IBC wire transfer."

Gunther's blood began to bubble. "What kind of problem?"

"In place of a verification, I'm receiving this message, 'ERROR, Please re-enter your account number with your personal code.' Since we don't have your code number, there isn't much we can do."

"Damn. Thank you, Mr. Raymond. I'll come down and we'll try again." He was sure he had double-checked the numbers when he sent the transfer information, but he could have transposed something, or, more likely, the machinery failed. Mr, Raymond was all business when he met him at the door.

Gunther carefully entered each number and letter to assure accuracy. Holding his breath, he reentered the transaction. The return message arrived in minutes. "ERROR, please......" Gunther felt a wave of panic as he drove to his office to call the Caymans. *I've got to get this mess straightened out.*

It took several minutes to get to someone willing to talk to him. The bank executive was emphatic, "Transactions on that type of account could only be initiated with an account number in conjunction with a correct personal code name or number." Gunther was frustrated but he realized the banker's voice vaguely emphasized, the words, "Personal code." Apparently that was the problem.

He started to mentally question the scenario. *Who knows about this account? Nobody, except the man who helped me set up the offshore business company, Mr. Smylee. Could he have had a hand in this? I doubt it; he only knows the account number, not my code number. I've never trusted the little twit, but I guess I better get together with him. He needs to know he'll have to deposit future money in a different account, at least until I get this mess cleared up.* He dialed carefully for a third time. "We're sorry, the number you are calling is no longer in service." Gunther had never used the emergency contact number before, and he became angrier each time he heard the recording. After seething for an hour, he decided to do the unthinkable, and call Smylee at his law office. Once he got the number from Information, Gunther closed the door at the top of the stairs and anxiously placed the call.

"Richardson, Deckmann & Smylee, how can I help you?"

"Mr. Smylee please."

"Who may I say is calling?"

"Mr. G," Gunther replied.

When the operator returned she told him Mr. Smylee wouldn't be available for several hours and wanted him to leave a message. Gunther thought, *like I have a choice.* "Must see you, important, G. Please advise."

Waking him with a jolt, Gunther's bedside phone was ringing in his ear. He picked it up as he swung his legs to get out of bed. "Hello." A brief recorded statement instructed him to be at O'Reilly's Shamrock Bar on 3rd and 38th at 3:00 this afternoon. He quickly packed a small overnight bag with a razor, underwear, socks, a clean shirt, and a .38 caliber revolver. With traffic light, he made it to the airport before 8:00 AM.

At American Airlines, the friendly, attractive brunette ticket agent's smile was replaced with furrowed eyebrows. "I'm truly sorry, Mr. Delmar, but your American Express card is coming up invalid."

"Young lady, that's just nuts," Gunther replied. "Run it through again."

"I'm sorry, sir. I'm getting the same results."

With his hand out, Gunther said in a huffy voice, "I don't have time to deal with this now; give me the card back. I'll pay cash."

"I sorry sir, but we have instructions to cut up all invalid credit cards."

"You're telling me you're going to cut my . . . " he said in disbelief, as he watched her snip through the card with an oversized scissors.

"I'm so sorry sir; we don't have a choice with invalid cards."

"You do take cash?"

She smiled, saying, "Sorry," for the last time.

Gunther pulled a handful of hundreds from his billfold and purchased a round trip ticket to Newark International. He was still frowning when she handed him the ticket. Then she asked, "Are you going to rent a car at Newark?"

"Why would you need to know that?" Gunther asked curtly.

"I don't," the agent said, "But I thought I'd warn you, most rental car agencies won't rent you a car without a valid credit card."

*****

"He went to New York City, first thing this morning," Charley reported. "And he's scheduled to return tomorrow morning."

"How can you be so certain?" Kristi asked.

"Remember the guy named Smylee?"

"What about him?"

"Gunther called his Manhattan office yesterday, but only got to leave a 'Can we meet' message.

"And?"

"He got a wake-up call early this morning – before five. It was a recording telling him to be at an Irish Delicatessen in Manhattan at three this afternoon."

"How do you know all this, Charley?"

"I got bugs in his office, and I managed to tap the phone line into his apartment."

"That's great work, Charley. And, before I forget, you know the pictures you sent us of the stuff in Gunther's office?"

"Sure, of course."

"It was fantastic," Kristi said. "John Snowden managed to shut down his island bank account with that info."

"I know," Charley said, matter-of-factly, "I'm pretty sure that's why he's going to New York."

"How did you find out he will be back in the morning?"

"Found his car at the airport. I have a homer on it, you know."

"I do now."

"Finding the right airlines wasn't so easy; he bought tickets under his Verner Delmar alias. The return was for 8:30 tomorrow morning."

"Maybe we can get somebody to that deli before he gets there. What's the name?" Kristi asked.

"It's O'Reilly's Shamrock Bar, on 38th and 3rd, 3:00."

"Thanks, Charley."

"There's one more thing."

"Okay."

"We're not the only ones watching this guy."

"Really? You have company out there?"

"I do. And, whoever the guy is, he seems competent, but a bit lazy"

"Make sure you don't end up being the target, Charley. I'll probably be there in the morning."

"That would be good. Bring an army; it's time to make our move."

Kristi said, "You mean, before somebody beats us to it?"

"Could happen," Charley answered.

"With a little luck, I'll see you tomorrow. Gotta go if I'm going to get one of Joan's people at Protection Forces to O'Reilly's before three."

* * * * *

Rather than carry the gun on the plane, Gunther checked the small bag when he picked up his ticket. The plane took off close to 10:30 – right on time. He devoured the scrambled eggs and link sausage American Airlines served on nonstop flights. Gunther would never admit, even to himself, that he was a little anxious, as the plane bounced around during its approach to Newark Airport. Fortunately, the landing was smoother than the approach. It was a little before noon when Gunther retrieved his bag and caught the bus to the Port Authority Terminal on 42nd. He could have easily walked to O'Reilly's from there, except his painful leg forced him to hail a cab.

Without the weekday turmoil, the cabby had no problem crossing Manhattan. On the ride to O'Reilly's, Gunther's suspicious imagination started him thinking. *What became of the emergency contact number, and was Smylee really too busy to talk on the phone? Why aren't we meeting at the Park Lake, as usual?* When he hobbled into the bar, he became even more leery. *This is a great place to get a sandwich, but it doesn't feel like a place Smylee would choose to meet.*

The place was usually barren on Sunday afternoons; today was no exception. Two couples at a table by the window were halfway through their lunch and three up-scale bar flies had settled in with their elbows firmly planted on the bar. Willis McQuillan, Lori's make-believe husband and protector, arrived a few minutes before Gunther. He chose a front corner table and sat dipping french fries into catsup and staring into his beer. He was there as an observer with orders not to initiate any action.

Gunther limped in slowly, quickly evaluating the patrons as well as the bartender. He ordered a beer with a corned-beef sandwich, then picked a booth close to the back door. At 3:00 sharp, a limo driver, in full uniform, stood inside the door and asked loudly, "Is there a Mr. Gunther here?"

Gunther waved to the driver thinking to himself, *something is wrong, where is Smylee?* The driver briskly walked to the booth. "Mr. Gunther?"

"Yes, I'm Gunther."

"I've been sent to been bring you to Mr. Smylee's home on Long Island."

"Have you now?" Gunther said, noticing the driver's beefy shoulders and tree-trunk neck.

"Yes. Please follow me, sir." As they walked toward the limo, Gunther realized that if he got in the limo, most likely, it would be the last ride he would ever take. Standing at attention, the driver opened the rear door.

Gunther bent down to see another man in the back seat. "Excuse me," Gunther said slowly, "I left my sunglasses. I'll be right back." As adrenaline kicked in, his heart raced, his senses heightened, and his limp vanished, as he moved quickly through the restaurant. With his revolver in hand, running low to the ground, he burst through the back door into the alley. Thud, thud, a few inches over his head, shots hit a stack of boxes in back of the restaurant. Once Gunther spotted his assailant, the shooter was a dead man. Without breaking his stride, Gunther's shot hit his chest dead center, blowing him back into a pile of trash.

The limo driver and the man from the back seat carefully went through the restaurant and out the back door. They found their associate on his back with a startled look on his face. His expression would never change; blood was everywhere. Gunther was nowhere to be found.

He hailed a cab and went to La Guardia. At the American Airlines counter, they let him exchange his Newark return ticket for one out of their airport. *The world was closing in on Victor Gunther.*

CHAPTER 46
HOMECOMING

Tootsie, sensing something was up, went from room to room, person to person, sharing in their apprehension. Ida retied her apron for the umpteenth time, and Sophia kept looking out one window, then another. Both tried to keep busy; waiting was always the worst part. They knew Joseph had some damage to his spine, but had no idea what to expect when he arrived. Jeff, seeing their apprehension, assured them everything would work out. It didn't seem to help.

Finally, a converted van ambulance, unsuccessfully avoiding the ruts, eased down the lake house driveway. The driver and one of Sandy's men opened the back doors, efficiently affixed a ramp, and wheeled Joseph out, where he found himself surrounded by Jeff, Sophia, and Ida. The moment he saw their happy faces, Joseph thanked God his family was safe and he was still here to enjoy them.

Hugs and tears dominated the reunion. It was hard for mere humans to compete with Tootsie's enthusiasm; she was all over him. Joseph paid special attention to Sophia, pointing out how pretty and healthy she looked. A blushing smile was her response.

As he wheeled himself into the front door, Joseph was hit with the welcoming smell of freshly baked bread. Ida, always the mother, had taken over the kitchen. Using olive oil, garlic, tomato sauce with an assortment of mystery spices, chunks of beef, and pasta shells, she had a casserole ready to serve whenever anyone wanted to eat. Seeing the table set with red wine and a salad, Joseph smiled, saying, "Looks like company."

"Are you hungry?" Ida asked, looking at Joseph.

"I wasn't until I smelled the food."

Enthusiasm replaced shyness as Sophia told Joseph about being saved by Modica and his team and whisked away to America so early it was still dark out. Ida was surprised to hear her telling more of the story than she thought Sophia knew. Jeff covered a few of the less violent details and they all enjoyed the story, as he explained how Alto's money found its way into the ProTect & Associates bank account. They talked at the table well into the evening. Jeff realized, not for the first time, but with clarity, how important Joseph's role had been in providing for them, and how important his mother and grandmother were to both of them.

Joseph made a mental note, *Modica's group did us a great service; tomorrow I'll have to write a thank you.*

At 8:30, answering the knock at the front door, Jeff welcomed Kristi, "Come on in. Everyone's in the kitchen." With an arm around her shoulder, he steered her in the right direction.

"Hi. This looks like a cheerful group," she said, as she went to Joseph and gave him a hug. "Welcome back. How are you doing?"

"With Ida's cooking, my biggest problem will be holding my weight down," Joseph replied. "How about a piece of her chocolate cake?"

"Sounds great," Kristi said, noticing Ida's beaming face.

The main reason she stopped by was to check on Joseph, but she also needed to bring him and Jeff up to date. After minimum chit-chat she started her report. When she went into the details, Ida and Sophia listened quietly, often with their mouths agape. Joseph and Jeff were too interested to notice.

Kristi started with, "We're definitely on the offense."

"That sounds promising," Joseph said.

"There's only one assassin; we're finally sure of that. More importantly, we know where to find him – Charleston, South Carolina." With a nod in his direction, she said, "Jeff arranged to have his friend Skyler, using the Wesfield company plane, fly several of us down there in the morning."

"No big deal," Jeff said. "Since we arrested the employees for corporate espionage, the board sees our efforts as their number one priority."

"Time may be more important than you know, Jeff. Yesterday the assassin – his real name is Gunther – was supposed to meet Smylee in New York. It turned out to be a set-up."

"You mean, somebody tried to kill him?" Joseph asked.

"That's right," Kristi said, "And I want to get him before somebody else does."

"Why? Does it matter who kills him?" Joseph questioned.

"I want that boy alive," Kristi replied. "Dead, he can't tell us who masterminded the conspiracy."

"Conspiracy?" Joseph said. "We're finally calling it what it is, a heinous conspiracy."

"There's too many components to call it anything else," Kristi replied.

"I know. It's just so outrageous."

"We have one other positive turn of events," Kristi paused. "I believe the killer is no longer in the area, and I can't imagine that he'd return."

"That is good news, but how can you be so certain?" Joseph asked.

"We've managed to cripple his finances," Kristi said with a smile. "I doubt he can scrape together lunch money."

"Was that your friend Snowden's doing?" Jeff asked.

"Yup, with Charley Tanner's help. I also believe the conspirators are trying to take him out."

"You mean vonLeer or Smylee is trying to kill him?" Joseph questioned. "Why?"

"Undoubtedly both. Look at what's happened. You and Jeff are the biggest obstacles to their acquiring Wesfield Lab. You are the majority stockholders, and you, Joseph, have a great deal of influence over the other stockholders. Gunther's assignment was to take you out of the equation. He failed twice. That's one more chance than people like Smylee usually allow."

"You think they'll kill him for that?" Joseph said.

"Not so much for failing, but his botched attempts have drawn very negative attention, and he knows too much. He's a liability, one we'd like to exploit."

*****

Kristi, Sandy, and Scott Scruggins met Charley in front of Charleston's Metro station. Before going inside, they all got in one car to hear what Charley had to report. They learned Gunther got to his car in the airport parking lot at 4:30 Monday afternoon. "Yesterday?" Kristi said.

"Right, yesterday. He checked his car before getting in, and, I'm sorry to say, found the homing device I had planted under his fender."

"How do you know that, Charley?" Sandy asked.

"Because I spent most of the day waiting in my car, which happened to be parked two rows in back of his."

"Oookay," Sandy said with a smirk.

"He spent the night in his apartment. At 2:00 AM, when he finally shut his lights off, I went back to my hotel."

"Nice work, Charley," Kristi said. "Gunther will be jumpy, defensive and extremely dangerous from here on out. In his mind, anyone who looks at him sideways could be one of Smylee's people trying to take him out."

Kristi went alone into the Metro Police Station to introduce herself and make sure they didn't have any surveillance people watching Gunther. She came out briskly, with two plainclothes detectives on her heels. They leaned into the open car windows, and Kristi introduced them as Detectives Connor and Sidney. Then she asked Charley if he thought he could find the other guy watching Gunther.

"So far," Charley said, "He's been showing up at the store about 10:00. I haven't seen him at the apartment at all. Whatever he's up to, it only involves his office. My guess is, he'd be there now."

"Let's take a look-see," Detective Connor said.

They drove down South Adger's Wharf, turned north for a block running along the park, then turned again up North Adger. "That's him," Charley said, as they passed a parked car along the park. Sure enough, he was slouching in his seat, right where Charley said he would be. They circled and came to a stop. Kristi got out of the car and walked across the street, directly to his car. A foul smell of stale tobacco came from the open window. "Hey, buddy. What agency are you with?" she asked, flashing the badge she'd never bothered to turn in.

"What?" He sat up straight in his seat.

"We both seem to be watching Gunther Imports. I assume you're with another agency."

"I'm not watching anybody," he said loudly. "What the hell are you talking about?"

"We both know what you're doing, so let's have it. Who're you with? Maybe we can work together?"

Visibly shaken, he said, "I'm private."

"Who are you working for?"

"I'm not at liberty to disclose that, Ma'am."

With a wave of her hand, the two detectives moved in behind Kristi. "Okay, Mr. Private. These two gentlemen will escort you to the station to check your documentation and get you approved to work in Charleston."

"I can't do that," he said.

"Wrong," Detective Connor said, sticking his gun barrel between his eyes. "Who the hell do ya think ya are? Get out. Keep yer hands in front of ya and don't even think of making any funny moves."

"Okay, okay. Take it easy."

"Leave the keys," Connor told him. "Walk slowly to the burgundy Ford at the curb." The incident didn't take more than a few minutes. Sandy moved the man's car to a parking lot and, after giving it a through search, called Detective Connor, telling him where they could pick up Mr. Private's mobile arsenal. Connor told him the man was turning out to be a very uncooperative character, and definitely not a private detective.

Returning to his team, Sandy said. "That's the most well-armed surveillance man you'll ever see. His car was a veritable gun shop."

"Apparently, he wasn't there to just observe?" Kristi said.

"Apparently not," Sandy replied, "I think guns could be the tools of his trade."

Kristi's two-way radio light began to blink. "Yes, Charley?"

"I'm at his house and the car is gone; I hope we haven't lost him."

*****

An hour earlier, Gunther, using 7 x 35 wide angle field glasses, looked out of his apartment front window thoroughly studying the street below. He realized his paranoia was in full gear – not a bad thing right now. A garbage truck, stopping noisily at every building, was the only questionable vehicle. After it cleared the intersection, he grabbed two suitcases, cautiously descended the steps, through the front door and into his black Mercedes. With one eye on the rear view mirror, he wove back and forth staying within the neighborhood until he was sure he didn't have anyone following.

Gunther thought, *I've got to get to the safe in my office . . . alive. With the money I stashed there, I can still live comfortably for the rest of my life. I won't be the millionaire I deserve to be, but I'll be comfortable.* He drove past the office at hourly intervals. No one appeared to be watching the place, but he felt certain that Smylee's assassins wouldn't give up with one failed attempt.

Kristi had arranged surveillance from inside the souvenir boutique across the street and the gallery next door. The shop owners were none too happy about the risk, but she compensated them handsomely, knowing full well retailing was a tough way to make a living. When closing time came around, the owners reluctantly agreed to let the watchers stay.

It was almost dark; shoppers had gone to restaurants to refuel and the Adger's Wharf, without shoppers, changed into a place of eerie shadow-filled silence.

Gunther parked directly in front of the store. First, he looked in all directions, searching for anything that might be out of place. Finding none, he cautiously got out of the car and moved to the building. He unlocked the door, turned off the alarm, and went straight to the safe. He thought, *maybe my precautions were unnecessary . . . better safe than sorry.*

CHAPTER 47
THE PICK UP

"Who can trust the banks?" Gunther's mother would say while stashing her pittance wages in nooks and crannies around the house. Good advice, he thought, neatly filling his suitcase with banded stacks of 20s, 50s, and 100s, along with bulky bundles of bearer-bonds. Carefully, he tucked in identification using his real name and two aliases. There were three: passports, driver's licenses, birth certificates, and documents showing that he belonged to several professional groups. Between the stacks of money and bonds, he stuffed a small black velvet bag containing personal jewelry and a few loose, but extremely valuable, diamonds. It's time to get the hell out of here.

Kristi was worried. With just four people, she'd only have two simultaneously watching each door of the shop. Apprehending him as he came out would be only two against one. Not good odds. *Not good enough when we're dealing with such a proficient killer*. Without any real authority, she couldn't ask for backup; after all, she told the Charleston police, it was just surveillance. She was ready to scrap the entire takedown, when she realized no matter which way he came out, Gunther had only the black Mercedes for his getaway. With nowhere for him to take cover between it and the building, the car became her main focus.

Kristi thought, *Darkness is my ally*. She stationed Charley in the deep shadow on the side of the souvenir shop across the street. Scruggins was positioned in the equally dark recessed entry of the gallery next door. She and Sandy were crouched down next to the driver's side door of the Mercedes. Back to back, they covered Gunther's approach from either direction. With all the stores closed and vacant, chances of a car coming down the bumpy deserted wharf road were minimal. They were on guard, impatiently waiting, and all thinking similar thoughts. *Come on, you devil; we're ready for you.*

Gunther turned out the inside lights and opened the back door a crack. It took a few moments for his eyes to adjust to the dark. The narrow alley had only one light, halfway up the street. It created several shadows an adversary could hide in. He decided to use the front entrance; it was slightly better lit and closer to his car. If there were a sniper out there, he would probably try for him the second he stepped through the doorway.

Peeking out the door for several minutes, Gunther watched for any motion, any sign of life. There was none; time to go. With a revolver in one hand, suitcase in the other, he moved swiftly through the door, keeping low, trying to look in all directions at the same time. No shots. He breathed a little easier. Then he moved around the front of the car.

"STOP," Kristi screamed.

He dropped the suitcase, diving to the cobblestones, raised his gun hand and focused on Kristi as his target. Too late.

Kristi's light .22 caliber pistol exploded first, with Sandy and Scruggins firing an instant later. Kristi's round spun Gunther around, hitting his upper arm, jerking him backwards from the impact. His gun flew high across the road almost hitting Charley who was running toward the action. One of the other shots hit Gunther as he rolled; it passed through one butt cheek and lodged deep in the other. The third shot grazed the top of Gunther's right shoulder.

Scruggins, Sandy, and Charley all jumped on the downed assailant with guns pointing at his head. Sandy drove his knee into the small of Gunther's back with all the force he could muster. With the wind knocked out of him, Gunther gasped for air as Sandy yanked his shattered arm behind his back, then twisted the other arm until they were together. Using a notched plastic tie-wrap strap as handcuffs, Sandy pulled vigorously, firmly locking his wrists together.

Scott bound his ankles with another tie-wrap, and Charley relieved him of his wallet and keys and quickly frisked his body for other weapons. "Go through his car, too, Charley," Kristi said.

"Right," he replied, heading to the Mercedes.

Kristi picked up Gunther's suitcase from the cobblestones and went to put it in their rental car's trunk. As she did, she thought, *I hope this thing holds the key to who he really is, and what he's up to.*

Blocking excruciating pain, Gunther searched his mind for a possible advantage. There was none to be found. Slowly he began to realize, *these were not the same people who tried to kill me in New York. If they were, I'd be dead by now. I'm in the hands of professionals, but who are they, and what do they want with me?* When the Charleston police car drove up it only further confused his thinking. *I've never broken a law in Charleston. Why are police interested in me? Why are they here?*

Detective Connor's car slid to a stop next to the group standing over Gunther. "You do realize this guy is bleeding all over our cobblestones," he said with a smile. "Did he give you much trouble?"

"We got lucky." Kristi said.

"Looks like this guy got unlucky with you bird-dogs on his trail," Connor commented.

"We need to get him to Ohio. Got any ideas?" Kristi asked.

"The university hospital is just south of here; I'll call, alert a doctor to be available, and get a couple of our people over there to help you keep an eye on him."

"Is that really necessary?" Kristi questioned. "Those wounds don't look life threatening to me."

"By getting us involved, it will show everything was done within the law."

"We need your help, Detective Connor," Kristi said, as a way of letting him know the delay was frustrating to her.

"It'll take a little time to get extradition papers anyway; we might as well make sure he doesn't bleed to death before you get him to Ohio."

"We'll appreciate anything you can do," Kristi replied.

"I checked our wanted file. Victor Gunther's name doesn't pop up. He's all yours."

"Good." Kristi said, thinking to herself, *Detective Connor is covering his butt....I can't blame him.*

"If you can get that plane back, we'll have him on it first thing in the morning."

"That's not a problem," Kristi said. "We held the plane – it's still here."

"You must've been pretty doggone confident you'd get him."

"We were hopeful," Kristi said with a smile. "If he didn't get us first."

"Well, congratulations to all of you," Connor said admiringly. "Great work."

*****

The ambulance made its customary noisy arrival, and the attendants scurried around Gunther, securely strapping him to an overly-designed stretcher. One of the ambulance personnel mentioned that she hadn't seen any hog-tied patients before. The other responded, "Seems like a good idea to me." While Sandy and Scruggins accompanied Gunther in the ambulance, Kristi decided to drop Charley off before joining them.

On the ride to the Lady Slipper, she said, "You and Bessie Mae stay and enjoy Charleston for as long as you like. You've earned it."

"Just doing my job, Ma'am."

"Unless you hear from me, I think you can go back to the big city whenever you're vacationed out." Kristi smiled affectionately, and said, "Send me a bill."

"No problem, Ma'am. Good luck gettin' him out of Charleston."

"Thanks. I don't anticipate any problems." She went back to Adger's Wharf, down the bumpy street, and brought her car to a stop in front of the import store. She needed to be alone, with time to gather her thoughts. She realized that, without a casualty, they had just defeated the most ruthless killer she'd probably ever encounter. The relief left her emotionally exhausted. After about 40 minutes of reflection, Kristi turned the car around and headed to Charleston's Medical University Hospital.

The emergency staff provided Gunther with enough temporary patching to enable him to take the flight to Ohio without extra risk. Scruggins, Sandy, and Kristi unsuccessfully tried to relax in the lounge while Gunther was being attended to. They didn't notice night had slipped away until 6:00 AM, when the smell of bacon signaled the cafeteria was open for breakfast. They had just finished eating when Detective Connor walked in, waving signed extradition papers. "Time to get that monster out of South Carolina, folks; we'll deliver him to the airport. Is your pilot ready?"

"He's waiting at the airport. I'll let him know you're on your way." Kristi replied. "Thanks for your help."

By the time she returned the rental car and got to the Wesfield plane, Skyler already had it warmed up, ready to go. Connor's officers had Gunther's good arm handcuffed to his seat and they stayed with him, waiting for Kristi's team to take over. After another "thank you," they exited the plane.

Skyler locked the door. "Everybody ready?" he asked.

Kristi, Sandy, and Scruggins fastened their seatbelts. "Let's roll," Kristi said, thinking to herself, *it's time to finish the job . . . time to go after the people who hired this devil.*

CHAPTER 48
INTERROGATION

The flight was smooth. Skyler didn't hear a word out of his passengers. Good and bad alike, they all were catching up on a couple hours of much needed sleep. "Ding, ding, ding, ding," the warning that the landing gear was dropping signaled the flight was coming to an end. Once again, Skyler set down at the little private airport outside of Tibbyville. As the door opened, Sheriff Surratt enthusiastically greeted them, "Welcome back. We're ready for you." He had an ambulance and both of Tibbyville's police cars waiting next to the plane.

Surratt climbed aboard to find Gunther face down, strapped to a body-board in the aisle, squeezed between the seats. Before taking him off, Surratt read him the arrest warrants accusing him of the murder of Sally LaPoint and the attempted murder of Joseph and Jeff Westerfield.

"Attempted murder?" Gunther said, shaking his head. "Are you telling me they're both alive?"

"I understand they're doin' great," Surratt said, enjoying Gunther's distress.

The words were a stake in the devil's heart. Failing once was frustrating; failing twice...... devastating. *How could they have possibly survived? I hit them dead center; I watched them fall. They have to be dead.*

Surratt and Sandy jostled the body-boarded captive through the narrow plane door, slid him down the steps and hoisted him onto a gurney and into a waiting ambulance.

When the three-car caravan got to Memorial Hospital, Gunther's gurney was wheeled into a private room. With guns trained on him, he was transferred to a bed and cuffed hand and foot to the rail. One of Surratt's people became a sentry outside the door with instructions to keep anyone out he couldn't recognize. No exceptions. After an attempt to eliminate him in New York, and a Mafia hit man in Charleston, there was no reason to think Gunther's bosses wouldn't try to take him out in Tibbyville.

Dr. Rand, scheduled to arrive after lunch, raced into the hospital with his usual forward lean at 1:00 PM. He turned abruptly when he spotted Kristi in the waiting lounge. "Hello, there, Chief Christopher," he said grabbing her arm, spinning her around and pulling her back out the front door.

"Hello yourself, doctor. Where are you taking me?"

"I'm gonna show you something." As they entered the parking lot, he pointed at a shiny new jet-black Cadillac El Dorado. "Now that's the car a successful doctor ought to be driving. Thank you, Kristi."

"Nice wheels; but don't thank me. It was the Westerfields' idea and their money."

"I'm sure you had a hand in it." Dr. Rand said.

"Not much," she said. "They do things pretty much their own way."

"I sent Joseph Westerfield a thank-you note, but he didn't acknowledge it," Dr. Rand said. "Please make sure they know how much it means to me."

"I promise," Kristi said. "I'll walk you down to see our boy."

"Well, lookie-here. He's back." Dr. Rand gleefully greeted the patient as he entered the room.

"Hmph," Gunther moaned, pulling at his handcuffed wrist and ankle. *First, I get taken down by a bunch of hayseeds, and now I'm going to be subjected to this old coot. I should have shot him when I had the chance.*

"I heard you managed to get a couple extra holes in your ass," the smirking Dr. Rand said, as he loaded an unnecessarily large syringe. "I suppose somebody caught you bending over with your dress up, aye, Bucko?"

"Just do whatever it is you're planning to do," Gunther said with a vein expanding on his forehead.

Jabbing the needle in Gunther's arm, Dr. Rand said, "This will put you to sleep while we take a few pictures of those new butt holes." He was out in a minute and on his way over to x-ray.

"Did you have to knock him out, doc?" Kristi asked.

"I've seen him in action, Ma'am. He's tough and ruthless. I don't take chances."

"I see that," Kristi smiled.

"He wouldn't get far anyway," Dr. Rand said. "Did you see the way his left foot drooped forward?"

"No, I didn't, really," Kristi answered.

"Drop Foot," he said. "I'd bet that shot in the butt severed the nerves he needs to flex his toes and ankle. Looks like Drop Foot."

"You mean he'll be crippled?"

"That would be my guess," Dr. Rand said. "We'll know a lot more when we see where the bullet ended up and what happens when we dig it out."

"Will he improve after you operate?"

"I doubt it," Dr. Rand said. "Once the nerves are destroyed, there isn't much anyone can do."

"So, he was already limping from the shot in his right thigh, and now his left leg is useless, too."

"Poor baby, he won't have any fun hurting people any more." Dr. Rand said. "I think from now on Mr. Bad-ass will be able to crawl faster than he can walk."

The X-ray tech had the films on a lighted wall display. "Is our bad boy still out?" he inquired, as he examined the negative.

"He is," a nurse answered.

"Is there anyone around who might be willing to handle the anesthesia?"

"I think so. Let me call the front desk to see who is still here." She flashed Dr. Rand the okay sign as she talked.

Fifteen minutes later, the country doctor became Rand, the skillful surgeon. The bullet was in deep, lodged along the femur bone, five inches below the hip socket. Because Rand needed to take a look at that bone, he chose not to try and retrieve the slug with forceps, but made a new incision in the back of Gunther's leg. It wasn't a complicated procedure and he had the bullet out in minutes. The bone contusion was not something Dr. Rand felt he could improve. Gunther was badly damaged, but nature would have to take care of the recovery. Rand knew his limitations only too well; he could sterilize and suture, but was unable to grow nerves, bone or muscle.

Gunther awoke nauseous, but only one wrist was cuffed to the side-rail. *I guess they don't think I'm much of a threat anymore.* He was right.

*****

Gunther was allowed two days to recuperate. On day three, Kristi and Sheriff Surratt came in shortly after breakfast. "You're going to be moving today, Mr. Gunther," Surratt said. "We have a private room ready for you to move into. You'll love it, it has your very own cot, toilet and wash basin."

"County or state?" Gunther responded without emotion.

"County," the Sheriff responded. "Here is a bullet-proof vest you'll wear during the trip,"

"Why the hell do I need that?"

"You know very well why." Kristi said.

"I do?"

"Of course you do." she answered. "Last week three men tried to kill you at Reilly's Bar in Manhattan. I'm sure you remember leaving one of them dead in the alley."

"How would you know that, lady? Was that incompetent one of yours?"

"You already know who set you up." Kristi said with an all-knowing smile. "It sure as hell wasn't us."

"Then how do you know about it?"

"We had an agent there, but only as an observer," Kristi replied. "He thought you were a goner when you were dumb enough to walk out to the car."

"How did you know I was going there?"

Ignoring the question, Kristi said, "For your information, this morning we also took a Mafia hit-man into custody a half-block down the street from your import company. Who do you think he was after?"

"Why didn't you just let him shoot me?" Gunther asked.

"Believe me, the thought crossed my mind," Kristi said. "But you're just a pawn. A ruthless evil pawn, I'll admit, but a pawn all the same. We're more interested in Mr. Smylee and the people who have been paying your way – the ones who are now trying to put you away."

"You think I'm gonna blow the whistle on them?"

"I could just let them take you out," Kristi said. "If I thought they'd given up on putting a bullet in you, I wouldn't be giving you the kevlar vest."

Paying special attention to how Gunther navigated the few feet from the wheelchair into the police car, Kristi thought, *the good doctor was right; that lame foot looks useless.* The trip to county lock-up was uneventful.

Gunther's new home was rather small, twelve by eight feet. One eight foot wall was made from concrete block and painted a pale mustard. The other three walls were floor to ceiling iron bars. Once in the cell, Gunther was handed crutches. His arms were strong and his right leg was agile enough to maneuver the few feet from the wheelchair to the cot.

Shortly after being served a meager lunch in his cell, Gunther was wheeled down the hall into an interrogation room. Seated between Kristi and FBI agent Marti Towne, Sheriff Surratt opened the discussion by asking, "Are you familiar with 'Old Sparky,' Mr. Gunther?"

"Your electric chair?"

"Sparky was put to work in April, 1897. The old timer delivers 1,950 volts a pop, and you, Mr. Gunther, may very well get a chance to meet her up close and personal."

"If you think I can be intimidated by talking about capital punishment, you're wasting your time," Gunther said with bravado.

"I was just enjoying the thought of it," Surratt smiled.

"If I should choose to cooperate fully, what can I expect in return?" Gunther knew as he spoke he should have waited for his interrogators to make the first move.

"That would depend on what you have to give us." Towne said. "Your crimes are part of a conspiracy that we are extremely interested in. If you can shed light on the people running the show, it would be worth something to us. If not, as the Sheriff put it, you'll get to meet Old Sparky."

"With witnesses like Kestler, from the funeral home, who saw through your old man disguise, and Doc Rand, you wouldn't have a leg to stand on in one of our courts," Sheriff Surratt added, pleased with his choice of words.

"Where would you like me to start?" Gunther said, with full knowledge he knew very few details regarding the clients Smylee represented.

The interrogating started with the congressman who arranged the meeting bringing Gunther and Smylee together. Gunther was given immunity for all criminal activity prior to his involvement with the Westerfields. They only talked three hours a day, because the interrogation was exhausting, filled with tedious detail.

Although he worked exclusively through Smylee, the scope of Gunther's activities was extensive. It involved a cross-section of businesses and countries. Gunther was impersonal in his descriptions; he didn't kill people . . . he removed obstacles. Surratt, Kristi and Towne were amazed as they listened to him pridefully tell how he had eliminated two Swiss biotech company executives by causing a car crash in the mountains. And how he killed a financial power broker in France, making it appear to be a street mugging. All in all, he had assassinated well over a dozen people, burned down an arms manufacturing company, and provided surveillance on chemical, pharmaceutical, and manufacturing company executives all over the globe.

Agent Towne evaluated the information daily. After two and a half weeks, he felt he had everything he was going to get. He was sure Gunther kept a few bargaining chips, but, accompanied with the statements made by the Wesfield saboteurs, he had more than enough to arrest Smylee for conspiracy. His plan was two-fold; while he arrested Mr. Smylee, other agents would present a subpoena to Manhattan Federal to gain access to the four Painter accounts.

CHAPTER 49
SMYLEE WHO?

Every weekday morning, a sea of executives and office workers rises up out of the subway to flood the sidewalks of New York. They are all nationalities, ages, shapes, and sizes. Like animals in heat, they plow through the humanity seeking their destiny. Immersed in the morning rush, Kristi said, "One thing I miss about not working here is seeing how the city comes alive."

"The pace can wear you down," Towne replied. "I'd say most of these folks are just trying to survive."

Kristi knew she was an unwelcome tagalong – the FBI seldom allowed outsiders to participate in their apprehensions. Marti Towne reluctantly agreed to let her watch from a distance because he realized this was, after all, really her ball game. Without Kristi, he wouldn't even know there was a conspiracy.

The four of them jammed into the elevator along with a dozen or so cookie cutter executives clad in pinstripe suits and shiny shoes. As the door swished open, a city policeman ushered everyone exiting at the 52nd floor into the hall. They were told to stay and not, under any circumstances, try to enter Richardson, Deckmann & Smylee. Towne flashed the policeman his FBI identification. "What's going on here, officer?"

"I'm not too sure, I was told some hotshot lawyer decided to end his misery."

"I need to see the officer in charge," Towne said, "Where will I find him?"

The policeman pointed down the hall, saying, "Go through the glass doors; ask for Captain Brown."

Towne found Brown just inside the doors, showed his ID, and extended his hand with a friendly smile. "Hello Captain, I'm Marti Towne."

"Is it Agent, or Marti Towne?" Brown asked skeptically.

"Marti will be fine. Can you give me a quick overview?"

"Why, may I ask, are you interested?" It was clear to Marti that Brown was ready to defend his turf.

"I'm not," Towne replied, "unless the victim happened to be named Smylee."

Brown's eyebrows raised, and he began to flush. "I'm not positive, but I believe the man was named Smylee."

Towne opened his briefcase, took out the Smylee arrest warrant, and handed it to the Captain. "If it turns out that Smylee is the victim, this will become a federal investigation. If that happens, I would prefer that we conduct a joint investigation."

"Who would be in charge?"

"You and I, Captain; I'm sure we'd work well together," Marti replied.

"That would be okay with me, but I'd have to call the chief. I don't get to call the shots."

"Let's try to get someone to give us a positive ID," Towne said. "And, I'd like to see the victim." They chose Mr. Deckmann, one of the partners, and escorted him to Smylee's office.

A determined policeman was on guard in front of the door. "No one is supposed to go in there before the forensics team gets here." Reluctantly, he stepped aside when Captain Brown pressed the isssue.

They stepped inside the door a few feet. Deckmann stared at the body for a few seconds, then slowly said, "Ooo. That's him. No doubt about it."

Smylee's head was on top of the desk lying in a pool of blood. The hole in his temple was clearly visible. His right hand, clutching a revolver, was also in the blood. With a gaping mouth and wide-open eyes, his face was a mask of fear.

"I'm glad you were treating this entire area like a crime scene, Captain Brown; it may very well be just that," Towne said, suspecting more than a simple suicide.

Brown smiled, "Standard operating procedure. I better call my chief and make sure he's okay with us working together." He got the joint operation approval without a problem.

While they waited for forensics, Towne used the delay to introduce his people. When he got to Kristi, he said, "Kristi and her people discovered the conspiracy we are looking into."

"It doesn't surprise me; I recommended some of her people." Brown stepped up and gave her a generous hug.

"It's great to see you, George," Kristi said, bending back from the hug.

"I take it you know each other," Towne commented.

"He's one of the loves of my life," Kristi replied, her green eyes dancing with mischief.

"I worked with Kristi when she was one of New York's finest," Captain Brown added.

An FBI forensics woman arrived to work with the NYPD team already at the scene. Their objective was to locate evidence indicating the presence of anyone who might have been involved.

Two pieces of evidence suggested the possibility of foul play. The slug entered the right side of Smylee's head . . . he happened to be left-handed. Even more unusual, the bullet exited the other side of his head hitting the desktop, indicating it entered his temple while he leaned forward with his head turned, a very unnatural position for a suicide. Most self-inflected temple shots are performed with the victim sitting upright with his eyes closed.

Towne and Kristi questioned co-workers together. The story was universal: no one really knew him. He was cordial but at the same time kept everyone at arms's length. Smylee was considered brilliant, tightlipped, and hard-working. As far as anyone knew, he wasn't married, nor did he show an interest in acquiring a companion. The man who seemed to know him best was Mr. Deckmann, one of the partners. "He's always been a loner," he told them. "He's had some devastating things happen to him the last few weeks."

"Oh? What exactly was so earthshaking?" Towne asked.

"First, Gudrun, his secretary, was found dead on the street in front of her home three weeks ago." Deckmann paused, "It was apparently a mugging. At least that's what the police said. She'd been his secretary since we formed the partnership."

"What's the other?" Towne questioned.

"Without warning, his main account, the Painter Organization, up and moved its business overseas. Painter represented over half our total billings," Deckmann said with another pause. "We may end up closing our doors if new business can't be found."

"You weren't given any notice at all?" Towne asked.

"Not a clue."

Kristi picked up the questioning, taking it in another direction. "Mr. Deckmann, what role did Hermann vonLeer play in the Painter organization?"

"Hermann vonLeer? I've never heard of a Hermann vonLeer."

"I see," Kristi said, thinking *I don't believe that for a second.* "What is your relationship with the Manhattan Bank & Trust?"

"They handle our business, but I can't see why that is relative," Deckmann said.

"Relative to what, Mr.Deckmann?"

"To anything," Deckmann stammered. "To Smylee's suicide."

"Why do you think it's a suicide, Mr. Deckmann?"

"What else . . . what else could it be?"

"It could be murder, Mr. Deckmann. Couldn't it?"

"Who would do such a thing?"

"You tell me, Mr. Deckmann," Kristi said, with her face inches from his.

He slowly shook his head, "I have no idea."

Employee questioning went on for several hours, but little was accomplished. On their way out, Towne told Kristi, "Too many questions for us to buy the suicide."

She nodded her head in agreement.

"The bureau will take a closer look," Towne assured her.

*****

Using a pay phone along the wall at LaGuardia, Kristi dialed the lake house. "Westerfields," Jeff answered.

"Hi Jeff. This is Kristi, How are you and Joseph doing?"

"I'm fine. He's using a walker, but getting stronger everyday."

"I thought I'd bring you and Joseph up to date."

275

"Let me get Grandpa on another phone."

"Hello Kristi, this is Joseph. Sounds noisy where you are."

"LaGuardia," she said. "Let me make this short or my time will run out."

"Shoot."

"Okay. Smylee is dead, the assassin is crippled and in custody, the Painter organization has left the country, and vonLeer is still a mystery man."

"Wow. You've been a busy woman. I can't wait to hear the details. That's great news," Joseph said. "I got a note from vonLeer, but it can wait till you get back. Again, thank you."

One more call. "Hello, this is Russ."

"My plane is leaving for O'Hare in fifteen minutes. Are you going to stay up late, by any chance?"

"I am now," he said. Then he went to take a shower.

CHAPTER 50
AWAKENING

Joseph's sleep was interrupted as cool evening air, freshly scented by an autumn shower, filled the room. Moonlight replaced the darkness by slipping between trees and through the lakeside windows. Chirps and burps of the evening critters, so abundant in the spring and summer, were scarce in the fall. *Silence has a sound all its own*, Joseph thought, as he lay quietly enjoying the peacefulness, and thanking God for his blessings.

The tranquility eventually merged into the realization that without making a trip to the bathroom, he probably wouldn't go back to sleep. I can do this, he thought, as he pushed himself to a sitting position by simultaneously swinging his legs over the side of the bed. Grabbing the walker, he lifted himself and shuffled across the room. *How about this? I'm mobile.*

During the tedious trek back to bed, Joseph noticed Tootsie making gentle whimpering sounds in front of his bedroom door. There was light coming from beneath it. On the other side, Sophia was slowly moving along the great room's fireplace wall. It was filled with pictures of all the people Joseph treasured throughout his life. She stopped from time to time, taking a photo from the wall, holding it in her delicate hands, and studying it with a fixated interest. *Why does this house have pictures of my Mama and Papa? Why are there so many pictures of me?*

The most puzzling picture, the one that captivated Sophia the most, was of a handsome soldier with his arm around a young woman holding a baby, and a small boy tugging at the woman's skirt. The soldier, the woman, and the children – she knew she knew them. The soldier was the man in her dream, standing on the unreachable cliff with the beautiful young girl. *Where have they all gone?*

Through the door, Joseph heard a woman's sobs. He couldn't

distinguish whether it was Ida, Sophia, or Lori, who was staying with Jeff for the weekend. He didn't want to intrude, but the sobbing went on and on. He decided no matter who it was, she might need a comforting shoulder.

Waving Tootsie aside, he managed to open the door a crack, but, before he could get it totally open, he had to back up the walker and pull the door handle. The new maneuver proved to be difficult. *Maybe I'm not so mobile after all.*

Sophia, with her face in her hands, was bent over in despair, totally unaware that Joseph was coming to her. She looked up, blurting out, "Grandpa." Leaning over the walker, she buried her head in his shoulder and held tight to his waist. "There, there, Sophia," he said, struggling to keep from falling. "Let's sit on the couch before I topple over."

"Oh. I'm sorry, Grandpa," she said between sobs, "I forgot you were hurt."

"It's okay, sweetheart," he said, realizing that she hadn't called him that in 25 years. She started calling him Grandpa the day Jeff was born. He always loved hearing her use it.

Joseph was thankful they managed to get to the sofa; his legs were ready to fail him. She snuggled close to him. Without any idea of the problem, he quietly put an arm around her and waited. Be patient, he reminded himself; she will tell me in her own time.

The sobs subsided. "I miss Freddy so. Why did he have to go off to war?"

Stunned, Joseph suspected she was finally allowing herself to deal with the loss of her husband Frederic, his son Frederic. "I understand," he said, tears spilling from his eyes. "God, how I understand."

"Sally, my baby, was taken from me. Then Freddy had to go to war. God took him, too. I don't know what happened to my wonderful boy. When did God take him? I can't remember what happened to my boy."

"Jeff, the man that brought you from the airport, is your boy. Jeff is your son."

"Jeff? The man who calls you Grandpa, is my Jeff?"

"Yes, Sophia, Jeff is your boy. He loves you. We all do. He's going to be very happy to learn you remembered he's your son."

"But, my Jeff is a boy, not a man."

"You've been in a world of your own for a long time, Sophia. You couldn't accept losing your loved ones, and your mind wouldn't allow you to go on without them."

"My boy is a man?"

"Your beautiful boy," Joseph said slowly, "has grown into a wonderful man."

He held her for the longest time; eventually the tears subsided. She realized that Jeff, a man she liked, a man who was always kind and gentle, was *her* Jeff. The positive jolt to her psyche may have cleared the way for her recovery. Sophia pulled back, looking Joseph in the eye and asked, "How long have I been away?"

He couldn't believe what she was saying: it meant after 20 years abroad, through the turmoil of almost being kidnapped and rushed off to America, Sophia had somehow managed to find her way back to reality. "I know it's late," he said, "But how about some coffee? I don't think either of us is going to sleep for awhile."

"I'd like tea, if that's okay?"

"It surely is," he said, thinking, *This is truly remarkable.*

"You sit, Grandpa," she said with her shy little smile, "Just tell me where things are; I can make tea."

They talked, and laughed, and cried, and talked some more. The answer to one question only seemed to be a foundation for the next. She understood the things Joseph said to her, but often asked him to elaborate on one point or another. By the time the sun peeked in the kitchen window, she was a little girl no more.

It was close to 6:30 when Ida, still in her nightgown and robe, came down the stairs to put on a pot of coffee. As she entered the kitchen, Sophia said, "How about a cup of coffee, Mama?"

"What's this?" she said. "What are you two up to?"

"I think you might want to sit down, Ida; we have something to tell you." Joseph said, as Sophia poured Ida's coffee and brought it to the table.

"You're serving me now, Sophia?"

"I can," Sophia said with a little smile. "Don't you think it's about time for me to wait on you?"

Ida was taken aback with her answer – this was not a Sophia she knew. Joseph said. "Ida., this may be a shock to you – Sophia's memory has returned."

She gazed straight ahead, her eyes welling with tears, as she realized that when Joseph said something of that magnitude, it was fact. Ida rose and grabbed Sophia, hugging her with all her might. Joyously crying for several minutes, neither woman let go of the other.

An hour later, the smell of bacon brought Jeff and Lori down the stairs and into the kitchen. Sophia, half-crying through a happy face, went to Jeff. She looked into his eyes, saying, "I remember when you were a little boy; you look so much like your father."

Totally confused, "Mother," was all he said.

"Your mother has regained her memory, Jeff," Joseph said.

"I'm speechless. That's fantastic," Jeff said, swallowing her slight frame in an extended hug. "When did all this happen?"

"I think being back in this house had something to do with it. Freddy and I were always so happy here." Sophia said, with happiness spilling from her gentle doe-like eyes. "I lost you for a long, long time. I'm so sorry, but now I have you back."

After catching his breath, Jeff motioned Lori to come to him. "Mother, I'd like you to meet Lori Smith. We're going to be married in the spring." Joseph's eyes widened – that was news to him.

With tears running down her cheeks, Sophia took Lori's hands in hers and looked lovingly into her face, as she said, "I am so fortunate, now I also have a daughter . . . once again."

"Who's ready to eat?" Ida asked joyfully.

"Let me help," Lori said, trying to escape being the center of attention. "I'll need a lot of cooking experience if I'm going to be a married woman."

Ida was happy to get the help.

Breakfast lasted several hours, filled with story upon story. Sophia had center stage. As she recalled her past, the others listened in awe. Her eyes lit up as she spoke of events in Jeff's life, from the 18 hours of labor giving him birth, to the day her world fell apart. As the conversation progressed, she seemed to remember more and more, but only positive events; she ignored the tragedies altogether.

One of her favorite memories started with a question. "Do you remember Grandpa Westerfield's sailboat, Jeff?"

"I sure do. It was a beauty."

"When you were little, Freddy, your dad, would bring us here to the lake house almost every weekend. Whenever it was warm enough, Grandpa would take us all for a sail. We spent many afternoons with wind and water splashing in our faces. Sometimes Grandpa would put you between his knees and let you take the wheel. You were always saying, 'Let's bring'er about, Captain Grandpa.' He would respond, 'Aye aye, matey.' Usually soaked, we would come back here for grilled hamburgers, hotdogs, chips and ice cream. You loved those hotdogs. It was always such fun."

Jeff smiled as he said, "Things really haven't changed much."

The reality was sinking in. No one was happier than Ida; her little girl had a new world where she belonged. *Sophia will be safe and happy long after I am gone.*

That evening, when Sophia said her nighttime prayers, they ended with, *"please, God, let me remember in the morning."* Her prayers were answered.

*****

Under an overcast sky, winter wind howled through the barren trees surrounding the Westerfield lake house. Whipping off Lake Michigan, it felt colder than it actually was. It was raw, it was gloomy, it was winter in southern Michigan.

Inside, burrowed into his favorite overstuffed chair, Joseph enjoyed the warmth of a crackling fire and a cup of coffee. Sophia and her mother hummed little tunes he didn't recognize as they scampered about, trying to put a feminine touch back into his surroundings. The lake house had never felt warmer. With both women pampering him at every turn, he was enjoying his recovery. It had been a long time since he had lived with a woman in the house, and now there were two, both treating him like royalty.

Having just finished shoveling a light snow from the porch steps, Jeff warmed both hands around a cup of coffee. As he walked into the great room, he saw Joseph hang up the phone shaking his head with a grin on his face. "What's tickled your fancy, Grandpa?"

"Hi, Jeff. You'll never guess who that was."

"By the look on your face, it must have been Jack Benny."

"Close. Marion Cooper."

"Sorry, Grandpa, but I've never seen Marion's humorous side."

"Remember when Kristi talked him into getting the environmental people to put the kibosh on the Mac Orchard project?"

"He got it done. I have to hand it to him."

"True enough," Joseph said. "He did a great job."

"So, what's so funny?"

Did you know the place has been put back on the real estate market?"

"No, but I can't say I'm surprised. Without getting Wesfield Lab, Bayer big shots won't be needing a place to stay."

"Exactly. Who do you think is trying to buy it at a 'fire sale' price?"

"Marion Cooper?"

"He's trying to put together a small group of investors to share the load."

"That is funny," Jeff said, seeing the irony. First, he sinks the ship, then tries to buy it at salvage prices." It was his turn to shake his head with a grin on his face.

"He would like us to get involved," Joseph smiled.

"What does he have in mind?"

"He, Bailey, and Kristi's friend Russ Atkinson think they can convert what's already partly constructed and turn it into a condo and office building project. They are also considering creating a trout hatchery."

"Is there any profit in that?" Jeff asked skeptically.

"They're looking into it. I think Marion might have some connection with the fish and game people."

"What happened to the environmental restrictions that crippled the original project?"

"Marion told me, 'No problem.' That's what I was smiling about."

"He's a dandy," Jeff said. "Politicians should be called opportunists."

They were both smiling as Joseph asked, "Well, what do you think? Want to put a few bucks in?"

"When we needed Marion's help, he came through for us."

"I'll let him know – we're in."

"All right then," Jeff said, with an apprehensive smile. "Who knows, we may end up in the fish business."

CHAPTER 51
SPRING 1975

"New York, New York." It can be a wonderful town. But, after spending a couple of big city months working with Marti Towne, trying to build a conspiracy case against Richardson, Deckmann & Smylee and the people who controlled Painter Inc., Kristi began to remember why she took the job in South Station.

Gunther's information was more than enough to create a strong case against Smylee, the dead man. Unfortunately, it did little to pin down his associates, and offered nothing that tied Hermann vonLeer to the grand scheme. Evidence was evaporating, people were mysteriously unavailable for questioning or missing altogether, and key correspondence couldn't be located. With her energy level ebbing, Kristi was beginning to realize the case was thinner than they had hoped for.

After pondering the facts over the weekend she concluded her only contribution would be grunt work from here on out. She went to the office prepared to tell Agent Towne he was losing his volunteer; this was going to be her last week. As she walked in, Marti handed her his phone, "It's for you. Jeff Westerfield."

"Hi Jeff. How you doin'?"

"We're doing very well; thank you," he said. "How is the conspiracy case coming along?"

"The real estate management company looks like they're legit," Kristi said.

"That figures," Jeff said in a conciliatory tone. "How about the legal group?"

"The money trail evidence is solid between Richardson, Deckmann & Smylee and the Wesfield saboteurs, as well as ties to Gunther. We'd have a stronger case if Smylee hadn't blown his brains out, but we're okay. Being unable to put names on the accounts that funneled money into the Painter Group is disappointing and frustrating. We believe it's the same greedy people that backed IG Farben, who in turn funded Hitlerism, but others do their bidding. We don't have hard evidence."

"Sounds like Towne is doing a thorough job."

"He always does," Kristi said with a friendly glance toward Marti.

"The main reason I called was to see if you could attend a get-together at the lake house Saturday."

"This coming Saturday?" she replied, happy to have another reason to leave. "I'm sure Marti is ready to get me out of his hair." Towne shook his head agreeably.

"If you can come a day early, Joseph and I would like to spend a little time with you on Friday."

"Sounds good. I'm ready to come home."

"See you Friday," Jeff said. "I'll arrange to have the Wesfield plane pick you up Thursday afternoon. I'll let you know the exact time."

"Thanks."

When Kristi arrived at LaGuardia, Skyler met her with a smile and a hug. "Good to see you, Kristi. Welcome aboard."

"It's nice to see you too, Sky; how's the baby?"

"She's an adventure," he said proudly, helping Kristi with her suitcases.

Three cavalier corporate types were already on board. They introduced themselves, complete with their titles. When they learned she wasn't a gear driving the Wesfield engine, they quickly lost interest and began to talk shop among themselves. Kristi got to sleep all the way back to South Station.

Russ and Sassy met the plane. Getting hugs and kisses from both immediately lifted her spirits. Russ asked, "How about stopping for a fish fry on the way home?"

"Sounds fantastic.". . . It was.

*****

It was an unusually warm day for early April. Trees were showing a faint promise of budding, and early-bird robins labored to find a worm in the winter-cooled earth. The off-lake breeze that swirled around the house carried the inviting aroma of charcoal-grilled burgers and hotdogs.

On the far side of the backyard, knock-down tables placed end-to-end were filled with condiments, bowls of chips, a variety of salads, melons, and an abundance of goodies. At the head of the table, paper plates, plastic utensils, and napkins signaled the starting place. Two ice- filled washtubs containing an assortment of beers and soft drinks were on the ground at the end of the tables. A large chocolate cake iced with the words, "Congratulation Kristi and Crew – A Job Well Done," was displayed on a separate table.

Kristi, Russ and Sassy were the last guests to arrive. They were surprised to find Kristi's east coast colleagues, Charley Tanner, Joan Voss, Sandy, and John Snowden, along with their spouses and children, had all been flown in for the party. They, along with Jake Jacobson, Gus Arven, Skyler, and their families had joined the Westerfield clan and were well into the festive reunion.

Milling around together without protecting, planning or plotting any life-or-death event was a welcome experience. *How precious safety and freedom are*, Kristi thought, not realizing she was the person most responsible for providing that safety and freedom.

"Joseph, how did you get God to provide this weather?" Kristi said, greeting him with a hug.

"We were going to have this shindig inside until I let Tootsie out this morning."

Most guests filled their plates with Chicago hot dogs and cheeseburgers more than once. They introduced their families to each other and enjoyed reminiscing about the details of their success. John Snowden was the welcome stranger, the mystery hacker who uncovered much of the information the others acted on. He loved getting a little recognition and being included in this close-knit talented team.

After everyone got to mingle to their satisfaction, Joseph decided it was time to have his say. He had recovered much of his mobility, but didn't trust himself to stand in one place for any length of time. He rose, holding tight to the table, and said congenially, "If I can have your attention for a moment, I'd like to say a few words." The adults closed in while the kids roamed around the grounds. "Thank you all for coming. I know you all have lives away from the world of Westerfield, but I have you for one more day."

"Thanks for letting the families come along," Sandy's wife said.

"You have been more than patient with us, ma'am," Joseph said directly to her. "It was the least we could do."

She answered with a smile.

Joseph continued, "I wonder if any of you realize what an amazing job you've really done." He paused to glance at each member of Kristi's team. "By working together, combining your talents, you defeated one of the most powerful and evil groups of men the devil ever spawned." Joseph raised his glass saying, "I salute you. I'm grateful to you."

"Hear, hear," someone said as glasses went up and clinked.

"You people are the best at what you do," Joseph went on. "You don't quit. You have good judgment. You are people of integrity. You are the type of people I want owning Wesfield Laboratory. In a way of thanking you, 1000 shares of Wesfield stock has been purchased in each of your names. Stock certificates are in the mail."

The bewildered group accepted the gift with thanks, not quite knowing what to make of it.

"Don't be so quick to thank me," Joseph said. "Without recovering some of the money we spent on ProTect from Gunther's Cayman Island account, the stock purchase probably wouldn't have been possible. So, in many ways, you can thank yourselves. Also, you might like to know, in dollars, 1000 shares is worth about $40,000. With the success we've had with ExRelief, we'll be paying a nice dividend this year, and the stock's value should increase for several years."

His words were received with positive nods and smiles, and a hint of disbelief.

"The main reason I asked you to be here today is to help me honor the woman who masterminded our success. I first met Marilynn Christopher in a waiting room after my grandson was attacked. I must admit I was skeptical with our fate in the hands of a woman Chief of Police. Little did I know, the Almighty must have arranged for her to be there, because that's where she was needed . . . No one could have been more well-suited for the job.

"'Fidelity, Bravery, Integrity,'" Joseph continued, "That was the motto that began Kristi's career. She has lived up to the FBI pledge, proving herself to be a courageous, cunning crime fighter and loyal friend. I'm proud to announce that in the future, she has agreed to continue with the ProTect Company, expanding it and making it available to anyone who finds himself under attack." Handing her his treasured trophy, The Toppled Pawn plaque, Joseph again raised his glass and tilted it toward Kristi. "You are the master, Kristi. I salute you."

A variety of congratulations came from her friends.

With her green eyes dancing, she blushed as she stood up "Thank you, Joseph. I had no idea what you were up to."

"I know. But it's too late now," he said with a smile.

"Thanks for the support and confidence you showed throughout this entire ordeal," she said, realizing this was a special moment. "Together, we 'fought the good fight,' but I must admit, I'm glad it's over."

The crowd murmured agreement. "It's been my honor to work with each of you. I'm proud that we were not satisfied with just protecting the Westerfields, but chose to take the fight to their enemies. Evil people will always be with us. The fight against them will never be over, but this chapter is. You, Joseph, allowed me to recruit the greatest team anyone could possibly hope for. Thank you. And thank you all."

As she sat down, Joseph got back up. "There is one more thing I would like to share with you," he said, taking a piece of paper from his pants' pocket. "This is a note from the man I met in 1972, who made the first offer to buy Wesfield Laboratory. When I declined his offer, he warned me with a veiled threat on my life. I believe his is the voice that speaks for the evil men we defeated.

"It reads: 'Congratulations to you, Mr. Westerfield.
We are no longer interested in acquiring Wesfield Laboratory.

Respectfully,
Hermann vonLeer.'"

When the chess game is over, the pawns and
the king go back to the same box

BIBLIOGRAPHY

Ambruster, Howard Watson. *Treason's Peace, German Dyes & American Dupes,* The Beechhurst Press, 1947

BayerAG. http://www.bayer.com/en/History.aspx

Borkin, Joseph. *Crime and punishment of I.G. Farben,* Simon & Schuster, 1978

Dwork, Debórah and van Pelt, Robert Jan. *Auschwitz, 1270 to the Present.* Norton in NY, 1996

Coalition Against BAYER Dangers. http://www.cbgnetwork.org

Corporate Watch, Freedom Press, London, England *corporatewatch. org*

Czech, Danuta. *Auschwitz Chronicle, 1939-1945* 1st American ed., H. Holt in New York, 1990

DuBois, Josiah Ellis in collaboration with Edward Johnson. *Devil's Chemists.* The Beacon Press, 1952, *Generals in Grey Suits,* London: The Bodley Head, 1953

Nuremberg Military Tribunal VI, Germany, August 8, 1947. American-Israeli Cooperative Enterprise --The Jewish Virtual Library

Russel Mokhiber and Robert Weissman. *Corporations Behaving Badly: The Ten Worst Companies of 2001',* Multinational Monitor, 2001

Sutton, Antony C.. *Wall Street & the Rise of Hitler,* 1976, available - pfd and E-books

AUTHORS NOTE

The "Painter Group" is pure fiction, based on my belief that countries, as well as powerful companies, are pawns being manipulated by the world's financial powers.

Today, BayerAG claims to be a totally detached from I.G. Farben and the Bayer Company that provided munitions in WWI.

The Coalition against BAYER Dangers is a watchdog group that monitors BayerAG activities around the world. They helped me locate research material for my book and I found them to be a very friendly, conscientious group. Their website is filled with interesting information.

www.CBGnetwork.org